TWO *of the* DEADLIEST

ALSO BY ELIZABETH GEORGE

FICTION

A Great Deliverance
Payment in Blood
Well-Schooled in Murder
A Suitable Vengeance
For the Sake of Elena
Missing Joseph
Playing for the Ashes
In the Presence of the Enemy
Deception on His Mind
In Pursuit of the Proper Sinner
A Traitor to Memory
I, Richard
A Place of Hiding
With No One As Witness
What Came Before He Shot Her
Careless in Red
This Body of Death

NONFICTION

Write Away: One Novelist's Approach to Fiction and the Writing Life

ANTHOLOGY

A Moment on the Edge: 100 Years of Crime Stories by Women

TWO *of the* DEADLIEST

NEW TALES OF LUST, GREED, AND MURDER
FROM OUTSTANDING WOMEN OF MYSTERY

Edited by
Elizabeth George

HARPER

NEW YORK • LONDON • TORONTO • SYDNEY

HARPER

A hardcover edition of this book was published in 2009 by HarperCollins Publishers

TWO OF THE DEADLIEST. Compilation copyright © 2009 by Susan Elizabeth George. All rights reserved. Printed in the United States of America. No part of this book may be used or reproduced in any manner whatsoever without written permission except in the case of brief quotations embodied in critical articles and reviews. For information address HarperCollins Publishers, 10 East 53rd Street, New York, NY 10022.

HarperCollins books may be purchased for educational, business, or sales promotional use. For information please write: Special Markets Department, HarperCollins Publishers, 10 East 53rd Street, New York, NY 10022.

An extension of this copyright page appears opposite.

FIRST HARPER PAPERBACK PUBLISHED 2010.

Designed by Emily Cavett Taff

Library of Congress Cataloging-in-Publication Data is available upon request.

ISBN 978-0-06-135034-4 (pbk.)

10 11 12 13 14 OV/RRD 10 9 8 7 6 5 4 3 2 1

Copyrights

Contents

INTRODUCING . . .

INTRODUCTION

Motive. Whenever a crime is committed or even merely contemplated, something lies behind the commission or the thought of commission, and this is motive. When investigating an act of violence, the police are never *required* to identify a motive for later presentation to the prosecutors. They are only required to seek the evidence—either physical or circumstantial—that proves or strongly suggests who bears the guilt for an illegal act. But conditioned by everything from true-crime television programs to passionate proclamations from defense attorneys, juries look for motive. In the case of the written word, readers demand it and, indeed, the success of a story often hangs upon the realistic nature of the motive.

Time was when motives in literature could be drawn from just about anywhere, when the morals and values of the day were far more rigid than they are now, and when it was not inconceivable that someone would kill to keep the fact of an illegitimate child secret, to hide an addiction to drugs or alcohol from employers or the public, to prevent a mistress from telling her tale to the tabloids. Things that are now accepted with a shake of the head, a shrug of the shoulders, and laughter generated from jokes made on late-night television once were matters that could bring down entire governments, destroy careers, and devastate families. Now, however, so often those who at another time would have had strong motives to hide information about themselves instead step forward, claim to "take full responsibility" for their actions, frequently wave Bibles in the air and testify to their miraculous conversion, or go "into treatment" to take care of the problem, emerging later rejuvenated, recovered, and reinvented. So it is for everyone from pop stars to politicians.

Because the world has become a more tolerant place—at least regarding certain aspects of daily life—the search for a motive behind a character's behavior is rather trickier than it once was. Children "born out of wedlock" are paraded in public, and those born to dubious starlets often seem to be used as a means of getting one's photograph placed in supermarket magazines. Politicians who engage in extramarital dalliances may lose their footing momentarily, but more often than not, they purify themselves and rise, phoenix-like, to run for another office or, more probably, to run a corporation and scoop up stock options like confetti at a ticker-tape parade. Athletes who abuse women, animals, or their own bodies tend to be judged not by the enormity of a crime they might commit but rather by their potential to take their teams to the playoffs.

In this climate, what is a writer to do in the creation of character and the development of motive? My editor once said to me, "It all boils down to sex, power, and money," and perhaps she was right. Indeed, so many of the antique motives used by the *grande dame* herself, Agatha Christie, can be examined in this light. But I think there's a lovely and fertile ground for motives in looking at the Seven Deadly Sins, for not for nothing are they deemed *deadly*.

Anger, jealousy, gluttony, sloth, lust, greed, and pride. Isn't the truth of the matter that every major crime committed has one of the deadly sins at its root?

In this volume, we're looking at two of these sins, lust and greed. As editor, I laid down a challenge for the contributors herein: to create a new story that had as its backdrop either lust or greed or both of them. Some of the contributors are crime writers. Some are not. Included in this volume is something a bit different. In the second portion of the book, you will find "Introducing . . . ," a section devoted to a group of writers who are either largely unknown or who have not been published before. These women come from various backgrounds—they are journalists, educators, and techies—and they have all been students of mine at one time or another, in one venue or another. I have asked them to participate in order to bring them to the readers' attention and, perhaps, to the attention of editors and publishers. It's a rough publishing world these days, and people of note are often disregarded.

Throughout *Two of the Deadliest*, all of the contributors have taken a different look at what constitutes lust and greed and at where submitting to the calls of these sins can lead a person. You'll find good guys, bad guys, and in-between guys. You'll find mystery, mistakes, misunderstandings, and murder, generated from the minds of a group of terrific women writers. In all cases, I hope you enjoy.

Elizabeth George
Whidbey Island, Washington

Two *of the* Deadliest

Dark Chocolate

Nancy Pickard

Seven inches high in the center, sloping gently from that center to the perimeter of the perfect circle, this was her cake.

"My cake," Marcie whispered, alone in her kitchen.

All hers. All of it. Every. Single. Bite.

"Mine."

Before she frosted it, there was white lacework around its dark sides, a residue of the flour with which she had dusted her pans. *Cake pan, cake pan, better than a man can.* She rhymed, she sang, as she swirled her frosting spatula along the steep sides and mountaintop of the tall, dark, luscious beauty.

Finished frosting, she stepped back to admire her work.

Behind her, the old refrigerator hummed along with her.

Ice it, ice it, slice it, slice it.

"Perfect," she whispered, as if she were afraid to wake the dead.

Perfect, perfect, perfect, hummed the refrigerator.

Now to cut into it. Always tricky. Always challenging. It made her nervous. Things could go wrong so fast, even after so much planning and work. Even after the mixing, stirring, baking, cooling, icing, things could still go wrong at the last minute. The cake could fall. It could fail to satisfy, could be too done, too dry, or not quite cooked clear through. She had stuck toothpicks into the very center of both layers while they were still in the oven, at the end of the baking cycle, and they had emerged clean. Nothing had clung to them. She had thrilled to see the toothpicks, which suggested she had cooked a perfect cake this time. But there was still time for it to go wrong. It could still fall, all tumbled down in the middle as if somebody had punched a fist into its face. She hoped it wouldn't fall or fail like that. She wanted this cake, her cake, this particular cake on this day, to be perfect.

Marcie picked up her special cake knife.

Silver-plated wedding gift from she didn't remember who.

One of those people,

Under the steeple.

She held the knife above her cake, hovering, anxious, afraid of messing up. Hard not to mess up. Easy to fail. Hard to lay a perfect thick triangle on a pristine plate. *Glass plate, clear plate, what will be my life's fate?*

She held her breath as she lowered the knife to the frosting.

It hurt. It almost hurt to do that, to touch the chocolate, to move the knife slowly through the icing and down to the firmer substance, the cake below it. She wanted to hurry, to rush through it so she wouldn't have to feel it, the pain of slicing through her cake. *No push, no shove. That rhymes with love.* Once she made the first cut, there was no going back. No taking it back, no changing her mind.

The knife slid through the cake until it struck the glass below.

So far, so good, Marcie thought, and began to breathe again.

The next bad moment would come when she pulled the knife out, so she delayed it. She stood there in the kitchen with her fingers around the silver handle, its shaft still stuck fully into the heart of the cake. *Dead, dead, running red.* When she pulled out the knife, too much cake and frosting might come with it, leaving a rough cut.

Slowly, with exquisite caution, she withdrew the knife.

It was a smooth cut. There was only a little cake and frosting stuck to the blade.

Marcie felt relieved. This could be a perfect first slice of cake.

After the initial cut, the next one was even harder, but she was ready for it. She had put a glass of water beside the cake, and now she plunged the sticky knife down into the glass and then slid one side of the knife and then the other side of it carefully over the glass edge to clean them off. Then she used a fresh dish towel to wipe the knife perfectly clean for the next stab.

Perfectly clear, perfectly clean, who was nice, and who was mean?

I could write nursery rhymes, she thought.

Heaven knew, she'd read enough of them.

Finally, the first piece of cake lay on her perfect plate.

Marcie picked up her fork.

She ate one bite, taking it from the thinnest tip of the slice.

Oh! It was delicious. It was the best cake she'd ever baked, or eaten.

If you're good, you'll do what you should.

As she held the bite in her mouth, savoring its flavors, she thought about a news article she had read recently. Scientists claimed they had proved that the first bite of any food was always the best. They said every bite diminished in satisfaction after that. Marcie couldn't remember why they said that was so, but she didn't believe it anyway. When she ate the second bite of her cake, it was just as good as the first one had been, and maybe better. It brought tears to her eyes, it was so wonderful to taste. It felt so good between her teeth, on her gums, and going down her throat.

"Oh." She whispered a moan. "It's so good."

Every bite after that was equally scrumptious.

Delicious, delicious,

People are vicious.

She cut a second piece no bigger than the first one. She didn't have to hurry. There was no cause to gobble the way she gobbled down the family's leftovers before she stuck their plates in the dishwasher after meals. She had all the time in the world this afternoon, or at least until six o'clock, when Mark came home from work. An entire world, a whole lifetime, could be contained in those two and a half hours. She wanted to savor every bite of it.

The second piece was better than the first, and she was still hungry after she finished it. Starving. Only a thick piece could begin to fill her up, she decided, but when she ate a third, thicker slice, it only seemed to whet her appetite for more. *Good, good, knock on wood.* She was glad she still felt so hungry. This was her cake and she wanted to eat all of it.

Marcie savored her fourth piece.

The phone didn't ring to interrupt her.

Well, of course it didn't, Marcie thought, because she had unplugged it. One of the phones. She'd only had to kill one phone to kill all of them.

A noise, possibly a laugh, or maybe a sob, rose into her mouth.

It made her cough, which made her choke on the bite she was swallowing while the laugh or sob was trying to get up and out. Marcie panicked, afraid she could choke to death on her own cake, leaving the rest of it for somebody else to find, and maybe even to eat.

She ran to the sink to spit out the cake in her mouth.

She took a long drink of water to wash away the coughing.

The water filled her up a little, the way the cake had not so far.

Marcie put down the glass so she wouldn't drink any more.

Then she got back onto her kitchen stool, at the counter where the cake was, and cut the last piece of the first half of the cake.

Maybe it was time to bring the phones back to life?

So nobody would worry if they couldn't reach her. So nobody would come over to check on her before Mark came home. They would worry, she realized, if they couldn't at least get the answering machine.

She got up and plugged in the phone attached to the machine.

"Hi!" she whispered in a bright tone. "You've reached the Barnes family!" Then she dropped her voice to a lower register. "Mark!" Then back up to her own voice. "Marcie!" And then she imitated her children, in the order in which they chirped their names, in order of their births, starting with "Luke!" who was six, then "Ruth!" who was five, and then the twins, "Matthew!" and "Mary!" who were three. Then she yelled, "We'll call you back!" just as they all did on the tape. Only the baby, John, wasn't there. The baby was silent.

It startled Marcie to hear her own voice so loud in the quiet house.

Her mother said they shouldn't have a recording that yelled in people's ears. Her father said it was annoying to wait for it to play through every time. Her minister's wife said it was adorable.

Marcie started on the second half of her cake.

Her glass plate was not pristinely clean anymore.

Her two bathtubs weren't clean anymore.

Some of the beds weren't clean anymore.

"You should be ashamed of yourself," she said in her mother's voice.

"What did you do all day?" her father's voice chimed in.

"You're so lucky you get to stay home," her sister said.

"What did you guys do that was fun today?" Mark asked her.

"We missed you at circle meeting," said her minister's wife.

Wife, wife, for all of your life.

Mother, mother, smother, smother.

"Shut up," she whispered. "Shut up. Shut up. Shut up."

Hands shaking, she dipped the cake knife in the glass of water, which was murky now, and wiped it on the chocolatey dish towel. Then she cut the rest of the cake in even pieces so they'd be ready for her when she was ready for them. Time was running faster now. It wasn't all that long before Mark would come through the door.

At least the cake knife was clean again.

She held it up to let it shine in the light from the window.

Yes, it was clean as a whistle.

The word "whistle" made her think of the dog, who wasn't barking. Wasn't that the name of a story? About a dog that didn't bark? It was supposed to be important, somehow, the fact that the dog didn't bark. A clue. But to what? Maybe if she'd gotten her college degree, she'd know. Marcie wondered if it would be a clue to Mark. When he approached the house, when he stuck his key in the lock, would it be a clue when the dog didn't bark?

Mark was smart, but she didn't think he was that smart.

He'd probably need more clues than that before he ran to see what was wrong.

Marcie finished the first piece of the second half of the cake, and then laid the next piece on her plate.

She estimated there was a little over one-quarter of her cake left to eat now. If it was more than a quarter, would that make it a third? She wasn't sure. She'd never been good at math, or at estimating things.

Never been good, never been good,
Never done what they said she should.

Married before she ought to.

Had babies sooner than they said she should—but not as many as they said she could. ("Do you think our baby stuff will last through at least one more?" Mark had asked her last night.)

Kept the house too clean.

Vain, vain, windowpane.

Didn't keep it clean enough.

Make a mess, and then confess.

Spent too much money.

Never had enough of it.

Sang too loud. Talked too much.

Said the wrong things.

Dressed the wrong way.

Couldn't please.

"Please," Marcie whispered, remembering a Beatles' song. "Please, please, please me."

She didn't think it would please anybody to find out she had eaten an entire cake, but it pleased her. It pleased her so much to eat the. last. bite. Surprisingly, it only left her wanting more.

She glanced at the kitchen clock.

There was still time to mix another one. If she couldn't bake it, maybe she could eat the batter and lick the bowl, all of the bowl, all to herself.

When Mark came home, she could give him a chocolate kiss.

She walked to the cupboard to pull out another cake box, but discovered to her dismay that there wasn't another chocolate one. There was only vanilla. At first she felt deep disappointment, excruciating disillusionment. No chocolate! Only vanilla! But then she thought, No! That was all right. That was fine. It was great, in fact. She was the only one in the family who liked white cake. She was the only one left in the family who liked it . . .

Marcie reached for the cake mix box.

Vanilla had its own special delights, in her opinion. It was tangy, it smelled wonderful, it looked so pure. And you could do anything with it. Put on any flavor or color of frosting. Sprinkle it with candy. Squeeze frosting into roses and squirt them onto it. Use it for weddings, for birthdays, for special days like this one.

Her mouth watered, thinking of the flavor of the batter that would be hers alone. She was so hungry all of a sudden, so hungry, as if there were a huge hole in the middle of her. A huge empty space. She felt as if she were falling into the space, and that she might keep falling and falling forever with nothing making a sound around her, and with the space getting bigger and bigger until there was nothing in the universe except her and space.

Maybe another cake would fill it, if she could only finish eating it before Mark came home to their very quiet house.

THE OFFER

Patricia Smiley

Mari Smith limped onto the escalator leading to the baggage claim at the Los Angeles International Airport and began her descent into hell. She was already dispirited, but the hoard of disembarking passengers, all babbling and pushing to get out of the terminal, made her so tense that she waited fifteen minutes at the gate for the crowd to dissipate before heading to claim her suitcase from the carousel on the lower level.

To compound her distress, she had broken off the heel of one of her sensible navy pumps in the Jetway in Seattle as she'd entered the airplane. The flight had already been delayed an hour, so there was no time to get down to the tarmac to search for the heel of a tired old shoe. Now she had to find a way to repair the thing before morning or she'd be forced to arrive at her interview lurching like Quasimodo.

She'd come to Los Angeles to compete for a marketing job at a drive-through pet-wash company that planned to expand its operation to the Pacific Northwest. Even if she got the position, her financial future wasn't assured. The company was a start-up with no money to cover her airfare or even her hotel room. She'd maxed out her Visa card to pay for travel expenses, and now the only pair of shoes she'd brought along was out of commission, a predicament that left her feeling defeated.

At the bottom of the escalator, Mari stumbled through a revolving glass door leading to the lobby just outside the baggage claim. As she scanned the vicinity for a sign pointing toward carousel 5, she found herself face-to-face with a barrel-chested man with spiky platinum hair that reminded her of quills on an albino porcupine. He was standing near a bank of telephones, wearing a black suit that seemed funereal and too heavy for the August heat. He was holding a sign partially obscured by his hands. All Mari could make out were the letters *MARI* and *SMI*.

Excitement ricocheted inside her head like a cartoon bullet. Maybe the wet-pet entrepreneurs had found some wiggle room in the budget for a limo ride to her hotel. For a fleeting moment she wondered if her luck was changing.

Truth be known, the broken heel was only one setback in a cascade of recent disasters. Her bad luck had started with a letter out of the blue from the Nigerian minister of education. It seemed that he was having a problem transferring his son's college expense fund into the country in time to meet the enrollment deadline. If he failed, the young man's lifelong dream of attending the University of Washington would be destroyed. Would Mari be kind enough to help?

The plan seemed simple enough. He would send her a check for thirty thousand dollars, which she would deposit in her savings account and then wire twenty-five thousand dollars to the son. The additional five thousand dollars was hers to keep as compensation for her trouble. She coveted the extra cash, because her car needed new tires and the dunning messages on her dentist's bill had turned impolite.

She realized too late that she had erred by wiring the money before confirming that the check had cleared the bank. It was little consolation that she had been one of the first to fall for the scam. The con man had wiped out her entire savings, and she was still struggling to recover. Then two months ago she'd lost her job as office manager for an auto-parts store and hadn't been able to find another despite an exhaustive search. Landing the pet-wash position was her sole hope for financial salvation.

Mari met the limo driver's gaze and smiled. He took a step forward. As he did, his hand moved, exposing the full name on the placard—MARION SMITHSON. A seed of resentment sprouted in Mari's chest. She should have known better than to hope.

"Ms. Smithson?" he said. "I'm here to take you downtown."

Downtown? Mari *was* going downtown. She'd booked a room in an economy hotel, the cheapest one she could find. She'd been warned that the taxi fare would set her back at least forty dollars, so to offset the cost, she'd packed some of her own food: several cartons of tuna salad and crackers she'd purchased from a supermarket.

"I wasn't expecting a ride," she said.

The driver glanced at his clipboard. "You're on my pickup log. Says here I'm supposed to take you to the hotel. The company prepaid, so I guess you're in luck."

Luck was for people like Marion Smithson, not for her. She was going to tell the driver about the mistake but paused a moment to glance around the area. There was no likely Ms. Smithson in sight. Perhaps she had missed her flight. If so, the limo driver had made the trip for nothing, and that was a shame. Mari needed a ride downtown. The driver needed a passenger. It seemed like a waste for both of them.

For a moment, Mari basked in the fantasy of accepting his offer. She had always dreamed of riding in a limo but never had, not even to her high school prom. The driver would probably never realize his mistake and she'd save a precious forty dollars. If necessary she would admit to the error when she arrived at the destination. Poor old Marion Smithson would have to take a taxi to the hotel, but if the company could afford to pay for a limo, they could certainly afford to reimburse her for cab fare. Mari wondered if the limo had tinted windows like the ones movie stars rode in.

"Why don't you wait in the car while I get your suitcase?" he said. "It's just outside."

Mari handed him her baggage claim ticket and followed him out of the terminal building. As soon as she hit the sidewalk, she was assaulted by blaring car horns, rumbling bus engines, and toxic exhaust fumes that burned her lungs. Heat licked at her face as she climbed inside the stretch limousine, clutching her battered carry-on. By comparison, the serene feel of climate-controlled air was a godsend.

An open bottle of champagne lolled in an ice bucket next to a crystal flute. The label read Krug, Clos du Mesnil 1995. Mari didn't know much about champagne, but the high-class label gave her the impression that she was in the presence of greatness.

"Would you like me to pour the champagne before I get your bag?" the driver said.

Mari hesitated. She had accepted Marion Smithson's ride, but drinking her champagne seemed dangerously close to stealing.

"I shouldn't," she said as her voice faded into a wistful sigh.

The driver smiled. "I've already picked up several of your competitors. They all got the same treatment. Life is short. Enjoy."

Mari studied him with interest. "Competitors?"

"I hope you didn't think you were the only one interviewing for the job."

Mari was taken aback by the coincidence. Marion Smithson was in town for an interview too. Regardless, Mari was certain it didn't entail shampooing uncooperative dogs and cats for a financially challenged start-up operation. She gazed at the empty glass. After the turmoil of the day, she could use a little pick-me-up. The bottle was already open and the champagne would lose its fizz long before Marion Smithson breezed into town.

"Perhaps one glass wouldn't hurt," she said.

The driver filled the flute to the brim and then disappeared into the terminal to retrieve her suitcase. After he loaded her luggage into the trunk, he slid into the front seat of the car and handed

Mari an azure cloth bag with drawstrings that were as soft as silk threads.

"It's a welcome gift," he said. "All the candidates got one. You're free to keep what's inside even if you don't get chosen."

Mari studied the bag. The color reminded her of water in a tropical lagoon. She wanted to strip down and dive in, knowing she'd break the surface feeling refreshed. She yearned to open it and see what was inside, but a twinge of conscience forced her to leave the bag on the seat.

The limo exited the airport through a ring of tall cylinders set ablaze by multicolored lights. They reminded Mari of a hip L.A. version of a pagan stone circle. She pressed her cheek into the cool leather seat and allowed the dry champagne to tickle her nose.

The limo wended its way past tawdry billboards, dusty palm trees, and cell towers ridiculously disguised as conifers. Mari barely noticed. Her focus remained on the azure bag. She'd always believed that curiosity was a virtue, so she wondered how inspecting the contents could possibly be wrong. It wasn't as if she planned to keep whatever was inside.

Her fingers tingled as they parted the tissue, going deeper into the bag until they'd unearthed a bottle of Hervé Léger perfume, an Hermès scarf, and a svelte case that held a gold Cartier watch. She lifted the watch from its repose and stroked it gently with her fingers. The burnished gold was smooth and achingly beautiful. She wondered what the watch would feel like on her wrist.

She removed her Timex and slipped the Cartier over her hand, allowing it to caress her skin. She knew she would have to remove the watch before she got to the hotel, but until then, she decided to accept her good fortune.

As the limo snaked along the ribbons of freeway toward downtown L.A., Mari spritzed perfume in her décolleté, draped the silk scarf around her neck, and counted each minute of pleasure on her Cartier watch.

She waited until the limo rolled to a stop in the circular driveway of an upscale hotel with a French name before returning the watch to the azure bag. The thought of parting with it created waves of envy that threatened to scuttle her resolve. The driver opened the door, and Mari slid out with her purse and her carry-on, feeling as if she'd just gotten away with something naughty.

"Thanks for the ride," she said, handing the driver a modest tip.

He smiled. "My pleasure."

Mari glanced around to get her bearings, hoping her hotel was close by. She didn't want to walk far, because her uneven gait had already caused her hips to ache.

As she was making her way toward the lobby to ask the concierge for directions, she saw a middle-aged woman in a business suit walking toward her. The woman seemed intense, as though the worries of the world were lodged between the furrows of her brow.

"Welcome to Los Angeles, Marion," the woman said. "I'm Lisa Beaudry, Weylin Prince's executive assistant. We spoke on the telephone."

Mari had not expected to be greeted when she arrived at the hotel. She felt a twinge of trepidation that subsided only when she realized that Lisa Beaudry had never met Marion Smithson in person or she would have known Mari was an impostor. Still, the game had gone on long enough. She had to set things right.

Mari took a step forward. "Thank you, Ms. Beaudry, but I have to tell you—"

Lisa frowned when she noticed Mari's lopsided stride. "What's wrong with your leg?"

Mari wondered if her concern was random or if the job required some sort of physical exertion and couldn't be performed by a candidate with a bad leg. Still, it was no concern of hers, so she explained about the crack in the Jetway and the broken heel. Lisa seemed relieved. She took Mari's arm and guided her toward the door.

"Your room isn't ready yet," she said, "so I took the liberty of booking a spa appointment for you. Choose any treatment you want. I've left instructions for the staff to charge it to our account. Meanwhile, I'll see what I can do about your shoes."

Mari felt as if she might swoon. A warm soak and a massage would go a long way toward easing the stress she'd been under. With any luck at all, she could slip out after the spa treatment and make her way to her economy hotel before Lisa Beaudry even knew she was gone. If Lisa discovered the pretense, Mari would apologize and explain that she and Marion had both come to L.A. for a job interview and that she'd misread the limo driver's sign. It was a simple mistake. Anyone could have made it.

"A spa treatment would be lovely," Mari said.

After her massage, Mari showered and dressed. The champagne had made her tipsy, but the masseur's hands had kneaded the tension from her muscles and sent her on a slow journey into Nirvana. He had also given her directions to her own hotel, which was about six blocks away.

Mari picked up her carry-on and her purse, and was preparing to leave when she felt a pang of alarm. She had forgotten about her suitcase. It must still be in the limo. She didn't have the license number or even the name of the company. Getting it back meant explaining her deception. Lisa would make her pay for the ride from the airport, plus the spa treatment, which would take all the cash she had left and leave her stranded in downtown L.A.

Mari hurried toward the elevator, praying that the limo driver had left her suitcase with the doorman. She had just reached the hotel lobby when she heard a woman's voice calling her name. She turned and saw Lisa Beaudry walking toward her. Apprehension ignited the flowery scent of perfume between her breasts.

"There you are," Lisa said. "Guess what I found."

Mari hoped it wasn't Marion Smithson.

Instead, Lisa handed her a shopping bag that held a pair of suede shoes—three-inch heels, apple red, with a navy bow that matched her navy suit.

Mari stared at the shoes in awe. "They're . . . beautiful."

Lisa handed her a plastic key card. "I thought you'd like them. Look, your suitcase is in your room. There's a cocktail party for all the candidates at six thirty, followed by dinner. I saw by the clothes you brought along that nobody told you it was formal. Not to worry. I found you something appropriate to wear."

Mari was relieved that her suitcase was safe but she was also concerned. Lisa Beaudry had not only taken her bag to the room, but she had gone through Mari's things, as well. Her name was clearly written on the tag on the suitcase handle. If Lisa had inspected it, she knew Mari was an impostor. Perhaps the police were waiting in the room to arrest her and take her to jail. The situation was mushrooming out of control. All she could think about now was finding her suitcase and leaving before her charade was exposed.

Mari took the proffered key card. When she got to the room, she pressed her ear to the door, listening for sounds from within. Silence. She opened the door. The room was empty, except for her suitcase and the azure bag on the bed. She scrambled to inspect her luggage and found that her name tag was missing from the handle. She assumed it had been torn off in transit. For once, she wouldn't complain about the baggage handlers' abuse of her personal belongings.

Relief lowered her pulse rate and her resistance. She picked up the azure bag, feeling as if she'd just been reunited with a former lover. Her breath quickened as she slipped the Cartier on her wrist one last time and felt the warm glow of desire.

She lifted her gaze from the watch and saw a sleek navy cocktail dress hanging in the closet. The silk rose pinned to the bodice was the same red as her new shoes. She held the dress up to the light. It was lovelier than anything she had ever owned. She decided to try it on, just to see what it looked like on her figure. If it suited her, perhaps she would buy one just like it with her first paycheck from the pet-wash company. She undressed and slipped the dress over her head, keeping a close watch on the door. If Marion Smithson arrived, she would leave immediately, telling her there had been a mix-up in rooms.

Mari admired her image in the mirror. Her plain facial features were married to a well-proportioned body and girlish breasts. Her skin and medusalike hair glowed with health. Nobody had ever called her sophisticated, but people always seemed charmed by her look of youthful innocence.

She turned away from the mirror, wondering what it would be like to work for a company that lavished expensive gifts on its job applicants. She considered Marion Smithson's professional credentials. She was obviously vying for a position of great importance to warrant such singular treatment. Perhaps the post required technical expertise, like engineering or computer science. If the job were geared toward sales or marketing, Mari's liberal arts education would surely put her in the running.

Since Marion Smithson had not yet arrived at the hotel, Mari decided to attend the cocktail party, have a drink and a few hors d'oeuvres, and find out more about the position. She had no plans for the evening except for tuna and crackers *à la maison*. In fact, she had no plans at all until the following morning at ten thirty when her interview with the start-up company was scheduled. Lisa hadn't discovered the ruse as of yet. A couple more hours seemed unlikely to change that. Perhaps, Mari thought, she might even score points with Mr. Prince and become Marion's competitor instead of her impersonator. She found the thought amusing.

At precisely six thirty, Mari stood outside the door leading to the hotel's grand ballroom, dressed in her sleek navy dress, apple red shoes with the navy bows, and the Cartier watch. She felt glamorous and sexy.

"Marion, you look beautiful," said Lisa Beaudry as she nudged her inside the room. "Come with me. There are people who want to meet you."

Mari wasn't beautiful and she'd never pretended otherwise, but the sound of the word lifted her spirits. She followed Lisa into a room full of people dressed in tuxedos, formal gowns, and glittering diamonds. The crowd was a mix of couples and singles of varying ages but most of them looked older, fifties or higher, and all of them looked rich.

Across the room, a stout man, whose uneven complexion looked like the surface of the moon, had just skewered a strawberry on a silver pitchfork and placed it under a fountain spewing chocolate. Lisa waved to him. He nodded and waddled toward them.

"That's Mr. Dolan," Lisa whispered in Mari's ear. "He's on our board of directors. Be nice to him."

Mari wasn't sure what Lisa meant by that statement. Of course she would be nice to him. She was here for a job interview, after all. She intended to be nice to everyone.

Mr. Dolan bit off the tip of the chocolate-covered strawberry. "I understand your background is in advertising."

Mari had once sold classified ads over the telephone during the summer between her junior and senior years of college, so it wasn't much of a lie when she said yes.

Dolan ran his tongue over his lips, capturing the last remnants of cacao. "So tell me about your family."

Mari was taken aback. It was inappropriate and probably illegal to ask a job applicant a question like that. A board member should know better. She didn't want to spoil her chance to curry favor, but she wasn't about to discuss her personal life.

"I'm an orphan," she said.

Mari didn't know what had possessed her to say that. Perhaps she'd been distracted by Mr. Dolan's rapid-fire blinking, which periodically pulled his face into a grotesque grimace. She wasn't an orphan. Her parents and her four siblings wouldn't find the lie funny, but she doubted they would be amused by any part of this escapade.

Dolan brushed his sticky fingers over her arm as if he wanted to take a bite out of that too. "Such a lovely young woman to suffer such loss."

He continued asking questions about her life and her job history until Lisa beckoned him toward another young woman whom Mari assumed was also an applicant. She waited until Dolan moved on to another hors d'oeuvre table before strolling over to speak with the woman.

"When is your interview?" Mari said.

"Tomorrow at ten. How about yours?"

"Ten thirty. I wanted to read through the job description one more time tonight, but I must have left it at home. I don't suppose I could get a copy of yours?"

The woman seemed surprised. "I didn't get one. Lisa told me the position was so new they hadn't had time to formalize anything. It doesn't really matter. Regional sales rep jobs are all the same. You call on customers, bring in new business, and write reports. We'll be on the road a lot, so I think they want somebody who's single. I'm sure they'll tell us more in the interview. Are you working now?"

The blood in Mari's veins felt clogged with ice. She couldn't tell the woman she'd been unemployed for months and was in L.A. to apply for a dead-end job with a start-up company, not while the dress, the shoes, and the Cartier were making her feel more successful than she'd ever felt in her life.

Mari smiled. "I'm the director of sales and marketing for a French lingerie company called C'est Bon."

She had no idea where that had come from either. Her underwear generally consisted of the equivalent of Big Mac work shorts. Cotton. Sturdy. Dependable. Maybe the navy dress and the watch were altering her DNA, because she was beginning to feel as if she *could* be an executive with an international lingerie company.

During the next hour, Mari spoke with several job applicants. All were women. Most were beautiful. She learned the company was called the Pleasure Club, an exclusive, members-only organization that specialized in adventure travel. Mari was surprised. The crowd seemed a bit too old for adventure, but she admired seniors who stayed active in their so-called golden years. The company's name was somewhat ambiguous. If the members hadn't looked so upstanding, she might have thought the organization was some sort of illicit sex club.

As the cocktail party wore on, Marion Smithson had still not arrived. Mari assumed she'd been delayed but would probably show up by dinnertime. She couldn't risk running into her, so she left the ballroom and headed toward her room.

"Marion? Where are you going?"

Mari whipped around and saw Lisa Beaudry standing behind her.

"Something came up at work," she stammered. "An emergency. A shipment of silk from China held up in port. A big order to fill. Nobody knew what to do."

Mari realized too late that she had made a mistake. Marion Smithson didn't work for a French lingerie company. That was a lie Mari had just made up.

"Perhaps that explains the message I just picked up at the front desk," Lisa said. "It said you'd been delayed but you would arrive in time for your interview in the morning. The wording seemed odd since I'd just seen you a few minutes ago."

Beads of perspiration began forming on Mari's upper lip. "Yes. The wording. The desk clerk must have misunderstood. I only wanted you to know I had to make a few telephone calls and may not make it to dinner."

Lisa frowned. "Okay. Just don't work too late. Your interview is at nine o'clock tomorrow morning. Mr. Prince will announce his selection by noon."

The burst of adrenaline subsided, leaving Mari feeling drained and anxious. She'd come so close to being exposed. Her nerves couldn't take much more.

"Look, Lisa. There's something you should know about me. I don't belong here—"

"I hope Mr. Dolan didn't intimidate you. People like him are the glue that holds this organization together. If you please him, it's like winning the lottery." Beaudry smiled and patted Mari's shoulder. "Get some sleep. You'll feel better tomorrow."

Indulging this fantasy was madness. Mari had to get out of the situation before she crossed the imaginary line that would leave her no avenue of retreat. She headed back to her room, listening at the door for what seemed like an eternity. Hearing no sounds, she entered, changed back into her navy suit, and returned the watch to the azure bag. She had no choice but to keep the shoes. It made no sense to limp to her real job interview in the morning when she had alternatives. She'd try to find some way to repay the Pleasure Club.

Mari collected her belongings and left the room. She was heading down the hallway toward the elevator when she heard Lisa Beaudry's voice in the distance. She peeked around the corner and saw Lisa walking toward her, accompanied by a tall man with a pointed nose and a swarthy complexion. He had unusually small ears, and his dark hair was slicked back with some sort of pomade that made him look like a harbor seal. Mari wondered if he could balance a rubber ball on that sharp nose of his. She didn't want to be caught sneaking out of the hotel, so she ducked into an alcove near an ice machine and waited for them to pass by.

"What about Marion Smithson?" the man said. "Dolan liked her."

"I don't know, Mr. Prince. That picture she sent us must have been taken years ago. I hardly recognized her. Plus, she seems skittish. I'm not sure she's right."

"Who else looks good?"

Mari couldn't hear the response, but she was crushed that Lisa hadn't defended her. Lisa who had touched her arm so gently and reassuringly, Lisa who had called her beautiful. How could she doubt Mari's ability? She hadn't even applied for the job, and yet she'd passed Dolan's litmus test. That had to mean something.

Mari would definitely be interested in landing the Pleasure

Club's regional sales rep job. In fact, she was beginning to think she was not only qualified, but also deserving. If only she could impress Weylin Prince before Marion Smithson arrived, she just might be able to pull it off. Besides, there was nothing to lose. Mari could meet with Prince at nine, and still make her real interview at ten thirty.

It was late and Mari dreaded the thought of lugging her suitcase six blocks to her real hotel. It was dangerous to venture out at night alone in a strange city, but it was also risky to sleep in a hotel room reserved for another guest. Marion Smithson might show up in the middle of the night and then what?

Besides, if Mari hoped to compete for the Pleasure Club job, she had to do some research on the travel industry. She checked her suitcase with the bell captain and hurried to the business center to search the Internet. By the wee hours of the morning, she had compiled an impressive array of statistics. She printed out her research and then slipped into a vacant meeting room where she assembled a makeshift bed out of dining room chairs and fell asleep.

The next day, after washing up and carefully applying her makeup in the mirror of a public restroom, Mari loitered outside the interview room waiting for Marion Smithson to show up. When she still hadn't arrived by five minutes after the hour, Mari strolled into the room with a head full of facts that she was sure would impress Weylin Prince. Even though she caught him staring at her breasts several times during the meeting, Prince seemed impressed by her knowledge and enthusiasm. Twenty minutes into the discussion, he leaned back in his chair.

"The job is yours," he said.

Mari felt bold and empowered. She had just won a job for which she hadn't even applied. Of course she would have to explain the mix-up in names when she filled out the official paperwork, but that seemed far away and unimportant.

"What's the starting salary?" she said.

Prince raised an eyebrow. "What's your pleasure?"

Surely he was joking. He almost seemed to be inviting her to name her price. Even though the job was new, the company must have established some sort of salary guidelines. She wracked her brain for a ballpark figure, given that she had never actually seen a job description. Fifty thousand seemed too low even though it was more than she'd ever made before. Fifty thousand and Cartier watches did not go hand in hand.

"A quarter of a million." She almost giggled as the words left her lips.

Weylin Prince's grin seemed wolfish. "That's a lot of money."

Mari was just about to tell him she'd been joking when he added, "How does a hundred thousand sound?"

Mari was dumbstruck. What quid pro quo would Prince want in exchange for a hundred thousand dollars?

"When do I start?"

He smiled again. "Tonight. We begin with a dinner party. Until then, enjoy your freedom."

Doubt bit into her thoughts as she considered his words. He was joking, of course. He only meant that she would be working hard, schmoozing with existing members and recruiting new ones. A job that paid so much money would certainly require long hours, but getting out of debt was worth the price.

"I accept," she said.

After the interview, Mari returned to the spa for a trio of treatments: facial, makeup application, and a manicure. By the time the staff had completed the beautification process, Mari looked more like a goddess than a regional sales rep for a travel club.

At six o'clock she donned the sleek navy dress and the apple red shoes with the navy bows and fastened the Cartier watch around her wrist. She was strolling across the hotel lobby heading for the limo that would take her to the Pleasure Club's dinner party when she saw a bedraggled young woman standing at the reception desk.

"Excuse me," she was saying to the clerk. "My name is Marion

Smithson. I was supposed to arrive yesterday, but I missed my flight and couldn't get another one. I left a message for Lisa Beaudry, but I'm not sure she got it. I need to speak to her. Can you ring her room?"

The clerk looked as if he was typing something into a computer.

"I'm sorry," he said. "Ms. Beaudry checked out."

Mari felt sorry for Marion Smithson, though as her mother always said, that's the way the cookie crumbles. Mari had won the job fair and square. She had competed with a roomful of candidates and had triumphed over all of them.

Once outside the hotel, Mari slid into the waiting limo and settled into the leather seat. A glass of champagne was waiting. This time it was meant for her.

Soon the streetlights of L.A. disappeared in the rearview mirror, leaving only the limo's headlights to illuminate the night. After what seemed like a long time, the limo stopped in front of a rustic lodge in the middle of nowhere.

Moments later, the driver escorted Mari inside the candlelit foyer of the lodge where she was greeted by spontaneous applause. She couldn't see well in the dim light, but she guessed that twenty to thirty people were in the room, many patting her back and murmuring congratulations.

The champagne had made her woozy. She shouldn't have had a second glass. She felt unsteady on her feet, so she was relieved when Lisa Beaudry took her arm and led her into a great room decorated in what looked like jungle vines and odd-looking trees. Mari thought they must be artificial, but when she reached out to touch one, she realized it was real.

Her eyes began adjusting to the dark, and she could see what looked like a replica of an ancient stone pyramid. Mayan perhaps. Some of the people in the room were wearing masks and others were dressed in ridiculous costumes—loincloths and feathers. Mari remembered thinking that the club's membership seemed too old for adventure travel. Maybe they only re-created the experience in theme parties like this one or maybe the event was just a teaser for an upcoming trip to Belize.

"Are you ready for the presentation?" Lisa said.

"Of course."

Mari's mind was racing. No one had told her about any presentation. Did they expect flow charts and PowerPoint slides? How could she get up and talk about her sales and marketing plans when she barely knew what the job entailed?

She felt dizzy and lethargic. She squeezed her eyes closed, but it didn't improve her focus. A moment later, she felt someone grabbing her hands and the Cartier watch slipping off her wrist. Something rough brushed against her skin. Rope. Somebody was tying her hands behind her back. No. That couldn't be right. The champagne must be making her hallucinate. Words seemed difficult to form but she tried nonetheless.

"What are you doing? Let go of me."

A wave of panic hit her as two burly men dragged her toward the opposite end of the room. The red shoes scraped against the floor. Her toes hurt, as if a snake from the fake jungle had slithered out to bite them. Just ahead she saw what looked like a large stone altar on a dais. She considered the lodge's jungle motif, with its Mayan ruins and loincloth costumes, and prayed this was merely some sort of kinky initiation ritual.

Mari had precious little time for speculation. Her feet lifted off the ground and the red shoes fell away. She smelled something metallic and saw dark stains embedded in the stone. Her eyelids fluttered and then closed. She felt cool air caress her body, as if her clothes had been stripped away. The last thing she heard was Mr. Dolan's voice.

"So glad you accepted our offer, Marion."

E-Male

Kristine Kathryn Rusch

Every morning, Gavin got up, fixed himself a mocha grande with sprinkles, and padded barefoot to his computer. He kept the computer in the second bedroom of his rent-controlled apartment. The bedroom was the size of a closet, but he didn't need much. Besides, the apartment itself was big, considering that most places in Manhattan were the size of a shoe box, and he paid one quarter what the square footage was worth. He'd been here since he was a student, only then he'd had to share with three other people.

Now he had the place to himself—him and the cat—and he preferred it that way. He had his routines and his rituals, and he valued all of them. They got him to work by noon, and that was saying something for a man who had been self-employed most of his adult life.

He would set the mocha on the second shelf of the desk and log on, careful to check his firewalls and his virus protection first. Then he'd download his e-mail, with its insistent spam (BIG BREASTS—THIRTY DAYS!) and even more insistent business matters (*Need the drawings for the Peterson account Friday. Have any prelims yet? Don't want to be surprised.*). Sometimes, he'd find a letter from his sister, filled with news about his niece (first grade and liking it), his nephew (coasting through the second grade), and her husband, who had the uncommon good sense to stay home to raise the baby.

Gavin would answer what he could, delete what he couldn't, and then he'd go to his morning treat: Stella's e-mail.

Stella, his almost-wife.

Stella, his now-ex-girlfriend.

Stella, who hated him almost as much as he hated her.

Stella's e-mail was rich in metaphor, lacking in love. But Stella had never been rich in love. Stella preferred lust. Good, old-fashioned, I-want-you-baby-in-the-worst-way lust.

Not hers, naturally.

His.

And he rarely got a chance to use that lust—in a constructive manner at any rate. Or, at least that was what Stella had told the judge when she got the restraining order.

Gavin seems to think he owns me. He watches me all the time. I'm afraid of him, Judge.

Gavin clenched a fist and then made himself relax it slowly. She was such an actress. Such a *bad* actress. But the judge had fallen for it.

Men *always* fell for her.

Even that judge.

When Gavin looked at Stella's e-mail, his memories of falling for her would come back. Stella had a wide variety of correspondents, most of them male, and most of them elderly pretending to be younger.

The slang always gave them away. They wrote, "Hey, baby," or "You look like one cool chick." They wrote in full sentences with capital letters and real punctuation instead of e-mail shorthand. It seemed strange to see someone type out "in my humble opinion" instead of using imho.

Gavin wondered if Stella was bright enough to catch these subtle clues, or if she thought all these men writing to her were young and handsome and interesting. Unlike him, as she had told him often enough.

"Yeah? So what am I?" he had asked, later realizing such a question had been the beginning of the end.

She had actually thought about the answer. Then thought about it some more, and then revisited it, like a hole in her tooth, something she couldn't ignore.

First she'd said, "You're okay in bed."

Then she'd revised it. "You're an artist."

Finally she'd ended with, "And you've got money."

The okay in bed had bothered him. He was fucking great in bed. Every woman except Stella had told him that. He saw to them first, and then he took care of himself. What more could a woman want? But Stella hadn't been that enthusiastic about sex in the first place.

She loved teasing. She loved being the object of lust. But she hated the fluids, the time, the sheer physicality of sex.

He'd thought about e-mailing that to her admirers. Sure, her picture on her Web site was hot. He'd taken it after a moment of passion, and yeah—artist that he was—the stuff he'd Photoshopped out was barely noticeable. You thought you saw a nipple, an attractive nipple, unless you looked closely. Then you'd realize you saw the suggestion of a nipple, not a real nipple at all.

The real nipple was disappointing. Large and bulbous and clearly a tool for child feeding, not for male entertainment. It made her entire breast look like the end of a baby's bottle instead of something a man wanted to wrap his hand around.

Whenever he took naked pictures of her—and he took a lot more than she realized—he always had to deal with the nipple problem. He'd become an expert at the nipple problem by the time he designed her Web site. She hadn't even noticed how he'd tucked in her waist to make it look just a bit smaller, or brought the color from the blanket over her hips to hide what little hair she had just so they wouldn't get in trouble with her Web-hosting service (which actually defined pornographic pictures as ones that showed everything, as opposed to artistic photos that did not).

Of course, all these idiots who e-mailed her read her blog and thought they knew her. Her blog was 90 percent fantasy and 10 percent reality, and that 10 percent only showed up when she was pissed off.

Any guy who was paying attention would know she was a real piece of work, a woman with a lot of issues and even more hang-ups, and one beaut of a temper.

But guys didn't think of that when a woman described how she liked to spend her evenings alone, just her with Mr. Buzzer and a package of microwave popcorn. All the guys figured they could make her give up the buzzer.

He was here to tell them that they were wrong.

That's what he'd initially thought he'd do, e-mail every Joe Asshole who e-mailed her, warning him away in creative and untraceable e-mails. Instead, Gavin got caught up in reading her made-up blog, comparing it to the e-mails she sent and received, and wondering if she really felt better about her life now that he wasn't in it.

To his friends, he said he didn't miss her. His work certainly didn't suffer. He had his commissions, mostly for ad agencies and Web sites and magazines, and he had two gallery shows this year in Boston, which was the next best thing to New York.

Anyway, he wasn't really without her. He had her cat—well, the cat she'd abandoned to him, even though she still used said cat's name as her password—and sometimes, in the middle of the night, he could pretend that little ball of warmth against the middle of his back was Stella.

He had her words too, and not the ones she'd sent him in anger the day she left (he kept those e-mails as well, downloaded and backed up, just in case). He had her Sent mail, which he read religiously, and her unsent mail—her Drafts folder—which he only opened on Sunday.

He loved unsent. Drafts were written in anger, and Stella excelled at anger. Once he'd found a letter that verged on the pornographic, and he'd wondered if she'd meant it for him until he found the name Tom halfway down the page. In no way could Gavin be made into Tom, not even when you squinted and blurred the letters together.

There were five Toms in her e-mail list, but none of them had that particular e-mail address, an address she had never sent anything to before or since. Gavin could've traced it, he supposed, but he saw no need since she'd never sent the letter.

She might've fantasized about this Tom, but she never consummated the fantasy, and that was enough for Gavin.

Lately, though, her e-mail had become a little staid. Almost boring. At first, he attributed it to the fact that they'd been broken up for more than a year. She'd never been much of a rocket scientist. She hadn't even graduated from college, preferring to pad her résumé so that the four years she spent at an elite school looked like a complete education.

Then, she stopped corresponding with most of her men. Her letters took on a terse note, as if she was too busy to be bothered to write anything.

At that point, Gavin realized that she hadn't used the e-mail account for nearly three days. No Sent mail, no unsent Drafts. She hadn't even responded to the real letters—the ones from family members whom he'd met once and hated—and that was unusual. In the past, she would let the men hang for days, letting them think maybe they'd screwed up by sending such a needy letter to a woman they'd never met, but she never, ever (not even when he'd begged) ignored her family.

That was the first sign that something was wrong. The second was subtler. A man whose handle was jondoe61 had disappeared from her regular e-mail. Gavin had to dig deep into her files to realize that Stella had actively blocked him.

It had to take something incredible to make Stella block anyone. She didn't even block spammers most of the time. She had blocked Gavin, of course, but that had been on the advice of her attorney.

And Gavin had known how to get around it.

Blocking jondoe61 got Gavin's curiosity up. What had it taken for Stella to decide this guy had to stay away from her, even if it was only in e-mail?

First Gavin checked the Junk file, but the Web-mail provider that Stella used actually had an efficient junk filter. The junk went into the Junk folder, then got permanently deleted after seven days.

Stella had blocked jondoe61 nearly sixteen days before. So Gavin couldn't find what had provoked her, and he certainly couldn't remember. All of her mail from men he didn't know seemed vaguely pornographic to him. He blamed her for this: No one should be that explicit in her blogs without expecting some kind of nasty e-mail in return.

But Stella had never had an Off switch. She didn't seem to realize that things she said, and, by extension, things she wrote had repercussions. She coveted the lust, although she did want it couched in romantic terms ("You're so beautiful" instead of "I want to fuck your lovely ass").

If men were savvy, they understood that she didn't want honesty. She wanted poetry. But she also seemed to understand that you had to read a lot of raunchy e-mail to get to the pretty ones.

And she never blamed herself for the content. If men wrote her nasty letters, it was because men wrote nasty letters, not because she talked about sex toys and orgasms in her nightly online ramblings.

Gavin sighed, sipped his now cold mocha grande, and realized he'd wasted half a morning on Stella's e-mail. She hadn't logged on either—which would have chased him out of there in a heart-beat—and he'd lost track of the time.

If he wasn't careful, he would lose the entire day. He couldn't afford that.

Well, he could, but it wouldn't be a good precedent to set for himself. A man who was self-employed had to have an asshole for a boss or he'd get nothing done.

At least, that was what Gavin told the cat. The cat, who had been licking her back leg when he spoke, showed her disagreement by sticking out her pink tongue and keeping her leg raised in a sort of feline finger gesture.

However, cats knew nothing about employment, the little free-loaders, so he decided to ignore her and get to work.

He had a commission to finish.

He actually forgot about Stella until the next morning. He made his mocha grande with extra sprinkles, padded barefoot to the computer, and logged on, thinking about his half-finished painting instead of the mystery of jondoe61. Only by habit did Gavin go to Stella's e-mail—and discovered that she hadn't written a thing all week.

He scanned through her Sent mail, wondering if she was on to him. Maybe she had realized he'd been reading everything, and as a result, she hadn't saved copies of the Sent mail. But he diddled with the e-mail himself, sending mail to one of the spammers as a test, and the mail he sent in Stella's name and with her account showed up in the Sent mail just like it was supposed to.

He deleted the test e-mail and remembered jondoe61.

Stella kept her answered mail. She was too lazy to delete a letter after she had responded. Gavin scrolled down through nearly a thousand messages, searching for jondoe61. When Gavin finally found an e-mail from jondoe61, he clicked on it then reset the e-mail program's perimeters so that all of jondoe's letters grouped together.

After reading six of them, he pushed aside the mocha grande, wondering if he could ever drink one again. He knew that both breakfast and lunch would be out of the question.

Gavin wouldn't have blocked jondoe61. Gavin would have reported him to the e-mail provider and maybe to the police.

This man was sick, his letters so twisted and perverted that Gavin doubted he'd ever get the images out of his head. Jondoe61 described what he wanted to do to women and when Stella answered him—

"Babe, what were you thinking?" Gavin whispered, knowing she hadn't been thinking at all, just answering her mail like she always did—

Jondoe61 told her that he hadn't just contemplated these things, he had actually done them, and he could prove it to her. One little meeting and she'd never think about Mr. Buzzer again.

Gavin's nauseous stomach clenched. Only great self-control and an unwillingness to believe that Stella was dumb enough to meet this creep kept him at the computer.

She had blocked the guy, Gavin reminded himself. She hadn't met with him. She'd blocked him.

And that, in Stella's mind, was worse than going to the police. Denying the man the comfort of her presence was the severest punishment she could conceive of. Gavin knew that too. He also knew the lengths she would go to punish a man, a man who only wanted a little time with her.

Really, was a little time too much to ask?

His fists were clenched again. He had to work at opening them. He took three deep breaths, like that court-appointed counselor had ordered him to do, and then he made himself concentrate.

He checked the Junk file. Five letters from jondoe61 mixed in with the Viagra offers and the Nigerian scam artists. Five letters, all of which grew progressively angrier as Stella refused to respond.

Five letters sent on the same day.

The day Stella had last accessed her e-mail.

Monday.

This was Thursday.

Thursday morning.

Gavin made himself breathe three times again. She had probably just changed her e-mail address. He would have to do a search and find the new one.

But changing her e-mail address wasn't like Stella. She hadn't changed her real address in more than a decade. She had kept the same telephone number her whole adult life, and had asked for a variation of it when she got her cell phone.

When Gavin's lawyer had told her that moving with no forwarding address would solve all of her problems, Stella had looked at him as if he had just suggested she jump in front of a moving bus.

Gavin sprang out of his chair, startling the cat. She looked up at him with green, expressionless eyes. He told himself that he spent way too much time alone, that isolated people made up shit.

But he couldn't shut off his brain.

So he picked up the phone and dialed Stella's work number from memory. The receptionist who answered was someone new who didn't recognize his name and therefore was willing to tell him that Stella hadn't shown up all week.

"She called in sick on Tuesday," the receptionist said. "Frankly, I've never heard her sound so bad."

He didn't like that. He also didn't like the fact that the answering machine picked up on her landline and her cell's voice mail was clogged. He went back to the computer and looked at the stupid letters from her annoying family.

They were wondering why she hadn't answered her phone either and how come she'd missed some baby shower and why the heck she'd suddenly gotten so rude.

He went back to the Sent mail, and when it told him nothing, he broke into her work account. That took some doing. Even though the company kept its e-mail on its corporate Web site, the Web-mail portion wasn't as sophisticated as the main Web providers. He had to keep his fingers crossed, hoping some antispyware software wouldn't find him, and then he had to use the password-cracking program that he'd downloaded months ago to access the entire system.

Once he was in, getting to Stella's e-mail wasn't hard. And dumb bitch that she was, she used the cat's name as her password at work as well. When he found her, he'd tell her to be more original.

Then he remembered that he wasn't supposed to talk to her, and thought maybe he'd send her an anonymous e-mail just to piss her off.

When he found her.

Which he hadn't, so far.

What he had found was a letter to everyone in her personal address book telling them that she had a major project at work and asking them to refrain from contacting her until she contacted them. She misspelled "refrain," and that wasn't like her. She always spell-checked, saying that a correctly done e-mail was like dressing properly for a party.

Gavin's hands were shaking as he examined the other major e-mail she'd sent late Monday.

> Hideous flu. Doc says it's extremely contagious. Should be back on my feet in a week or so. Staying off e-mail till the dizziness goes away. Sorry—

She hadn't even signed it, and that was the tip-off. Stella had an automatic sig line in her work e-mail that gave her mailing address, her e-mail address, her cell, her business phone and fax number, as well as announcing to each and every person she had contact with that she had been promoted to executive office assistant, which sounded like a glorified secretary to him, but she was pretty damn proud of it.

He scanned through the rest of the e-mails.

Nothing sent or received that held the slightest bit of interest. Nothing about her illness except a few queries from higher-ups trying to find out when she planned to return.

No answer to those either.

Gavin didn't like this. At all.

And there was nothing he could do. He couldn't go to her apartment because of the restraining order—the damn neighbor had called the cops when he was on the stoop the last time—and he couldn't call her family because they'd just hang up on him.

He couldn't go to the cops because they'd want to know why he was spying on her. They'd pick him up for violating the restraining order.

Damn Stella. If she hadn't been trying to punish him so hard, he could help her now. She had shut down all his options.

He had no way to prove that she was missing.

Except his gut.

And the ugly tone of the letters from jondoe61.

That was what Gavin kept going back to, jondoe61. The stuff he'd said in his e-mails was beyond disgusting. No one should imagine those things, let alone inflict those images on naive and somewhat innocent women like Stella. Hell, she couldn't take Gavin's anger or his explanations that yelling and throwing were reasonable responses to adverse stimuli.

He'd "scared" her, poor baby, and she'd fled.

No wonder she'd blocked jondoe61. The asshole had raised the stakes considerably, and he hadn't even met Stella.

Or had he?

Gavin went back to jondoe's original e-mails. They sounded a bit too familiar, like things a man might say to a woman he'd met, not one whose blog he read every night.

Not that Gavin knew the difference between an in-person stalker and an online one. Not really. He wasn't even sure if online stalking was illegal.

Except for him, of course, and only when it concerned Stella. He was barred from contacting her, and in that court order someone had the brains to add "through all forms of communication in existence or to be developed in the future." Meaning, his stupid overpriced lawyer said, no e-mail and no chat rooms and no texting.

Gavin was just guessing about jondoe61. But his guesses were based on his knowledge of Stella, and the things she'd tolerate.

She would never tolerate jondoe61.

Since Gavin couldn't check up on her—at least not any further without breaking a court order—he decided to check on jondoe61.

It took Gavin three hours and two newly downloaded hacker programs to get to the site without paying for it—which should have been a tip-off to him, but wasn't, damnit, not until he was in—and what he saw made him glad he hadn't eaten all day.

The man's Web site was a study in perversion. Women in states of bondage, women glassy-eyed and black and blue, women looking sad and resigned . . . and dead, if you came right down to it. Gavin didn't think anyone could pose that kind of dead, the pasty-skinned empty-eyed version of dead that never showed up on television crime dramas.

He studied the photographs, not because he was perverse (he most decidedly wasn't) but to see if they were Photoshopped. He had a good eye for photo doctoring—he'd done enough of it himself—so he knew he would be able to spot when someone else did it, and he didn't see any of it here.

What he did find, almost accidentally, was that a lot of the photos were of the same group of women. If you clicked in the center of one of the early photos, the link led you to other photos of her.

They had a sequence: scared woman, bound woman, terrified woman, glassy-eyed woman, and empty-eyed woman.

He found dozens of these sequences, all of them posed—if that was the right word—in the same place, all of them with different women, all of them clearly taken over a period of time. How long, he couldn't tell. When, he couldn't tell either.

But it was definitely a period of time because the woman's hair went from pretty and clean to tangled to tangled and greasy. Her face went from well scrubbed to scratched to sallow. Her eyes went from emotional to vacant.

Gavin looked away.

He wanted to take a shower. He wanted to toss his computer out the window.

Hell, he wanted to burn it—and the inside of his mind.

Instead, he sat back down and found the part of the Web site that he knew had to be there. The special members-only part, the section for members who paid extra.

Two more hacker software downloads and one frozen screen later, he found it. It was labeled IN PROGRESS.

And damned if it didn't have a photo of Stella inside.

Gavin had dialed 9 and 1 before he set the phone down. How stupid was he? He had a restraining order, for crissakes. Cops always suspected guys with restraining orders of illegal activity.

Hell, he'd called Stella to explain the night he got the order, and then found himself hauled to jail the next day for a violation. His lawyer had played for the judge's sympathy—and since Stella wasn't there, had gotten it with a simple (and true) argument: *Gavin's never been subjected to such treatment before. He has no idea what the order means. Besides, he hasn't threatened Stella McAllister in any way. He has never physically harmed her.*

She's just trying to make his life miserable. And, Judge, it looks like she's succeeding.

Gavin had gotten off with a night in jail and a warning that next time, he'd get a lot more time and a hefty fine.

He couldn't afford either.

Then there were the other matters that the police would frown on: He had just downloaded four different hacker programs and illegally penetrated a for-profit Web site; he had downloaded what looked like snuff photographs, the worst kind of porn; and to top it off, what had set him on this journey was his own illegal hacking of his ex-girlfriend's e-mail.

He had broken he didn't know how many laws, and he didn't have any reason to except simple curiosity. That he'd stumbled on something bad was purely accidental, and proving that it had been accidental stumbling might be dicey at best.

But Jesus, he couldn't let anything happen to Stella. He didn't love her, not anymore, but she was an okay person. He didn't wish anything bad on her.

He had to tell someone.

He just wasn't sure how.

He made himself think it through. The key, for him, was to save her without getting caught. That meant that someone else had to do all the heavy lifting. He could hire a private detective, but how the hell would he know the guy was competent or would protect him from the cops or would even do *anything* besides collect money and sit on his ass?

He wouldn't. So that was out. Just like calling the cops directly. Or calling her stupid family.

Except . . .

One of the benefits of living in New York was that everything was close. The spy store always creeped him out when he went in it, but he went in it all the same. They sold devices that altered a person's voice over the phone. He could make himself sound like a five-year-old if he wanted to.

Instead, he chose to sound like an older woman. He bought the stupid device, then read the dumb manual, then stopped at one of the few remaining pay phones on the island.

He made sure he was wearing a pair of gloves (thank God it was cold enough that this didn't look unusual), and before he went anywhere near the phone, he tugged a ball cap low over his face, making sure he didn't look at any buildings or traffic lights or banks, so no automatic cameras could get a clear shot of his face.

Then he plugged in some newly acquired quarters (which he had touched only with his gloves) and dialed her mother's number from memory.

(It scared him that he had that number memorized too. How pussy-whipped had he been in this relationship? Jeez, maybe he'd been the one lucky to escape with his dignity intact.)

When her mother answered, he said in his old lady voice, "Stella hasn't been to work in nearly a week. She's not home sick like they think. She's disappeared."

Then he hung up. He used the same phone, and the same voice, to leave a similar message on her boss's voice mail.

But he didn't call 911. Instead, he called the regular police line and asked if they had an e-mail address, something they used for disturbing photographs.

"What do you mean, ma'am?" the person answering the phone asked.

"I've seen a naughty Web site," he said, "and I do believe there are children on it."

"Can you give me the URL?" the person asked.

"The what?" he asked, just for verisimilitude.

"The Web address?"

"Oh, no. It's on my son's computer. When I'm babysitting my niece the next time, I'll just e-mail you."

"Ma'am, who is your son?"

"Who do I send it to?" Gavin asked, as if he hadn't heard the previous question.

"We have a computer crimes division, but, ma'am, it might be easier if we just visited your son and—"

Gavin hung up. Quietly, quickly. He stuck the device in his coat pocket and, keeping his head down, walked to the nearest deli, ordered a hamburger to eat in, and a cake to go.

Then he went into his favorite bookstore, and chatted up the pretty clerk like he usually did in the afternoon. She was petite and redheaded and nothing like Stella and he'd initially thought that was the attraction, but then he realized that the clerk incited the same kind of lust that Stella had, a long time ago.

Only with this woman, he never let on. He'd learned *that* lesson. Better to fantasize.

So he visited her as a treat for doing a good deed. He bought the latest *New Yorker*, and went home, his heart pounding. He felt like he had done something wrong.

But he always felt like that after he talked to a pretty woman, and he blamed Stella for that. She had made him ashamed of his own lust.

She had also made him worry that other women wouldn't be interested in it, when they had been in the past. In the past, redheads had found him as attractive as he had found them. They'd enjoyed each moment with him, whether it was in the darkness of their own bedroom or a quickie in an alley after they'd gotten off work.

He'd tried to go slower with Stella, and look where that had gotten him. Making anonymous phone calls and being afraid to ask the pretty clerk for a cup of coffee.

If he hadn't been so upset, he might have gone to his bedroom and worked off some of the tension. But he didn't have time. He had to finish what he'd started.

He had to execute the next part of his plan from his home computer and he prayed his skills were up to it. If not, the cops would come after him anyway.

He needed to send the URL for the jondoe61 Web site to the police computer crime unit.

He'd thought and thought about that all the way home, and finally he decided to have Stella do it.

He sent an e-mail from her personal account, back-dated the damn thing to the day she'd disappeared, and added this cryptic note: *If anything happens to me, check out the man who runs this Web site. He's been threatening me.*

As a last-minute thing, he decided to attach all of jondoe61's letters. Then he sent the mail to the police, CCing her mother and her employer.

When he finished, he paced for another hour, knowing he wasn't done, but he wasn't sure what was left.

Finally he realized what was making him so damn nervous.

He had to trust someone else. He had to hope he'd done enough to save her before the scratched-face stage. Or the glassy-eyed stage. Or, God forbid, the empty-eyed stage.

He had to trust.

And he'd never done that before.

He couldn't sleep. He couldn't eat. He couldn't check on anything. He couldn't even break into Stella's e-mail anymore, not without raising suspicions.

And those images from jondoe61's site kept haunting him. Gavin wanted them to go away.

He wished he could scrub out his mind.

Then he realized he had to scrub out his computer. Deleting stuff wasn't enough. Putting things in the trash didn't clean it off the hard drive, and doing a disc cleanup didn't do it either.

He had to make the information impossible to access. He had to make it go away.

Finally he settled for moving his important files to another hard drive. Then he switched drives. Once the new drive (which was really an old drive he hadn't gotten rid of yet) was up and running, he took the drive with all the incriminating material, and set all of his kitchen magnets on top of it. Then he poured coffee into it while it was plugged in. The resulting electrical surge popped two breakers in his apartment's circuit box, but fortunately didn't cut the power anywhere else in the building.

In his closet, he set the stained and ruined hard drive, which no longer powered up (and God, he hoped the information on it was long gone).

Then he prepared for the worst.

The worst happened two days later when the police finally visited him. Two rather bored-looking detectives, neither of whom resembled the handsome and ambitious detectives on television, came inside and asked him when he'd last seen Stella.

Gavin could honestly say that he hadn't been near her since the restraining order, and why, he wanted to know, were they looking into this?

Because she was missing, one of them said as if he didn't care.

Gavin wanted to tell him to care. Gavin wanted to say that Stella had probably progressed from scared woman to terrified woman. But he didn't say anything. He answered the questions, let some of his peevishness show because peevish was how he'd feel if Stella had gone on an extended vacation without telling anyone.

The detectives made some cursory notes, told him everything was routine, reminded him to stay away from her, and left.

And he didn't hear anything for another two days.

In the end, he heard only because he'd been living with New York 1 as if it were the last television station in town. NY1 broke every damn story in the city, and they would love a kidnapping if they knew about it.

The story came across at 9:21 PM as breaking news. The police had found an executive secretary, held captive for days in a Web site designer's warehouse. The designer had found her through her blog, traced her address through her Web server, and stalked her. He kidnapped her, sent dismissive e-mail to her friends and family, forced her to call her employer, and set about turning her into one of the horrible before-and-after montages he created for his site.

The story had to sound bizarre to the layperson—what Web site designer would need a warehouse?—but it soon became clear that this guy and his little circle of friends photographed their grisly pastimes, used their captives until the captives lost their usefulness, and then murdered them.

The cops even found a nearby dumping ground.

Stella was alive, but she'd never be the same. Gavin could tell that from the few glimpses of her he got on NY1 and in the papers. The *Daily News* had a tearful shot covering its front page.

Stella never used to cry like that.

He nearly sent condolences, but he couldn't. He had to stay uninvolved. A mystery tip had led the police to the designer, a tip, they thought, from a subscriber who had finally gotten fed up with the Web site. The paying customers were all being investigated.

Gavin hoped to hell that the cops weren't as good at digging through computer records as he was. He hoped they wouldn't notice that the site had been hacked about the time of Stella's disappearance. He hoped that he had wiped all traces of his own e-mail address from the Web site itself.

But he wasn't sure he had.

He and the cat lived in fear for weeks, fear that turned into a nagging worry for a few months, and then into relief after a year.

A year. And he got no thanks because he couldn't take the credit.

He couldn't even check Stella's e-mail anymore without fear of being caught.

His mornings were ruined. He needed a new routine.

He finally found one when he realized the pretty bookstore clerk used her own name as part of her e-mail address on a Web-based mail server. Her password was, of all things, "password," and her e-mail wasn't as interesting as Stella's, probably because he had no real vested interest in the clerk, but it gave him something to do while he sipped his mocha grande.

And he could think about her, both at home in his private moments and when he visited every afternoon, careful only to say hello. Because if he said more, she'd know he knew too much about her.

Not that he thought he knew too much. He wanted to know a lot more. Where did she live? What did her bedroom look like? Did she close her eyes when she kissed a man or did she like to watch him?

He liked it when they watched.

But he couldn't tell her that. He couldn't tell her anything. He didn't want her to stop him.

For, in addition to performing a private service for his own momentary entertainment, he was also performing a public service. He was guarding her against creeps and stalkers and people who wanted to hurt her.

Because they were out there. They were all over the place.

And he was a silent superhero, keeping a vigilant eye on her life.

Just in case she needed him.

Like Stella had.

Enough to Stay the Winter

Gillian Linscott

Peter waited by the giant agave plant at the gatepost of the villa. Across the drive, the spikes of a matching agave were silhouetted against the fading blue of the evening sky and the intense violet of the Mediterranean, forty feet below. His right hand closed around the knife handle. The thought came to him, with the satisfaction of a new answer to an old puzzle: Yes, I can kill. He supposed that any other Englishman who happened to be nineteen years old in that summer of 1921 would be saying much the same thing. If born two or three years earlier, he'd probably have been dead in the mud of Flanders. Dying wasn't the problem. It demanded no decision from you. But it was likely that, before dying, he'd have been expected to kill somebody with a gun or a bayonet. Could he have done that? He'd supposed so, but until a few hours ago he hadn't known for sure.

There was a stickiness on his palm where it rested on the handle of the knife. He sniffed. Pine sap. He realized he must have put his hand on a trunk seeping clots of resin as he hurried up the steep path from the beach to the headland. He kneeled down and used the dry, sandy soil to clean his palm and the knife handle. If he turned away from the sea and looked inland, he could just make out the white walls of the farm in the dusk. It was set halfway between the village of Èze on its high summit of rock and Èze-sur-Mer, the fishing settlement down on the bay. He knew that if you came close to the farm, you saw that the paint on the white walls was flaking, the stones of the terrace were uneven, and the remains of the olive orchard that surrounded it were no more than five gnarled trees in rough grass burned to the color of an old lion's mane.

"It's practically a ruin, darling, but at least it's cheap."

Margot had said that within a few minutes of his arrival on that first visit two weeks ago, stretching out her silk-stockinged legs and leaning back in her chair, wineglass in hand. He'd met her only that morning, in the market. She'd recognized his accent as English, introduced herself, and put him through a swift cross-examination of who he was and what he was doing in the South of France. The answers seemed to satisfy her, because she'd invited him to join them that evening for drinks after dinner.

"There are just the three of us, a household of women, practically a convent."

The three of them were Margot, her sister, Donna, and Donna's seventeen-year-old daughter, Janine. Donna, in her early forties, was a widow, rather plump, with a gentle face but wary eyes, like an animal expecting something to creep up on it. Margot, five years or so older and thin as a whip, was a divorcée and didn't care who knew it. She smoked cigarettes, wore her blond hair cropped and tightly curled, and favored dresses short enough to show shapely calves. Peter was both fascinated and shocked, though he was careful not to show it. He'd never met a divorced woman before. He assumed she was the wronged party, because the woman almost always was. When he arrived that first evening, the three of them were sitting on the terrace around a table of sun-bleached wood under a vine that sprawled over a rickety framework of pine branches. Margot poured wine for him and continued the examination she'd started that morning. He was happy to tell her all she wanted to know: he was on vacation after his first year at Oxford, alone abroad for the first time and still dazed by his good luck.

"Mr. Hoddy was looking for somebody to read Latin poetry with him. A friend of a friend knew my tutor and he recommended me. I was on the train to Nice within three days of term finishing."

Margot was hungry for details. Mr. Hoddy was from Chicago, where he'd built up a fortune in the canning trade. In his late fifties, with more than enough money, he'd decided to spend a year in Europe, educating himself in the things he'd missed when he was too busy making his fortune. He'd rented a stone house by the harbor for the summer and set about finding a young man with a public school and university background to improve his self-taught Latin. He was a genial employer. The pay was excellent and the workload light, mostly consisting of reading Latin poetry aloud to Mr. Hoddy in the mornings and before dinner, to give him an idea of the sound of it, and guiding him through his efforts at translation. For the rest of the day, Mr. Hoddy liked to go out in a boat fishing and did not expect Peter to accompany him. He retired to bed early.

"Then you must come and see us often," Margot said. "Heaven knows, we don't get much civilized company."

Donna nodded. She'd said little but listened intently to the conversation. As for the girl Janine, she seemed hardly concerned with the rest of them. Her glossy brown hair, cut in a page-boy bob just above the shoulders, swung over her face, so that Peter couldn't tell if she was listening or not. After a while she got up from the table and knelt on the terrace, stroking one of the two cats that had been prowling around. Donna's eyes followed her, full of pride.

"They're mine," she said. "They're called Kala and Kaga."

"She insisted on bringing them from England," Margot said.

"Well, I couldn't leave the poor darlings, could I? Besides, they're valuable, pure-bred Siamese."

They had sky blue squinting eyes, ivory fur, brown muzzles and paws, and bodies as sinuous as boa constrictors. Peter preferred his cats rounded and purring, so hadn't taken much interest until he saw how the cat was reacting to the girl's stroking. Kala, or Kaga, had stretched herself into an inverted bow shape, greedy for pleasure from nose to outspread back toes, so that Janine could run her hand along the length of her stomach. Peter went to kneel down beside them and stroked gently with one finger along the cat's outstretched throat. Janine's hand and his touched accidentally and she looked up at him. The look of entrancement in her eyes sent a shock through him. He saw that the pleasure she was giving the cat had transmitted itself back through her stroking fingers into her own body. Her eyes were a strange brown that seemed to him both calm and bright at the same time, like sun on river water. Her hair swung back, showing the clean line of her jaw and white neck.

"I'm sorry," Peter said.

He went back to his place at the table, not sure what he was apologizing for. Margot gave him a look that showed she'd noticed his confusion.

"Is your Mr. Hoddy married?"

It was only much later that he realized this was why she'd made his acquaintance in the first place. As it was, he answered cheerfully, glad of the chance to get back his self-possession.

"Yes. His wife's back in Chicago. She had to go home because one of the grandchildren was ill, but the kid's getting better and she'll join him again as soon as she can."

Margot grimaced and stubbed out her cigarette.

"End to your hopes, then, Donna darling."

"Speak for yourself."

Donna said it unexpectedly savagely, glaring at her sister. Peter looked from one to the other. Were they joking? If so, there was no sign of it. He glanced toward Janine, who was still kneeling by the cat. Their eyes met and he caught a look of pain in hers. That was when he knew he was falling in love with her. He sensed in that moment that her apparent self-possession was as fragile as the skin around a bubble. He'd admired beautiful girls before, even been a little in love before, but in his experience beauty brought arrogance along with it and that always made him uncertain. She was as beautiful as any of them, but vulnerable. What was more, she'd trusted him enough to show it.

Over the next two weeks, Janine and Peter met most afternoons at the gate to the olive orchard, when most living things were sunk in siesta, the sun a disk of brass and the metallic rasp of cicadas the only sound apart from the soft fall of their rope-soled espadrilles in the dust. Sometimes they'd go down to the sea, sometimes climb up to the village of Èze and walk through narrow streets between shuttered houses to the ruined castle at the top. One day, as they looked out over the long sweep of bay from Cap Ferrat to Cap d'Ail, he let the back of his hand brush against hers and asked if she was lonely. She raised her brown eyes to his, considering it like a new idea.

"Perhaps."

"You have no friends here?"

"They're all at home. They write sometimes."

He slid his hand around hers so that their palms were touching.

"Is there a particular friend back home?"

She shook her head, her fingers linking with his.

"Aunt Margot says I've got to marry a rich man, to look after them in their old age."

He couldn't tell if she was joking.

"You wouldn't do that, would you?"

"I suppose you could like a rich man as much as a poor man, couldn't you?"

She turned to him and smiled when she said it. There was something in her smile and her voice that reminded him of Margot.

"If you liked him, would it matter if he were rich or poor?" he said, trying to keep the anger out of his voice.

"Oh look, a lizard," she said.

He didn't get his answer but she left her hand in his as they walked back down through the village.

Now, waiting in the dark by the agave, Peter found his fingers had closed tightly around the handle of the knife, as if they were trying to burn their way into the wood. He unclasped them, flexed them, and made himself breathe slowly and deeply. No point in wasting energy. He'd have to move decisively. As soon as he heard their footsteps coming up the path, he'd step back behind the gatepost and let them go past. Briefly, he'd considered waylaying them to reason with Margot, to give her a last chance to turn back, but rejected this. The woman was beyond shame. She'd only shout out and D'Abitot's servants would come running. So he'd let them go inside and then hurry through the garden to the terrace and into the house. Would it be just the two women, or all three? Surely Donna wouldn't come too. There must be limits to her terrible passivity, her subjugation of herself to Margot. Surely she couldn't walk beside her daughter in the dark like some tawdry priestess escorting the sacrifice. His fingers went to the knife handle again. He prised them away. Not yet, but soon.

Oddly, for a man who had no great interest in being sociable, it was Mr. Hoddy who had brought about the visit to Maurice D'Abitot in his villa on the headland. Mr. D'Abitot was seldom seen in the village, although his housekeeper had been pointed out to Peter in the market, fingering gleaming tomatoes and aubergines as if doubtful about their pedigrees. D'Abitot was reputed to be the product of an aristocratic French father and an English mother, his villa stuffed with artistic treasures that included two Monets. Mr. Hoddy was interested in Monets too and had bought one for a public gallery back home in Chicago. He longed to see Mr.

D'Abitot's but was too polite to present himself at the villa without an invitation. He asked Peter diffidently if he could arrange an introduction through his English friends. Peter promised to do what he could, but had no great hopes, guessing that Margot and Donna were a notch below D'Abitot in the social life of Èze.

That evening, as on most evenings of the previous two weeks, he walked up the pathway of the old farmhouse to where the women were sitting around the table on the terrace. Although Margot had never taken the same interest in him as when she thought his employer might be a bachelor, she tolerated his presence, especially when he remembered to bring with him a bottle of wine or a fruit tart from the village bakery.

"Thank you, darling. Every little stick feeds the fire."

That was a favorite saying of Margot's. She was as open about the household's financial straits as she was about her divorce— amazingly so to Peter, who thought it vulgar to discuss money. She'd made it clear that they'd moved to the south of France because it was cheaper to live comfortably there than in England.

"It was either this or a semidetached in Basingstoke, traveling on buses and going to bridge parties smelling of damp mackintoshes. At least the sun shines here."

Peter caught a look on Donna's face that suggested homesickness for Basingstoke and mackintoshes, but she said nothing. When he tentatively raised the subject of Mr. D'Abitot, he was surprised to find that Margot had made his acquaintance.

"He had two friends staying last month and they were desperate for a fourth hand for bridge, poor dears. I went up there twice— after dinner." The fact that she hadn't been invited to the meal itself clearly still rankled.

"She says it's beautiful inside," Donna said wistfully.

"The Louvre in miniature," Margot said, kissing her fingertips. "He has things in there that must be worth tens of thousands."

Peter watched Janine stretch out her bare brown arm to take

an olive from the dish. He imagined that one evening he might summon up the nerve to choose an olive for her, hold it out between finger and thumb the way you'd feed a bird. He saw the tilt of her head, the swing of her hair, her parted lips moving toward his fingers. But at that moment something started wailing like a vengeful ghost. The image shattered.

"What's that?" Janine said.

She jumped up, sending her chair clattering. For a moment Peter thought, terrified, that he'd actually done what he'd imagined and this was somehow the result. But the olives were still in the dish, his fingers still around the stem of the wineglass. The wailing was coming from something just out of sight, toward the house. Janine ran in the direction of the sound and Peter followed, with Margot and Donna shouting something from behind that he didn't hear.

"Kala!"

In front of him, Janine called out the name. The cat was writhing at the foot of the steps to the house, stomach uppermost, grinding her hindquarters against the flagstone as if in intolerable pain. At first Peter thought the animal must have been poisoned and ran to protect Janine from the sight, but Margot pushed ahead of him.

"I said she was coming into season, didn't I?" She scooped up the cat, flung her inside the house, and slammed the door.

"Don't be cruel to her, poor thing," Donna protested.

"You fuss over them far too much," Margot said. "Now I suppose we'll have all the stray toms from the village in the garden. Damn."

Peter's face turned as fiery red as the sun over the sea. He'd never before seen or heard the urgency of a female cat's desire. The air actually seemed to vibrate with it. Janine glanced at him, saw his blush, and smiled.

"Poor Kala," she said.

Peter could hardly look at her as he said his good-byes and fled. That night, he lay awake naked in the heat, hearing the sea shifting on the beach in the pine-and-thyme-scented breeze off the land. The sea was saying, "Poor Kala, poor Kala," in Janine's voice.

Next evening, Margot was triumphant. "*We're* all invited, half-past five tomorrow."

"Do you suppose that's teatime or champagne time?" Donna said.

"We'll wear tea gowns, darling, but hope for champagne. He is half French after all." Peter was disconcerted, sure that Mr. Hoddy had hoped for a lone visit to Mr. D'Abitot's rather than a social occasion. Still, it would have been ungrateful to object and Mr. Hoddy was too pleased about the Monets to mind.

It turned out to be not champagne but a white wine that was undoubtedly more expensive, an aristocratic wraith of alcohol that lingered in the nose and on the palate, served in slim crystal glasses glinting rainbows in the sunlight. It was poured for them by a white-gloved manservant named Pierre at a table under a sun umbrella, in a garden laid out in the Italian style, with clipped lavender and rosemary hedges and marble statues.

Peter guessed that Mr. D'Abitot was in his midforties, but it was hard to tell. His tall and supple figure, fine features, and glossy dark hair could have been newly created that morning to suit the occasion or miraculously preserved from the courtly Middle Ages. He wore a cream linen suit that matched the painted walls of his villa, his cravat the exact purple-blue of the Mediterranean beneath them. Peter, disliking him on sight, wondered if he kept a whole range of cravats to reflect changes in the weather and time of day and if his valet would come rushing out with a darker one if a cloud happened to pass over the sun. He was feeling light-headed, partly from the wine and the sense of floating like a gull above the sea in the cliff-top garden, far more from Janine. He'd never seen her in formal dress before. Her tea gown was blue silk, sleeveless except for a knot of ribbons hanging from the shoulders down each arm, hem cut out in points like the petals of a harebell, swaying in the breeze around her white silk calves. She was standing on her own by a stone nymph, sipping her wine. She must have felt his eyes on her because she looked across at him. He smiled and she smiled back, but she looked nervous.

Margot, in lime green crêpe de chine with a low neckline, was doing most of the talking, too loudly, inquiring about the health of Mr. D'Abitot's bridge-playing visitors as if they were dear friends of her own, sympathizing with the poor darlings who had to stay in Paris in July. Peter could see that it came as a relief to Mr. Hoddy when Mr. D'Abitot suggested they might go inside and see some of his little collection.

They went in procession through the villa. The Monets had a room of their own. Mr. Hobby and Mr. D'Abitot discussed them learnedly, with Margot adding an occasional "Divine" or "Absolutely," as Donna surreptitiously fingered the fabric of the curtains.

Janine stood looking at the pictures, with Peter as close to her as he dared. He was fighting an urge to trace one of her ribbons with his finger, from her shoulder to her wrist. He thought that if he did, his fingertip would make a long burn on her skin.

After the Monets came the Whistler room, daringly decorated in white, black, and eau de nil, and the master bedroom with its two small Fragonards. The bed was a four-poster with hangings of white muslin and a white-and-gold coverlet.

"*Très* Versailles," Margot exclaimed. "And Marie Antoinette *elle même*." With a varnished fingernail, she touched a china figurine on the mantelpiece. Immediately D'Abitot went toward her, hand raised and an expression of intense pain on his face. She looked alarmed.

"I wasn't hurting her."

"She's very delicate," D'Abitot said, hardly trying to hide his annoyance.

Peter realized his dilemma: Mr. D'Abitot needed admiration for his beautiful possessions as a drunkard craved wine, but he was in constant anxiety that a touch less expert and loving than his own might harm them. Peter felt no sympathy for the man. Twice already, once as they left the Monet room and again with the Whistlers, D'Abitot had moved in to part Peter from Janine. Now he did it again, coming to stand between them as they stood looking at one of the pictures.

"You'll recognize the shrubbery, of course—almost identical to his arrangement in *The Swing*, only this is earlier." He said it to Peter, turned slightly away from Janine, but his purpose was clear as daylight. D'Abitot wanted to steal the privilege of standing close to the girl. Worse, Janine was looking far too impressed with him, hanging on his every word. It was torment to be parted from her, even by the narrow width of D'Abitot's body. Peter wasn't able to work his way back to her side until the end of the tour, when they came to the terrace. One side was open to the gardens, another made up of arches framing the sea view. Janine, alone for once, stood looking down to the sea and Peter went to join her. She turned to him, eyes bright, lips apart.

"Look."

The terrace was on the very edge of the headland. The part where they were standing was cantilevered so that it hung over thin air, with the sea washing against sharp rocks forty feet below, nothing but a waist-level stone balustrade in between. Janine leaned over for a better view. Peter, fearing for her, kept his arm curved close to her waist, not quite touching but near enough to save her if she overbalanced. It was both a pain and a relief when she turned away to admire the terrace. It was as carefully designed as the rest of the house, whitewashed walls, bright-colored rugs and cushions giving it a Moroccan feel. More wine was served—this time red, but cool and with a faint smell of violets. A Siamese cat was lounging on a red-and-gold cushion, the same coloring as Kala and Kaga, but larger. It was so elegant and still that Peter thought it must be a model until it opened its mouth in a cavernous pink yawn.

"A Siamese, how lovely," Margot enthused. "They're terribly fashionable now, aren't they? We have two of them at home."

"It's Tamburlaine's bedtime," said D'Abitot.

A corner of the terrace was taken up by a cage large enough for a lion, if anything so grand could be called a cage. The sides were pierced and patterned brickwork, the front wrought iron in the shape of lotus leaves. A carpet-covered platform took up the back wall. The servant Pierre carried in a terra-cotta dish of what looked like minced chicken and set it on the floor of the cage while D'Abitot himself placed the cat carefully beside the dish.

"He's so beautiful," Janine breathed.

Peter's patience snapped.

"Do you mean the man or the cat?" he asked her under his breath. She stared at him, surprised. "Not that it makes much difference," he said. "They're both pampered to the point of being ridiculous."

"Peter, why are you so angry? Mr. D'Abitot knows so much and he's being so kind to us."

Pointedly, she walked over to D'Abitot as he latched the cage door. She thanked him.

Peter thought, If he as much as lays a finger on her, I'll hit him. He imagined his fist striking home on the perfectly tied cravat, red-wine stains on cream-colored linen. It seemed to him that D'Abitot was looking at Janine exactly as he looked at all his possessions. She was beautiful, so he needed to have her in his collection. The thought was so intolerable that he took a step toward D'Abitot. Margot's voice checked him.

"Maurice, how do they do the wonderful glaze on this bowl?"

D'Abitot's duty as a host dictated that he must go to where she was standing. Peter moved in beside Janine, trying to control his anger. She glanced sidelong at her aunt and Mr. D'Abitot, their heads bent over the bowl.

"I think she's asking him for something," she said.

"What?"

"Money, probably."

"No!"

Their eyes met, his shocked, hers sad.

"She can't help it. It's like a bee scenting pollen. There, you see. He's saying no."

He glanced across and indeed there was a denying look on D'Abitot's face, mouth pursed and eyes angry. He turned his back abruptly on Margot and started talking to Mr. Hoddy. Soon after that the party broke up, with the usual courtesies but a feeling of strain in the air.

Mr. Hoddy wanted to talk to his fishing skipper at the harbor, so he parted company at the foot of the rocky path down from the villa, suggesting that Peter should see the ladies home. Margot insisted on walking alongside Peter on the path up through the pinewoods, with Janine and her mother behind.

"I think he rather took to you, darling," she said to him. Her tone was acid.

"D'Abitot? I don't particularly want him to take to me. Didn't you notice how he kept looking at Janine?"

He was angry with her for not protecting the girl from that covetous collector's look. Donna was too passive to be of any use, but surely worldly-wise Margot could have done something if she hadn't been more concerned with her own affairs.

"Do you think so, darling?" She gave one of her high, artificial laughs. The smell of the spicy perfume she used was radiating off her, face flushed under her makeup. He'd have said she was drunk, but there hadn't been enough wine served.

"He's worth millions," she said. "What we saw this evening was nothing. They say he has ten times as much in Paris. It all goes to a nephew."

He realized that it was money, not wine, making her drunk. D'Abitot's refusal had done nothing to take away the power of his wealth. Peter escorted her home without another word.

Next day, as soon as he'd finished reading with Mr. Hoddy, he went walking all around Èze-sur-Mer and Èze, hoping to meet Janine and make sure no harm had been done by his flash of bad temper. He hoped that the glamor of the villa might have worn off and in the light of noon she'd see, as he did, that D'Abitot's display of luxury was unmanly, laughable. By lunchtime he hadn't found her, so he made his way down from the village to the farmhouse. There was nobody on the terrace, but the back door to the house was half open. He padded toward it on his rope soles, but before he got there he heard Donna's voice, unusually loud and angry.

"I know what's best for her. I don't like it."

Then Margot, sounding amused. "It's going to happen sometime, darling. Why not now?"

Peter stopped and listened, any thought of calling out gone.

"She's not old enough," Donna said.

"You make too much of a baby of her. We all have to take our chances."

"She could wait until we're back in England."

"He won't be in England, will he?"

"There are others."

"Like him? It's a question of seizing the moment. Suppose he takes it into his head to pack up and go back to Paris. The rich move quickly."

"I still don't—"

"Oh for heaven's sake, where's the harm? It should bring us enough to stay the winter at any rate."

A silence. Peter listened, willing Donna to stand up to Margot for once. Then Donna's familiar, defeated voice.

"It doesn't feel right to me."

And Margot's laugh, knowing she'd won.

"Tonight, then, while the iron's hot."

Peter turned and walked fast under a sky throbbing with heat down to the fishermen's shop by the harbor. He reached it just before it closed for the afternoon and bought the knife.

It was a knife of the sort the fishermen used to gut their catch, a broad blade about a foot long attached to a black wooden handle with brass rivets. When Peter tested the blade against his finger, trying to look as if he bought knives every day, his skin sprang apart, beaded with blood, and the man behind the counter laughed and told him to take care. He bought a small leather satchel that a fisherman might use for carrying hooks, put the knife inside, and walked back up to the village. In a street leading to the castle he found Janine at last. It was an amazement to see her looking so much as usual in her white-and-green-print dress, bare legs dusted with sand. She smiled and started saying something, then stopped at the look on his face.

"Peter, what's wrong?"

"Do you know what your aunt Margot's planning?"

She stared at him, biting her lip, then dropped her eyes and nodded.

"And you're just accepting it?"

"Is it so very wrong? Besides, once she's made up her mind to something, there's no stopping her." She sounded abashed and yet there was that hint of laughter in her voice that chilled his blood. He shivered at Margot's power of corruption.

"Of course it's wrong. It can't be what you want."

"Oh, me." A sigh, as if she never expected her opinion to matter, but there was still a laugh mixed in it.

"You could stop it. You know that."

"Peter, why are you so angry?"

He felt like shaking her. Her brown eyes seemed wider than he'd ever seen them, but unreadable. He moved toward her. "I'm not going to let you do this."

She was angry now.

"Peter, it's nothing to do with you after all." She turned her back on him and began to walk away down the narrow street. He plunged after her and caught her by the arm, fingers digging into muscle under smooth skin.

"Come with me, now. Mr. Hoddy will let you stay tonight then we can discuss—"

She pulled away. "Have you gone mad? I can't do that."

As he tried to hold her back, the satchel slipped from his shoulder. It fell to the cobbles and the knife slithered out. She looked down at it then up at his face, eyes frightened. Then she ran away, lurching and stumbling on the cobbles, so that he was afraid she'd fall. He couldn't risk scaring her more by following her, so he stood and watched as she rounded the corner. Two of the villagers strolled past, looked at him as he knelt and fumbled for the knife, and wished him good afternoon. He didn't go back to Mr. Hoddy's villa for Latin poetry and dinner. That was all in the past now. Instead, he walked down the path through the pinewoods to the beach and strolled by the sea like any tourist, until dusk.

It was dark now. He was sure he'd been waiting for an hour or more and he began to worry that he'd missed them. Perhaps she was inside with him already. There might be a back way up to the villa. Why hadn't he thought of that while it was light? Even as he waited there, D'Abitot's fingers might be stroking their way from the nape of her neck, along her shoulder, down her arm, as his own had burned to do. Peter groaned and started up the path to the villa, careless of the noise the gravel made as it spattered under his feet. He was too late, he was sure of that now, but at least he could still kill D'Abitot. The scream came just as he got to the garden. It was unmistakably a woman's scream, clear and jagged as forked lightning, and it came from the terrace.

"Janine! I'm coming. Janine." He shouted it, running toward the sound, stumbling over bushes with the sharp scent of lavender like a taste in his throat. The white arches of the terrace were in front of him, glowing with lamplight. He jumped up the low wall between terrace and garden and threw himself into the light. The first thing he saw was Donna. She was standing at the seaward edge of the terrace with her hands over her face, rocking from side to side. Two men were watching her, D'Abitot barefoot and in a blue silk dressing gown, the servant Pierre in shirt and trousers. Peter ran to Donna and grabbed her by the shoulders.

"Where is she? What have you done with her?" She slumped against him and opened her eyes, looking crazy with fear.

"He pushed her. He pushed her over."

D'Abitot made a sound halfway between protest and disgust, as if accused of a vulgarity. Peter's eyes went to him, then to the darkness beyond the terrace. He let go of Donna, not caring if she fell, and leaped back over the low wall and into the garden. He went down the steep steps through the pinewoods to the beach, not conscious of moving from one to the other, as if the darkness itself were carrying him. He was aware of men's voices above him, D'Abitot and Pierre he supposed. Once, at an angle on the path, a torch beam cut across him and D'Abitot shouted something. It didn't matter to him what it was. He'd deal with D'Abitot later, after he'd found her. The steps ended and his feet sank into the soft sand of the beach. There was more light there, reflected from the sea, enough to make out the foot of the headland. The rocks beneath it were black and jagged. Far above, the villa lights shone as if nothing had happened. He thought of Janine standing on the edge of the terrace the day before, his arm not quite touching her. In his mind, he saw her body falling toward the rocks, pale as a moth against the dark.

He ran toward the headland, his progress slower when the pools and rocks began. His ankle caught between rocks and he had to use both hands to free it. Looking back, he saw the beams of two flashlights coming across the beach. He plunged on, into a pool that came up to his knees, making for the larger rocks below D'Abitot's terrace. When he came to them he climbed up, first slipping on seaweed, then tearing his hands on barnacles. Something dark was flung across a great wedge of rock in front of him, dark and limp as seaweed but more substantial. A streak of white cut across the blackness. He clawed his way up the rock. The whiteness was a neck, stretched back. He had to slide a hand under it to see her face.

"Oh thank God. Thank God."

He clung to the rock, sobbing and shaking with relief. He was still there when the others arrived at the edge of the rock pool and flashlight beams hit him.

"Is she alive?"

Donna's scared voice. D'Abitot, sleek head rising from a waterproof cape, was standing on one side of her, Pierre on the other.

"No, of course she's not," he said. Then added, relief and wonder in his voice, "But it's Margot."

D'Abitot came splashing toward him with a flashlight, Pierre just behind him. Peter yelled at him from the top of the rock, "Where's Janine?"

"Janine?"

D'Abitot's pale face in the torchlight looked genuinely puzzled.

"The girl," Peter shouted. "The girl you were seducing. Where is she?"

D'Abitot's face went blank. "I don't know what you're talking about. If you can help us lift her . . ." Pierre was already clambering up the rock. Peter slid down and splashed back across the pool to where Donna was crouching, sobbing.

"What have you done with Janine?"

"*Nothing.* Is Margot dead, really dead?"

"I told you yes. For heaven's sake, what have you done with Janine?" He was kneeling beside her, shaking her. She raised a hand and flapped him in the face.

"Stop it. She's at home, in bed."

"At *home?*"

"Of course. Where else should she be? Margot, oh poor Margot."

D'Abitot and Pierre carried Margot's body back across the sands, while Peter supported Donna. They stopped at the first fisherman's shed they came to, where Pierre, who seemed to know his way around, found a tarpaulin to cover the body.

"I'll send men down for her at daylight," D'Abitot said, quite gently. "You'll want her carried up to your home?"

Donna had sunk down on an upturned rowing boat and seemed incapable of answering. D'Abitot went over and sat beside her, said something, and actually took her hand. After a while she nodded. Peter couldn't believe what was happening. D'Abito had murdered her sister and yet she seemed to be letting him comfort her. He knew he should be talking about police, magistrates, charges, but the only thing that mattered was to know that Janine was safe. D'Abitot stood up and spoke to him.

"I shall see to the arrangements then."

"The police . . . ?"

"They will be informed," D'Abitot said. "You will see her home?"

Peter's voice, as he guided Donna up the path to the farmhouse, must have roused Janine. She came out to meet them carrying an oil lamp, a coat flung over her nightdress, eyes wide and frightened, and helped her mother sit on a chair on the terrace.

"Margot's dead," Donna told her flatly. "She fell off Mr. D'Abitot's terrace."

"You said he pushed her," Peter said.

Donna raised her eyes to him. "No I didn't. Nobody pushed her. She just fell."

She put her hand in the pocket of her jacket and brought out a handkerchief. Something else fell to the floor and Peter bent to pick it up. It was a wad of French banknotes, tightly folded. Donna snatched it from him.

"He gave it to me, for expenses, for burying her."

"D'Abitot gave it to you? When?"

"Just now, on the beach."

Peter stared at her, sickened. So the man could even buy his way out of murder. And why had he pushed Margot over? He might have asked Donna more but she screwed up her eyes and let out a wail.

"Where's she gone? She's out there now, all on her own in the dark. I'll never see her again."

This cry of what sounded like real grief for her sister silenced him. Janine put her arm around her mother.

"Come inside. You'll get cold."

He waited a long time, watching moths battering against the lamp. There was a bottle of wine on the table, half full, and two glasses. The one he picked up had Margot's lipstick print on it, bright red. He put it down and drank the harsh wine from the bottle in gulps. Janine came out as the sky was turning the grainy white color of predawn.

"She's asleep," she said. "She's had two of her pills."

"D'Abitot pushed Margot," he said. "Your mother screamed it out just after it happened. He's bribed her to lie about it." He was so confused he was past caring if he hurt her. She shook her head.

"D'Abitot didn't push her over. My mother did."

"What!"

"She told me, when I was putting her to bed. She and Margot quarreled on the terrace and my mother pushed her. She says she didn't really mean to push her over but she was so angry she didn't think."

"But D'Abitot paid her money."

"Yes, it was kind of him, wasn't it? Or perhaps he just doesn't want fuss and having to be a witness." She sighed and sat down heavily beside him.

"But what were they doing there in the first place? Were they trying to rob him?"

"Of course not. You knew what they were planning. You wanted me to stop them. I wish I had. And now poor Kala's gone as well."

"Kala?"

"Yes, that's what my mother was crying about, Kala out in the dark on her own." She seemed impatient with his bewilderment. "You knew they were taking Kala to mate with Tamburlaine. Margot suggested it to D'Abitot when we were visiting. That's what he was angry about. He said he didn't know enough about Kala's pedigree and she might not be good enough for Tamburlaine. But Margot said they should do it anyway. She knew a back way into the villa and it would take only a second or two once they got her into his cage and then it would be too late for D'Abitot to do anything about it. I don't know how you knew but . . ."

"I overheard them arguing about it, only . . ."

His voice trailed away. He couldn't tell her what he'd thought. He didn't know whether the tightness in his chest came from wanting to laugh or cry.

"Only, poor Kala was frightened when they took her out of the basket," Janine said. "My mother wanted to bring her back and not do it after all, only Margot tried to grab Kala. My mother was only protecting her, she says. I don't think she really meant to push Margot." But there was a world of doubt in her voice.

"But why was Margot so set on mating them? I didn't think she cared about the cats."

"Pedigree Siamese kittens can sell for a lot of money. She said if Kala had five or six, that would pay our rent for the whole winter. You know what she was always saying." Until then she'd been dry eyed, but now she was crying.

"Every little stick feeds the fire," Peter echoed Margot.

It had been, after all, such a small greed.

"Poor Kala," Janine said. "Poor all of us."

"We'll find her. We can do that at least."

The two of them looked for her as the sun came up and found her curled on a pile of nets in a fishing boat, deeply asleep, all the lust gone out of her. They suspected that would be because of one of the lean tomcats who prowled around the harbor.

"But we can't be sure," Janine said. "Not until the kittens come."

Playing Powerball

Elizabeth Engstrom

"Wretched excess." Davison Tollifer muttered the words as he drove his ancient wreck of a Jetta up the long curving drive toward the family overindulgence of a house. The staff of gardeners kept the boxwoods trimmed within a millimeter; the rolling lawns sprouted not a weed; flowers bloomed on demand and faced the house with precision, their colors in perfect—and irritating—harmony. He knew that the inside of the mansion was just as perfect. No dust mote, cobweb, or blade of grass tracked in on someone's shoe would be on the marble floors for more than five minutes before a uniformed maid had it swept away.

Davison observed it all and wished he had a memory of playing catch with his father on that lawn, or riding a tricycle around the circular drive, or picking flowers with his mother, but there were no such memories. He rode a horse instead of a bicycle. He played soccer at school. And flowers were delivered daily.

Nobody should have this much money, he thought.

And now, apparently, he was going to receive precisely one quarter of it all: this estate outside Pittsburgh, the Manhattan penthouse, the Tuscan villa, the stock portfolio, and who knew what else. He'd long understood the time was coming, of course, but now that it was here, he was appalled by the whole idea. What if

Richard, Katherine, and Peggy decided that *he* should have this horror of a house? What would he do then?

Turn it into the headquarters for Greenpeace? Give it to some other worthy cause? Sell it and donate the money?

Keep it?

No, never. He'd never keep it. He did just fine on his community college salary, teaching environmental studies, adding religiously to his 401(k), and living in his third-floor walk-up apartment. He didn't want anybody in his world to know he came from this. Steel money. Money made from the mills in which poor men labored. The whole package had been a horrible embarrassment as he was growing up, and his feelings about it had never changed. He'd let his parents pay only for his Yale education, then set out on his own. He'd never taken another dime from them.

Unlike his siblings.

He pulled up next to Richard's Mercedes, and turned off the engine.

He checked himself in the rearview mirror, ran his fingers through his hair, wished he'd taken the time to get a haircut, and grabbed the gym bag that was serving, this weekend, as his overnight luggage.

Despite the monumental waste that this estate represented to him, the mansion was situated perfectly in the peaceful countryside, just outside the reach of the steel-mill stench. He took a moment to appreciate the quiet and the smell of the twilit air before approaching the front door. For a moment, he didn't know whether to ring the bell or just open the door and go in.

He needn't have worried. Richard, a tumbler of their father's best scotch already in hand, opened the door with a smile that said it wasn't his first drink of the day.

"Dave!" He grabbed Davison in a hug that squeezed the breath out of him. "Good to see you, man."

Davison set his gym bag on the marble table in the center of the foyer. The house, never warm, echoed with silence. Twin curving staircases, inspired by Tara in *Gone With the Wind*, flanked the foyer. To the right was the library. To the left, the dining room. Straight ahead, the doors were open to what their mother always referred to as the salon.

A familiar feeling of melancholy and isolation settled over him, as it always did whenever he came into this house.

"Kathy!" Richard called. "Dave's here."

Davison cringed at the use of his childhood name. "Davison," he said.

"Davison. Right. Sorry. Davison. And Katherine, not Kathy."

Richard, always larger than life, robust and barrel chested, had a bit of a sunken air about him. At fifty-one, his face looked gray, except for his nose, which was covered with a starburst of red and purple veins. His hair was considerably whiter and thinner than the last time Davison had been home, and his normally taut stomach had relaxed into a bulging belly for the first time. While Richard didn't look very healthy, Davison had the feeling he was still the same bully he had always been.

"Hey," Richard said, looking through the windows to the circular driveway, "maybe you'll buy yourself a decent car now, eh? One you won't have to park on a hill? You'll have the bucks for it now."

Davison ignored him. Before Richard could speak again, Katherine glided into the foyer, immaculate in crisp linen slacks and a silk blouse that matched the champagne in the glass she carried. Tall and pencil thin, the very image of their graceful mother, Katherine seemed genuinely happy to see Davison, although the touch on his shoulders was light and she kissed the air near his cheeks instead of his flesh.

"You look good," Davison said. "As always."

"Thank you, darling. It's lovely to see you too. Put your things upstairs and freshen up, then come join us in the salon."

"Is Peggy here?"

"We don't know where Peggy is," Richard said, the foyer table steadying him against the effects of the scotch. "Seems she's given the staff some time off. P'rhaps she's taking a little break herself."

"I'm sure she'll be back tonight," Katherine said, "since the funeral's tomorrow."

The funeral.

Davison nodded and grabbed his bag. "I'll be down in a minute." He took the south staircase steps two at a time and walked down the long hall to his old bedroom.

He hesitated at the door, however, his hand on the ornate lever. This room had been a guest room for him to sleep in since the day he was born. Nothing of a personal nature had been allowed, except on the shelves of his small bookcase, on his student desk, and pegged to the corkboard on the wall behind it. Everything else was placed just so by professional decorators and had to be maintained in its strictly defined position.

That had been Father's decree, and nothing would be different now.

He pushed the door open and entered. It looked exactly as it had last Christmas, and when he had returned home for his mother's funeral three months before that. The massive room was larger than his entire apartment in Charlotte, with floor-to-ceiling windows that looked out over the formal knot garden and reflecting pool on the south side of the house.

His mother had redecorated it right after he left for college. That had been a shock the first time he came home to visit. He felt she wanted to erase his entire presence in the family's life. But then he realized it was *he* who wanted to do the erasing. Mother was merely redecorating.

That was when he stopped coming home. Only at Christmas was he here in body, but never in spirit. And even then his presence was due to Katherine and the guilt she had long been able to induce in him.

Without thinking, Davison set his worn bag on the bed. A moment later, horrified at the inappropriateness of it—this unsightly thing lounging on the perfect bed like a malignancy—he moved it quickly to the floor.

But then . . . Wait a minute, he thought. Nobody was here to reprimand him. This was *his* bed for the night, and he could put his tattered gym bag on it if he damn well wanted to. So he did. He unzipped it and took his toiletry kit to the bathroom.

Hell, the *bathroom* was bigger than his apartment in Charlotte, he thought.

He brushed his teeth, splashed cold water on his face, dried it with a scented towel that had apparently been dyed to match the accent tiles, and then went downstairs to see how long he had to stay here. He wanted to leave tomorrow, right after the funeral, and drive straight through, so he could be back in class on Monday.

But something told him that this wasn't going to happen.

In this family, nothing was ever that easy.

Davison found his brother sprawled on the sofa in the living room. Silk. Chenille. That sofa would have cost Davison an entire month's salary, and there was Richard with his shoes on it, an empty scotch glass dangling from his hand.

"Think I'll move in here," Richard announced. "Let someone else take care of me for the rest of my life."

"Dad leave this place to you?" Davison asked. He realized he'd spoken far too quickly when Richard directed a slow and easy smile his way. Davison saw he'd risen to his brother's bait.

"Interested, are you?" Richard asked him.

"Not particularly." He was just annoyed with the fact of Richard's having information. He didn't *care* if Richard got the mansion. He didn't want any part of the place. The daily upkeep of this place could probably feed a small village in South Africa.

"It's a default position," Richard said. "I'd arm-wrestle you for it, but I'd bet that Matisse over there that you don't want it, and Katherine would rather have the villa. So I might as well take it."

"Where is Katherine anyway?" Davison went to a drinks cart. He poured himself a glass of water from one of the carafes standing on it.

"Upstairs. She wanted to see the old man's bedroom. People are apparently coming tomorrow to take away all the hospital crap." Richard shivered. "Pretty goddamned ghoulish, if you ask me."

Davison perched on the edge of an ottoman—Venetian silk and velvet, as his mother would have pointed out. He still felt like a guest in this, his boyhood home. But no, he corrected the thought. *His boyhood house.* This place had never been his home. He took a moment to appreciate the sweeping view as the sunset colors in the sky faded and the lights of the city below began to come alive.

Richard stretched. "Might make some changes around here," he said. "This room needs a decent media system, or maybe I'll turn the library into a real theater—"

"Dad might have left the whole shootin' match to the ASPCA," Davison told him.

Richard threw his head back and laughed, too long and too hard. Booze was fueling his mirth. "ASPCA. They'd take one look at Dad's big-game trophies and give the money back." He laughed again, so hard he began to cough.

"Enough scotch for you," Katherine said as she soundlessly appeared at the doorway. She glided to a wing chair near the sofa and lightly sat. "Upstairs is ghastly. Ugh! I'm sorry he had to go through all that. Mother's sudden death was much . . . neater."

Neater? Davison thought. *Neater?* Even death had to be tidy in this house.

"I was just telling Dave here that I would take this house, and you the villa," Richard said.

"And that leaves?" Davison asked, then cursed himself for even being interested.

"That leaves New York," Katherine said. "And the stocks."

"We'll have to divide up the stocks to pay for the upkeep on the places," Richard said.

"What about Peggy?" Davison asked. "Don't you think she'll have something to say about this? And what about Father himself, in his will?"

"Well, of course," Katherine said. "I believe the attorney is coming to the funeral and we will meet with him afterward."

"Peggy doesn't want any of this shit," Richard said. "We'll give her a million and she'll be happy."

"Whoa," Davison said, getting up to refill his glass. "That's pretty harsh."

Richard shrugged. "So you'll take New York, eh?"

"I'm happy in Charlotte," Davison said, "doing exactly what I'm doing."

Richard smiled at Katherine. "Then it's you and me, babe. A mil to Peggy and the rest divided two ways," he said.

"Now wait a minute," Davison said. "Let's not get ahead of ourselves."

"Ignore him, Davison," Katherine said. "He's had too much to drink. Of *course* we'll abide by Father's wishes. And if he didn't leave anything concrete, then we'll work it out among ourselves. It will be fair."

"Fair schmair," Richard said, with a sudden burst of venom.

Davison stood, his back against the view, and sipped his water. Richard couldn't hurt him anymore, he reminded himself. The power of the bully had been equalized over the years. Still, Richard's attempts at intimidation had the power to make his face flush and his heart race.

"You spat on everything Father accumulated during his life," Richard said to Davison. "You sneered and turned up your nose, and now you don't get to have it. Any of it. I'll fight you if you even try—"

Katherine stepped to the sofa and put a hand on Richard's shoulder to stop him. She took the empty glass from his hand and set it on a nearby table. "Nobody's going to fight, Richard. We'll see what tomorrow brings."

Richard scowled.

"When we're all sober," Katherine added with a knowing look at Davison.

"Good idea," Davison said, grateful to his big sister for always being the peacekeeper. But the fact that she still had to adopt that role said a lot about the nature of their family dynamic. Eager for a change of pace, he said, "I've had a hell of a drive. What's there to eat?"

"I don't know," Katherine said. "Shall we raid the fridge?"

"Do you remember Alabama?" Katherine asked as she dipped the tips of her salad fork into a small dish of dressing.

Davison set down his tomato sandwich. "How could I forget Alabama? It had to be the only family vacation we ever took."

"Why the fuck did they take us all to Alabama?" Richard spoke around a mouthful of deli roast beef, speared directly from the unwrapped package.

Mother would have been horrified, Davison thought. She'd be aghast that they were eating in the servants' kitchen too. But that was where they'd found the food. The regular kitchen had been filled with cases of a canned prescription drink for their father's last meals, and little else.

They had each fixed their meal and then sat at a central, scarred table to eat. As a child, Davison had eaten here with his nanny when his parents weren't home. It always made him feel a little bit naughty, and he'd enjoyed keeping the secret.

"Strange, wasn't it?" Katherine toyed with her dainty salad, but she didn't put a single lettuce leaf onto her fork. "I went everywhere with Mother." She smiled. "Paris, London, Geneva. I remember she once took me on a trip just to study art in Florence. That was a nice time. You took trips with her and with Father too, didn't you? But for our only family vacation, all six of us together, we went to Alabama. Isn't that odd?"

"They were busy," Davison said. "Mother had her charities, and Father, well, you know. He worked."

"He *always* worked," Richard said.

"Dad must have had a business meeting there," Davison said. "In Alabama. I remember us going to the beach together, but I don't remember him with us at all."

"That would be typical," Katherine said.

True, Davison thought. Their father had been absent most of the time. How odd it was. While the Bible thumpers in Charlotte rattled on about the love of money being the root of all evil— something Davison heard every time he turned on the television on a Sunday morning—in his experience, it was more like the *pursuit* of money to the exclusion of all else that was the root of all evil. "Anyway, it's too bad we never did it again, even here in Pennsylvania. Seems like we could've gone camping or something."

"Camping?" Richard and Katherine said in unison.

"Guess not," Davison said wryly. "Mother would never have gone camping. She might have wrinkled something silk."

"Well, we could go now," Katherine said.

"*Camping?*" Richard asked, grabbing a slice of bread and spreading it thickly with butter. "You said *camping?*"

Katherine laughed. "God, no. But the four of us—since none of us is married at the moment—we could go *somewhere*, have a vacation together, have some fun for once."

"That's a great idea," Richard said. "Where?"

"The Galapagos?" Davison offered.

Katherine wrinkled her nose. "Bird poop and walruses. How about Dubai?"

"African safari?" Richard tossed in. "They have some deluxe ones these days."

"What about Sydney? Or Rio? A world cruise, even?" Katherine looked at Davison as if expecting him to react with his usual liberal disdain. "Money is no object, remember."

Money is no object, Davison thought. *Money is really, finally, no object.*

Davison considered his colleagues, those of them who regularly went to Harrah's in Cherokee to gamble. As intrigued as he was, he never had gone. His thrifty soul would not allow it, nor would he support the thugs who bankrolled the tribal casinos. But now . . .

"If money really is no object," he said slowly, "why don't we spend a week in Monte Carlo?"

"Monte Carlo! Davison!" Katherine said in delighted surprise. "I would never have expected that from you. What would you do there? Lie on the beach? Drink in a luxury bar? Gamble?"

He shrugged. "I always thought if I won the lottery, I'd set aside a modest amount and try my hand at poker. Or blackjack. Just a bit."

"About time you took a little risk," Richard said. "But the lottery? D'you actually buy lottery tickets?"

"My whole *life* is riskier than yours," Davison said. "And yes, occasionally I buy a lottery ticket."

"You're too much." Richard shook his head and laughed. "All this"—he waved his hand to take in the room and what lay beyond it—"and *you* buy lottery tickets. You kill me."

Katherine rerouted the conversation. "Monte Carlo is a brilliant idea."

"Let's go this summer," Davison said. He felt pleased that she'd warmed to his suggestion. "I'm not teaching summer term this year."

"Jesus. Quit that dead-end job," Richard said. "You're a man of independent means now."

A man of independent means.

"Think Peggy would enjoy Monte Carlo?" Davison asked.

"Of course!" Katherine said. "What's not to love? We'll have a ball! It'll be the family vacation our parents should have taken us on all along, only more fun. There's sun and beach."

"And that damn casino," Richard said. "The last time I was there, they took too much of my money. I need to get it back."

"It's where millionaires go to meet other millionaires," Katherine said. "It might be good for all of us. We could jump-start our pathetic love lives."

"Has Peggy ever been out of the country?" Davison asked. "I mean, apart from trips with our parents?"

"Peggy has never been anywhere," Richard said.

"Then it'll be our thank-you gift to her," Katherine said. "Taking care of them couldn't have been easy for her."

"Why not? Mom went fast," Richard said dismissively. He stuffed the last of the roast beef into his mouth, let his fork clatter to the empty plate, and leaned forward, elbows on the table, chewing. "And Peggy always had adequate staff."

"Still," Katherine said, pushing her own plate away, "you haven't seen his room upstairs. It was no picnic for Peggy."

"Hey," Richard said, "growing up with them as *parents* wasn't a picnic either. We all got out as soon as we could."

"Peggy didn't," Davison said. His appetite had disappeared at this turn of conversation. He had always felt guilty that Peggy had been the one to stay home, the one left to care for their parents when they had fallen ill.

"Peggy made her choices," Richard said. "Just like you did. Like you were some saint while the rest of us—"

"Richard . . ." Katherine murmured.

Davison waved off her attempt at intervention. He knew what his brother was talking about: his refusal to take a monthly stipend from their parents. Both Richard and Katherine had gladly lived off the generosity of their father for decades, but Davison had chosen a different path. Richard never passed up an opportunity to jab at him about it, and Davison was just beginning to understand why. Richard was envious of Davison's independence.

"I'm sure we're all happy with our choices." Katherine picked up her champagne glass. "And thrilled with the way our lives have turned out." She drained the glass and set it, just a little too hard, on the tabletop.

"Things will be different from here on out," Richard said. "You'll see."

Davison wondered how. But some things weren't worth discussing. He looked at the mess they'd made of the servants' kitchen, all over table and across the countertop. "Shall we clean this up?" he suggested.

"Peggy'll be home soon," Katherine said. "Let's go back to the salon." She picked up her glass, refreshed it with champagne, and glided from the room.

Davison put his plate in the sink, filled a glass with water, and followed her. "Shouldn't Peggy be back by now?" He checked his watch. He'd been home for less than two hours, but it felt like two days.

Richard grabbed a handful of chocolates from a candy dish on a side table, then flopped again onto the sofa. It had been replaced often since their childhood days, but Richard's propensity for flopping on whatever was long enough to hold him had never shifted. "What are you really asking, Davy-boy? Can't be *that* worried about Peggy, eh?"

Katherine laughed, then folded herself into the wing chair, tucking her feet underneath her. "What are we all really asking?"

Davison wasn't sure what they were talking about. He leaned against the fireplace mantel and looked questioningly at Katherine, who laughed again. He knew if he closed his eyes he could believe it was his mother, sitting in that chair, laughing that charming and meaningful laugh that Katherine had inherited.

"Oh, Davison," Katherine said. "You are *so* sweet. It's the *will*, darling. We all want to know what's in the *will*."

"Do you think Peggy knows?"

"Hard to say," Richard said, chewing a chocolate. "Probably. Maybe that's why she's not here. She doesn't want to lie to us by telling us that she doesn't know, and she doesn't want to spill the beans before the appointment with the attorney tomorrow."

"What I would like to know," Katherine said, "is why *you* don't know, Richard. Surely you've asked."

"I've asked," Richard said. "Of course I've asked, but the old man wouldn't tell me. 'None of your business, you vulture,' he said."

Davison carefully wiped the condensation from the side of his water glass, hoping he looked calmer than he felt. "He called you a vulture? He actually called you a vulture?"

Richard raised an eyebrow. "Yep," he said. He seemed unperturbed.

"I don't think he was in his right mind at the end," Katherine reasoned.

"He was in his right mind, all right. He was a bastard. We all know that."

Davison felt his face grow hot. "How can you say that about him? He supported you in a fancy lifestyle for years. You could show a little gratitude."

"Yeah, right," Richard said. "That's *just* what I feel, gratitude." Richard pulled himself up off the sofa, dropped his handful of chocolates onto the glass-topped coffee table, and headed back for the scotch decanter.

"Richard, darling." Katherine put her half-empty champagne glass on the side table. "Let's not drink any more."

"Good idea," Davison said. "Alcohol has a way of . . . I don't know. Exacerbating emotions."

"Not for me," Richard said. "Whenever I'm in this house, I want to get numb, and this does the trick." As he tried to put the heavy crystal stopper back into the decanter, it slipped from his hand and smashed on the marble floor.

"Oops." He kicked the larger shards aside, threw the scotch

down his throat, and returned to the sofa. Once again, he flopped. "As to *gratitude*—well, a bastard is a bastard, Davy, and money has nothing to do with it."

"He was generous with you," Davison said. "With both of you."

"And with you," Katherine said. "You took something as well. Let's not forget that."

"Yes, of course, okay," Davison agreed. "Tuition for college. My point is, he didn't *have* to be generous."

"Yes, he did," Richard said. "He raised us to expect to live like this."

"No, Davison is right," Katherine said. "He didn't have to be generous. I think Mother and Peggy convinced him to continue our allowances, Richard."

Richard rubbed his palms together. "How nice of them. And now we're about to get our hands on the whole enchilada."

"*If* he left it to us." Davison found he was tired of this conversation. He was tired of his drunken, greedy siblings. He was tired of this house; he was tired of his parents. He was tired of feeling guilty about not visiting them, tired of worrying over them as they grew older, tired of feeling horrible that he had moved so far away and left Peggy to take on everything that rightly should have been shared among all four of them.

He just wanted to be *done* with the funeral and get the fuck out of Pittsburgh. If he never heard the term "steel money" again, he'd be happy. "I hope he left it all to charity," he muttered.

"He wouldn't dare," Richard said.

"It's *his* money, Richard," Davison continued. "*He* made it. Why do you think you have a right to it?"

"Because it's my birthright," Richard said. "One-quarter of the Tollifer estate belongs to me, and that's all there is to it."

"But you've got to have planned for your future," Davison said. "You've put some money away after all these years, haven't you?" He looked at Richard, who looked blankly back. "*Haven't* you?"

Katherine barked out a laugh.

"I just don't get how you can feel entitled to all this"—Davison gestured around the expansive room—"this wretched excess."

"Wretched excess is our bare minimum, Davison," Katherine said. "You'll learn. You'll see how easy it is to become accustomed to nice things."

"No shit," Richard said. "Once you fly to Europe—or anywhere else, for that matter—in a Lear, you won't be too happy catching JetBlue."

"Oh my God." Davison ran his hands through his hair in frustration. "Father may not have been perfect, but he and Mother *did* do some good. Especially Mother, with her charities, and the foundation. Shouldn't we be talking about *them* tonight? Shouldn't we be talking about who they were and what they did for us, for the community, for all the people they employed over the years? Shouldn't we be a little grateful?"

Richard stared into space.

Katherine picked at a cuticle.

"I think I'll go to bed," Davison said in resignation. "What time is the funeral?"

"Ten," Katherine said. "We meet with the attorney at one."

"Fine." Davison was eager to be finished with the entire situation. He thought he just might keep his mouth shut until it was time to say good-bye to them. There wasn't any point he could argue that would make a difference to his siblings, and he knew it.

As he stood up, he took one last look around. He knew that this might well be his last trip to this house, this weekend the final time he saw any of his siblings. They had nothing in common, and perhaps it was time to be rid of them all in one fell swoop.

The feeling made him uncommonly sad.

"Good night," he said.

"'Night," Katherine said.

Richard said nothing.

But as Davison got to the foyer, he heard a car door slam.
Peggy was home.

Davison helped her bring grocery sacks into the house. He was
appalled by her appearance. Peggy looked pale and exhausted.
Always tending toward pudgy, she was now obese, her hair straggly and an inch of gray showing at the roots. She wore black
sweatpants and a man's shirt, and her complexion was marred by
blotches and pimples. She hadn't looked like this last Christmas.
Ten months with their dying father had taken a toll.

Yet once the grocery sacks were on the counters in the kitchen,
she gave Davison one of her trademark hard, heartfelt hugs.

"Before you say anything"—she looked pointedly at Richard
and Katherine, who stood in the doorway—"I have a new dress for
the funeral and an appointment to have my hair done early tomorrow, so I won't embarrass either of you." Then, with a deep breath,
she turned to the bags on the countertop. "I bought food."

"Where's the staff?" Richard asked. "Why are *you* shopping for
groceries?"

"Father gave them each fifty thousand dollars and a month off,"
Peggy said.

Katherine gasped.

"It was the right thing to do," Peggy went on. "They'll be back
in October."

"Fat chance," Katherine said.

Davison wanted to slap Katherine. The wear on Peggy's face
was more than obvious, and he was sick with guilt. The fact that
his brother and sister felt nothing—the way they were treating
Peggy—made his blood pressure rise. His heart pounded in his
ears.

"Let's talk about Father's will," Peggy said.

"Will I need a drink?" Richard asked.

Peggy showed her familiar, crooked smile. "It couldn't hurt."
She pulled a Snapple from a grocery bag.

Back in the salon, Richard went immediately to the scotch, and
Katherine refreshed her champagne. Richard didn't seek the sofa
this time. It was as if he needed to be vertical to understand everything correctly. For her part, Katherine took up her perch in the
wing chair, and Peggy relaxed in another. She kicked off her shoes
and put her feet up on the ottoman. She opened her Snapple and
drank half of it down. Davison took a place on the grand piano's
bench, a strategic position where he could see everyone and hear
everything.

"It's nice, isn't it?" Peggy said. "I mean us being together."

"It's good to see you," Davison said. "I'm sorry that you had to
endure all this alone."

"It was hard," Peggy admitted. "Father fought to the end."

"When did he have the presence of mind enough to give the staff
such generous bonuses?" Richard asked.

"He was a generous man, as you have, no doubt, noticed. He
was a good man, a brilliant man, and our staff understood that,"
Peggy said. "You have no idea what they did for us. Until we hired
a full-time nursing staff, Martha and Klaus did everything. Martha
ran the household, Klaus took care of the property, and in addition
they also took care of all Father's needs."

"Then what did you do?" Katherine asked while sipping her
champagne. "Besides eat, I mean."

Peggy paused. She looked directly at Katherine. "You have no
clue about anything, do you?" She spoke without rancor. Her
self-control amazed Davison. He could never have responded so
calmly.

"Shut up, Kathy," Davison said to her. "Just stop it, all right?"

Katherine raised her eyebrows and pursed her lips.

"Where have you been all day?" Richard asked Peggy.

Peggy fortified herself with another swig of her drink, set it down, and began rubbing her swollen feet. "I had to have one of father's suits altered to fit him, so I picked that up and took it to the funeral home. I went to the caterer's, the attorney's office, and then bought groceries," Peggy recited. "The caterer will be here early tomorrow to set up for the reception after the funeral."

Richard keyed in on the only words important to him. "You went to the attorney's office? Why? Don't we all have an appointment there tomorrow after the funeral?"

"We made that appointment in case you wanted to talk with him, but there is really no reason, as the estate is all settled."

"How can that be?" Katherine asked.

Peggy took a long drink of her Snapple, then looked briefly at each of her siblings. "Father left everything to me," she said.

"You mean the arrangements," Katherine said.

"I mean the estate," Peggy told her.

Richard relaxed against the couch, amazement on his face. "You're fucking kidding." He looked at Katherine.

Davison smiled. This went a *long* way toward assuaging his guilt. Peggy deserved it all.

"I think we *will* go to that appointment tomorrow," Katherine said. "A man can do things at the end of his life when he's sick and not in his right mind."

"He was in his right mind," Peggy said. "The attorney will tell you that. There were physician certifications and witnesses, just to keep it incontestable. And he left provisions."

"Such as?" Richard asked.

"Such as the fifty thousand each to Martha, Klaus, and Henrik."

"Henrik?" Richard said. "Who the fuck is Henrik?"

"The groundskeeper."

"And *he* gets *fifty thousand dollars?* Just like that?"

"Not only Henrik," Peggy told him. "Dad also left a nice gratuity to the people who manage the Italian property and the Manhattan property."

Katherine said, "Jesus God. Anyone else?" as Richard asked, "How *much* of a gratuity?"

Peggy was silent. She regarded Richard with exaggerated patience. Davison knew exactly how she felt. "I know that you have every right to this information," Peggy finally said, "but could you ask your questions without the accusatory attitude? These were Father's wishes, Richard."

"*Maybe* these were Father's wishes," Katherine said. Her eyes narrowed as she regarded Peggy.

Davison saw Peggy gather her resolve around her. As if watching her father waste away wasn't horrendous enough, she still had two terrible events yet to endure. This was one of them, and the funeral was the other. But that would be the last. Peggy was strong, and she'd get through both, despite Richard and Katherine. After that, Davison realized, she deserved to do whatever she wanted with her life and her money.

Admiration for his baby sister flooded through him as he waited to hear what she had to say next. He made himself ready to come to her defense if Richard and Katherine got nasty with her.

"*Whoever's* wishes they were," Richard said, "let's hear about these provisions."

Peggy took a deep breath. "As I said, the bulk of the estate was left to me to manage. I'll keep up the foundation and carry on Mother's philanthropy. You, Richard, and you, Katherine, will retain your allowances until your deaths."

"With the standard annual cost-of-living increases?" Katherine asked shrewdly.

A cloud of disapproval crossed Peggy's face, but instead of saying what she was thinking, she politely said, "Of course."

"Well, I can live with that!" Katherine held up her champagne glass. "To us, then, Richard!"

"To us!" Richard raised his own glass, then drained it of scotch.

Davison waited, but Peggy seemed to have nothing more to say.

"What about . . ." He hated the sound of the word he was about to say. "What about me?"

"You never wanted anything, Davison," Peggy said. "Father respected that. He admired it, actually. He assumed it would continue to hold true."

Davison found himself stunned to speechlessness. He'd been prepared for just about anything this weekend, but he had not been prepared for this.

If there were ever an injustice in the world . . . Richard and Katherine assuming their useless lifestyles while *he* continued to slave away at a wretched community college job?

In one quiet moment, Peggy had taken away the car that would have replaced his old Jetta; his middle-finger salute to the community college board of directors who *never* fucking approved a single idea he had; his trip to Monte Carlo in a Lear jet—oh the *chance*, just once, to gamble; his PhD; his life of leisure; his *everything*. Peggy had pulled it all out from beneath him.

Or had she? No. Wait.

This had to be a joke. Katherine and Richard had put Peggy up to it, and they were waiting, in their twisted type of glee, for his reaction.

"Very funny," he said, managing a smile. "Joke's on me. You guys got me."

"But it's no joke, Dave," Peggy said. "Father never wanted what happened with them"—she nodded toward Katherine and Richard—"to happen to you. I'm so sorry if you're disappointed. He thought . . ." She made a futile gesture.

Disappointed? Davison looked over at Katherine, who was gazing at him with an amused expression. Richard too was smiling at him, waiting for his reaction.

"Disappointed?" Davison asked. "That's what you think I am? Disappointed?"

He had *never* wanted his father's money, but he had always wanted the option. He'd always wanted to be able to say "no, thanks," and to say it nobly because it felt so good to be better than the others. It felt so good to avoid the strings that he knew—could swear—had been attached to everything their father gave, because if there weren't strings, if *he'd* refused and all the time the money had come and gone for free . . . But Richard and Katherine *had* danced like puppets to their father's whims, hadn't they? Hadn't they? While he, Davison, the noble and self-sufficient one . . . He'd chosen to take *no* money from his father just on the chance that taking it in the first place had meant being at his father's beck and call and he hadn't wanted that, couldn't have borne that.

And now, to be cut completely out of the will? Just for saying no? Just for being noble? Just for doing what seemed the right thing to do? Without a penny?

No. No way.

He was the one who was self-sufficient. *He* was the one who provided for himself, paid his taxes, and added value to the community.

He was the one who *deserved* an inheritance.

In fact, he was the *only* one who did.

He stood up from the piano bench. He looked directly at his youngest sibling. "No," he said to Peggy and then to them all, "it's my turn now."

As soon as the words were out of his mouth, he saw the truth in them. The courage of the righteous began flowing through him. "*No,*" he said again. "It's my turn. It's my *goddamned* turn. One-quarter of the Tollifer estate belongs to me, and that's all there is to it. At *least* one quarter. I'll fight you for it. I'll fight *all* of you." He headed out of the room.

Behind him, he heard Katherine laughing. It was their mother's laugh, as before. But this time, he heard something else:

It was a dizzying moment as they both laughed, both his mother and his father behind him, laughing wildly and in collusion and watching with great amusement as he acted out the script they had written for him so long ago.

CAN YOU HEAR ME NOW?

Marcia Talley

"*When you take public transportation,* sit next to a serviceman. You hear me, Marjorie Ann?"

Of course I heard, and the hundred times before that too, but I suppressed a sigh, and tried not to roll my eyes.

"Memorize his rank and insignia," Mama added. "If he tries any funny business, Uncle Sam will know where to find him. That's what Papa always said."

The only thing Mama ever got from following her father's advice was knocked up, but she married the guy, and the result was me, so I guess it'd be small of me to complain.

Actually, I hadn't taken the kind of transportation Mama was talking about—bus or train—for quite some time. My late husband had had many faults, but dying penniless wasn't one of them. Since Stephen, I usually fly first class, particularly after Delta sent my luggage to Chicago and me to Las Vegas, where I ended up crying on the shoulder of an oilman from Houston who . . . well, never mind.

I go first class by train too, but old habits die hard, so when I boarded the Acela in D.C., bound for New York, with the specter of Mama practically perched on my shoulder, what could I do but wander down the aisle, scanning the rows, looking oh-so-casually for a serviceman to sit next to. Halfway through the car I had one of those head-smacking moments like, duh, Marjorie Ann, whose army is going to pay a per diem for a soldier to ride first class on the Acela? So I picked a seat next to a long-legged businessman with a profile chiseled out of marble and a laptop perched on the fold-down table in front of him.

"Is this seat taken?"

He glanced up with a languid, "Be my guest," blinked twice with eyes the color of the Mediterranean flecked with gold, and grinned. I often have that effect on people. It's my hair, Mama says, quoting Sylvia Plath: *Out of the ash, I rise with my red hair / And I eat men like air.*

I was in a relationship, as they say, so this guy was in no danger of being eaten alive by me. I also wasn't in the mood to encourage him, so I sat down, melted into the plush blue upholstery, and dug around in my bag for a book. I'd brought two along: a thriller that had just hit number three on the *New York Times* best-seller list, and a copy of Agatha Christie's *Mort sur le Nil*. In French, *bien sûr*. Another one of Mama's tricks. If you're stuck next to a busybody who wants to talk until your ear melts down about her grandchildren or her hysterectomy, you can look up from your *roman policier*, flash a sweet, slightly puzzled smile and say, *Je ne parle pas l'Anglais*, even if that's the only bit of French you know. I'd done that once, but trust me, thumbing dumbly for hours through pages of gibberish is *très* dull.

Thankfully, my seatmate already had his nose glued to his laptop, where a Gantt chart he'd created in Excel pulsed across the screen in a rainbow of living color. He frowned, studying it—a serious, silent type—so I picked up the best seller and began reading where I'd left off.

The guy might have been serious, but I was way wrong about the silent. From the confines of a tooled leather holster attached to his belt, a cell phone launched into Papageno's theme from *The*

Magic Flute. I got a gentle elbow in my arm as he dug it out. "Brad here."

I don't know about you, but listening to anyone rattle on for—I checked my watch—ten minutes about rearranging plane reservations had me wishing I'd sat in the quiet car. Brad was giving some travel agent a hard time about switching tickets from San Francisco to Belize, poor guy, adding an excursion to the Altun Ha Mayan ruin. Honestly, it just about broke my heart.

Eventually Brad got things sorted out, and I returned to my book. Ness, Joel, and Toby had just been dumped on their aunt's London doorstep, when Brad's cell phone rang again. Clearly he'd taken the time to personalize his contacts with customized ring tones, because this time, instead of Mozart, the phone began buzzing like a demented insect. *Psszt psszt psszt* it rang, like bugs being fried by an ultraviolet zapper on a hot August night. I shuddered.

"This is Dave," Brad answered, sweet and smooth as chocolate-cream pie.

Dave?

"The market was up yesterday," he drawled. "Let's sell a hundred thousand of the index fund."

I kept my eyes on my book and my curious ears cocked while "Dave" dumped Time Warner and picked up Kraft, sold pounds and bought francs, bought December coffee at one ten, and liquidated his position in Futurepharm based on a phone call from a friend at the FDA. Why anyone'd risk being jailed for insider trading in order to save a lousy twenty-four thousand bucks was beyond me.

Make laws for the needy, not the greedy. Shades of Mama again, pontificating in my ear, misquoting Roosevelt.

Need can make men desperate, but greed, in my experience, makes men stupid. I needed twelve forms of ID to cash a check at Wal-Mart, but anyone could move millions on the telephone. Four phone calls later, I knew Dave's bank account number and pass code, his VISA card number (and expiration date!), and his passwords to Schwab and Ameritrade. Math had never been my strong point, but give me a string of numbers—TU 9-1997 (my grandmother's phone number); 25 left, 35 right, 21 left (the combination to my gym locker in junior high); 766-42-1057 (my first husband's Social Security number)—and my mind was a steel trap. I could be dangerous.

Good thing for "Dave" that I'm an honest kind of girl.

As I listened, pretending to read, Brad gave his cell phone a workout, didn't even let it cool down before calling home. "Melissa, sweetheart, it's me. I'll be late for dinner."

I'm sure Melissa knew what a hero she was married to, and how grateful she should be that his long hours and almost supernatural genius kept champagne in the fridge, Escada on her back, and a Mercedes-Benz in the driveway, but apparently Brad felt obliged to remind her of it anyway. In a déjà-vu haze—Harrison, my first husband, thought he was God almighty too—I found myself rooting for Melissa. I prayed for a dead zone, a tunnel, a weak battery, anything that would shut the arrogant SOB up. I was hopeful when the train rumbled out of Baltimore and into rural Harford County, but alas, not even crappy one-bar reception discouraged the man. Brad simply twisted in his seat, pressed the phone between his ear and the window, and barked, "Can you hear me now?" every few minutes before bidding his long-suffering wife a desultory good-bye.

I was sipping in silence, enjoying a glass of chilled tomato juice delivered to my seat by a uniformed attendant, anticipating the imminent arrival of a Greek salad with lamb, and appreciating the view as the train sped across the Susquehanna between Perryville and Havre de Grace, when Brad really harshed on my mellow. His blasted phone rang again, a jazzy piano tune this time, kind of classy, so I thought it might be Melissa calling him back.

"Hello. This is Phil."

I nearly swallowed my straw. Phil? What happened to Brad? Or Dave, for that matter?

"Oh, Annie," Phil cooed, slipping into his new identity as slickly as an undercover operative for the CIA. "Have I got a surprise for you."

I stole a sideways glance over the rim of my glass to see him pause, smiling, thoroughly appreciating (I imagined) the oh-ing and ah-ing going on at the other end of the line. "How'd you like to spend a week in Belize, babe?"

Annie liked it, and was already packing her tankini, if the tinny shrieks of joy leaking out of the receiver were any indication. The way Phil practically drooled into the cell phone, I felt like handing him my napkin. From some hidden corner of my brain a phrase leaped out, an escapee from a poem I'd been forced to memorize in high school: *And her well-tanned arms held hidden charms / For the greedy, the sinful and lewd.* Something like that, anyway.

While Phil made kissy-face with Annie, I tried to remember the title of the poem. Something about Alaska. I closed my eyes and pondered, as if the answer might be written on the inside of my eyelids. I was still teasing it out—"The Yukon," maybe?—when Phil said, "Well, hot *damn!*" and my eyes flew open.

After a few sentences, I deduced that he was in touch with a banker, discussing hedge funds, AAA-rated Eurobonds, and bearer shares in Panama. And I couldn't help overhearing when "Phil"— sounding veddy veddy British—arranged a private offshore bank account, set the password to his wife's birth date, and began redirecting his assets into it, with no more effort than applying for a rental card at Blockbuster. You had to like that in a banker. Last time I opened a bank account, they gave me a travel alarm.

When everything was arranged to his satisfaction, the guy made another call. I hoped he was going to share news of his good fortune, whatever it was, with his wife. But, no.

"Melissa, it's me again," my seatmate purred, wearing his Brad voice. "I'm sorry, but I won't be home tonight after all. They're flying me out of JFK on the red-eye. Hong Kong this time."

Liar, liar.

Did Melissa believe one word of the bullshit Brad was shoveling? Hard to tell from my end, what with Brad listening thoughtfully and nodding agreeably—yes, dear; no, darling; whatever you say, sweetheart—all the way to Wilmington. Barf. I felt like putting a muzzle on the guy, maybe a straitjacket too. Poor Melissa!

When the train stopped for passengers in Philadelphia, I closed my eyes and crossed my fingers, praying he'd get off and leave me to my book in peace, but it simply wasn't my lucky day. *Yada yada yada* for the hour it took to streak north at 120 miles per hour through the backyards of suburban New Jersey. *Blah blah blah* past the belching smokestacks and steaming garbage hills that spoiled my view of the Empire State Building, five miles in the distance, across the Hudson. As the train slowed to rumble through Newark Airport station without stopping, I remembered the nail file in my purse, a serious, old-fashioned metal one that TSA would have confiscated in an instant. I could put it to use! I could insert it neatly between Brad's ribs, and thrust, and twist, hard. I didn't know Melissa, but somehow I knew she'd be grateful.

Fortunately for Brad, I missed my chance. In no time at all, the conductor informed us we were arriving at New York's Penn Station, and it was time to gather up our belongings and leave the train and have a nice day. By that time, Brad had apparently smoothed things over with Melissa and was fussing over Annie again as he hurried out of the train and along the platform, his cell phone mashed between his palm and his ear, his laptop case swinging wildly from a strap looped over one shoulder.

I fell several passengers behind as we merged into single file to ride the up escalator, which spit everyone out into a vast concourse among the huddled masses, flanked by their luggage and the roaming homeless. Overhead, a prehistoric departures board whirred to life, informing everyone, letter by letter and number by number—snick-snick-snick—that the Regional 171 would be departing, twenty minutes late, from gate 11.

After surviving the stampede, I caught sight of Brad again as he passed Houlihan's pub. I was headed in the same general direction myself, but by the time I trundled past the new-books display at Book Corner, Brad was some distance ahead. I watched as he finished his call, and slipped the phone into his belt.

Or so he thought.

Instead of nesting neatly in its holster, the cell phone slid down his pants leg, did a somersault on the polished marble floor, and spun away in the direction of Kabooz's Bar and Grill. Surprisingly, Brad didn't notice.

A kid toting a backpack sent the instrument skidding another two feet with the toe of his Birkenstock, and a woman pushing a stroller drove right over it before I was able to scoop it up.

"Wait!" I yelled, rushing after Brad . . . Dave . . . Phil . . . whoever . . . as fast as anyone could while dragging a wheelie bag behind. I followed him up the escalator at Madison Square Garden and out to Seventh Avenue, but Brad was unencumbered and well ahead of me by the time I emerged, dazed and blinking, into the bright sunshine.

"Hey!" I yelled. "Hey, you dropped your cell phone!"

Brad plunged on, oblivious, elbowing his way through the line of people waiting for a cab. I nearly caught up with him then, but he veered left, and crossed with the light at Thirty-third and Seventh, leaving me standing stupidly on the curb.

If I could just get his attention! But, what name should I use?

Brad, the family man?

Dave, the biz whiz?

Phil, the international playboy?

Who *is* this guy when he talks to his mother?

"Brad!" I shouted.

Across the busy street, Brad turned his head, puzzled, scanning the faces of the pedestrians snaking around him.

I waved the cell phone in the air. "You dropped this!"

Brad paused under the WALK / DON'T WALK sign, cupped his ear with his hand, stared at me, and shrugged.

"Your cell phone!" I screamed over the roar of noonday traffic.

Brad patted his empty holster, waved in cheerful acknowledgment, smiled, and stepped toward me from the curb. That was when it happened.

It wasn't my fault. Honest. The cab had the right of way when it sideswiped the jerk and sent him sprawling in the crosswalk, where a bus barreling down Seventh applied its brakes but . . .

My God, it was awful!

Tires squealed and passersby screamed as I turned away from the gruesome residue and stared at the cell phone in my hand, at the four-bar signal, at the tiny screen with its AT&T logo superimposed over a movie poster of Michael Douglas in *Wall Street* saying, "Greed is good."

That figured.

Naturally, I used Brad's phone to call 911.

Then, just as naturally, I thumbed through his directory, looking for Melissa. She deserved to be the first to know.

"Home" popped up before "Melissa," so I highlighted the entry and punched Send.

"Melissa," I said, when she came on the line. "You don't know me, but I'm a friend of Brad's. Do you have a pencil?" I waited for her to find one, and then said, "Write down this number. It may come in handy."

"Thanks," she said, "I guess."

"It's a bank account," I explained. "And the password is your birthday."

"How did . . . ," she began, but I mashed my thumb down on the red button, cutting her off.

I was booked into the Marriott on Times Square, so I waited until the cab dropped me off before turning Brad's phone off, wiping it clean on the hem of my jacket, and dropping it into one of the green trash cans in the median at Forty-sixth and Broadway. As Brad's phone sank like a stone amid a sea of newspapers, fast-food wrappers, and crushed soda cans, I noticed a billboard over-head, a kinetic light sculpture that proclaimed in flashing blue and yellow, "Thank you for using AT&T."

I'd been married to a cheating worm like Brad once myself. So I saluted the billboard. "You're very welcome," I said.

GOLD FEVER

Dana Stabenow

A few minutes after he'd gotten home from work, the doorbell rang. He carried the beer he'd just uncapped to the door. On the landing stood two men in suits. "Okay," he said, "this can't be good."

The younger one blinked at him through black-rimmed glasses. "Mr. Nelson? Gilbert Nelson?"

"That's me," he said. "Let me guess. Cops?"

"Were you expecting us?" the older man said, stepping inside without invitation. The younger man was quick to follow his lead.

"No," Gil said amiably, shutting the door behind them, "you've just got the look, is all." He sat down in his recliner, put the footrest up, and gestured at the couch with his beer. "Have a seat. You're looking like you're on a mission, so I won't offer you a beer." He grinned. "After, if you like. It's five o'clock somewhere."

"I'm Detective Lipscomb, Anchorage Police Department. This is Detective Tanape."

"How you doing. What's up?"

The younger man, Tanape, consulted a file folder. "Do you own a Cessna 170 with the tail numbers November zero seven six eight Alpha?"

The footrest dropped with a bang as Gil sat up straight, no longer amused. "It's a 172, and yes, I do. What's happened to it?"

"Nothing, so far as we know."

Gil was not reassured. "I was just out at the tie-down at Lake Hood. It was fine then," he said. "Has it been broken into? Vandalized?" He was on his feet. "Jesus, did somebody take off in it?"

"Mr. Nelson, really, calm down." Tanape patted the air soothingly. "There's nothing wrong with your plane. That's not why we're here."

"Well, why the hell *are* you here then?" He sat down, a little pissed off at being alarmed unnecessarily and not unwilling to show it.

"Were you flying in the Skwentna area last week?"

Gil's eyes narrowed. "Yes. I was on my way back from a hunting trip."

"Where and what were you hunting?"

"Mulchatna and caribou. Look, what's this all about?"

"Anybody with you on this trip?" Lipscomb said.

"Yeah, my buddy Ralph flew up from Naknek to meet me there."

"May we have his name and contact information, please?" Tanape said.

Gil gave it to them.

"Did you get anything?" Lipscomb said.

"Four, two each. And some ptarmigan."

"Got it on the premises?"

"Yeah, freezer in the garage. You want to see?" Gil laughed and shook his head when they said they did, but he led them through the kitchen to the garage, opened the freezer, and displayed the shelves full of meat wrapped in white butcher paper, all carefully labeled in Marksalot with the cut of meat and the year.

Back in the living room, Tanape said, "When did you come home?"

Nelson thought back. "The fourth."

"And you came straight home?"

"Yeah. Ralph went south, I came north, and home."

Lipscomb's eyes were steady on his face. "Didn't stop along the way?"

"No."

"Not even once?"

"No." He shrugged. "Well, you know. Once. To take a leak."

They exchanged glances. "Where was this?"

"About an hour out of Skwentna, or I would have waited for the outhouse at the strip there."

There is no place to pee in a Cessna 172, so he was forced to either use the Ziploc bag that had held his sandwich or find a landing strip. Ziplocs were without question the pinnacle of modern technology—he didn't know a hunter in Alaska who didn't pack out their kill in Ziplocs—but they worked less well as urine-collection bags.

Fortunately, landing strips in Bush Alaska weren't that hard to come by, and he found one mere minutes after he started looking, a pale scar on a leveled-off foothill at the mouth of a canyon carved out by a rushing, unruly creek. There were the remains of some buildings barely visible through the birch and the spruce. They looked deserted.

He dropped down to fifty feet and made a pass down the strip, inspecting the surface. Someone had cleared it not too long before. He banked, turned, and sideslipped into a landing that he was a little sorry no one was there to see.

The 172 rolled to a stop and he opened the door and got out. Movement caught the corner of his eye and his first thought was a bear. He reached for the .30-06 in the back.

"Step away from the plane," a voice said.

He smelled him before he saw him, a thin man who hadn't shaved in a month and who hadn't showered in longer than that. He was dressed in a pair of ragged shorts and he held a pump-action twelve-gauge shotgun, the business end pointed at the Cessna.

"Whoa," Gil said, raising his hands, palms out. "I just stopped to take a leak."

The man looked at him for a long, considering moment that had Gil's hair crawling on the back of his neck. Finally he gestured with the shotgun. "Get your business done, then, and be on your way."

"*It was the fastest piss I* ever took," Nelson said to the detectives.

"Had you ever met him before?"

"No. Like I said, I just needed to take a leak, and I landed on the first airstrip I saw."

"Why do you think he was so confrontational?" Tanape said.

Gil snorted. "Come on, guys. I'm thinking this isn't your first rodeo. The guy was working a gold claim. You know how miners are."

"How are they, Mr. Nelson?"

"Insane. Terrified everybody wants to jump their claim, and willing to kill over it." He swigged his beer. "Gold fever, they call it. You're not born in Alaska and don't learn that it's real, believe me. Especially when your grandfather was a stampeder during the Klondike." He shook his head. "I don't know what it is about gold. It's soft, it's the Play-Doh of metals. It won't hold a shape if you don't mix it with something else, silver, copper, nickel, palladium. I guess it's pretty, if you like yellow. And they make some pretty things out of it, but I've never been much for jewelry, myself."

"You ever done any mining, Mr. Nelson?"

"Hell, no. I've never wanted to work that hard." He regarded them over the mouth of his bottle. "You ever going to tell me what this is all about?"

They looked at each other. Lipscomb shrugged, and said, "It'll be on the news tonight, probably. The miner's name was Rudy Gorman. His partner flew supplies into the mine the day after you landed at the strip, and found him dead."

"Dead as in—"

"Dead as in murdered, Mr. Nelson. Shot at point-blank range. With his own shotgun." Lipscomb looked at him. "Your plane was spotted by someone else in the area, and they got your tail number. Which makes you the last person to have seen him alive."

Gil followed the story on the news, but it was soon supplanted by a gang shooting in the Dimond Center parking lot and then two trials. One featured an Alaska Bush Company stripper who had seduced the new boyfriend into killing the old one, and the other dealt with a state senator caught on camera taking a fistful of hundred-dollar bills from an oil company executive during a contentious legislative session featuring a wellhead tax increase on North Slope crude. In the meantime, Gil went down to the cop shop on Tudor and gave Lipscomb and Tanape his statement for the record. They visited him at his home and had him run through it twice more, without much enthusiasm.

While he had the means to kill Gorman, the miner had been killed with his own shotgun, not Gil's .30-06, and he had no discernible motive, being gainfully and lucratively employed as an A&P mechanic in his own shop and having inherited the Turnagain house he lived in from his grandfather the stampeder.

The third time Tanape actually apologized for the intrusion. Gil waved it off. "It's okay, I get it. Like you said, I was the last person to see him alive."

"Unless it was the girlfriend, and she lied about finding him dead," Lipscomb said. By then they were pretty relaxed in his presence, and had timed their arrival at his house to coincide with the end of the workday. They'd both accepted a beer.

"Girlfriend?"

"One Elaine Virginia Brandon," Lipscomb said.

Tanape raised his eyes to the ceiling and gave out with a long, reverent whistle.

Gil grinned. "A looker, huh?"

"If I weren't married," Lipscomb said. "Anyway, she was also his partner in the gold mine, and she was the one flying supplies out to him."

"She's a pilot?"

"Yeah. Nice little Piper Super Cub."

"Haven't met her."

"You wouldn't have. She doesn't have floats. She parks at Merrill."

"You think she did it?"

Tanape shook his head and stood up. "Naw. Merrill tower corroborates her departure time, and the ME says the deterioration of the body matches her statement. We tested her for gunshot residue and came up with zip."

"I'm sorry, guys," Gil said, showing them to the door. "I wish I'd seen something that would help."

"Not your problem, Gil," Lipscomb said. "See you around."

The following spring, Gil signed up for AT 231 in the Av Tech department at the University of Alaska Anchorage. He'd soloed at sixteen and had flown for the Civil Air Patrol, but, as he told his pilot friends when they gave him a hard time, a refresher course in search, survival, and rescue never hurt. "You should take it too," he told them, and one of them, a hard-assed pipe fitter named Joe Denham, actually did.

They walked into the classroom together, and as Joe later described it, "I never saw anyone struck by lightning before." A blond pocket Venus named Ginny was also taking the class, and Gil was smitten at first sight. "God, I got horny just watching them, they couldn't keep their hands off each other," he said at the stag party. "For a while we were all scared to go into the hangar when they were in there together. Mile-high club, my ass. I think Ginny and Gil were in the on-the-deck club the first day of class." He toasted Gil. "Lucky bastard."

Gil laughed but didn't contradict him.

Their courtship lasted the length of the semester, and the entire class was invited to the wedding, at which the instructor officiated, bride and groom both being orphans.

They honeymooned at the gold claim that Ginny, née Elaine Virginia Brandon, had inherited from her boyfriend, an hour south of Skwentna. They sold it to a Canadian company the following year, at which time the company announced the discovery of the eighth-largest gold mine in the state, with estimated assets of over three hundred thousand troy ounces. At the current price of almost $800 per ounce, that was well over two billion dollars waiting to be scooped out of the ground. There was a photograph on the front page of the *Anchorage Daily News* of a beaming Ginny and Gil accepting a gigantic check from the CEO of Northwest Minerals and Mining.

Tanape and Lipscomb were at Gil's door before the paper had been on the street an hour.

"Guys," Gil said. He looked over his shoulder. "Honey, it's those two cops I told you about."

Ginny walked into view, a curvaceous blonde with tousled hair that looked as if she had just rolled out of bed, and a swollen pout that gave a pretty good idea of what she'd been doing there. No one had ever made jeans and a plaid shirt look that good.

Gil's hand slid around her waist to rest against one round hip. "You remember Ginny." He leaned down to kiss her, and she arched into it so his lips slid from her cheek to her neck, eyes half closing, her left hand coming up to rest on his chest. On her ring finger she wore a lustrous gold wedding set, the bands chased with intricate figures and mounted with a princess-cut diamond that had to weigh at least five carats.

Gil straightened up and saw the two cops looking at the rings. He held up his left hand, a matching band minus the diamond on his ring finger. "I kept back enough for the rings." He smiled at the two cops. "Come on in and have some coffee."

"This wasn't a good idea," Lipscomb told Tanape. "Let's go."

In the car on the way back to the cop shop, Tanape said, almost imploringly, "But they killed him. You know they did."

Lipscomb sucked hard on his cigarette, his first in three years. "Sure, I know it. I can't prove it, though, and in our job that's all that counts."

"We should have tested him for GSR. I know, it was a week later, but there might have been something. Even a trace and we could have gotten a warrant."

"For what? Gorman was shot with his own gun. It had his prints on it, and hers. And hers were easy to explain away. Nelson had to have worn gloves."

"Gorman wrote the will in her favor the year after they hooked up. Do you think they had been planning it that long?"

"They're both pilots. Just because he parks at Hood and she parks at Merrill doesn't mean they didn't know each other. The Alaska aviation community is pretty incestuous."

With dawning horror, Tanape said, "You think they met *before* she met Gorman? You think her relationship was planned?"

"He's an A&P mechanic. Good ones are like, well, like gold. Ask any pilot, they'll tell you the same. He could have annualed her Cub, and it started there. They weren't in a hurry, they took their time about everything else. Long-sighted, our young friends, and good actors. And very, very good liars."

He glanced at Tanape, slumped beside him, suffering through

subsequent stages of frustration, rage, and, most especially, embarrassment. Tanape had really liked Gil Nelson, and it was humiliating to realize just how wrong he'd been about him. It stung in particular for a practicing law enforcement professional whose first lesson as a matter of survival on the job was to learn that everyone lied.

It probably wasn't the moment to suggest that Brandon was very probably the one who had called in the sighting of Nelson's plane. It had been an anonymous call, after the news of the finding of Gorman's body. If Nelson's plane had been seen by someone else, the call preempted their reporting it to the police, pushed the investigators to Nelson, whose testimony corroborated Brandon's and the ME. So long as Nelson had no motive and there was no evidence to the contrary, the result would be death by person or persons unknown.

He went over Nelson's statement in his head. Had to pee, landed, menaced by Gorman, peed, took off. He realized that even if they had suspected him, Nelson's plan B would have been self-defense. Had to pee, landed, menaced by Gorman, defending himself the gun went off accidentally, Gorman dead. With one in every thirty-seven Alaskans holding a pilot's license, there was rarely a jury without one on it, and they would all have had the same thought. It could have been them on that strip that day. A self-defense plea would have been a slam dunk.

But Lipscomb and Tanape had made it easy for him. The cigarette suddenly tasted bitter in his mouth. He rolled down the window and flicked it out. "Look at it this way, partner. They got what they wanted. They won't be reoffending. They're no risk to the general population, and that's who we're sworn to serve and to protect."

They drove the rest of the way to the cop shop in silence. As they pulled into a parking space, Tanape said, "Did you notice? Her hair is almost exactly the same color as the gold of their rings."

Lipscomb slammed the gearshift into park. "We'll drop in on

them from time to time, see if any tarnish is starting to build up on our little golden couple. See if one of them wants to roll on the other."

"What if they don't?"

They got out and Lipscomb paused next to the open door of the police cruiser, his breath making a white cloud in the frozen January morning, the dawn a faint pale gold streak throwing the sharp-edged peaks of the Chugach Mountains into stark relief. He looked over the top of the car at Tanape, shivering in his topcoat. "Nelson told us the truth about one thing."

"What?"

"Gold fever. It's real."

Your Turn

Carolyn Hart

Terri stared outside at a crimson cardinal, and her surroundings receded, no more real than a shadow. The silk sheets on Greg's bed were rich, red as the bird's feathers. The tip of his index finger caressed her chin, slipped in tantalizing slowness to her breast, touched a nipple—

The sharp clang of the desk bell shocked her into awareness, and she steeled herself. As she turned her face toward the hospital bed, the nurse entered from the adjoining room.

Leo's hand waved in dismissal. "I don't—need you."

The nurse was middle aged, with a worn, incurious face. She nodded and slipped away.

Leo stared at Terri. "You forgot we were playing."

He looked down on her from the hospital bed, which seemed out of place in a man's baroque bedroom with heavy mahogany furniture.

Leo's dark eyes still burned with life even though the rest of him was burning out, just as all the cigarettes had smoldered to ash through the years. He was as comfortable as could be managed for a man dying of lung cancer: propped up with three down pillows behind him, his pain dulled by morphine. He was dependent upon oxygen from the tank beside the bed. The oxygen flowed through plastic tubing into two hollow prongs that fit into his nostrils. He was too weak to rise. His voice was a hoarse whisper. He summoned attention with the old-fashioned silver desk bell. He insisted the nurses, three of them, each on an eight-hour shift, stay out of his presence unless he needed them. "I'll ring—when—I want you."

"Penny for—your thoughts." The sound was a ghostly rasp. Leo's face was unsmiling, held no warmth. Once he'd been imposing, six feet tall, with a brush of inky black hair, a long bony face, a wide mouth with an almost perpetual sardonic smile. Now his face was gray and drooping, defined by fatigue and pain.

Terri was careful not to look toward the elegant cheval mirror in its pewter frame. Would her face betray her? For she found Leo repellent now. She hated his illness, hated the smell of a room burdened with ebbing life. Death was present; waiting, beckoning.

She needed a man, not an invalid, and from the moment she'd first glimpsed Greg at the tennis club, she'd wanted him. She'd loved his tousled thick blond hair, the faint stubble on his face, the power as he threw a ball high and arched to serve. When he touched her to show her how to swing her arm higher as she served, she'd looked at him and the bargain was made though not a word was said. He was waiting at her car when she left the club that day.

Every time she moved from Greg's embrace to Leo's sickroom, she struggled to hide her aversion. She'd never loved Leo, but he had been exciting and rich, and an accomplished lover. It had been a fair enough bargain. She'd been young and beautiful, an acquisition other men might envy. She wasn't as young now. Ten years had left lines no matter how much cream she smoothed into her skin. But her status as his wife had opened wide a world she'd always longed for: Paris in the spring, safaris in Africa, fashions and jewels, whatever luxuries she desired. Leo took pleasure in her body. Most of all, his dark and jealous nature enjoyed flaunting Terri to prove to the world he was unaffected by his first wife's inexplicable defection. He was baffled that Diana had discarded him for a pudgy lawyer with thinning hair and a weak chin.

Terri realized she was holding a red checker piece. "I was thinking about my next move." She glanced down at the black-and-red board. Stupid game. She would never play it again after Leo. . . .

Terri swerved away from the thought, though more and more she'd been counting the days. He was dying. Why didn't he die?

"At least you realize it's your turn." His eyes were hot, black.

Terri forced a smile. "No matter what I do, you always win."

"Try harder." The husky whisper was cool.

She would have liked to upend the checkerboard, fling it at him. "You don't like to lose, Leo."

He gave a short laugh, then choked. He struggled for breath. He gestured peremptorily.

Quickly, she hurried from her chair, bent to the oxygen tank, and turned the valve to increase the flow.

In a moment, his chest heaving, his breath quieted. He lay back against the pillows. He looked old and frail, though he was only a few months past sixty.

Terri waited, then turned the valve back a little.

His eyes flickered open. "You weren't thinking—about your move." His lips twisted. "You're more interested—in a different game."

She stood very still, her reflection in the cheval mirror rigid as steel. She'd dressed with care, a pink silk bateau blouse and trousers, matching pink high heels. Not for Leo, though. For Greg. He'd undressed her, his hands . . .

Leo's eyes glittered. "You could have—waited until I was—dead."

In the mirror, her face suddenly looked pinched. One moment she was an immaculately groomed honey blonde dressed in expensive silk. The next she was a shaken woman in her late thirties, sharp nails digging into her palms. "I don't know what you're talking about." She felt a sickening twist inside. She saw knowledge in

Leo's burning eyes. It wouldn't make any difference what she said. He knew about Greg.

Thoughts fluttered, aimless as confetti thrown high. *Someone must have told him. . . . Leo was dangerous when he was angry. . . . He was cruel and sly. . . . What could he do? . . . Could she calm him—*

His look was a sneer. "Won't do—any good—to lie." He pointed toward the door. "I should—send you away."

She looked at the door, and, next to it, the mahogany étagère crammed with Leo's favorite keepsakes, a hideous head of Medusa with its writhing snakes, a bronze owl with an empty gaze and slightly parted beak, and a shining white ivory temple.

"I could do that." He gave a strangled laugh. "I know all about—you and your lover. That wasn't—a good move—on your part—Terri." His breathy delivery pushed out the words in bits and pieces. "You should have—remembered—the prenuptial agreement—has a clause—null and void—in event—adultery."

She clutched at her throat. "Leo, please—"

"Don't interrupt me—lawyer—coming—tomorrow." His gaze was as bleak as iced granite. "Kiss the money—good-bye. See if—pretty boy—wants you—without it."

Terri gripped the handrail above the pond. A half dozen times she'd almost reached for her cell, then made no move. She didn't dare tell Greg over a cell. Her understanding was imprecise, but messages could be overheard. What would she say if she reached him? *Will you love me without any money?* Damn Leo. Damn him for his nasty, ugly mind. Greg didn't care about the money. He loved her.

Hate coursed through her. She'd never hated Leo until now.

The harsh glare of the sun made her head ache. Of course Greg knew she'd be rich when Leo died, but they'd never talked about it. She didn't blame Greg for counting on a comfortable future.

He loved fine things, cashmere sweaters, Veuve Clicquot in crystal flutes, Four Seasons hotels, fine leather from Italy, Armani suits, but that only showed how cultivated he was. His discerning taste made his desire for her all the more wonderful. She, of all the women at the club, was his choice.

There was a Tibetan carpet he wanted for his bedroom. She wanted to give the carpet to him for his birthday. She wanted to give him everything. She'd never felt truly alive until she met him. She blinked against the sharp reflection off the water. Greg would be pleased by her thoughtfulness and yet, a little thread of worry swirled deep within; sometimes she felt as though he was as cool and remote as the carved wooden Abyssinian cat he kept on his bedside table and always touched for luck.

Terri jerked away from the railing, walked swiftly toward the garage. A feral black cat ran across her path and she drew in a sharp breath. It didn't *mean* anything. Superstition was for fools.

She felt a surge of relief as she slid into her Lexus. She had to get away. She had to think. She had to decide what to do. As she eased the car into the circular drive in front of the Tudor mansion, she heard the distant wail of sirens. The shrill cry was familiar, always a little sickening. She'd heard sirens too often this last year, an ambulance racing up the narrow, twisting road for Leo to take him to the nearby hospital on the other side of the woods. She'd always known one day the ambulance would come, and he would be dead. She wished . . .

Terri drove slowly and carefully, her hands clamped on the steering wheel. More than ever before, she hated the steep drop off the side into the wooded ravine. She hated the lack of guardrails. Leo had always laughed at her, told her she drove like an old woman, that his first wife always went as fast as she could, squealing around the turns. Terri knew Leo enjoyed taunting her, but, more than that, she knew he was remembering the woman he'd loved and lost, remembering her as daring, mercurial, enchanting.

When Terri made the last hairpin curve, she experienced the familiar relief. At the stop sign, she hesitated. She wanted to see Greg.

But deep inside, she didn't want to tell him Leo was changing his will, that she would be penniless when he died. Of course, Greg wouldn't really care. . . .

When Leo had become too ill to have dinner in the dining room, she began to have her meals on the balcony of her bedroom in fine weather. Even though it was March, the weather was warming, the trees beginning to green. The view from her balcony was such a relief from the dining room with its heavy dark furniture, austere green walls, and gilded trompe l'oeil paintings. The dining room made her feel insignificant and alien. But the balcony made her feel like a queen surveying her kingdom, elevated and free.

Tonight, however, she'd scarcely managed to eat a bite though the food was, as always, superb.

Morgan's face was impassive when he came to remove the dishes. "Mr. Leo wished to know if you will join him at lunch tomorrow with Mr. Stewart."

Terri stared up at the stocky, impeccably attired servant. Sprigs of graying hair lay lank on his skull and tufted above his ears. His eyes seemed to mock her. Did he know? Did *everyone* in the house know that she was to be cut from Leo's will?

"Mr. Stewart?" Her voice sounded thin, even to her own ears. Charles Stewart was Leo's lawyer as well as an old friend.

Morgan's sandy lashes blinked above those knowing eyes. "As you may recall, it is an annual occasion. They always celebrate the anniversary of their yacht's triumph in the Pineapple Cup. That would be"—his manner was patronizing—"twenty-two years ago tomorrow."

She'd been married to Leo for ten years. She would have liked to claw Morgan's puffy face. She forced a smile, and pushed words out. "I will look forward to luncheon tomorrow."

As she spoke, she heard the stilted words. If she were Leo's languid daughter, Kate, she'd have shrugged and said, "Sure. Tell Pops it's a date. If I don't get a better offer." His son, Barron, would have given an energetic, distracted nod. "Tell Dad I may run late. Got a deal going, but I'll come." She should have simply said she'd be there.

Why did she always feel uncomfortable when she spoke with Morgan?

Because she didn't belong.

She sat stiffly while Morgan finished clearing. As the door closed behind him, she looked out at the darkening sky, at the setting sun streaking the woods with mauve and crimson, at the Tennessee hills darkening in the twilight.

Damn them. Damn them all. Damn Leo and Kate and Barron and that moon-faced Morgan. She'd been glad to sign the prenuptial agreement. She'd agreed not to proceed against the estate, and been thrilled at the prospect of five million dollars.

That money belonged to *her*. She'd earned it. She'd given Leo what he wanted, youth and beauty and sex. It wasn't her fault he was sick and dying. If he cared for her, he'd understand.

But he didn't care. No more than she cared for him.

That money was hers!

The digital clock glowed in the darkness. She'd not slept. It was almost two in the morning, the morning of the day the money would go away.

Terri threw back the covers. She slipped into a soft velour robe.

If Leo died before daylight, the money would be hers.

Terri sat in a small gilt chair in front of her dressing table. Moonlight silvered the room. Her reflection in the mirror was shadowy, almost as if she were a ghost. She flicked on a small lamp, saw her staring eyes, turned it off.

The doctor had been amazed that Leo had lasted so long. Just last week, he'd stepped out into the hall with her. "He's slipping away." His voice had been gentle. "The oxygen is keeping him alive, but his lungs are weakening. Any day now, Terri."

But not soon enough.

Leo must have hired a private detective. He would have proof of what she'd done. He would present Charles Stewart with everything needed to turn her out of the world of the rich, where fine clothes were a given and cost no object.

Will you love me without any money?

Fury swept her. Just because Leo saw her as bought and paid for, he didn't want to believe Greg loved her.

Of course Greg loved her.

Terri pushed up from the chair and hurried to her desk. She picked up the telephone. Landlines were all right. It would be hard for anyone to overhear, not like a cell. Was the line tapped? It might be, but it made no difference now. She'd leave in the morning. Maybe she'd leave tonight. The car was in her name. She'd pack her clothes and go.

She dialed the number she knew so well.

The call was answered on the third ring. Greg's voice was wary as he said hello.

She felt a tightening in her chest. Her eyes darted to the clock. He sounded wide awake. At two in the morning? She heard faint sounds of music in the background.

"Greg, I'm coming over. Leo knows about us. He's changing his will tomorrow. I have to leave." That was the answer. Leave it all behind, leave Leo and his rasping voice and burning eyes and hissing oxygen tank. "I'll get a divorce. He won't care. Greg, we can get married." Her voice rose in eagerness.

Silence.

"Greg?"

"Baby," he said, his voice smooth and easy, "you've had a bad dream. Whatever's wrong with you and Leo, work it out. We don't want any scandal. Convince him he's wrong."

"You don't know Leo."

"He's old. He's sick. Hold his hand. Look beautiful. That's your specialty, babe."

Terri felt a quiver of nausea as she pictured the dying husk of a man lying in the hospital bed. "I can't."

"You will. Come on, Terri," he said, his voice warm as honey, "we're going to have a good life together. Let's start it off right. No scandal. No trouble. Let Leo die in peace and then we'll have smooth sailing."

The minutes were running out. She was an heiress until noon. The redrafting of the will might take several days, but once Leo told Charles Stewart, she was done. For Stewart had *never* liked her. He'd enjoy proving she didn't qualify for the money.

Yet she knew it wouldn't do any good to argue with Leo. He had looked at her with loathing.

She pushed up from the chair, moved toward the door. Maybe—just maybe—Leo had died. The doctor said it would be quick, that death could come at any time. She moved down the wide, moonlit hallway, her slippers soft on the marble floor. She hesitated at Leo's room, then eased the door open a fraction. If he died tonight, she would be all right. She would have Greg.

She slipped inside Leo's bedroom. A bronze lamp sat on the bedside table. At night the shade was turned to keep light from his face, but the room was dimly lit by its bulb. The night nurse slept in an adjoining room, the door slightly ajar.

Terri watched her husband. She finally discerned the almost imperceptible lift and fall of the sheet across Leo's chest. He was alive. Damn him. But if he died tonight . . . he *was* going to die . . . she'd earned that money . . . he couldn't survive without the oxygen

. . . the doctor said they had to have electricity . . . the house now had a generator . . . if the oxygen went off . . .

The hiss of the oxygen tank seemed to grow louder in the stillness. It seemed, even, to beckon. Terri took one step, then another. The tank sat in front of the bedside table. It was plugged into the same outlet as the lamp.

Terri knelt beside the tank. If the oxygen stopped . . . She covered her fingers with the hem of her robe, reached behind the bedside table, felt the hard rubber of the plug. Her fingers closed around it.

She knelt until her knees hurt from the unyielding wooden floor. Her shoulders ached. The hiss of the oxygen seemed to surround her like a cloud of flies. As long as the oxygen flowed . . .

With a harsh intake of breath, a pulse quivering in her throat, she yanked the plug from the outlet.

Silence.

One moment, the tank buzzed. The next, nothing.

Quiet pressed against her, heavy as a rock.

Leo jerked.

Terri stared up at the bed.

Leo gave a strangled gasp, shuddered.

The sound was small, though it seemed loud as a scream.

Her heart thudded. Desperately, she jabbed at the socket, inserted the plug. The oxygen tank hissed. She came to her feet, backed away from the bed. She stopped at the door, clung to it. Her heart pounded as if she'd run a race.

On the bed, Leo's body shuddered. He flung one arm to the side. The arm slid down. His hand dangled. The fingers splayed open, limp, unmoving.

The knock on Terri's door was urgent.

She fought free of tortured sleep. She didn't want to wake up. Something was wrong. Something bad had happened. Then memory came, the memory of Leo's lifeless fingers. She pushed herself up. She stared as the door opened.

The night nurse, Mona Riley, stepped inside, her face grave, but composed. "Mrs. Lewis, I'm afraid I have bad news."

Terri made a sound deep in her throat.

"Mr. Lewis died in the night . . ."

The doctor came. The funeral home removed Leo's body.

The day seemed interminable. Every time the phone rang or the door opened, Terri stiffened, fear writhing within her, wild as a serpent.

Leo's son and daughter arrived. They treated Terri civilly, but when she walked into a room, they fell quiet, making her the outsider, their veiled glances dismissive.

Through restless nights, until fatigue brought burdened sleep, through the dreary days of flowers and cards and callers, through the somber visit from Charles Stewart to inform her of the bequest through the prenuptial agreement, she waited.

Nothing happened. She began to relax. It was over. Leo was dead. No one questioned his death. Not a single person. Days passed. She pushed away the memory of the heavy quiet when the oxygen stopped, the jerking shudder when he died. Death had been certain. He was going to die. He was almost dead. It was natural, really. He was very sick. If he couldn't breathe, that was because he was sick.

The house was busy. Barron and Kate were in and out as they chose mementoes, his secretary Elinor Griffin boxed papers in his study, appraisers took inventory, readying the mansion's contents for auction. Terri agreed to move within a month. She would have loved to be gone in an instant, but she wanted to act as if everything was normal.

Everything *was* normal. She had to remember that.

She'd had no chance to see Greg, had only spoken with him

twice. Both times he'd told her to wait. After she moved, she'd keep up her membership at the club. They'd take their time, he said. They'd seem to discover each other. There was no hurry.

Will you love me without any money?

When that thought came, she pushed it away. That was an ugly memory because of Leo. What he'd said didn't matter now. The past didn't matter.

She found the envelope beneath her pillow a week after the funeral. She was startled when her fingers touched stiff paper. She pushed aside the puffy feather pillow and found her name inscribed on a creamy envelope, written in Leo's thick black distinctive writing.

She couldn't breathe. A letter from Leo. It took every ounce of will to pick it up. She ripped open the envelope, pulled out a stiff white card embossed with his initials in gold: LBL. Leo Barron Lewis. The writing was uneven, shaky, but unmistakably his:

> Murder will out, Terri. Perhaps the reference eludes you. No matter. You found it tedious to play checkers with me, so I've planned a more exciting game for you. I believe you'll be challenged. More so than with checkers. You'll be hearing more, Terri, never fear.
>
> *Leo*

Terri ran to the bathroom, where she tore the cardboard into tiny strips. She flushed them away. But she couldn't flush Leo's words from her mind. She walked feverishly about her room. Toward morning, she flung herself across the bed to slip finally into hag-ridden sleep.

She stood in the shadow of the pines that screened court 7. Greg's deep, smooth voice was encouraging. "Stretch tall when you serve, Anna. Up like this."

Terri watched his hand slide along the willowy brunette's arm.
The woman turned and leaned against him. "Sorry. I lost my
balance." She didn't move away.

Greg didn't step away. "Practice makes perfect."

Terri felt a surge of fury. She knew Greg was paid to keep the
members happy, but she desperately wanted to have him hold her,
have him reassure her. Her fingers hooked on to the fence wire.
What would he do if he knew? . . . What would he say? She couldn't
tell him that she had . . .

Terri stumbled away from the court, hurried to her car.

She found the second letter in her jewel box on Saturday:

> I assume you destroyed my previous note, Terri. Good
> move. Let's talk about the proof you committed murder.
> Are you familiar with UltraMax 800 film? You needn't
> trouble yourself with technical knowledge. It photographs
> in very little light. A camera whirred that night, a cunning
> device secreted in my owl. That amused me. My bronze
> owl couldn't see you, but the camera in its beak will turn
> you into a convicted felon. In due time.
>
> *Leo*

Terri's heart thudded. She felt the pulsing in her head. Leo's
room was dark. She flipped on the overhead light. The hospital bed
and oxygen tank were gone, but everything else remained as it was
on the night Leo died. Except the étagère next to the door. One
shelf was empty. The owl was gone.

Terri hurried downstairs to the study.

Elinor Griffin looked up from the desk. In her late forties, she
had an interesting angular face with catlike green eyes, high cheekbones, and a broad mouth that could slide into an engaging smile.
Lean and athletic, she was an excellent horsewoman and had been
Leo's confidential secretary for fifteen years. For an instant, disdain

was clear in those brilliant green eyes of hers, then her expression became bland. She said nothing, merely looked inquiring.

Terri felt as if she'd turned to stone. She felt like that awful statue Leo liked, the one on the top shelf above the owl. Leo had laughed. "Imagine how those snakes would feel?" Now she knew. *In due time.* Terri struggled to breathe. "Elinor, where's the bronze owl that was in Leo's room, next to the door?"

Elinor looked surprised. "Is it gone? As far as I know, nothing's been taken from Leo's room. Except the hospital bed." Suddenly, her face drooped. Her lips pressed together.

Terri knew she was grieving. What right did she have?

Elinor blinked and, once again, she was the composed secretary. "I'll ask around. I can't imagine what happened to it."

Terri swallowed. "Leo liked it, and I wondered where it had gone. I'd like to have it. It means a lot to me."

This time the note was in her closet, tucked in a chest with her nightgowns:

> Have you been looking for my owl? You won't find him, Terri. Possibly you are claiming sentimental attachment? That won't help. An old friend of mine has it and will think it is nothing more than a memento until he receives instructions to retrieve the camera. Perhaps this week. Perhaps next. One day soon . . . In due time—
>
> *Leo*

Terri pushed away the plate. Food nauseated her. She'd scarcely eaten for a week. Often she felt dizzy, especially at the top of the stairs. She seemed to hear Leo's voice, mocking her: *In due time. In due time.*

Day followed day. One week passed. Two. Three. She leased a condo. She bought new furniture, everything bright and cheerful and modern. She picked out drapes. She was counting the days until the month was up and she could move.

She overheard Morgan speaking to the cook: "Mrs. Leo has taken it hard. I thought she was a gold digger, but she's been struggling. She hardly eats a thing. I guess you never know, do you? Mr. Leo was a fine man."

She wanted to cry out that Leo was a devil. Instead, she slipped away.

Terri enjoyed breakfast, French toast and sausage and a ruby red grapefruit. Sunlight spilled onto the balcony. Tomorrow she'd leave this house forever. Then she'd be free. Leo couldn't do anything to her. She'd thought it out very carefully. He'd been cremated. He was gone. Ashes. Nothing could ever be proved. If anyone accused her, she'd tell them Leo was confused and rambling and mean.

But if there was a film from the owl . . . All right. She'd say she came in and found the oxygen off and plugged it in. No one could prove anything. Could they?

She picked out a Riviera blue turtleneck and a swirling white skirt and white kidskin sling-back shoes, everything springlike and cheerful. She admired her image in the mirror.

The knock on the door was polite.

Terri wished she'd chosen any top but the turtleneck. She felt as if she were choking. But if it were the police, the knock would be demanding. Didn't they shout, "Police! Open up!"

The knock came again, subdued but insistent.

Terri forced herself to cross the room. The doorknob felt cold to her touch. She turned and pulled.

Elinor Griffin's pale lemon suit was crisp, but her face was drawn and weary. She swallowed, finally spoke. "Here's Leo's last letter. He asked me to bring them to you. I don't think he should try and hold on after he's dead. I guess he loved you terribly." She hesitated, then the words came in a rush. "Damn him. I don't know why I care so much." Her face crumpled in tears. She thrust the envelope at Terri, turned away, and hurried down the hall.

> Did you think I'd forgotten you, Terri? Not likely. You won't likely forget me either. You don't qualify for the death penalty. The bar is high in Tennessee, murder during the commission of a felony or other strictures that don't apply to you. Still, twenty to thirty years in prison will give you time to ponder what could have been. You might be interested to know I'd decided to let the prenuptial agreement stand if I awakened the morning after our last chat. If you are reading this, I did not awaken. Your pretty boy won't be with you in prison, Terri. You can think about him, about me, about your choice. You're a good-looking woman now, and that will get you some attention, but not the kind of attention you will enjoy. I hope I'm not boring you. You often seemed bored when we played a game, but I doubt you are bored now. I've given you a great gift, honing your awareness of life's unpredictability. It cost me a pretty penny. I made several arrangements through Morgan, others through Elinor. My moves, if you will. Soon enough it will be your turn. My only regret is that I won't be there to see what you do. Will you win or will I? Go to your balcony and look down now. Enjoy taking your turn.

> *Leo*

Terri opened the balcony door as a dark sedan slid to a stop. Two young men got out, men in dark suits, with stolid, impassive faces. They walked toward the steps. As they disappeared from view, Terri heard the click of their shoes.

She whirled and ran across the room. She grabbed her purse. In the hall, she heard Morgan at the door. "May I give Mrs. Lewis your names?"

A deep, husky voice said, "Samuels and Brown. We're here to interview her. Official business."

"I see." Morgan sounded uncertain. "Gentlemen, if you'll step this way . . ."

Terri ran to the end of the hall. She plunged down the back steps. She ran through the kitchen, leaving the plump cook staring after her.

She rushed out the back door. Her chest ached as she ran to the garage. She flung herself into her car, fumbling to insert the keys. The motor roared as she backed out of the garage. She yanked the wheel and sped down the drive. She drove with one hand, fumbled in her purse for her cell. She flipped it open, speed-dialed.

As the car screeched around the first turn on the narrow road, Greg answered. "I need help." Fear lifted her voice. "The police are after me. Please, meet me—"

"Police? What the hell are you talking about?" His voice was distant.

She jammed on the brake, slowing the car. Sweat beaded her face. That *curve*. She had to go slower.

The wail of a siren sounded.

"Oh God." Terri's heart thudded. The police. They'd arrest her. Was the siren coming up the road? Was it behind her? "Greg"— it was a scream—"shut up and listen. They're coming after me. Because of Leo. They're going to arrest me. I'll meet you at the club. You can get some money—"

The connection ended.

The siren sounded louder and louder.

Terri hunched over the wheel, her hands sweaty. Hot tears blurred her vision. Coldness spread within her.

Will you love me without any money?

She pushed on the accelerator. She came to the sharp curve, the horrible curve, the deadly curve. Her tires squealed as she yanked at the wheel. The car slid to the right. For an instant, the Lexus hung in midair before turning end over end, banging and crashing against the limestone outcropping, exploding in a fiery ball of flame.

Thad Samuels and Garrett Brown looked much younger in polos and Levi's. They sat at the bar, their faces solemn.

Thad swiped a finger on the salty rim of his margarita. "Do you suppose her brakes went out?"

Garrett took a deep swallow of his Bud. "What else? Damn, what a weird deal it all was. I guess it's okay we didn't hang around. Especially since that ambulance that was coming up the road saw her go over. What could we have told anybody? The car was going too fast and flipped out."

"Makes you think." Thad's frown was profound. "Too bad she left before she knew we were there. If we'd caught her, given her the birthday balloons, maybe the accident would never have happened."

Garrett sighed. "I wish we knew who hired us. Somebody went to a lot of trouble to try and make her day special, huh? I was real glad to be paid up front in cash, but now I wish we had a name."

Thad blinked in surprise. "What for?"

Garrett looked embarrassed. "Well . . . we could send a card or something."

Thad munched on tequila-spiked ice. "Better leave well enough alone. Whoever the poor bastard is, I don't think a condolence card from Party Pals Inc. would brighten his day."

A CAPITOL OBSESSION

Allison Brennan

I.

Well ventilated though it was, the senate minority leader's spacious office couldn't mask the smell of a corpse in the middle of summer.

Detective John Black flashed his badge in the general direction of the California Highway Patrol officer who guarded the door. The CHP handled capitol security and they had secured the office as soon as the body had been discovered, but murder was under the jurisdiction of the Sacramento Police Department. All staff, media, and other onlookers had been banned from the third floor. Already the capitol press corps had broadcast the news and John had ignored two messages from the chief of police.

It was the most political of crimes: murder in the capitol.

Conspicuously tall at six foot seven, John didn't attempt to survey the scene discreetly. Instead, he crossed into the middle of the room as he pulled on gloves. The victim was female, blond, in her early thirties, seated in a wholly unnatural position, crammed into the armoire, a man's suit pushed to the back. A sleeve obscured part of the victim's face.

The smell was awful, as gases and bodily fluids had released after death. John unconsciously breathed through his mouth. One of the crime scene people offered him Vaseline. He declined. He'd smelled worse decomps during his twenty years on the force, but it took only one summer working Sacramento's streets to learn quickly what heat did to a dead body.

The victim's skin had taken on a greenish discoloration, her face was bloated, and the skin had started to marble. Dried blood covered the woman's chest. One of her legs was under her body, the other straight up. She was fully clothed, her skirt bunched loosely around her thighs, revealing black lace underwear attached to garters. One garter was missing.

John visually inspected the wound in her chest. It didn't look like a bullet—the dark red hole appeared elongated and narrow.

Knife wound. By the looks of it, only one. No passion, then. Crimes of passion usually resulted in multiple stab wounds as the killer released his anger and frustration in a blind rage.

John looked away from the dead and inspected Senator Bruce Wyatt's office. It was decorated like the rest of the restored capitol, adorned with antiques in the Renaissance Revival style. A little ornate for John's taste, but it suited the architecture. No arcs of blood on the ceiling or any sign of disturbance. But the room was full of heavy, antique furniture; an array of period paintings; and covered with a dark burgundy rug. If the woman was killed here, there would be evidence somewhere.

"What do you think, Simone?" John asked the supervising criminalist.

The woman didn't glance away from her examination of the wardrobe. "I'll know more when we can remove the body."

"What's the medical examiner's ETA?"

"Thirty minutes."

"But you have a guess."

This time she did look at him, a hint of humor in her eyes. "I didn't get to be in my position by guessing. I'll wait until we have the room processed before I posit a theory. But," she added, "I know one thing with certainty."

"What?"

Simone nodded toward the corpse. "Look at her. I think you know what I know."

John stared at the body. "She'd been dead awhile when she was put inside."

"Bingo. Rigor had set in. You're looking at her being moved into the armoire roughly twelve to twenty-four hours after death. But the body isn't in rigor anymore, so she's been here a couple of days. The ME should be able to give you a better timeline."

Interesting, John thought. Had the body been lying around the office for a day before the killer decided to stuff her into the armoire? Had she been killed in Wyatt's office or moved here? Where were the security cameras? He made a mental note to talk to the senate sergeant-at-arms as soon as he spoke to those who had discovered the body. He'd learned long ago not to take security for granted.

"Process all adjacent offices and hallways," John said.

"Already on the list." Simone turned back to her work.

John said to one of the CHP officers in the room, "Who found the body?"

The cop approached, flipped open his notebook, and read formally, "Senator Wyatt called us at nine twenty-five this morning. He was in a meeting when they discovered the body."

"Who was in the meeting?"

"Chief of Staff Rob Douglas and Senator James."

Lara James. Perhaps there was a silver lining. After months of avoiding him, she wouldn't be able to ignore him now.

The cop continued, "Senator James smelled what she thought was a dead rodent. She opened the armoire and found the body."

Dead rodent? No way a woman—an ex-soldier—like Lara James would mistake a human corpse for a rat carcass.

"And Wyatt didn't notice the smell?"

It was more a rhetorical question, which John would ask Wyatt himself. The armoire itself was solid wood, enough to mask the smell for a time. The foul odor would begin to emanate from the chest, slowly worsening as the body decomposed. Whoever put the body inside had to have known it would be discovered. By the looks of it, she'd been dead more than forty-eight hours, but not longer than a week. At a week under normal indoor temperature conditions, the gases would have accumulated to such a degree that the smell couldn't have been masked.

They had no ID on the body yet, but John suspected she was known in the building. Once Simone and her team finished processing the scene and he could remove the suit obscuring her face, he'd bet dozens of people would recognize her.

He said to the CHP officer, "Take me to Senator Wyatt, please."

II.

The California state capitol was divided into two distinct, connected buildings. Home of the California legislature since 1869, the original building had a fourth story added in 1908 and had been completely restored in the early eighties. At one time the four-story structure had housed the entire legislature, the governor, and the staff. But as the state grew, so did the politics. Hence, the east wing annex had been built. It was substantially bigger than the original building, less attractive but more practical.

The designers had done the best they could to connect the new six-story building to the original four-story structure, but the entire place was a maze of slopes, stairs, and shortcuts that only experienced staff could navigate. The state assembly occupied the north side of the capitol; the state senate dominated the south side. John would have gotten lost if he hadn't been following the uniformed cop from Wyatt's office through two halls and down a seemingly hidden staircase to the third floor.

"Senator Wyatt has been in the Members' Lounge since the incident," the cop said.

Incident. Murder was not an incident.

The Members' Lounge—also known as the Maddy Room—was accessible from the senate chambers. It had only artificial light. A long, dark-wood conference table sat on plush red carpet that bled out into the hall and the senate chambers beyond. Couches framed the perimeter. A refreshment center in the corner provided water and soda. The buffet could be used to bring in lunch or dinner for the elected officials. The large painting of former Senator Ken Maddy was almost lost among the cluttered mishmash of art that lined the walls, from modern to antique and everything in between.

John wondered if they'd named the room for Senator Maddy because he had been one of the few likable people in politics. He doubted it. John hadn't met a politician he himself liked, Senator Lara James excluded. Could be his job, of course. He didn't meet many politicians until they broke the law.

Senator Bruce Wyatt sat alone at the table, talking on his cell phone. He was in his midforties, physically fit, and he still had a full head of graying light-brown hair. The sleeves on his white Oxford shirt were unbuttoned and rolled up just below the elbow, his burgundy tie loose around his neck.

Wyatt had been in elected office for twelve years, John knew. Six years in the state assembly, he was now in the middle of his second senatorial term. That meant term limits loomed up ahead for the senator, and because of this Wyatt was now running for U. S. Congress, his opponent Assemblymember Kevin Andersen. It had so far been one of the most talked-about, scandal-ridden primaries in the state. Wyatt and Andersen had a long-time rivalry and a scandal wasn't in Senator Wyatt's best—or even worst—interest.

John motioned for the cop to leave him alone with Wyatt, and closed the door. Wyatt jumped up, snapped his cell phone closed, and demanded, "Who was she? What happened?"

John motioned for the senator to sit. Wyatt hesitated, then

complied. John pulled out a tall-backed black chair opposite him and sat comfortably on the soft leather.

"You didn't recognize her?"

"I—I couldn't tell. I may know her, but I'm not sure. Maybe she's someone I've seen on occasion? Familiar, but . . ."

Wyatt knew her. John would swear to it, but he didn't push. Not yet.

"Let's go back to the last time you were in your office."

"Today?"

"Before today."

"I drove back to the district—Shasta—Thursday. Early afternoon. I had an evening event, and a full schedule there on Friday. I spent the weekend with my family."

John made a note. "I need a copy of your schedule for the last week."

"I'll have my scheduler print it out."

"Who has access to your office?"

Wyatt leaned back. "My staff. Department of General Service. The sergeants, janitorial staff, rules committee. I think state parks has a master key because the building's a historic landmark."

Great. Who didn't have a key?

"How did you find the body, Senator?"

"During a meeting. Senator James thought she smelled something coming from the armoire. The key wasn't there, so she picked the lock."

"How long has the key been missing?"

"I don't know. I put a clean suit in there Monday. But I always leave the key in the lock. I'd planned to wear the suit on Thursday, but I was running late and didn't have time to change."

Easy enough to verify. But it still didn't clear Wyatt of murder.

"Did you touch anything in the armoire?"

"I don't think I've touched it since I put my suit in there on Monday. And I can assure you, Detective, there was no dead woman in the armoire then."

III.

State Senator Lara James paced her office, running her hand impatiently through her short dark hair. She didn't want to be stuck in here, but the CHP officer had told her to sit tight until the Sacramento PD talked to her.

Patience was *not* one of her strengths.

The face of the dead was imprinted on her mind. Not just the dead woman upstairs in Wyatt's office, but each dead soldier and each dead civilian Lara had faced during her nine years of military service.

A bullet to the leg had ended her career two years earlier, and she didn't want to see any more death. Wasn't that one of the reasons she'd run for public office in the first place? To work her way up to a position where she could do more good than harm? How laughable. What had she been thinking?

She was neither a warmonger nor a peacekeeper. She was a soldier who believed in right and wrong, who knew the threat and was willing to fight for freedom. But she'd seen far more evil during her time abroad than she'd known existed. For it was one thing to read textbooks about mass murders and war atrocities; it was quite another to dig up a mass grave of women and children.

A voice and a memory popped into her head.

"Women and children first!" It was a familiar voice followed by a woman's laughter, and Lara recalled the swish of a door and more voices. The California Restaurant Association had converted an old bank into their offices, and the main floor still had heavy, old-fashioned glass doors. Why would she think of this . . . except that female laughter tickled a memory.

Lara rolled her chair over to her bookshelf and pulled out a volume: *2007–2008 Lobbyist Directory*.

She sat behind her desk and flipped through the pages, each quarter-page a photo and bio of a lobbyist registered with the state of California.

And there she was.

Lara stared at the woman with short, slick blond hair and vibrant green eyes, her smile sweetly seductive for a canned shot.

Lara realized that she hadn't immediately recognized the lobbyist because not only had her face been partially obscured, she'd met her only a few times. Wyatt had introduced them at a fundraiser. He'd offered them both a ride home, and Lara had gratefully accepted. Her sore leg had been bothering her, and she'd been too proud to use a cane.

"Women and children first!" Bruce had said when he pushed open the heavy door for her and Tiffany Zaren. The lobbyist had laughed.

Lara's secretary Bonnie knocked on the door, then opened it and said quietly, "John Black from the Sacramento Police Department is here to see you."

Lara looked up. She couldn't believe . . . "Black?" she repeated.

"Hello, Lara."

John smiled at Bonnie and walked around her. Bonnie shrank back and closed the door, leaving Lara alone with him.

He didn't sit, and in her position Lara felt unusually vulnerable. Not because she was a woman, but because John was very tall and broad. A ruggedly handsome detective whom she'd slept with on more than one occasion. Some might have called it a relationship.

"Can't avoid this call, can you?" he said as he slid into the chair across from her desk and crossed his legs.

Lara bit back a nasty comment and flipped the lobbyist directory toward the detective. She tapped her finger on Tiffany Zaren's picture. "I think she's your victim."

John snatched the book and examined the photograph. "You could be right."

"I *am* right."

He kept the directory. "You discovered the body, I'm told."

"Lucky me."

"How?"

"I smelled it."

"Senator Wyatt said you smelled a rodent."

"I *said* I smelled a dead animal. But I knew that wasn't accurate."

She didn't need to elaborate.

"And you just opened the armoire?"

"I took out my trusty-rusty Swiss Army knife." She cracked a half smile and waved the knife in front of her. "The file is a multi-use tool."

John grinned. Damn, but was he sexy when he smiled. "What else did you touch?"

"Wyatt's desk and probably the conference table. The armoire. I didn't touch the body or anything inside."

"Where was the key?"

"Wyatt said he noticed it missing last week." John wrote something down. Lara leaned forward. "Okay, what's going on?"

"Not sure yet."

"Did you notice the position of the body?"

"What do you mean?"

"I mean the legs. They were broken. I think the body was moved."

"There's no proof—"

She waved her hand. "Look, I may not be a cop, but I've been around enough dead people in my life to know what happens when you move them. Rigor mortis had set before she was crammed into that space. So my question is, where was she until she was moved into that cabinet?"

He didn't answer her question. Instead, "What do you know about Wyatt?"

"Bruce is one of the good guys," she said without hesitation. "He served in the first Gulf War. He's the one who talked me into running for office in the first place."

"And that makes him a good guy?"

She laughed. John was one of the few people who amused her.

"I know him, John. Murder? No. He'd be a congenital idiot to kill someone in his private office, then stuff the body in a piece of furniture."

"He's looking at a congressional seat."

"This is America. You don't kill the competition. Lie about them, maybe; kill them, no."

"Could have killed her in a panic, thought he could dispose of the body later."

"That's ridiculous."

"You know as well as I do that killers don't always think ahead." He made a note, then asked, "What about Wyatt's staff?"

"I really don't know any of them, except Rob Douglas, Bruce's right-hand man. He seems okay."

John's cell phone went off. He answered it, said two words, and hung up. "Let's go identify the body."

"Me?"

"You."

"You have the photograph."

"Maybe I just want more time with you, Lara."

"You could have called."

"I did. You ignored me."

Touché.

IV.

John introduced Lara to the investigators in Wyatt's office as he signed her into the log. "Don't touch anything," he admonished.

She slipped on latex gloves nonetheless. She'd done six years in the Military Police before taking the three-year tour of duty in Iraq.

Wyatt's office had been transformed into a crime scene. The body had been removed from the armoire and now lay on a plastic tarp to preserve evidence.

The victim was indeed Tiffany Zaren and the first thing Lara noticed was that lividity was set on her left side.

"So she *was* moved," Lara said.

John turned to a uniformed officer standing near the door and handed him the lobbyist directory. "The vic is Tiffany Zaren. Get her address, employer, associates, the whole nine yards. Call her office and find out the last time anyone saw her, if she's married, has kids, elderly parents living with her, a boyfriend, an ex."

Lara interrupted, "She's divorced, no kids, and lives in one of those new lofts downtown. Sixteenth and J. She's a lobbyist with Nygrant, Prescott, and Zaren. Her big clients are Indian gaming."

John raised an eyebrow. "I thought you didn't know her well."

"I've talked to her a couple of times. I have a good memory."

John caught her eye. "So do I."

She turned back to the victim, flustered, and hating being flustered. She'd been avoiding John for the last couple of months. The intensity of their relationship unnerved her, and she thought a break was in order. He just didn't know when to give up.

And she didn't know if she wanted him to.

"You're correct, Senator James," Simone Charles said. The criminalist turned to John. "The ME confirmed it. She was on her left side for at least twelve hours. But she had to have been moved in a fairly narrow window—twelve hours after her death up to twenty-four. There's no ID or purse in the armoire or the office. She's missing a garter and a shoe."

John asked, "Have you finished sweeping these offices?"

Simone replied, "We're still collecting potential evidence. We'll be done in a few hours, then can expand the search to the rest of the floor."

"I'll check for any security tapes," John said. "And have—"

The sergeant-at-arms interrupted, "Detective, we have some sensitive issues here—"

"We also have a dead body here."

"There are one-hundred twenty elected officials in this building, plus the governor's office—"

"Ms. Zaren's body was moved. We don't know if she was killed in this room or in another part of the building. Or outside the building and brought in. Did you get the security tapes I asked for?"

"For the last forty-eight hours."

"Make it for the last week," John said. He glanced around the office. "There's no security in here?"

"Not in the offices. Most public areas are covered, entrances, elevators. It would be virtually impossible to pass through the halls without being caught on at least one camera."

"What about security to get into the building?"

"All entrances have cameras, metal detectors, and X-ray machines. Staff and guests are required to pass through them."

"Not after hours," Lara interjected. "Any staff can come in using their ID card. Legislators can walk around the screening or come in through the garage."

John said, "I want all security tapes of everyone who has come in and out of this building, from elected officials to janitorial staff. Are there cameras in the garage?"

"Yes."

"I want those tapes too. Digital?"

The sergeant shook his head. "Analog."

"Get it all to Officer Smiley here." John gestured toward a dour-looking cop standing by the door. The two left, and John turned to Lara. "What else do you know about the victim?"

"Not much. She went to all the fund-raisers, which isn't surprising for a lobbyist. She knows I'm not one of her votes, so I don't see her much."

"Detective?" Simone approached. "The ME is bringing up a gurney to transport the body. He shared his preliminary findings."

"What do you have?"

"She was stabbed once in the chest. The weapon hasn't been found, but it's likely a narrow, nonserrated knife. She's been dead over seventy-two hours, less than one week. Some of her smaller muscles were already relaxing, so she was moved close to twenty-four hours after she was killed."

"A full day? What about smell? Why didn't anyone notice her earlier?"

"The building is air-conditioned. That's going to slow the rate of decomposition. And the armoire trapped the smell for a time. It takes a couple of days before a body starts to really stink. The victim wasn't killed in this room," Simone added. "The only blood we've found is dried—"

"She's been dead for more than three days, why wouldn't it be dry?"

"I should say *flaked*. If she were killed here, I would expect to see blood in the carpet or furniture, even with a thorough cleaning job. If the killer tried to clean with bleach or another caustic chemical, that would show. Everything is pristine. But there are some blood flakes all around the armoire, and several just inside the side door."

John said, "Someone would certainly notice if a dead body was being carried through the building. Are you certain she wasn't killed in this room?"

Simone shrugged. "There's also an odd mark on her back." The criminalist rolled the victim to her side and lifted her white silk blouse. On Tiffany Zaren's flesh was an impression, almost like a white stamp, in a perfect two-by-three-inch rectangle. There appeared to be small letters within it.

"I can't make out the words," John said.

"Because lividity was on her left side, I think her back was against some sort of metal plate for several hours. I'll work on it and get back to you, but so far we haven't been able to find anything in this office or the adjoining offices that match this shape and size." She rolled the body back over. "The knife pierced her lung and she probably suffocated, or died of bleeding into her pericardium. There's not enough blood here for her to have bled out. But look at her hands—" Simone lifted one arm. Dried blood coated Zaren's hands, with more streaks and marks on her arms, skirt, and blouse.

"She was trying to stop the bleeding."

"Either she pulled the knife out herself, probably stunned or in shock, or the killer pulled out the knife and she grabbed her chest. Wherever she was killed, there's going to be blood evidence."

"I'm going back to my office," Lara said.

John glanced at her over his shoulder. "Good. Then I'll know where to find you."

v.

John went back to the Maddy Room. Two men in crisp suits were arguing with the haggard-looking senator. "I'd like to speak with Senator Wyatt in private," John said.

"This is an embarrassment to the institution!" one of the men exclaimed.

Wyatt was pale. "But what happened? *How* did she get into my office?"

John escorted the two men to the door, closed it behind them, then sat on the table, his height giving him additional psychological leverage over the sitting Wyatt. He hadn't decided whether Wyatt was guilty or not—Lara was right, only an idiot would stash a body in his own office. But Wyatt wasn't acting as John would expect an innocent man to act.

"You know the victim," John stated.

"I just found out. Tiffany Zaren. Of course I know her. I'm carrying one of her client's major bills."

"Indian gaming?"

"Yes."

"Is the bill controversial?"

"Anything related to Indian gaming is controversial," he said. "That doesn't have anything to do with this."

"Then what does her death have to do with?"

"I don't know. I—I still can't believe it."

"When was the last time you saw Ms. Zaren?"

Wyatt paused, as if thinking. But John suspected that he knew exactly the last time he'd seen the pretty lobbyist, just as John was positive Wyatt had recognized her when he'd first seen the body. Was he trying to protect himself or someone else?

"Wednesday at a fund-raiser."

"Where?"

"Chops."

"Who put on the event?"

"It was an assembly leadership fund-raiser."

"I need a guest list."

"My secretary can get it."

"And Ms. Zaren was there?"

"Yes."

"What time did you arrive?"

"Six, six thirty."

"What time did you leave?"

"Eight. I had another event to go to, a dinner."

"With whom?"

"Several people, including another senator and two assembly members, a couple of major donors. My wife, Cindy. My secretary has all that information."

"Where was the dinner?"

"Morton's."

"And you didn't see Ms. Zaren after leaving Chops at eight?"

"No."

"I'll need information about the legislation you were working on together."

"Why?"

"Gambling is a touchy subject. It's a good place to start." But a better place to start, John thought, was to find out why Wyatt was acting guilty if, as Lara believed, he was innocent.

VI.

After speaking with Tiffany's partners in the lobbying firm of Nygrant, Prescott, and Zaren, John went to her loft. Her car was in its parking slot, and he confirmed with the landlord that the last time she'd entered the garage was at eleven PM the previous Monday. That correlated with Nygrant's assertion that she usually walked the five blocks to work.

Something in that conversation bothered John. When he'd asked about a boyfriend or ex-boyfriend, the men shifted uncomfortably and Prescott said, "Tiffany has been involved with several men."

"Who?"

"I couldn't say."

"Why not?"

"I don't know anything firsthand, just rumors. She'd been involved in a very public affair with Kevin Andersen, the assembly minority leader, last year. It's over. He wasn't married, there was nothing controversial about it, but some of our clients felt it could compromise their position. Since then, she's dated several other men."

"So she broke it off with Andersen?"

"As far as I know."

And while there was nothing unusual about an attractive lobbyist being a revolving door for relationships, it gnawed at John.

Nothing was amiss in her loft, which could have been called "minimalist." The mail on her desk had been opened and dealt with. Nothing past due, bank statements showed a healthy but not excessive balance, and her expenses were in line with her income. Organized. Tidy. No journal or diary. A laptop computer sat on her desk. John called Simone and asked her to come and pick it up, as well as Zaren's computer at the lobbying firm. He'd ask for extra help to work the gambling angle. He'd read an article a while back that implied Nevada gaming interests weren't pleased with the expansion of Indian gaming in California. But he couldn't figure out how killing a lobbyist would help either group. Unless it was to cast suspicion on Wyatt. But if someone was smart enough to frame someone, John didn't think they'd be so damn obvious about it. That whole scenario just didn't feel right to him, and after twenty years as a cop, John trusted his instincts.

By the time he arrived back at the capitol, it was well after five. The crime scene people were done, the victim had been taken to the morgue, and Wyatt's office was still sealed. John spoke to his officers, who were reviewing security tapes starting at eight PM Wednesday night, when Tiffany had last been seen. So far, there was no evidence of foul play anywhere. John wanted to seal off the entire historic building, but he came up against brass who said that if she'd been killed elsewhere in the building, the scene was already compromised, and the chief wasn't going to take the heat for further inconveniencing staff and elected officials.

Damn politics. A woman was dead and his boss kept catering to the politicians.

John went down to the assembly minority leader's suite hoping he wasn't too late to speak with the victim's ex-boyfriend. The secretary immediately escorted him to Kevin Andersen's private office. Though not in the historic building with the gravitas of history and period furniture, Andersen's office was well appointed, with awards and diplomas covering the wood-paneled walls. His desk was clear except for an expensive-looking silver pen-and-pencil set positioned dead center and a short stack of files in the corner.

"I'm stunned." Andersen was in his early forties, with perfect hair that might have been a rug.

"When did you last see Ms. Zaren?"

"I don't recall."

"It was your fund-raiser Wednesday, correct?"

"Yes, but she left before I did."

"You were involved with her for how long?"

"Why is this relevant?"

John simply watched him, reminded of how much he disliked politicians.

"About eight months," Andersen said.

"And she broke it off."

"It was mutual."

"Alleged impropriety because of her gaming clients?"

"It was mutual," he repeated.

"Do you know if she was currently involved with anyone?"

"I don't keep tabs on her."

Andersen stared him in the eye. Good liars can do that, but good liars were rare. Still, he was in the lion's den.

"Where did you go after the fund-raiser?"

"Home."

"Alone?"

"Yes. Is this an interrogation?"

"I'm just asking questions." John put on his simpleton face. Andersen wasn't buying it.

"Do I need a lawyer?"

"Do you?"

Andersen tensed, then responded curtly. "I went home alone around ten thirty. After the fund-raiser, I took my staff out to dinner, then walked two of the girls to their parking garage because I don't like the idea of women walking in downtown Sacramento alone at night. Julia and Hilary. They're in the office today, you can confirm with them. Then I walked back to the capitol, got in my car, and left. I ran upstairs to my office to get something, but I wasn't in there long."

"Where was your car parked?"

"In the capitol basement."

"Did anyone see you?"

"Probably. Couldn't say who."

"Thanks for your time."

John found his officers viewing security tapes in the CHP office on the first floor of the annex, across from the governor's office. He said, "It's after six, I'm going to head back to the station and write up a report. I want someone on Wyatt's office all night, and if you see anything on the tapes, call me. I need a list of everyone entering and exiting the building and at what time."

"Yes, sir."

John was about to leave when he saw someone familiar on one of the closed-circuit screens. "Is this live?" he asked.

"Yes," the commanding officer said. "These are coming in from all the cameras. Some are fixed, some rotate in five-second intervals."

What was Lara James doing looking at the camera on—"Where's this?" He tapped the screen.

"Third-floor annex. Outside the main elevator bank."

What was she up to? John left and found the camera—but Lara was gone.

VII.

At first glance, security appeared tight in the capitol building. Visitors and staff entered through metal detectors, their possessions scanned by X-ray machines. Throughout the public areas of the building were both CHP officers and extensive security cameras, which fed live to the CHP office as well as copied to tape. CHP monitored the cameras, walked the halls after hours, and were posted at key positions on the ground floor.

Even with all the precautions, however, there was a huge hole in camera security. While the public floors were well monitored, upstairs, where staff and legislators worked, there were fewer cameras. And in the historic building where Tiffany Zaren's body had been found, the only security above the first floor was cameras aimed at the elevators.

What the criminalist had said to John bugged Lara. Someone had intentionally moved Tiffany's body into Wyatt's armoire. Why? Convenience? To frame him? Or maybe both? More important, how? So Lara walked both the annex and the historic building, top floor to the basement, to map out a path where someone could theoretically bypass all security cameras.

She came to a startling conclusion: If someone knew the building well, it was possible to get almost anywhere above the first floor in the historic structure—and certain areas of the adjoining annex—without being caught on camera.

"What are you doing?"

She spun around. It was John Black.

He raised an eyebrow. "I was checking the tape in the CHP office and saw you staring at one of the cameras, with that expression you get when you're deep in thought. I've been tracking you since. I figure you have some thoughts in that smart head of yours that relate to my case. Will you share?"

"Of course," she said.

He started up the stairs, and she swallowed her embarrassment to ask, "Can we take the elevator?"

John's expression showed concern, but he simply said, "Sure."

She sighed, relieved he didn't comment further. She'd walked far too much today, and she hated having a bum leg. She hated being unable to continue her career in the military; she hated living with constant pain.

Lara shared with him her observation about the security cameras and concluded by saying, "It makes me think Zaren's murder was premeditated. Unless the cameras picked up something that wouldn't seem strange to the security guard monitoring the camera bank. Like someone who wouldn't raise suspicions." *Staff or a member.*

"Why would someone bring her here to kill her?" John asked. "Then plant her body in Wyatt's office?"

"The crime lab hasn't discovered where she was killed?"

"Not yet. But it has to be in the building. Even if someone could get her body into the building, I can't see why they'd do so."

"To embarrass Bruce? To prove they can? There've been some wacky stunts around here by people trying to get political or media attention."

"But murder?"

Lara didn't have an answer to that.

They exited the elevator on the sixth floor. Most people had left work—it was well after six—but a few stragglers remained. Lara spoke quietly as she led John through the corridor that led to the historic side of the capitol.

"Someone wanted to frame Bruce Wyatt."

"Maybe he killed her."

She shook her head. "I don't buy into that. He's not that dumb."

"Maybe he's counting on people to think that." Lara didn't say anything, and John continued. "I know he's your friend, but you know as well as I do that sometimes the people we think we know are strangers." John rubbed his temples.

"Headache?" she asked.

"I missed lunch."

Without thinking, Lara said, "We should get a bite to eat."

"We?" John grinned. "It's a date."

"I mean—"

"Too late to backpedal, Lara. I'm holding you to dinner."

They found themselves on the assembly side of the historic fourth floor. "This place is a freaking maze," John said. "I don't know how anyone can find their way around. Was that passage we just walked through on the roof?"

"Yes, the original capitol roof. A couple of protesters broke through the maintenance door a few years back and draped banners over the side," Lara said. "Now there's a dedicated security camera there and alarms on the door."

John glanced around; they were standing outside the freight elevator. "There're no cameras here," he said.

He punched the button and stepped in when the doors opened. Lara followed, not sure what he was thinking.

"There're no cameras on any of the historic stairwells, only on the public elevators," Lara said. "I've been thinking about this all day, Tiffany had to have been killed on the historic side. The annex has far more security. No one can walk down the halls without being observed. And while staff and members come and go at odd hours of the day and night, wouldn't a killer try to hide?"

"Unless he had a reason for being here," John said.

The freight elevators opened. She pointed to the door on the right that led to the stairwell. "See? No security." She opened the door and gestured. "None inside either." She stared at another door across from the banister.

"What's wrong?" John asked.

She didn't respond, but walked around the landing of the stairwell to a door that looked exactly like one she'd often walked past on the senate side. Expecting it to be locked, she tried the knob.

It opened.

"Lara—"

"I rarely come over to the assembly side of the building, but in the senate stairwell there's a door like this. I think they connect."

The hallway was dark and Lara couldn't find a light switch, but saw light coming from under a door about thirty feet away. Shelves lined the walls, stocked with supplies like toilet paper and toilet-seat covers. A maintenance closet?

"Lara?"

Suddenly fluorescent lights came on. John had found the switch.

"This goes directly to the senate side," she said. "I never knew this was here. I thought the only way to get to the senate side of the building was the front hall, by those ornate staircases under the governors' portraits. Very visible. But this . . ."

"Coupled with the fact that there is virtually no security over here and, frankly, few people."

"There are only four legislative offices, and some staff and committee rooms, but most of the people work in the annex."

"And at night?"

"Zero, unless they're late on passing the budget. Do you know the time of death?"

"Simone said more than seventy-two hours. I'll know for sure after the autopsy tomorrow. I'll have Simone's team check out this hall."

"If no one saw her on Thursday, wouldn't it stand to reason that she was killed Wednesday night?"

John nodded. He walked down the corridor and put on a glove. He tried the door. It opened.

"It was locked from the other side."

"You tried it earlier?"

"I was curious."

He closed the door and faced her. "You've always been curious, haven't you?"

Lara swallowed, anticipating a change of subject to one she wasn't as comfortable with as murder. "Is that a problem?"

He shook his head, his mouth firm but his dark eyes lit with something that made Lara's heart flutter. "I've learned something in these last couple of months."

"What's that?"

He took a step forward and she had to look up at him. She was considered tall, but standing next to John she felt petite and feminine. "My feelings for you have never changed, but seeing you again, face-to-face, they are more intense. I shouldn't have called you. I should have come to your office and not left until you agreed to move in with me."

"John—"

He kissed her. For a long moment, her mind went blissfully blank, her entire body focused on his mouth. She wanted to protest, she wanted to tell him it wasn't the same for her.

But that would be a lie.

John stepped back, a grin on his face. "I love you too. Let's get dinner."

He opened the door.

VIII.

John learned several things during the autopsy on Tuesday morning. Time of death was established as Wednesday night between ten PM and two AM. Tiffany Zaren died of massive internal bleeding when a knife—likely a letter opener—punctured a corner of her heart and her lung.

And she'd had sex less than an hour before she died.

DNA samples were taken and sent to the lab, but it would be at least two weeks—even with the rush John put on it—before he had anything useful. And he needed to make an arrest before he could compel a suspect to submit his DNA. Still, the information would be useful during his next conversation with Senator Bruce Wyatt and every other man who had been in the building after nine PM Wednesday night.

John returned to the capitol with the new information. The officer who was viewing security tapes called on his cell phone and said, "I have a list of everyone who came and left the capitol from eight PM Wednesday to four AM Thursday morning."

"Meet me in Senator James's office."

Lara was at her desk, glowing. At least he imagined she should be after their night together. He wasn't going to let her walk away this time. He was in it for the long haul. For the first time, her attitude told him she believed him. Trust didn't come easy for Lara, and John was honored he'd earned it.

"I have—" he began, but his cell phone rang. It was Cindy Wyatt, the senator's wife.

She said, "You left a message for me yesterday. I'm sorry I didn't get back to you right away. I was out most of the day. Bruce told me about that poor woman."

"I was calling to verify a dinner you had at Morton's Steakhouse last Wednesday evening?"

"With my husband and his colleagues and their wives."

"What time did you leave?"

"I'm not sure. Between ten and ten thirty."

"Did you go straight home?"

"Yes. We drove right to our town house on the river. Then on Thursday afternoon we drove to our home in Shasta."

"And you and your husband were home all night?"

"Yes."

When he hung up, Lara said, "You're verifying Bruce's alibi?"

"A dead body was in his office. I have to verify his and everyone else's on his staff, just for openers." John tapped his pencil on the pad. "His wife says he was home all night. Wives have been known to lie." He made a note to verify Cindy Wyatt's statement.

"What are you doing here anyway?"

"I missed you." He smiled when Lara blushed. "Seriously, I wanted a private place to talk to my officers. You don't mind, do you? I figure this is the most secure place in the capitol, away from controversy and probing press."

"That's fine. I have something to do. I'll be right back."

John watched Lara leave. Something was wrong. He'd have gone after her, except Officer Smiley came in ready to report on the tapes he'd viewed. "Eight legislators entered the garage after eight PM Wednesday night," he said, "and three staff members. Staff are required to use their passkeys to enter, not exit, but we identified them on camera when they left."

"Someone could have come in during business hours and hidden somewhere in the building," John noted. He glanced at the staff list. One name stood out: Robert Douglas, Wyatt's chief of staff. He entered at 9:50 PM and exited an hour later.

Smiley nodded. "I identified Tiffany Zaren entering the building at ten forty PM with Senator Wyatt. She never left. Wyatt exits the garage at eleven thirty-five PM."

"I want to view those tapes." Douglas had been in the building at the same time as Wyatt and Zaren.

"You asked me to check for Assemblymember Kevin Andersen? He came in at ten thirty, just like he said."

"When did he leave?"

"He didn't. At least not through the garage."

"Find out which exit he used and when he used it. I need to talk to Wyatt."

First Wyatt lied, then Andersen. Why?

IX.

Lara's fists were squeezed tight. She stood in front of Bruce Wyatt in his temporary office one floor beneath the crime scene.

"You had Cindy lie for you!"

"I—what?" Wyatt looked stricken.

"I called your house at eleven Wednesday night. Cindy said you were out. She told the police you were at home. You're a bastard."

"I don't know what—"

"Were you having an affair with Tiffany Zaren?"

"I—no—not like—"

She knew as soon as he stuttered that he was guilty. He'd cheated on his wife and Cindy was covering for him. Why? Because she *loved* him? How could she love a man who didn't take his wedding vows seriously? How could Lara respect a man who cheated on his wife, who lied to her, who was possibly a killer?

"You killed her."

"I didn't. I swear to you, Lara, I didn't kill Tiffany. Yes, we were having an affair. It didn't mean anything, just one of those things. . . ."

Lara felt betrayed. She had admired this man. She'd always understood where he was coming from, even when they disagreed on policy. She had *respected* him more than anyone else. More than her father, more than her commanding officer. Bruce Wyatt was like an older, wiser brother. A mentor.

Now he was nothing but a fraud. How could she believe anything he said?

"Tell the police."

"No, I—"

"Dammit, Bruce! They're not stupid. They're going to see you coming in with her on the security tapes!"

His face fell as he remembered security. "I didn't think——"

"You can say that again." If Bruce was so stupid as to think that he could get away with having an affair, maybe he *was* stupid enough to stuff his dead lover in an armoire.

"It's not what you think."

"What a cliché. You have no idea what I think."

"I didn't kill Tiffany," he whispered.

"I'm telling the police about my conversation with Cindy. I'm not lying for you, Bruce."

John walked into the office. "Let's start from the beginning." He didn't look at Lara and she realized she should have gone to him first. But she'd been so angry with Wyatt, and herself, for her bad judgment, she'd wanted to confront Wyatt herself.

Wyatt seemed to shrink, becoming older and defeated. "I was having sex with Tiffany. We came here after the dinner. Cindy and I had taken two cars, I told her I had to pick up some papers. Tiff and I had never, um, 'been' in my office before. She left around eleven thirty. Said she didn't want anyone seeing us together. I wanted to drive her home, but Tiff . . . She said she'd be fine. I left right after, went down to the parking garage. I didn't think anything of it. I tried calling her on Thursday before I left town, but she didn't answer."

"You lied to me. You didn't think we'd see you and the victim on the security tapes?"

"I didn't think anyone would have a reason to!"

Lara interjected, "Even after her murder? What were you thinking?"

Bruce was flustered. "To be honest, I thought the security cameras would show her talking to someone else—after she left me—and prove I wasn't the last one to see her."

"You should have come clean from the beginning," Lara said, disgusted with her former friend and mentor.

Lara watched John answer his cell phone. A minute later he said to Bruce, "We found the murder weapon. A letter opener. In your middle desk drawer with Tiffany's missing garter wrapped around it."

x.

Wyatt lawyered up. He claimed he didn't recognize the sterling-silver letter opener, and that was it.

John pushed the senator hard before letting him leave, but he didn't have anything more than circumstantial evidence. There were no prints on the letter opener, and he couldn't reconcile where and how Wyatt had killed Tiffany, or why he would move her after twenty-four hours to hide her in his office. Security tapes showed he used the elevator five minutes after Tiffany went down the staircase, and he exited the building from the basement shortly after that.

While John had believed in the possibility of a crime of passion and Wyatt panicking, stuffing the body in the armoire, he simply had a hard time believing that the senator would have left the murder weapon in his own desk.

But maybe someone with free access to the office would have.

John met with Robert Douglas in the CHP office, having no intention of pussyfooting around with Wyatt's chief of staff.

"You were in the building late Wednesday night," John began.

Douglas nodded. "I came in to pick up some papers."

"When?"

"Around ten. It was after I made my rounds at the fund-raisers. Why?"

John ignored the question. "What time did you leave?"

"I don't know. It wasn't that long." He glanced away. This guy wasn't a good liar.

"Did you see Senator Wyatt at any time Wednesday night?"

"At Chops, for a fund-raiser."

"And?"

"And what?"

"That was it?"

"I don't understand."

John slammed his fist on the table. "Yes, you do understand, but I'll ask clearly. When you were in the building between nine fifty and ten fifty-five Wednesday night, did you see, hear, talk to, or otherwise know that Senator Wyatt was in the building?"

"Yes."

"Was he alone?"

"No."

"Who was he with?"

"I don't know."

"If you're trying to protect your boss, you're doing a piss-poor job of it. Spit it out or I'll charge you as an accessory."

Douglas blanched. "I was in my office working. I often work at night, when it's quiet. I heard someone moving around his office and thought it was odd, because the janitorial staff is long gone by then. I opened the door and—"

"And what?"

"Bruce was with someone. I didn't see her face. He was sitting in his chair and she was under his desk and—"

"I get the picture. You didn't recognize her?"

"I just saw blond hair."

"And you didn't think to say anything after we found a dead blonde?"

"I—no."

"Did Wyatt see you?"

"Yes, but I left right after that."

"And?"

"The next day he came up to my desk and joked it off."

John took out his ace. He had Douglas's personnel records. The top page was a copy of a request for a raise submitted to the Senate Rules Committee. "On Thursday, the senator approved a raise for you. A nice bump."

Douglas didn't say anything.

"Was he paying you to hide the fact that he was having an affair, or that he killed someone?"

"The affair," Douglas whispered. He cleared his throat. "I swear, Bruce didn't look or act like he killed anyone. We had a staff meeting in his office after he left Thursday afternoon and everything looked like it always does." He sat up straighter, as if trying to please a strict teacher. "In fact, Kris—the scheduler—opened the armoire to put Bruce's shoes inside. He keeps an extra pair and she'd taken them down to be shined. I swear, ask her."

With one sentence, Robert Douglas had cleared both himself and his boss of murder and provided another witness.

Unless the substantial salary increase was for moving the body Thursday night and Douglas was far shrewder than he appeared on the surface.

"What time did you leave Thursday?"

"Five thirty or so."

"Did you return at any time Thursday night or early Friday morning?"

"No. I took Friday off. Felt I'd, um, earned it." He stared at his hands.

Which led John back to, who wanted Tiffany Zaren dead? And why would they frame Senator Wyatt?

After Douglas left, John studied the tapes again. Officer Smiley had marked all key segments. "The place was Grand Central Station between nine and ten," Smiley said. "But after eleven, the only people in the building other than security personnel were Wyatt, the vic, and Assemblymember Andersen."

Smiley continued, "I traced their steps, and Wyatt's statement holds up. See—here—Zaren leaves Wyatt's office."

"That's what you said on the phone, but I don't see anything."

"Here." He paused the tape. An arm appeared in view. He slow-motioned the tape and Tiffany came into the frame briefly, then disappeared two frames later. "By the shadow, she must have taken the stairs."

"Taken the stairs where?"

"Don't know. She doesn't show up on any other camera, but the stairwells aren't monitored in the older building."

John remembered his walk with Lara through both sections of the capitol. "What about Andersen?"

"He was in his office briefly, from ten thirty until ten fifty. He was talking on the phone with someone when he entered. Then he left and took the elevators to the garage."

"But you said earlier that Andersen didn't leave through the garage."

"Right. He didn't. He is on tape leaving through the north entrance at twelve ten."

Where in the building was Kevin Andersen for over an hour? He told Smiley to expand beyond the garage. "Review the tapes starting at eight PM on Wednesday through six AM Friday and tell me everyone who comes in or leaves the building."

XI.

Lara was furious at herself and at Bruce Wyatt, but she didn't believe he was a killer.

She retraced the steps she'd taken with John the day before and found herself in the same assembly corridor on the fourth floor of the historic building where she and John had gone down in the freight elevator and discovered the passage to the senate side of the building. A long, narrow hallway curved around, leading to three different committee rooms. She'd never been in any of them. The doors were locked. Contemplating picking the locks, she decided against it. She'd call John and ask him if the CSI had extended their search for evidence into the assembly side.

She rounded the corner near Committee Room 437 and practically ran into a credenza. It stuck out like a sore thumb in the narrow hall. No other furniture had been in any of the halls she'd been roaming. She sat down on top of the credenza to rest her bum leg, disturbing a fly that buzzed by her head.

Lara rubbed her eyes. She was more disappointed than anything else. Why had she run for office in the first place? Her mentor had turned out to be an adulterer, legislation she felt passionate about was killed unceremoniously in committee, and nothing worthwhile was accomplished.

Maybe she should try not to take it all so seriously. John had walked back into her life, and she didn't think she'd be able to get rid of him this time. She smiled, remembering last night, thinking about what it would be like to let someone fully into her heart and share her life.

Her leg wasn't feeling any better and Lara accepted the fact that she was going to have to take a pain pill to make it through the rest of the day. When she slid off the credenza, three more flies flew off as well.

What were *flies* doing here in a climate-controlled building?

She squatted in front of the credenza, putting most of her weight on her good leg, and used a tissue to ease open the doors from the bottom.

The smell of death assaulted her, though there was no longer a dead body in this space. There had been—the bottom of the credenza was covered in dried blood. On the back panel was a two-by-three-inch metal plate with SAMPSON FURNITURE COMPANY stamped on it.

Other than the memory of death, a bright red spiked-heel shoe was the only thing inside.

Lara called John.

XII.

Lara sat alone in her office while John and the crime scene investigators worked in Committee Room 437. As soon as she'd shown them the evidence, they searched the entire floor and found blood evidence in the unlocked committee room closest to the credenza. It now looked like Tiffany had been murdered in that room, then stuffed in the credenza, where rigor took hold. The killer had to break rigor to move her the next night to Wyatt's armoire.

John didn't have much time to talk, but he said that it looked like Wyatt's alibi held, and the security tapes showed it would have been impossible for him to kill Tiffany Zaren unless there was some huge conspiracy to protect him. Both Lara and John doubted that—secrets didn't last long in this building.

If Wyatt wasn't guilty, who had killed the lobbyist? Lara wondered. It mattered for justice, but did it truly matter to *her*? Bruce had still lied to her. Everything she'd believed in was . . . gone.

Everything except the solid and reliable John Black.

She was surprised when Assembly Minority Leader Kevin Andersen walked into her office. "Do you have a minute?" he asked her.

"I have several," she answered.

He sat down and leaned back in his chair. "I hear Bruce was arrested."

"You hear wrong."

"Oh?"

He was pumping her for information. It was politics as usual. Andersen and Wyatt had a rivalry going from way back to their college years, and Wyatt had defeated Andersen the first time they both ran for the same seat. And now they were running against each other for Congress. Of course he would gloat over the tragedy.

"What do you want, Kevin?"

He put his hands up. "Nothing, nothing. Just wanted to talk about what happened, I guess."

"A woman is dead and you want to gloat over Bruce's downfall. Asshole."

Andersen's expression hardened. "He was having an affair with a lobbyist. That's not a crime, but murder is." How did Andersen know about the affair? Had it leaked out that fast? She wouldn't be surprised.

"I don't believe for a minute that Bruce killed her. I don't know what happened, but I do know that the police are investigating every possible scenario."

"It doesn't matter. They might not be able to *prove* Wyatt killed her, but they can't disprove it. And he knows it. You need to convince him to resign. He won't listen to anyone else, but he might listen to you."

"The police are going to figure out exactly what happened. They have security tapes, they have witnesses, it's just a matter of time. Bruce may be an adulterer, but I don't think he's a killer."

Something crossed Andersen's face, then he jumped up and slammed his fist on her desk. "Who's going to give him money after this scandal? And you, little lady, would be wise to distance yourself from that fool."

Little lady? She should kick the smug expression off that bastard's face.

He walked out and she fumed. *Asshole.*

But how did he know Bruce Wyatt was having an affair with Tiffany?

XIII.

The nighttime basement supervisor, Benjamin Jackson, normally came on duty at eight in the evening, but John had asked that he come in earlier. It had already been a long, long day.

Because the evidence proved that Tiffany Zaren had been kept in the credenza for a full day before her body was moved to Wyatt's armoire, someone else had to be involved if Wyatt was guilty. John had pushed Robert Douglas and the rest of Wyatt's staff, but no one acted like a guilty accomplice.

But there was one piece of evidence he couldn't reconcile, and he hoped Jackson had the answers.

Jackson was at least sixty and wore a defeated expression, like Morgan Freeman in a prison film.

"Mr. Jackson, I have a couple of questions. On Wednesday night, cameras show Senator Wyatt leaving the garage at eleven forty-five PM."

"Yep, white Chevy Tahoe. He drives his district car, doesn't use a fleet vehicle."

"I also have the cameras showing that Assemblymember Andersen came down to the basement just before eleven, but I don't have a time that he left. I'm still going through film, but I was hoping you might remember."

"Wednesday or Thursday?"

"Both days."

Jackson rubbed his chin. "Well, on Wednesday he came down about eleven and sat in his car for a time. Then I saw him get out and go to the little boys' room."

"Where?"

Jackson pointed in a westward direction. "It's near the stairwell to the historic building. You can't see it from here, but there's a corridor that goes to the older side. Only staff use that bathroom, but I thought he might have been a little tipsy."

"And then?"

"I saw him in his car after midnight. Don't recall the exact time, but there he was, sitting in the driver's seat, sleeping."

"Sleeping?"

"Sure, eyes closed, just sitting there." Jackson winked. "It's known to happen. They drink a little too much, don't want to be caught driving—the scandal of a DUI is more serious nowadays than ten, twenty years ago."

"Did you wake him?"

"Naw, he got out a few minutes later and told me he'd drunk too much and was going to walk home."

"And Thursday?"

"Came in at eleven, gone before midnight."

John went back to the CHP office and had Officer Smiley run the garage tape from that time period Thursday.

Sure enough, Kevin Andersen drove in at eleven. He parked, and the tape had him going up to his office. He left almost immediately, went into the staircase—

But the next time he showed up on tape was a full forty-three minutes later, when he entered the basement. The CHP commander confirmed that the hall provided access to the historic stairwell. The stairwell without security camera monitoring.

More than enough time to move a body.

XIV.

It was late when Lara was leaving the office. She had half-expected John to come in and suggest they have a drink or relax at his place.

He didn't. Of course, he was working.

Their relationship was complicated only because she made it that way. She saw that now. *Why* was she playing hard to get? The fear of a lifetime commitment? But life was too short. Shouldn't she take a chance now and again? She had willingly risked her life for her country, why couldn't she risk her heart for the man she loved?

She called John's cell.

"I'm about to talk to Andersen," he told her. "Are you in your office?"

"Yes."

"I'll come up when I'm done."

When he hung up, she thought about that snake Andersen

coming into her office and threatening her—calling her "little lady" and telling her to distance herself from Wyatt. If he'd been a friend, she might consider it an act of kindness. But Kevin Andersen had never been a friend of hers. What a jerk. She figured John was in the leader's office, and walked down the one flight of stairs.

His door was unlocked. She walked in; the office was empty.

"Hello?"

No answer. She heard voices in Andersen's office; the door was ajar. She heard John say, "You don't want to do this, Kevin. Put the gun down."

She peeked in and saw Andersen with a revolver aimed at someone. She couldn't see John from this angle, but it had to be him.

There was no other way into the office. She tiptoed to the secretary's desk and pressed the panic button—it alerted the assembly sergeant-at-arms when there was a security problem in the office.

Kevin Andersen was definitely a *major* security problem.

"Get your handcuffs. Cuff yourself to the chair. I don't want to kill anyone, I just need time."

"Let's talk about this," John said.

"It was a mistake, and I fixed it!"

"I'm sure you had a very good reason for killing Tiffany—"

"I didn't kill her! Wyatt did it."

"We both know that's not true."

"Did he buy you off?"

Lara could almost feel John bristling from the accusation.

Everything clicked. Andersen's previous relationship with Tiffany, Bruce's affair, the tapes— *"I fixed it."*

Andersen's finger was on the trigger. His eyes were wild, and his once perfectly coiffed hair was hanging in front of his face.

"You knew about Bruce's affair, didn't you?" John said.

"His *wife* called me. Told me they were in the building."

Lara was stunned. *Cindy Wyatt?* Why on earth would Cindy

Wyatt call her husband's biggest rival? A woman scorned . . . she must have known about the affair. What had she planned to accomplish if Andersen found out about it? Did she really want her husband to lose the congressional primary?

"You didn't mean to kill her."

"I didn't. Bruce did. I saw him."

"You saw him kill her?"

John was buying time. Good. When were the sergeants going to get here? Lara feared Andersen would lose it.

Andersen nodded frantically, sweat on his brow. "They were having sex in the committee room. I was just going to get pictures, threaten him with exposing the affair. He went for me, Tiffany got in the way, and he killed her."

"Well, let's get your statement on the record then. Why don't you—"

"I see through your game! I know what you're doing! You're trying to get me to come down to the station." He barked out a laugh. "I didn't kill Tiffany. I loved her!"

Lara sensed Andersen was about to fire. She kicked open the door and startled him enough that he shifted the gun from John to her.

That was all John needed. He leaped over his desk and tackled the assembly member. Andersen kept hold of the gun and hit John upside the head.

Lara grabbed Andersen's wrist and slammed it against the corner of his desk. He dropped the gun and yelped in pain. She kneed him in the groin with her good knee, then retrieved the gun from the floor while John cuffed and Mirandized him.

Two sergeants rushed in and John flashed his badge. "Sac PD."

"My career is over," Anderson sobbed.

"Your freedom is over," Lara said. "And to think that I spent nine years of my life fighting for it."

"You don't understand!"

"Tell me."

"I loved Tiffany. I would never have hurt her. Not on purpose. It was an accident. An awful accident."

Lara leaned forward. John had pushed Andersen into a chair, cuffed, and was calling for a car to transport the prisoner to the city jail.

"Let me tell you what I think happened. Cindy Wyatt was furious with her husband about his affair and wanted to hurt him. The best way to hurt Bruce would be to damage his career. She called you and told you about Bruce and Tiffany. You snapped. You were already in the building. You had to see for yourself." She tapped his sterling-silver pen set, which, not surprisingly, had an empty slot for a matching letter opener. "You grabbed the letter opener on your way out.

"You then caught up with her in the stairwell. Maybe fought with her, maybe confessed your undying love. You got her into the committee room and stabbed her—"

"No." He shook his head back and forth, his hair falling into his eyes. "Bruce has taken everything that was ever important to me. My first election. My girlfriend. And he moved into my congressional district just to run against me! And Tiffany . . . I loved her. I loved her and she slept with *him*! I didn't mean to hurt her." Suddenly he closed his mouth, looked at the sergeants, his eyes wide, then from Lara to John. "I want a lawyer!" he demanded. "And a doctor! I think you broke my wrist, Lara. I'll sue you." He glared at John. "And I'll sue you for false arrest! Bruce Wyatt set me up. I know it!"

Lara glanced at John. He looked weary, but elated. "Thanks," he said.

"Anytime." She winked.

"Think Wyatt's still going to run for Congress?"

Lara nodded. "Yeah. Probably be a bloodbath with the scandal and the affair, but ironically, the more people in the race, the better chance Wyatt has of squeaking out a victory."

"Over my dead body," Andersen spat out.

"Ready to go home after I book him?" John asked her.

"Your house or mine?"

"I'll stencil your name on my mailbox first thing in the morning."

"What more could a girl want?"

CONTEMPORARY INSANITY

Marcia Muller

Five days before I turned nineteen, I ran off with thirty-year-old Jack Whitestone. We drove in his beat-up old Toyota Tercel non-stop from Winnetka, Illinois, to Las Vegas, Nevada, where we were married by a justice of the peace in a tacky little wedding chapel two blocks off the strip. Jack couldn't afford a wedding ring or even a decent motel for that night and he wouldn't touch the money I'd withdrawn from my savings and checking accounts. He was like that: always wanting to be the provider. Always wanting . . .

But at least now I was Julianna Whitestone.

Really, I didn't mind the shabby accommodations by the freeway off-ramp or the sound of the cars and trucks that never stopped, even in the middle of the night. I had Jack, and that was all that mattered.

God, I lusted after the man: his sleek, tall body; his smooth, summer-bronzed skin; his wild black hair that my fingers tangled in; his hazel eyes that seemed to see only me.

I didn't care that I'd aborted my college education, severed my ties to friends and family, been disowned by my wealthy real-estate-developer father. Jack was enough.

The next morning we headed for California and the American dream.

The American dream turned out to be a cramped, furnished apartment in a sixties-style building a few blocks off La Cienega Boulevard in Los Angeles. The boulevard itself was a dreary thoroughfare lined with marginal shops, fast-food restaurants, bars, and porno theaters; on our street similar apartment buildings sat cheek by jowl with old stucco bungalows—all of them in poor repair. I'd waitressed a couple of summers at the country club back home, so I got a job in a coffee shop on the boulevard. The pay was terrible, the hours long, and my feet constantly hurt. But it didn't matter; I had Jack.

Jack had given up a none-too-promising career as a furniture salesman in Evanston (I met him when I went in to buy a computer workstation for my room at Northwestern), and once we reached California, he couldn't find a job for weeks. Finally he got on as an attendant at an all-night convenience store. But things would get better, he promised. He borrowed five hundred dollars of my money and enrolled in acting classes during the day. And he went to them faithfully, in spite of being tired from working the night shift at the store.

On weekends, we'd ride around the beach towns in the old Toyota. "There," Jack would say, pointing out some beautiful oceanfront house, "there's where we'll live someday soon."

He didn't understand that I didn't care where we lived so long as we were together.

He wanted things, Jack did. Houses, electronic equipment, sports cars, swimming pools, the clothing and jewelry that we saw in the windows of the expensive shops along Rodeo Drive. I wished I could give them to him, but my father's lawyer had made it perfectly clear: I was cut off without a penny unless I opted to annul the marriage, return home, and go back to the university. I'd never known Daddy to be so harsh, and it shook my faith in him and in family ties.

At times it was a temptation to obey his dictum, I'll admit, particularly on the days when all we had for dinner were tacos from the fast-food place on La Cienega, where two people had contracted food poisoning the year before. I'd always been Daddy's little girl—pampered and sheltered from the real world. And in that world, people like me didn't waitress in coffee shops and eat tacos that might be poisoned.

But I couldn't leave Jack. No matter how tired I was after a day of waitressing, I wanted . . . no, *had* to have that lean sleek body. His slow smile as he touched me, those soul-searching eyes.

Near Christmas Jack dropped the acting classes and got the remainder of his tuition back. He wanted us to have a nice holiday, he said, but I sensed it was because he was frustrated by his instructors' negative feedback. We did have a good time, however, with a tabletop tree, turkey dinner, and presents. Jack gave me a gold chain, and I gave him a pair of L.L. Bean fleece-lined moccasins. If you're from a place like Illinois, you don't think it gets cold enough for those in California, but, believe me, it does.

And then, in February, our lives changed for the better. Matt Edwards, an old friend of Jack's from the furniture store, called. He now lived in the Bay Area. Come on up north, he said. I've got this investment company—Edwards Concepts—and I need your help.

We packed what we had; it wasn't much. Drove north, Jack's dreams of becoming an actor left behind.

The Toyota died south of the sprawling port city of Stockton, on the Sacramento River. Lights spread out in the distance—so near, yet so far.

We didn't have Triple A. Didn't have enough money for a tow or repairs. Jack checked under the hood, kicked the car's bumper, and called it a "piece of shit." Then we hitched a ride to the nearest freeway exit and found a Denny's. From a booth in the garishly lighted chain restaurant, he called his friend collect.

Nobody home.

We left a message giving our location and the number of the phone booth in the Denny's, then spent the night drinking coffee and eating pie that we couldn't afford. When the light was coming up outside the misted, badly washed windows, a shiny black car pulled into the lot and a man got out.

"Matt!" Jack exclaimed, and ran outside to embrace him.

Matt Edwards had the quick moves and grace of a quarterback—which, I later learned, he had been at Ohio State till a drinking and doping scandal got him tossed out of school. He was tall and lean like Jack, but blond and pale, with a gaze that slipped away from mine so quickly that I couldn't determine his eye color. He bundled us into his Mercedes sedan, said he'd send "his people" for the belongings we'd left in the Toyota, and drove us to our new home in San Carlos, a middle-class bedroom community on the San Francisco peninsula.

The place Matt had waiting for us was in a condominium complex in the hills west of town. Two bedrooms, two baths, a small kitchen, living and dining rooms, and a balcony whose views of gently rolling pine-covered hills misted by morning fog took my breath away. A futon lay on the floor of the master bedroom; we fell onto it as soon as Matt left, saying he and his wife would pick us up for dinner at seven.

We were too tired to make love.

As I drifted off, I thought, Why won't Jack's friend look me in the eyes?

The restaurant was Argentinian—what the foodie magazines called elegant but casual—on a sidestreet in Palo Alto. As we'd driven into town, Matt had pointed out the massive stone pillars and rows of tall palms that flanked the entrance to Stanford University. The main street of the town was composed mainly of older buildings, many of them what Matt's wife, Claire, called Spanish Revival; the shops looked interesting, and the sidewalks teemed with both students and older people.

The restaurant's decor was elegant: walls and ceiling painted in various orange tones, exotic plants separating the inlaid bamboo tables. They knew Matt and Claire there. The maître d' and waiters greeted them warmly and respectfully, calling them Mr. and Mrs. Edwards.

Claire was tall—close to six feet—with shoulder-length blond hair, and so thin in her clinging black dress that I wondered if she was anorexic. Matt looked handsome in a black polo shirt and fashionable trousers. I felt underdressed in my cotton pantsuit, and I knew Jack was ashamed of his cheap outfit from Wal-Mart.

The prices on the menu horrified me, but Matt said it was their treat and we should order what we wanted. And before we did, he asked the waiter to bring champagne, a basket of empanadas, and a basket of lobster corn dogs.

"Lobster corn dogs!" I exclaimed.

"They're wonderful," Claire said, putting a thin, gentle hand on my arm.

Matt still wouldn't meet my eyes, but he smiled at Jack.

Salad. Really good white wine. Steak. Really good red wine. Dessert—something rich and creamy. After-dinner drinks, and dark, rich coffee that was nothing like the instant we were used to.

Matt and Claire drove us back to the condo in San Carlos in her white BMW sedan. Matt told Jack he'd see him at the office the next morning. Jack asked how he was supposed to get there, and with a flourish Matt showed him a brand-new tan Volvo in our carport.

"The GPS'll get you there all right," he said. "I had the address programmed in."

"*I can't believe it. I fucking can't believe it!*"

Jack was pacing around the empty living room of the condo, sipping at a snifter of the brandy he'd found—among other luxury food and drink items—in the kitchen.

I didn't answer. I stood at the glass door to the balcony. The rolling, forested hills were faintly backlit by light from their other side. It was so beautiful . . .

"Julianna?"

"Yes?"

"Can *you* believe what a great situation we've fallen into?"

"It's . . . it's wonderful. I'm overwhelmed, but I'm sure I'm going to love it here. Let's go to bed now, Jack."

We did. And celebrated our good fortune in the appropriate manner.

Claire and our new furniture arrived simultaneously at two the next afternoon.

By daylight, Claire looked older, with fine lines around her eyes and mouth.

Her collarbones showed sharply through the nearly translucent skin above her scoop-necked T-shirt. She hugged me, her pungent perfume clogging my nostrils, and said, "Let's see what Matt has chosen for you."

The furnishings were beautiful: buttery leather chairs and sofas, intricately designed wooden tables and cabinets; a big-screen TV; a huge sleigh bed and armoire; thick, soft area rugs.

I wandered around in a near daze, touching our new possessions. Everything was exquisite, expensive. I should have been thrilled, and I *was* appreciative, but somehow it would have been nice if Jack and I had chosen our own furniture together.

As if she sensed my misgivings, Claire said, "Matt knew you'd want to be settled quickly, and since Jack's going to be working long hours and you don't know the area, he took the liberty of shopping for you. If there's anything you don't like, feel free to send it back. And of course you'll want to pick out the wall hangings and other accentuating touches."

"Everything's perfect. I wouldn't dream of sending it back."

She smiled, pleased. "Well, Matt knew your basic taste from his time with Jack at the furniture store."

Jack's basic taste. And only coincidentally mine.

To cover my surprise, I asked, "Were the two of you married back then?"

"Yes. We moved to California a year ago."

"Do you work?"

"Not really, although occasionally I help Matt with the business. You?"

"I've never done anything except waitressing. I hated it."

She patted my shoulder. "Well, you won't have to worry about waitressing anymore."

"Doesn't it seem sort of . . . weird to you?" I asked.

Jack was lounging in a recliner in front of the big-screen TV, sipping a glass of chardonnay that was a far cry from the Two Buck Chuck we'd usually had in L.A. "Weird, yes. Like going to heaven."

I sat in the matching chair beside his, set my wineglass on the table between them. "No, I mean . . . I don't know. It reminds me of that movie where the guy gets this great offer after he finishes law school and the company pays for everything but it turns out they're Mafia lawyers—"

"The Firm."

"Right."

"Well, for one thing, Matt's investment company doesn't have Mafia clients. And for another, he and I go back a long way; we were best friends as kids. He wants me to be happy now that I've given up my dream of being an actor."

"Best friends?" Why hadn't I heard of Matt before his phone call to Jack in L.A.?

"Oh, yeah." Jack began to reminisce. "We grew up in Gary, Indiana. Shabby neighborhood, working class, both of our fathers were employed at the mills. My dad drank, smacked the family around. Matt's did too. We just sort of figured it was the way families were. Still, we enjoyed ourselves. Pickup basketball and baseball games. Stealing beer from the 7-Eleven. Cutting classes and hanging out. Neither of us was much for school."

Things had gotten bad when Jack and Matt were seniors in high school, he said. Jack's father lost his job at the mill, emptied the family's small savings account, and left town. Matt's father also lost his job, but his solution to the problem was more extreme: He turned his hunting rifle on his wife and two daughters, then himself. Matt was working his Burger King shift at the time.

"A crappy job—only thing that saved him," Jack said. "He had an athletic scholarship to Ohio State. I moved to Chicago. Nothing was better for me there. I was a dumb kid with no experience except as counter help in fast-food joints. One day Matt showed up on my doorstep. Some guy he knew from school recommended him to his father, who owned a chain of furniture stores, and Matt got on at their Evanston branch. A few weeks later, an opening came up and he recommended me."

"But Matt wasn't working there when I met you," I said.

"No. He and Claire—she was the bookkeeper—split about a year ago. I didn't hear from him again till he called me in L.A."

"How'd he know you were there?"

"Said my mother told him."

Yet Jack's mother was a hopeless drunk; he'd written her after we got married, but we'd never heard from her. Would she even have saved our address or phone number?

Shortly after this, Jack began to bring things home. A bigger plasma TV. A better computer. A small speedboat for which he had to rent an extra parking space. Clothes that were more like Matt's. A one-carat diamond ring for me.

Knowing what he'd told me about his past in working-class Gary, Indiana, and his abusive father, I could understand why he needed such luxuries.

After our furniture was delivered, I hardly ever saw Claire. Just a few lunches at expensive restaurants in Palo Alto—which she paid for—and a trip to a personal shopper at Nordstrom so I could outfit myself properly. Most of the time, Claire said she was helping out in the business. I didn't see Matt at all, but he and Jack spent time together. Matt had interested Jack in golf and sponsored him for his country club. The one time Jack took me there for dinner, I was uncomfortable in spite of my designer dress and expensive jewelry. People weren't very friendly.

Still, I was enjoying our newfound good fortune. Jack had bought me a little red BMW convertible, and soon I knew my way around the peninsula. I shopped madly, even drove across the wooded hills to the coastal town of Half Moon Bay and hunted through its chic boutiques. I considered sending a postcard home extolling Jack's success, but decided against it. Let my father wonder what had happened to me; maybe he'd even worry. And while he did, I'd be happy.

Within two months I was bored, so I asked Jack if I could visit the offices of Edwards Concepts. Maybe I could help out like Claire did.

He laughed at the suggestion. "Honey, all you'd see is a bunch of desks and file cabinets. We keep operating expenses to a minimum."

"But what about helping out?"

"There's nothing for you to do. We're fully staffed." He ruffled my hair, kissed my forehead, told me to enjoy our new life.

Jack worked long hours, studying for state certifications in this and that, and our sex life had dwindled. I still wanted him, but more often than not when I made overtures he'd rebuff me. He kept bringing luxury items home, though: a sound system; artworks; a custom-made mattress; gold-plated showerheads and faucets for the bathrooms. Then he started talking about taking flying lessons and buying a plane.

"But don't flying lessons take up a lot of time?" I asked. "You're gone so much as it is."

"You need some new interests, Julianna. Why don't you take a couple of classes at the JC?"

In November, less than a year after we'd arrived in the Bay Area, we moved to the same posh suburb where Claire and Matt lived—Los Altos Hills, some fifteen miles south of San Carlos. The sprawling ranch houses in our neighborhood were set apart, on big lots. From our deck we could see the bay and the planes landing at the distant airport. I wondered how we could afford such a place, but Jack said Matt had cosigned the loan. I thought Jack had bought the house in an attempt to curb my dissatisfaction with our marriage, and I hated that he'd just gone out by himself, found it, and made a deal.

On the other hand, the house *was* beautiful: multileveled, with a series of tiered decks and a waterfall cascading into a custom-designed pool. The backyard was lushly landscaped. There were fireplaces in the living room, bedroom, and kitchen. Our possessions, which had overwhelmed the condo in San Carlos, didn't even come close to filling it.

So there were more opportunities for Jack to buy and buy and buy.

The night we moved in, we didn't make love. And, worse, I

didn't care. Somehow, in a house like this, it didn't seem so important. As I fell asleep I found myself imagining all the things I could buy too.

At the Christmas season I'd expected an office party, dinners with Jack's clients, maybe a reception at Matt and Claire's, but none of those happened. Instead Jack brought home extravagantly wrapped presents and a tree that had to be topped in order to fit under the high ceiling of our living room. When I asked what he wanted me to fix for our holiday dinner, he said he'd arranged to have it catered— hors d'oeuvres, standing-rib roast, horseradish sauce, Yorkshire pudding, assorted vegetables, everything down to the plum pudding. And champagne and expensive wines, of course. He'd invited Matt and Claire, and selected appropriate presents for them.

A design firm was coming to trim the tree. As they did, I found myself mourning the loss of our previous simple Christmas in Los Angeles. I'd felt so close to Jack then. . . .

On Christmas morning Jack and I had an orgy of gift opening. I'd bought him a few things I thought he'd like, but he'd bought dozens for both of us. For me: a mink coat (where would I ever wear *that*?); another diamond ring, bigger than the first; perfumes and silk garments and a gift certificate to a famous spa (did that mean he thought I was getting fat?); a new iPhone. For him—on our joint credit card—I'd bought a 1930s vintage silk robe and a smoking jacket; an old-fashioned fountain pen and assorted inks; a gold-link bracelet; a leather-bound set of his favorite author, Charles Dickens. Jack gave himself a set of professional-level golf clubs, all sorts of fashionable clothing, and an airplane.

"You can't fly it!" I exclaimed when he showed me a photo of it.

"Yes I can. I've been taking lessons."

I was dumbstruck. In the hours Jack had supposedly been studying for various state-investment certifications, he'd been soaring through the skies. Without me.

I thought about the money. Where was it coming from? My father was wealthy, and we'd always lived well, but this . . .

I had an overwhelming desire to call home, but the the flinty voice of my father's attorney intruded: "Cut off without a penny unless you annul the marriage, return home, and go back to the university."

No, Daddy can't control me anymore. From now on I'll take responsibility for my own actions.

Matt and Claire arrived for dinner prompty at eight. He looked trim and as handsome as ever in a dinner jacket; he enveloped Jack in a bear hug, took both my hands in his and said I looked lovely. This time he met my eyes. I guessed he'd had his doubts when he first met me, but now he seemed to have accepted me. Claire looked even thinner, clad in a tube of red velvet; when she hugged me her bones felt brittle. They'd brought a couple of packages, which they placed under the tree next to the ones Jack had gotten for them, and the waiter from the caterer's brought little mushroom tartlets, shrimp, caviar, and champagne. At first the conversation lagged; then we all began speaking at once.

"Claire," I said, "I love your dress."

"Julianna," she said, "the house looks wonderful."

"Great tree, Jack."

"Like that jacket, Matt."

Then we all laughed, toasted, and unwrapped presents.

Silver candlesticks and a trivet from them.

Silver cocktail tray and napkin rings from us.

We joked about our common tastes, and toasted some more.

During the dinner, I noticed that Claire's eyes were anxious— straying from Matt to Jack to me. The conversation was superficial: the San Francisco Forty-niners' so-so season; the best place in town to find good pâté; a new wine merchant who had opened nearby; the new house that Matt and Claire had made an offer on a few days ago; the changes in the restaurant scene; a play they'd recently gone to in the city that hadn't been very good. You'd have thought we were nervous and trying desperately to fill up dead air. And all the while Claire's glance skipped restlessly, questioningly, among us.

The waiter announced that coffee and after-dinner drinks would be served in the living room. Claire and I went ahead, but Matt and Jack held back. I excused myself and ducked into the powder room while Claire continued on. The door was thin, and I could hear what the men were saying.

Jack: "I don't think accepting ads from Google or Yahoo is a good idea. Their detection software is too good."

"But think of the revenues."

"We don't want to attract attention. It could affect the other side of the business."

"Maybe we should move headquarters overseas."

"Do *you* want to live in Turkey or Poland?"

"Christ, no!"

"Then let's keep things the way they are."

A silence while Matt considered. "Okay. For now."

They drifted on, past the powder room door and into the living room where Claire waited. I ran water in the sink for a few seconds, then followed.

For a while after Christmas, I let my questions about Edwards Concepts lie. I knew why: I was afraid of what I'd find out. Our luxurious life still pleased me, and I didn't want to disturb it. But then a distressing incident in late February brought the problem to the forefront.

A woman called the house. She had a pronounced southern accent. "Is this where Jack Whitestone lives?"

"Who's calling please?"

Silence.

Click.

I put it down to a crank caller; our phone number was unlisted, but that didn't stop everyone. Or maybe she was a client whose investments had gone bad.

Three hours later she called again. "I want to talk to Jack Whitestone."

"May I tell him who's calling?"

"Are you his wife?"

"Who's calling, please?"

"'*Who's calling, please?*'" She mimicked my voice.

Click.

My first impulse was to leave the phone off the hook or let the answering machine pick up in case she called again. But then I went to the family room—what family? Jack's never here—and got a glass of wine from the wet bar. I sat down to wait.

The phone rang, and I picked up. "Whoever you are, either stop calling here or tell me what you want."

"You're Mrs. Whitestone." Same voice, and it was angry.

"And who're you?"

"You'd like to know, wouldn't you?"

I wanted to scream at her, or hang up as she'd previously done. But I was curious about what could provoke such anger with me, a stranger, so I said, "Yes. Tell me what you want."

"What's due me."

"And what is that?"

"My wages. They're long overdue. Nobody at that office'll take my calls, and long distance is expensive. I've about wiped out my monthly budget."

"Give me your number and I'll call you back."

She told me her name was Bebe Kirby, in Anniston, Alabama. I called her back immediately. As things turned out, we had a lot to discuss, and afterward I had even more to think about.

Edwards Concepts was not an investment company. Matt, and later with Jack's help, had established dozens of Web sites that accepted ads, for which the advertisers paid so much every time someone clicked on them. They had employees in out-of-the-way places—such as Anniston, Alabama—or foreign countries who clicked on the ads repeatedly.

"They call it 'click fraud,'" Bebe Kirby told me. "It's not legal here in the U.S., but in some places in Europe it is."

I recalled Matt suggesting they move operations to Europe and Jack asking if he wanted to live in Turkey or Poland.

"They pay less than a cent a click, nothing compared with what they get from the advertisers. But people like me will settle for any kind of work. I'm disabled and I need something I can do at home to make ends meet. So that's why I'm calling your husband. I haven't been paid in two months."

"Click fraud," I said numbly. "Is that like spamming?"

"No, but that's the other side of their business. They also pay people to send out thousands of spam messages every day. They offered me that job, but it pays even less than clicking. I tell you, they're getting rich off powerless people, and now they won't even pay us."

"How'd you get this number, Ms. Kirby?"

Her voice turned sly. "When you're on the computer as much as I am, there're ways."

I felt sick to my stomach, my hands clammy. Jack and Matt were criminals, and Claire and I had been living lavishly off the proceeds.

Bebe Kirby said, "You really didn't know about this?"

I shook my head, realized she couldn't see me, and said, "I thought Jack was working for an investment company."

"Well, you poor thing. Men'll lie most any way they can, it seems."

"Ms. Kirby, I'll see that you get your money. How much are you owed?"

She named a surprisingly low figure. "But I don't want to start any trouble between you and your husband."

"It's already started."

I tried to call Claire. She and I had become more friendly since Christmas, talking on the phone a few times a week, and having lunch frequently; today she was supposed to be at the new house, consulting with a decorator. But I got no answer there or on her cell phone. I called Edwards Concepts and got the answering machine. I didn't try Jack's cellular: Our eventual confrontation would have to be face-to-face.

And what was I going to say?

You hid the truth from me, now get a legitimate job or I'm leaving you?

No.

Abandon all the possessions you've bought with your illicit money and we'll start over somewhere else?

He'd just laugh at me.

How had he been able to hide the truth from me? Because—in spite of all the signs—I'd wanted to believe him. And I had to face the fact that I'd become addicted to money and possessions myself. I hadn't wanted to give up our lifestyle, so I'd turned my back on my doubts and suspicions. Well, now I'd have to confront them.

That could mean the end of our marriage. Jack would never give up the money and possessions. They were his reason for existing, the loves of his life, not me. Never me.

I supposed I could go home. Buy a plane ticket, fly back to Illinois, and beg Daddy's forgiveness. But he'd insist I go to the authorities and expose Jack and Matt, and I wasn't sure I could do that. Besides, when I left I'd resolved to handle my own problems.

I'd just never imagined their magnitude. . . .

Six o'clock and still no Claire and no answer at the office. Outside the windows of the house that had never felt like a home, it had turned dark and rain began falling. I moved restlessly from room to room, and at seven tried Claire again. This time she answered, sounding out of breath.

"The decorator didn't bring the right samples," she said, "so I had to go to his shop in the city. Then I got caught in traffic. I had to stop to pick up a burger. I'm exhausted."

"You're not expecting Matt for dinner?"

"He and Jack are working on a project at the office tonight."

"There's been no answer there all afternoon."

"They're probably letting messages go to voice mail. They often do that."

"Claire, I need to talk with you in person. I'm coming over there."

"Julianna, please don't. As I said, I'm exhausted. The house is a mess. I've been packing breakables, and there're boxes all over the place—"

"Sorry. This can't wait."

Claire had apparently reconciled herself to my coming over, because the outside lights were on in the large white-shingled house a few blocks from ours. I went up the walk, tapped on the door, and Claire appeared almost immediately. She was beautifully dressed, as always, in gabardine pants and a silk blouse; she didn't look the slightest bit exhausted. I followed her to the nearly stripped family room, turned down the offer of a drink, and got straight to the point.

"I know about Edwards Concepts. I know what their business really is." I told her about Bebe Kirby's call.

To my surprise, Claire laughed. "Those people who work for us are such idiots. I'll see that she gets her little check."

"So you're aware of what's going on?"

"For God's sake, Julianna, I'm the company *accountant*. How could I not know? Besides, Matt and I thought up the business together."

"You thought up an illegal scam . . . !"

"Oh, stop being so naïve. You must've suspected."

"Well, I suspected something wasn't right, but—"

"Look, it's nothing unusual. I know at least half a dozen firms in the Bay Area alone that're pulling variations on the same scam."

I didn't know what to say to that.

Claire went to the wet bar, took down one of the remaining glasses from the shelf behind it, and poured herself some wine. "Sure you won't join me?"

I shook my head.

"Julianna, you're very young, but if you've been with Jack, you can't *possibly* be such an innocent. He's been scamming his whole life."

"He's never . . . What are you talking about?"

"That furniture store in Evanston? I was bookkeeper there, and we were embezzling like crazy. The three of us. When it looked like management might catch on, Matt and I split to establish something here in the Bay Area. Jack stayed on for a while, met you, and thought he'd gotten his hands on some real money." Claire smiled maliciously; she was enjoying this. "But your precious daddy derailed his plans by disinheriting you. Then Jack got it into his head that he might become an actor—after all, he'd been scamming for years—but his acting coaches told him he wasn't even third rate. Seems Jack can't act if the deal's legitimate. So he called Matt, and here we are now."

Jack, a scam artist who only wanted my money? I was so stunned I could barely speak.

All I could say was, "What you're telling me is that Jack never loved me at all."

"Oh, I think he loves you as much as Jack can love any woman. He's into material things, and women who can get them for him."

I thought back to Christmas dinner, Claire's anxious eyes roving around the table. I thought of the long hours Jack spent away from home and his slackening sexual interest in me when he returned. Suddenly I felt sick to my stomach.

I said, "A woman like you, Claire?"

"Well, why not?"

"Have you been having an affair with my husband?"

"Ah, the penny drops." She didn't look a bit ashamed.

"Oh God. Does Matt know?"

"I doubt it, but I can handle him if he figures things out. He doesn't want to rock the boat; we've got a lucrative deal going for us, and when that's pointed out to him, he'll look the other way. Frankly, you should do the same thing."

I'd been standing behind the massive leather couch. Now my knees threatened to buckle, and I had to grasp it for support.

I said, "I want you to break it off with Jack. Tonight."

Claire laughed as if I'd said something funny. "I'll break it off when I'm tired of him, Julianna. Till then, you'll have to cope."

I drove numbly toward Edwards Concepts. Out of curiosity I'd gone by there shortly before Christmas and had been surprised to find a nondescript stucco house in a shabby San Carlos neighborhood near the Southern Pacific tracks. Only a small sign identified the building as the Edwards Concepts headquarters.

Tonight when I parked at the curb, I saw lights on behind the covered windows of a front room. I hurried up the walk, my coat collar turned up against the rain. The front door was open. I pushed through, and turned left toward an archway.

Three metal desks topped by elaborate computer systems; bookcases stuffed with phone books and technical manuals; battered file cabinets; an old-fashioned fireplace, long unused.

And on the floor beside the fireplace, a man's body. His arms were outflung, and blood pooled under the right side of his head, which rested at an odd angle on the hearthstone.

Jack? No, he was heavier, taller.

I rushed forward, dropped to one knee beside him.

Matt.

"Don't touch him."

The words came from behind me. I stood up, saw Jack coming through the archway. He must have been in the bathroom; he was wiping his hands with a paper towel.

"My God, Jack. What happened?"

"He . . . he fell." Jack's face was ashen and drawn, his shirttail pulled out of his dress slacks. One shoulder seam was ripped, and there were flecks of blood on his sleeves.

Matt . . . *fell?*

"How did he fall?"

"He tripped over something."

"Did you call an ambulance?"

"No reason to. He's dead." Jack's voice sounded like one of those computer-generated ones that you get when you try to call the phone company and can't reach a real person.

"What about the police?"

He just stared at me.

He's in shock, I thought. Like I'd been at Claire's. Like I still was, standing there beside Matt. Shock after shock after shock.

"Jack? The police have to be notified. Claire—you and she . . ."

He moved toward a desk chair, sat down. "Look, Julianna, we have to decide what to do."

"What do you mean, decide what to do?"

"To get ourselves out of this."

"No."

He gave me a sharp, surprised look. "No? Are you insane?"

"Jack," I said, "I know what kind of business this is. I know about you and Claire."

"Oh Christ." He leaned forward with his elbows on his knees and cradled his face in his hands. "You didn't figure out about the business by yourself. How did you find out?"

"Claire told me," I said, omitting my conversation with the woman in Alabama. "She also told me why you married me."

"Claire. Yeah, she never could keep her mouth shut."

"She was right, wasn't she?"

He didn't say anything. He looked pale, sick. It was as if he was somebody I didn't know, had never even seen before.

I said, "Matt didn't fall by accident, did he?"

Jack's head snapped up. "What?"

"He found out about your affair with Claire and confronted you. There was a fight and you . . . you killed him. That's what really happened, isn't it?"

Jack's face contorted dramatically. "It was an accident! It was self-defense. It was Matt's fault, not mine. Claire spreads her legs for half the guys on the peninsula, he *knew* that, so why the hell did he have to make such a big deal out of finding out about her and me? Sure, we were friends, but so what? There he was, accusing me of crossing some damn line, then attacking me. I had to defend myself, didn't I? I didn't mean to kill him." He made a sound in his throat, motioned at Matt's body. "We have to cover this up, Julianna."

"Cover it up? *We?*"

"You and me. We've got a great thing going here. Why should Matt's crazy jealousy spoil it for us?"

He was on his feet now, looking into my eyes. His were pleading and about to spill over with tears. Fake tears, I thought. As Claire had said, Jack had been scamming people his whole life.

A man was dead. Not a moral or an honest man, but nonetheless a human being. And Jack wanted to cover up the way he'd died and go on as before, acquiring more possessions and probably more women who could provide him with the means to do so.

As for me, I was no longer in the grip of the contemporary insanity that was gripping him, gripping our culture.

Jack said, "We could claim you were here when it happened. We could say you saw Matt fall, that it was an accident. Or we could pin it on Claire, say she wanted Matt out of the way so she and I could be together. No, the accident idea is better. It would work, Julianna."

"Shut up!"

He stared at me with his mouth open. I'd never spoken to him like that before. Now I was as much a stranger to him as he was to me.

"I'm going to call the police," I said. "Right now, and tell them what happened to Matt. Don't try to stop me."

He didn't. I'd have scratched his eyes out if he'd tried, and he knew it. Jack was a coward as well as a liar, a cheat, and a scam artist.

When I put the phone down and looked at him again, he was pacing the floor, his stranger's face a match for the soulless voices on the automated telephone services. He was muttering to himself and seemed to have forgotten I was there.

He's planning what he'll say to the police, I thought. He's thinking of ways to save himself and put the blame on Matt or Claire or me. Scamming to the end, he was.

I was sick of him and I was through with him. Through with my earlier life too. I would never go back to Illinois. As soon as I could, I would leave northern California and find a new place to start a new life, one that would be all my own.

THE VIOLINIST

Wendy Hornsby

From the journal bequeathed to me by my aunt, Mary Carlisle, entry dated July 2, 1961:

My acquaintance Ernest Hemingway died today, by his own hand. There is suddenly such a public stir and notoriety about not only the fact of his untimely passing but also that he was a suicide that some of the old crowd are comparing his loss to the loss of our beloved Jack London so many years before. Of course Ernest never met Jack, a generation separates them, but Jack's influence over the younger writer cannot be disputed; many comparisons of their work and their exploits are still made by the public and the critics. Thus, though the instruments of their deaths were certainly dissimilar, one by shotgun, the other by morphine, the essential intentions of both were the same. Or so people assume.

Secrets, like promises, can be terrible responsibilities for the entrusted keeper. I have borne my secret about Jack London's passing for a very long time out of respect for the wishes of my very dear friend, now so long gone. Indeed, perhaps enough years have passed that there is no one left for the truth to haunt, except for myself. I believe that a correction in the record needs to be made, so I pass the obligation to you, my dear niece, along with other substantial considerations, as my legacy to you.

The particular event that occurred during the long night of November 21, 1916, only exists at the dark and distant end of a long passage of time. Nevertheless, there doubtless will be some fuss when the facts are revealed. I do grant you full permission to publish the facts as I know them, and I trust your judgment about how and when that should best be done.

Chapters in books will need to be rewritten, footnotes altered, certainties rearranged. Myths rethought. But after so many years, the little ripple this truth will stir will be nothing like the tsunami it would have caused had I come forward when the people involved were still alive and the public still worshipped my dear friend Jack London.

Jack was a bright star in his time, his fame unrivaled, surely unprecedented for a writer, greater in its way than Hemingway's. He was beloved or reviled in equal measure depending upon one's notion of the social proprieties; he was a radical and a rake. Early in the last century, millions read Jack's work. Millions more followed coverage of his personal exploits as if his life itself were a grand novel unfolding in the daily press expressly for their entertainment. He drank, he scrapped, he womanized, he proselytized. He escaped from South Seas cannibals and the jaws of a wolf. He was beautiful and young.

Jack aspired to literary greatness, but driven by the necessity to produce income at the rate of nine cents per word to support his many dependents, for the most part he churned out adventure stories to thrill the masses, and not great literature. The reality is, Jack was a hack.

An ephemeral phenomenon, Jack's renown was soon eclipsed by the rakes and radicals of the next generation, writers like Hemingway. Maybe it was a blessing that he did not live long enough to see his name pass into obscurity, even against the best of efforts.

I loved Jack, as did many. How shocked, how grieved we were when he left us so soon, dead in his fortieth year. There were many theories and rumors about what happened during that particular night in 1916. Was he a suicide? An accidental overdose? Natural causes? Murder? Which? There lies the crux of my secret.

For me, the story begins during the summer of 1903, at the Wake Robin lodge, a bucolic resort set in a lovely, grassy valley near the small town of Glen Ellen, a short train ride north from San Francisco. The lodge belonged to Netta and Roscoe Eames, who were the publishers of the literary magazine where my very first story appeared, and Jack's. Netta had invited me to come up from San Francisco so that I could meet some of her other authors. She generously gave me the use of a small cabin, which I shared with her niece Charmian Kittredge, whenever she came up from Berkeley.

Charmian was a decade older than I, a little bundle of anxious energy. Unusual for the time, she was self-supporting even though she had family who could provide for her needs. Charmian was a skilled typist and bookkeeper, and she worked for a shipping company in Berkeley, where she also owned several small houses that she rented out. She was skilled in business and enjoyed her financial success, flaunted it a bit with rather flamboyant dress. I had known her previously: Netta had asked Charmian to write a review of my first story, and I reciprocated by taking Charmian to dinner with Jack's mob of friends.

Charmian and I were correct with each other. But Charmian saw every woman as her competitor, so true friendship with her was not easy. To be honest, I did not admire her particularly. It seemed to me that Charmian always had to be at the front of every photograph, had to have the last word in any discussion. Overbright always in her manner, she wanted to be the center of all attention. I am reminded of the words of the first President Roosevelt's daughter, Alice, whose description of her father would be apt for Charmian when she said, "Teddy wanted to be the bride at every wedding."

Though never married and approaching her midthirties, Charmian Kittredge could never be described as an old maid. She was what was then called, with disdain in conventional circles, a New

Woman: sexually receptive, educated, outspoken, independent. She was far from pretty, too many teeth and a long, prominent jaw, but she had a trim, athletic body. Overall, I found her to be vain and materialistic, too proud of her slender figure and the clothes that covered it, and of her love affairs, several with married men who in the end failed to leave their wives for her.

That summer of 1903, Jack planned a long sailing trip up the American River, preferably with a female companion, as yet not selected. To tidy the edges around that tryst, he removed his wife, Bess, and their two pretty little daughters from their home in Oakland to a tent cabin at the same Wake Robin lodge in Glen Ellen. It was only after they were settled that he announced he wasn't staying with them. I loved Jack, but he generally gave in to base urges instead of following the more prudent course.

I liked Bess. Jack was a great entertainer and kept their home in Oakland full of guests, for whom Bess more or less cheerfully provided great pots of spaghetti and jugs of red wine. As those gatherings always became raucous, drunken brawls by the time they were over, I generally escaped early to help Bess with the washing up before alcohol overwhelmed the better instincts of the crowd.

At Wake Robin we two, Bess and I, could engage in quiet conversation uninterrupted, though many of the crowd were there. I found her to be intelligent, well read, and modest, and I sought out her company, especially when Charmian was in residence and I wanted to absent myself from our shared quarters.

When finally Jack arrived late in the summer, a frisson of excitement passed through the camp. The first alarum was raised by his girls.

"Daddy's here. Daddy's here." Little Joan led the greeting party to meet Jack's carriage, dragging her baby sister, Becky, by the hand. Before Jack had two feet on the ground she threw herself at him, still singing her refrain, "Daddy's here. Daddy's here."

Bess seemed truly happy to see Jack, relieved that he had come at all, I believe. She knew he regularly had other women, but so far, none of them had been more than an intellectual flirtation or passing sexual fling. Yet I know that summer had seemed different to Bess. Jack had never before sent his family away while he stayed behind.

The only person in camp who did not come out to greet Jack was Charmian.

Several days passed happily, with Jack leading the pranks, boxing matches and fencing bouts as usual. He taught his girls how to bait a hook and wait for a fish to bite, he took them riding through the hills. In the evenings, he gave his arm to Bess and escorted her to the dining room. I had never seen her happier, or him more contented.

Then, one afternoon, toward the end of that week, Bess came to my cabin. I was editing a manuscript that was due at my publisher and did not immediately answer her knock, hoping whoever it was would go away. But when I heard Bess's voice call my name, I rose and opened the door. I was shocked to see her face, the normally high color drained, her cheeks bloodless. Her dark eyes were bright, like a panicky colt's.

"Bess," I asked, "what's happened? The girls?"

She shook her head; they were fine. With some effort, she asked me to come out for a walk, to give her some counsel.

I took her arm and we walked, slowly, through the camp, past the lodge, the London cabin, the stables, crossed the creek, and, on the far side, walked along the back side of Wake Robin. Bess sighed as she raised her hand to direct my eye toward a rustic little loggia erected next to a swimming hole created by a dam across the stream. There were lounge chairs under a canopy and hammocks strung between trees. In one of the hammocks, with their backs to us, sat Jack and Charmian, deep in conversation.

"What do you make of that?" she asked.

"Charmian was asked by her aunt Netta to write a review of one of Jack's stories for their literary magazine," I said. "They are probably discussing it."

"They have been sitting there since breakfast," she said. Her chin began to quiver. "I can see them from my cabin."

It was almost supper time. I had not seen them at lunch.

I almost said that Charmian wasn't Jack's sort, not to mention that she was years older than Jack, but I stopped myself in time. One doesn't reveal to the wife one's knowledge of the husband's paramours, especially when one has been among the chosen, even if only briefly and long ago.

Instead, I said, "Shall we join them? He is your husband, she is your friend, there is no reason for you not to speak with them."

Bess shook her head. "I feel something dire is happening."

I could not refrain. I said, "Not Charmian, of all people. Surely Jack sees through her. We all do."

She looked at me, eyes narrow. "Men don't see women as other women do."

"Jack is devoted to you and the girls."

"I disappoint him in bed."

I took her arm again and we turned to retrace our steps. We lost sight of the loggia and the pair in the hammock before we reached the bridge over the stream. When it was back in view, we could see that the hammock was now empty.

Jack, alone, waited for Bess at their cabin door, pacing nervously. When he glanced up and saw us, he froze. I saw some wave of great emotion come over him.

"Shall I go with you?" I asked Bess.

At first she nodded, then she changed her mind. "As you said, he is my husband. And I believe he has something he wants to tell me."

I kissed her cheek and patted her hand. With a deep breath she squared her shoulders and walked straight to Jack. She was frightened, I knew, but also resolute; she had two young daughters to protect. Immediately I turned to remove an extra set of eyes from their private scene.

I found Charmian inside our shared cabin, packing her belongings into her valise, preparing to leave. I have read the phrase, "a look of triumph," enough times to reject it from my work as a cliché. But that afternoon I saw it: the look of triumph on Charmian's face. The victor, winner of another's husband. How damnably proud she was.

I said, "Charmian, what have you done? Have you thought about the children?"

"Jack and I have accepted the inevitable, embraced the path that fate intended for us," she said. "We are mates."

"You decided that today while sitting in a hammock in full view of everyone?"

"No." She had the grace to blush and lower her face, but her smile of triumph only widened. "We have been in love all summer. No one knows, and I trust you, out of loyalty to Jack, not to tell anyone until the appropriate time."

"When, exactly, would the announcement of a love affair become appropriate?" I asked.

"When the divorce is final," she responded.

I repeated, "Divorce," remembering all the men in her past who had not left their wives for her as promised.

"We have a plan," she said, as if what she and Jack wanted was sufficient justification for destroying the happiness of so many, two of whom were still young and tender.

She began, enthusiastically, to reveal the plan. To me it sounded like a business partnership with rights to the bed included, but Charmian believed with all her heart that she was talking about a love the likes of which the modern world had never seen.

Charmian would free Jack from all cares so that he could write uninterrupted. She would keep his house and oversee business matters, type and edit his manuscripts, divert distractions, and love him passionately, carnally, whenever he desired. She would be tolerant of his flirtations.

"And what do you get in return?" I asked.

"A magnificent life."

She went on to tell me that she had given him an analysis of earnings from his stories and books. Clearly, he gained more attention for, and therefore earned more, from tales based on his own adventures, in the Klondike, tramping across the country, tossed into jail as a vagrant, as an oyster pirate. Essentially, stories in which he faced down his own imminent death and won.

"We will sail the world, together," she said. "And tell the world of our adventures." She grew more excited as she related this plan: Her color rose and a fine bright sheen dampened her broad brow. Through all of this adventuring, Jack would write, she said, producing one thousand new words a day for the rest of his life. They would be famous. They would be rich.

I was shocked by that last. Her paramour, like her, was a Socialist. "Jack has no interest in acquiring wealth."

She looked at me through a vixen's eyes and challenged my understanding of Jack's heart. "*You* know what Jack wants?"

"He's a writer," I said. "He wants immortality."

"Mired in domesticity with Bess, how will he achieve that?"

"Mired in controversy and public shame, how will he?"

"Fame may take many forms." Better to be talked about than ignored, I learned, was Charmian's clarion.

And so it was that Jack London left a fine wife and his daughters, and eventually joined Charmian. It wasn't a smooth transition.

The divorce took two years, Bess fighting it with every resource she could muster. Charmian hid herself away with her aunt Netta at Wake Robin for most of that period, spending her days working hard for Jack, typing, editing, and sending off in polished form the manuscripts that Jack regularly sent her as bundles of crude, hand-written pages. They wrote many letters, but she and Jack were rarely together.

Jack moved in with friends and resumed carousing with his old crowd. In the company of his friend George Sterling, he was a regular visitor at the bars and brothels of San Francisco's Tenderloin. George, in common with most of Jack's crowd, had no affection for Charmian and could not understand what Jack's attraction to her had been. Delighted that the two were, apparently, parted, he encouraged Jack in a new affair with the lovely drama critic Blanche Partington.

While Charmian waited and toiled on his behalf at Wake Robin in Glen Ellen, Jack's affair with Blanche grew quite serious. I saw the two of them together on many occasions, particularly on a sail on the Sacramento delta that we all took on Jack's boat, the *Roamer*. Jack and Blanche seemed well matched. Clearly, with Blanche on his arm, and probably elsewhere as well, Charmian and her plan had faded from Jack's mind.

Charmian was as great a spinner of tales as was Jack, or maybe she was a great seller of fantasy. She seemed to have some power to hook into Jack's brain and make it turn toward her interests. On the day Jack traveled to Glen Ellen to inform her that their affair was finished, Jack told me of his surprise when Charmian, instead of creating a scene as the scorned lover, had offered companionably to ride along with him all the way to Sonoma to catch his train home.

When I saw him on the evening of his return to Oakland, he seemed dazzled as he recounted the day. A long journey on horseback through gently rolling foothills covered with grass burned to shiny gold by the long, dry summer. Above, the sky was a brilliant Botticelli blue. By the time he met his train, he was persuaded again to be her mate. Forever.

Yes, the two of them would sail the world together, Jack informed the crowd gathered for dinner in Oakland. But they would also invest in terra firma. They would buy land right there in Glen Ellen, on the beautiful slopes of the Valley of the Moon where they had ridden that very day. There they would create a new Eden as a model for the world, an agricultural utopia, the Beauty Ranch. They would build a mansion, to be called Wolf House after his most famous story. They would use timeless, immutable local material, native stone and whole redwoods, and it would last a millennium. Truly they would achieve immortality. Together.

He married her in a quick ceremony before strangers the very day his divorce from Bess was final.

Compared to his bride, Jack was an innocent, an ill-educated, quite gullible, idealistic tramp with a gift for storytelling whom she'd plucked up out of relative obscurity because she believed in his potential. Jack was no match for the wily Charmian: He was the violin, she the violinist who gave him voice. She molded him into his own image of the worldly wise adventurer, writer, rancher. Lover.

They sailed around the world. That they nearly died of sun poisoning and bad food and a variety of exotic parasites, not to mention an encounter with naked, spear-laden cannibals, helped to sell ever more copies of their books, articles, and stories about the journey. They built their model ranch on acreage in Glen Ellen, and Jack pioneered agricultural techniques based on theories he found in books. And he wrote one thousand words every day.

Charmian saw the crowd as a distraction from their work. Too much drink, too many temptations. On their sailing trips she could, of course, avoid the others and take full possession of Jack. But at home, on the ranch, Jack issued a blanket invitation: Come one, come all. Stay long.

Charmian kept herself away from the antics of their visitors for the most part, hers frequently an empty chair at table. She published a set of rules. No one except Jack, Charmian, and their houseboy could stay at their cottage overnight. To accommodate guests, Jack refurbished a bunkhouse a small distance from the main house. All were welcome to stay, to enjoy the ranch, to entertain Jack. But, no matter how much drink was consumed, how long into the night the conversation and high jinks lasted, mornings were sacrosanct. No one could approach the house or make noise until lunch was announced. Lunch was announced when Jack had finished his pages.

Jack and Charmian made and spent several fortunes, he on land and agricultural schemes, she on pretty things and comfortable travel. Charmian Kittredge London, an avowed Socialist, traveled first class, and taught Jack to expect first cabin in all accommodations.

I saw them rarely. But one meeting stands out.

It was 1907, the year after the Great San Francisco earthquake. Our mutual friend George Sterling had the grand idea that as so many of our homes and haunts were now gone to the fire that had come with the quake, we should all resettle down the coast, in Carmel. We would become a community of artists and writers and love one another forever.

Many of us trekked down and set up camp next to the ruined walls of the old Spanish mission, beside an inlet that was abundant with abalone. Few of us had money to speak of and the abalone provided many free meals, just as the remnants of the mission provided free shelter.

Among the group was a beautiful young poet named Nora May French whom George had brought down. Anyone could tell she was in a state of mental depression, and the rumored causes were many. Her sea-captain lover had left her; she had an unrequited passion for one of our number, curly-haired Jimmy Hopper; who remained true to his wife. But I believed that she simply had a melancholy nature. She did write some lovely poems, but she published few and earned very little for those that she did.

The summer was a grand frolic, but by its end most of us made plans to leave, driven by the practical problem of earning a living. We had one last big splash. Jack and Charmian came down for a few days. Jack, of course, was in his element. Charmian complained of the damp.

By Monday afternoon all of us were gone except for George's wife, Carrie, and Nora Mae. Carrie said she had some things still to pack up, but what she probably wanted was a little bit of quiet. Nora Mae remained, I believe, because she had nowhere else to go nor funds to get there.

In the night, after Carrie retired, she heard Nora Mae creep into her tent and lie down on George's empty bed. Believing the girl to be lonely, Carrie said nothing. When, shortly after, she heard some slight choking sounds she took them for quiet sobs. In the morning she discovered that Nora Mae had swallowed cyanide. An empty packet was found on the table beside her empty glass.

There was, at first, a great show of both shock and sadness. But within a short time the suicide of Nora Mae French seemed to the group to be an elegant, well-timed removal. A romantic, Byronic end, in its way. Why grow old and unattractive only to become a drag on friends and acquaintances when one could easily carry the means to one's end in one's pocket, as Nora Mae apparently had?

George saw to it that her poems were published in a beautiful little volume. The book was well received; a certain number of the public were thoroughly enchanted by the tragic end of the beautiful poetess. At last, in death, Nora Mae had the renown that eluded her in life.

Thus began a sort of cult of suicide among the crowd. Many of them began carrying around a lethal dose of cyanide to use when their Nora Mae moment arrived. Eventually, six would take the dose, including, separately, both George and Carrie Sterling.

Jack, alone among the crowd, found the notion appalling, although Charmian was intrigued by the power of posthumous fame.

It was several years after that when I first visited Jack and Charmian at their ranch. Jack wrote to me during the fall of 1911, imploring me to come. The previous months had been difficult for them. Charmian, though in her forties at the time, had given birth to a little girl during the summer of the prior year, but tragically the baby had lived only a few days.

Both Jack and Charmian were deeply grieved. Charmian expected Jack to sequester himself with her after their loss. Instead, desperate to be with his daughters after losing the baby, he proposed building a house for Bess and their girls somewhere on the ranch property and moving them up.

Bess thought about the proposal seriously enough to take the girls to Glen Ellen for their first visit. Their day on the ranch was spoiled by a willful act on Charmian's part. As the family, Jack, Bess, and the girls, sat down in the shade of a stand of live oak for a picnic, Charmian raced her horse too near, showering the picnickers with dust and ruining the food. Bess declared that the girls would not be secure under Charmian's roof, and left, never to return. Jack was furious, and launched into a protracted fight to gain more time with Joan and Becky.

During that year Jack seemed to abandon his fight against strong drink. Several of his drunken escapades reached the press, one in San Francisco with the old curmudgeon Ambrose Bierce, another in Oakland, that ended in a barroom brawl and landed Jack in jail and with a black eye.

The couple did get away twice on long trips, but the following year Charmian was still depressed. Though he was earning a large income, they were mired in debt and Jack seemed obsessed with that "other" woman's offspring, namely, his own girls. Jack thought that the company of females might cheer Charmian, and so I was invited up to the ranch in Glen Ellen, along with Carrie Sterling.

That fall, when Carrie and I arrived, the Londons were building Wolf House in earnest. Even in its unfinished state it was the largest house I had ever seen: four stories tall, as many bedrooms as a small hotel. No more bunkhouse for the crowd!

In the new house, Jack's room would be an eagle's nest alone at the very top, reachable only through Charmian's own room.

The ranch was indeed beautiful. I was happy to have the enforced solitude of the mornings there to write, and to have the company of good friends for long walks or rides in the afternoon. Jack made clear that I was welcome for as long as I wanted to stay, but I cut my visit short after happening upon an argument between these two eternal lovers, in the kitchen, when I arrived for dinner, apparently a few minutes before guests were expected.

"When will it end, Jack?" Charmian demanded, voice controlled but full of pent-up anger. "Every night at my table there are an extra dozen souls."

"My friends are not extra souls," he responded. "My friends are parts of my soul."

"They have the worst influence on you. You could hardly rouse yourself to work this morning, again. With debts piling up, you cannot afford the distraction."

I was reminded of the dining room that would seat thirty for dinner, being built in the new house, and I wondered what abuse Jack would suffer when that number of guests sat down to dine with them. And then stayed over.

I removed myself from the number at their table that night and took the train home in the morning.

We met again by chance that winter, shortly after the New Year, 1912, in New York City. The idyll between Jack and Charmian was not going well. He came out to dinner one night with George Sterling and several others, but without her. He made no excuses, no tale about a headache or such. Instead, he said he hadn't seen her for two days, dismissive of the question and, it seemed, of his wife.

I ran into Charmian the next afternoon at the Metropolitan Museum of Art, alone, and I invited her to join me for tea. I expected to hear that it was over between them, that he had found someone else; who that someone was I believed I knew.

But, to my surprise, she announced, "We're sailing around Cape Horn in March." She adjusted her mink scarf, face serene, as if her husband hadn't gone missing some days earlier. "From Baltimore to Seattle. It will be our longest trip since the South Seas. Another honeymoon for us."

A fantasy, I thought, and she was lost in it.

Jack was more or less continually drunk, without Charmian, between January and March, when the ship that was to carry them around the cape was scheduled to set sail. To my surprise, he was on the ship, with Charmian, when it left the Baltimore harbor.

George Sterling, who had been his drinking companion during that New York period, told me that after a full week of heavy drinking, Jack was frightened upon waking one morning to discover that he had shaved his head bald at some point, he could not remember doing it, and, worse, he realized that he had not so far written a single page in the year. There was a three-month accumulation of unpaid bills, nothing in the bank, and nothing new to submit to his publisher.

I believe that Jack returned to Charmian for refuge, desperate to be saved from himself. During their voyage he wrote *John Barleycorn*, his heartfelt tome about the evils of drink. And they renewed their partnership. Charmian returned home to Glen Ellen pregnant for the second time. But she miscarried shortly after their return from the trip around the cape, and there would be no third chance for a child for her. She was devastated.

One calamity followed another. Jack nearly died of a burst appendix. Then, in quick succession, his prize stud horse died, a late frost ruined their apple crop, a dry wind destroyed their corn in the field, and locusts infested their eucalyptus grove.

I believe that, in Charmian's eyes, Jack's potential, and perhaps charms, had begun to wither. She began to emerge again as an independent woman. She became herself a published writer, proud of her earnings. After editing and revising Jack for so many years, the writing process held no mystery for her.

Their single great success that year was the completion of Wolf House. By August there were only a few details to be finished before the house was cleaned in preparation for the master and mistress to move in. The massive raw redwoods supporting the structure wept pitch, and the final task was to remove it with turpentine. They set a date in late August for the move.

However, before they could move in, during the night of August 22 of that year, 1913, Wolf House, the grand edifice built to last for a millennium, burned down. For three days the ruins smoldered.

Their brilliant plans seemed to perish with that fire. The embers of Jack's vision for the ranch took some time to burn their way out, but cool they did. For most of the two years left him, he and Charmian traveled, up and down the California coast: They sailed the *Roamer* on the Sacramento River, and twice they journeyed across the Pacific for long stays in Hawaii.

In Hawaii, Charmian went out at night without Jack, who was frequently too ill to stir. Our friend George Sterling said Jack had a mistress there, but remembering Jack as I saw him soon after their return, I doubt he had the ability to please a mistress. Or perhaps even his wife.

Jack also made several trips without Charmian, but they went badly. On a solo visit to New York, the press reported that Jack and three "actresses" were slightly injured in a late-night carriage accident. Under contract to *Collier's*, he went to Vera Cruz to report on the Mexican revolution, but was sent home with "dysentery" before he had a chance to see anything of the revolution. With each episode, the press coverage grew less kind, the readership less tolerant; Jack became tedious.

At home during the fall of 1916, Jack had several projects under way that were full of new idealism. He had soured on socialism and replaced it with Jungian psychology as his driving philosophy. But he finished little during the last year of his life other than travel articles. He was drinking heavily and injecting himself with morphine against pains in his stomach. When his hands shook so violently that he could not drive the needle into a vein, his Japanese houseboy, Sekine, or Charmian, would do the favor for him.

Even though he had not been well, he planned another trip to New York, again without Charmian, who was volubly opposed to it.

Sometime during the day of November 21, Jack wrote a letter to his daughter Joan, inviting her and her sister for lunch and a sail on Lake Merritt during the next week when he would be in Oakland to catch his train for New York. He sounded hopeful.

On that day, the twenty-first, I was again at the ranch, again at

Jack's insistent invitation. I was the only guest in residence at the bunkhouse, as Charmian had sent the others away in the interests of Jack's recovery. They were happy enough to go. Jack had become quarrelsome and there were many angry words to be heard coming from the London cottage in the evenings.

During that visit, I generally managed to stay out of my hosts' way most of the day, joining them only for lunch and dinner, after which I would excuse myself early instead of staying long into the night for the customary discussion. Charmian seemed relieved to see me to the door before Jack had consumed his nightly quota of drink.

I happened upon Jack late on the afternoon of November 21. It was just about sunset. The land was still warm from the day, but there was a crisp wind gliding up the Valley of the Moon to ruffle the confetti of leaves still clinging to the vines in Jack's vineyard.

Winter was coming, and though the California winter would be mild, I felt, as the days grew shorter, the seasonal pall of melancholy descend upon me, a legacy of my New England upbringing.

Except for the break for lunch, I had worked all of that day editing some short stories of my own that were due at my publisher's. My eyes were tired and my back felt stiff. I felt the need for some fresh air and some exercise before dinner.

I gathered my camera, as was my habit, and went out for a stroll through the fields and eucalyptus groves. There was a large pond below the house—Jack called it a lake—where a fine variety of birds generally came to fish for their supper, and I had the idea that I would walk out on the wooden pier where Jack kept a little fishing dory tied up. There I would wait for whatever came by that might look interesting through my lens.

As I approached I saw that Jack was in the water, swimming slowly shoreward from the middle of the pond. I snapped a few photographs of him because I liked the way the low sun rays caught the water streaming from his arms as he stroked, cascades of bright crystals. When his feet could touch bottom he stood, shook his great thatch of blond hair like a dog. I continued to take photographs. He had not yet seen me.

I remember I was glad that Jack felt well enough to swim, because he had been ill off and on with stomach trouble since early summer. There was talk variously of ptomaine poisoning or kidney stones or uremia, but the true cause was surely a life of immoderate consumption of rich food and strong drink and late nights, and self-medicating. His show of energy was, I thought, a good sign that he was recovering.

As I snapped the shutter release, Jack rose, entirely naked, from the black water, his flesh pink from the cold, his legendary love staff no more than a pale pink knob amid the dark triangular patch below his protruding belly. When he saw me, he bowed, doffed an imaginary hat, and grinned as he reached for his old flannel robe and covered himself. I returned his salute, snapped one last photograph, and turned to take the path in the opposite direction.

My photographs from that evening are the last taken of Jack. They show him smiling, apparently, perhaps deceptively, robust. His spirits were high and his smile was natural, fond. He was, as always, a wicked prankster. I knew he was laughing behind my back, hoping for the possibility that he had shocked some remnant of Victorian sensibilities on my part. He had not.

I turned and walked away not because I was embarrassed by his nudity, but because I was saddened to see how bloated his lovely belly had become, how thin his sturdy arms and legs. Jack had once been a truly beautiful man. I wept for him.

The path I took wound through the fields, continued around the back side of a sharp stone outcropping, and came up through a stream-cut valley to the site of the ruins of Wolf House. The ruins were already covered with moss and native vines twining around the blackened stones and charred beams. It was certainly a ruin that would last a millennium, the eternal relic of a lost dream. My photographs from that evening show an ominous skeleton disappearing into the forest.

Later that evening, filled with a sense of dread that the old argu-
ments between husband and wife might recur during the meal, I
approached the front door of the London cottage at the appointed
hour. The Japanese houseboy, Sekine, opened the door before I
knocked. He must have been waiting for me.

"How is Jack feeling?" I asked.

For an answer he shook his head, not good. With a glance toward
the kitchen, where Charmian was softly humming, he gestured for
me to come closer. He whispered into my ear, "Mr. London ask,
you please go see him now, before you see missus." When I nodded,
respecting his quietude, he led me through to the sitting room.

Jack, sitting in his favorite old leather chair, held out his arms to
me. I knelt and leaned into his embrace.

"How is my friend?" I asked him, kissing his stubbly cheek.

"I am as you see me," he said.

"Sekine said you wanted to speak with me." I glanced toward
the kitchen. "Alone."

"A favor," he said, voice low.

"Anything," I said. "Almost."

He smiled, chuckled softly. "A small favor."

"Tell me."

"Will you watch over me tonight?"

"Sit up with you?"

"Not precisely, Mary." Again he looked toward the kitchen.
"Charmian ordered a new black silk dress in obvious anticipation
of an event we both can guess; the dress was delivered this afternoon. She tried it on and it seems to suit her."

"Good Lord, Jack."

"She is sorting through all of her many albums of clippings and
reviews and has begun to compile notes, *The Life of Jack London*
seems to be in the works."

"Every woman needs a good black dress," I said in hopes of
deflecting the conversation from the direction I knew he was headed.

"Charmian has put on a few pounds since the miscarriage."

"Black dresses for certain events, yes. Though I've told her, no funeral. No mumbo jumbo over my head."

For the briefest moment I risked Charmian's wrath by resting my head against Jack's chest, that loveliest of pillows. When I straightened again, I asked him, "Tell me what you want me to do."

"Tonight, will you sleep here in the house, in the room next to mine? Will you watch over me, but do nothing more?" He put up his hand when I started to interrupt, again. "Tonight of all nights I don't want to be alone."

"Of course." I remembered Nora Mae creeping into bed beside Carrie so as not to be alone. I was afraid I knew what Jack intended. And I was certain that if what I suspected was indeed his plan, I could not stop him. "I will bring my things over after dinner, if you are certain that Charmian won't mind."

"We won't tell her," he whispered. "Sekine will call for you after Charmian has settled in for the night."

"All right, if this is what you want," I said. "But Charmian's wrath will be upon your head if she discovers me."

He pulled my face to his and kissed me full on the lips, as a lover would.

"Be kind to her," he said when he released me. "I know what drove her, and it wasn't noble or fine. But consider what she gave me before you judge her. Let her create my legacy. Let her find a living from it. That much I owe her."

"Oh, Jack."

"She will, you know," he said. "In death I will become the great man I could never be in life."

Jack excused himself during dinner; he could not eat. As he exited in the direction of his sleeping porch, behind Charmian's back he pointed to me, squinting at me, until I nodded. I would do as he wished, bear witness and nothing more.

Jack and Charmian did not share a bedroom. Their rooms paralleled each other, separated by a set of concrete steps that led into a garden. The rooms were better described as sunrooms, wrapped halfway down with windows on three sides. If either of them leaned forward from their beds, they could see into the other's room.

Charmian, a chronic insomniac, frequently could not fall asleep until the hour before dawn. At night she pulled bamboo shades down over her windows so that the morning sun would not disturb her. Jack, on the other hand, slept like a stone, more frequently after a dose of morphine, and enjoyed seeing his ranch out his windows as he wakened.

I excused myself after dinner and walked down to the pier on the lake, where I had spied on Jack earlier, and waited until all of the lights in the house were out except for the little reading light over Charmian's bed, a diffuse bright spot seen through her shades.

Sekine, wrapped in a kimono, came for me. Like thieves in the night we sneaked in through the kitchen door. With my shoes in my hand, I followed him to Jack's room.

The only light in Jack's room came from a small votive on his night table. Sekine had provided everything Jack might need during the night. On the table beside the bed there were a carafe of fresh orange juice, a basin of cool water and facecloths, and a medical kit that held Jack's syringes and vials of morphine, in case he wakened in pain.

When we walked into his room, Jack gave me a silent salute. I kissed his forehead before Sekine showed me to a dressing room that opened off Jack's bedroom where a daybed had been made up for my vigil. With the door ajar, I could see Jack in his bed, though I doubt he could see me at all. The only light in my little room came from the candle beside him.

Jack waited for Sekine to leave before he picked up the medical kit and opened it. I braced myself, expecting this to be the moment. But all that he did was take an empty morphine vial from inside and set it next to his glass of juice. And then he saluted me again and settled back against his pillows.

I may have dozed, I may have been woolgathering. I came to awareness suddenly when some small object hit the floor outside my room; I don't know how long I had been at my post or what time it was. Startled, I rose to my feet and peered in at Jack. He looked in my direction and gave me a quick wave to retreat back into the dark, and then he dropped his head to his pillow and played possum. Standing in the dark, I heard light footsteps approaching down the hall.

Charmian came into view at Jack's bedroom door. I remained very still.

From the door, Charmian peered in at Jack, listening, I thought, to his breathing. Draped in a white silk robe, her waist-length hair loose and hanging down her back, she swept silently into the room, like a ghost. For a moment she stood beside his bed looking down at him. Then she felt his forehead, pulled his blanket up under his chin, and bent to kiss his lips. Jack did not stir.

She picked up the empty vial, examined it, looked again at Jack. She seemed to say something to him, but I could not hear her words and he did not respond.

After another short wait, she picked up the medical kit and lined up five vials on the table beside the empty one. Next, she took out the long, shiny steel syringe and expertly filled it with the contents of the five vials.

Horrified, I reached for the door, intent on stopping her. But remembering my promise to Jack, I did no more than bear witness to the events that followed.

Charmian, seated on Jack's bed, took one of his arms from under the covers. Holding his hand in one of hers, she gently guided the bright needle into the tender flesh on the inside of his elbow.

There was a quiet funeral in Oakland, against Jack's express wishes. Charmian did not attend, giving Jack's children that day to be with their father. Afterward, George Sterling and I carried his ashes on the train back to Glen Ellen.

At the ranch, we followed Charmian up to the knoll behind the ruins of Wolf House; her new black silk dress was indeed of an elegant cut and fabric.

Ranch hands had prepared a cement vault deep in the soil of his land for Jack's urn. There were no prayers or eulogies, following Jack's instructions. The vault's lid was lowered into place, and the hole filled.

With a gesture from Charmian, the ranch hands rolled a massive chunk of red lava stone, quarried to build Wolf House, into place over Jack's grave. There Jack remains, a great lover, adventurer, writer, captured for all eternity. His passing an enigma. As he wished.

Cougar

Laura Lippman

"Sorry," said the young man who bumped into her, although he didn't sound particularly sorry. Almost the opposite, as if he were muffling a laugh at her expense. At least it was water, and she could change into her other blouse, the one she had worn on the walk here, assuming Mr. Lee didn't object. Surely, Mr. Lee wouldn't make her work the rest of the shift in a soaked white blouse that was now all but transparent.

"Sean!" his girlfriend chided without conviction.

"Hey," said he-who-must-be-Sean. "It was an accident. I didn't even see her."

Of course, Lenore thought, going to the back to change. A five-foot-ten blonde in a sushi bar is hard to spot. Yet she knew he wasn't lying. He hadn't seen her. No one ever saw her. She was here every Friday and Saturday night—seating them at their tables, bringing them their drink orders when the waitstaff got backed up. But even the regulars didn't seem to recognize her from week to week. For young people who came here, the sushi dinner they gulped down was just preamble, preparation for the long night of barhopping ahead. If she wasn't their mother's age, she was close enough, forty-two. And, fact was, she had her own twenty-one-year-old son at home, living in the basement with his nineteen-year-old girlfriend, and she was invisible to them too.

Still, at least one young man seemed to register her presence as she walked to the back room to get her shirt. Well, he noticed her tits, given that the thin white blouse was now plastered to her front. "Nice," he said to his friend, not even bothering to lower his voice. "Check out the cougar."

So now she was presumed to be deaf as well as invisible. Deaf, or in some strange category where she was expected to tolerate whatever others said about her. Was it the job? Her age? But then, it was the same at home. Worse, actually.

"A kid at work called me a cougar last night," she said over breakfast the next morning, a Sunday. Not hers. Lenore had eaten breakfast at ten AM, a respectable time for a woman whose shift ended at midnight. Now it was almost one PM, but her son and the girlfriend had just roused themselves a few minutes ago and were nodding over bowls of cereal, their heads hanging so low that their chins almost grazed the milky ponds of Trix.

"Was he nearsighted? I can't imagine anyone thinking you was hot." That was Marie, the girlfriend, and the insult was so automatic that it carried no sting. As far as she could tell, it was the reason that Frankie kept Marie around, to insult Lenore. Otherwise, he would have to do it himself and that was too much effort.

"I think it's because my shirt was soaked through. Another kid bammed into me when I was carrying a tray of water glasses."

"Big thrill," Marie said.

"Well," Lenore said, "pretty big." She had a showgirl's figure and she didn't care what the magazines deemed fashionable—an hourglass figure would always be in style. Marie, meanwhile, was flatchested and soft with baby fat. Which made sense, because Marie was still a baby—lolling in bed all day, watching cartoons, eating all the sugar she could find.

"Shut up," Frankie said tonelessly. They did as he said. They always did what he said.

If Marie was a baby, then Frankie was a six-foot-two toddler, perpetually on the edge of a tantrum. He had returned home quite unexpectedly six months ago, with no explanation for where he had been or what he had been doing in the two years since Lenore had last seen him. She had offered him his childhood room, but he sneered at that, claiming the basement that she had just renovated into a television room. She had planned the room as a retreat, a place to watch television late at night, maybe work on her various craft projects. But now it belonged to Frankie and she had to knock if she wanted to enter, even if it was to do his laundry in the utility room in the back. Once, just once, she had walked in without knocking and she wasn't sure what scared her more—the drugs on the coffee table or the look on Frankie's face.

I could lose my house, she thought as she backed out of the room, laundry basket clutched to her middle. Until that moment, she had—what was it called?—plausible deniability. She had suspected but not known what went on in her basement. But now she knew and if Frankie got caught, the government could take her house. That very thing had happened to Mrs. Bitterman up on Jackson, and there were rumors that it was why the house on Byrd Street was going to auction at the end of the month. Lenore lived every day torn between wishing her son would get busted, and knowing that his arrest would probably destroy her life instead of saving it.

Kicking him out wasn't an option. She was scared of Frankie. *She was scared of her son.* It was such an awful thought, she hadn't dared to let it form, not for a long time. She had even daydreamed that the man in her basement wasn't Frankie at all, just some audacious imposter. Certainly, he bore no resemblance to the boy she remembered, a serious but sweet child who never quite stopped puzzling over his father's disappearance when he was still such a little thing. And he was so much bigger than the fourteen-year-old they had taken away from her, put in the Hickey school, then that weird place out in western Maryland, where they taught them to cut down trees or something. He didn't even resemble the nineteen-year-old who had moved out in disgust two years ago, when she had said he had to live by her rules if he wanted to stay under her roof. She had been shocked when he actually went, because she had no idea how to make him do anything—pick up his clothes, rinse a plate. If he had refused to leave, she would have been powerless.

In the two years since then, Frankie must have figured that out. And now he was in her basement, dealing drugs, running up her electricity bills, leaving crusty bowls strewn about, eating everything in sight and contributing nothing. Once, she had steeled herself to ask him if he might kick in for food or utilities. "Marie don't eat much," was all he said. His meaning was clear. She owed him room and board for the rest of his life, however long that might be. She owed him everything he wanted to take from her. She owed him for the big mistakes—not being able to hold on to his father—and the small ones, such as not getting him the right kind of sneakers when he was at Thomas Heath Elementary. Sometimes, late at night, when she heard police cars hurtling down Fort Avenue, she wondered where Frankie was, if he was dead, and she wouldn't have minded too much if that were so.

And then she thought how unnatural she was, how a mother should always love her child no matter what.

Frankie had come home in March and now it was August, the end of a miserable, fretful summer. Working two jobs—the sushi place on weekends, Sparkle-and-Shine cleaning service on Monday through Thursdays—she should have been able to save on her AC bill, but Frankie and Marie ran it full force, forgetting to turn it down when they headed out, which was usually about four in the afternoon. Every day, Lenore came home to a chilled catastrophe of a house. She tried to remind herself of how lonely she had been over the past two years, how empty her free evenings had seemed. That's when she had taken up various crafts in the first place, teaching herself crocheting and knitting, figuring out what her computer could do, where it could take her. But the computer was in the basement, along with the television, and it made her heart sore to see what that once-pretty room had become since Frankie took it over. She was stuck in the kitchen, listening to the Orioles on the radio, or sitting out in the living room with the newspaper, which she never had time to read in the mornings.

Only on this particular August afternoon, there was a man on her sofa. A young man Frankie's age, dressed like Frankie—T-shirt, baseball cap, jogging pants, as Lenore still thought of them, although Frankie insisted that she say "tracksuit." Dozing, he looked harmless, but Frankie probably looked smooth and sweet too when he was sleeping.

She cleared her throat. The stranger jumped, and his feet—huge, puppyish feet, as if he hadn't gotten his full growth yet, although he was already pretty big—just missed the porcelain lamp on the end table. As it was, he had already left vague scuff marks on the peach leather.

"Who are you?" he asked.

"Frankie's mother," she said. It took her a second to remember that she had a right to know who he was.

"Aaron," he said. "Frankie said I could crash here for a while."

Beaten down as she was, she had to ask: "Here, as in the house? Or here, as on my sofa? Because that's a nice piece, and your shoes have already—"

Aaron jumped to his feet and Lenore thought, This is it, this is where I get hit for standing up for myself in my own home. Until that moment, she had never allowed that thought to form, had never admitted to herself what it was that made her fear Frankie. Not just the drugs and the consequences of his business being discovered. And not just the physicality of a slap or a punch, but the meaning of such a blow. She hadn't been a good mother, or a good-enough mother, and Frankie, ruined as he was, had returned home to remind her of that fact for every day of the rest of her life and maybe his, depending on how things worked.

But this boy, this Aaron, actually felt bad. He kneeled to examine the mark. "That was stupid of me," he said. "But I know a trick my aunt taught me. She had six boys, so believe you me, she knew how to get any kind of stain out of anything. You got any talcum powder?"

She did, a rose-scented talc that she hadn't thought to use for months, years. He sprinkled it on the arm of the sofa, his fingers as light and gentle as the priest who had baptized Frankie, then said: "Now we let it sit overnight. The powder will draw out the grease."

"Like salt on a red wine stain," she said.

"Exactly. The main thing is, you don't want to use water, this being leather and all. It's an awfully nice sofa. I feel bad about not taking my shoes off. But Frankie and Marie were downstairs and wanted to be alone—" He actually blushed, as if Frankie's mother might not know why her son and his girlfriend preferred to be alone in the basement. "He told me to come up here, and I got so sleepy. I coulda gone upstairs, I guess, but that seemed forward."

He looked at her strangely and then Lenore realized the only thing strange about the look was that it was direct. He felt bad, he cared what she thought of him, at least for this moment. If he hung around, he would soon absorb Frankie's attitude toward her. But, for now, he was the kind of boy she always wished Frankie would bring home. She cast around in her memory. What did you do with your son's friends when they came to visit?

"Hey," she said. "You want a snack? Or a beer?"

Unlike Marie, Aaron didn't move in, but he was there more nights than not and Frankie offered him the guest room on the second floor. "Is that okay?" Aaron asked Lenore. Frankie didn't give her a chance to answer. "Of course it's okay."

She was the one who offered Aaron a key, however. It was over breakfast. Although he came in at three or four AM with Frankie and Marie, he would get up when she rose at seven for her cleaning job and share a cup of coffee with her. He said he couldn't sleep once he heard her moving about, and she believed him because she had found she couldn't really fall asleep until she heard the trio come home.

"You don't have to—" he began.

"It's no big deal," she said. "And this way, if you want to come home earlier than the others, you don't have to wait around with them." Then, after a moment's hesitation, she asked what she had never dared to ask Frankie. "Where do you go? I mean, all the places close down at two, don't they?"

"Most of them. But there are some. And—well, the corner, there's usually some late-night business. Although . . ." Now it was his turn to hesitate. He got up, rinsed his coffee cup out in the sink, placed it in the dishwasher. He was considerate that way. Sometimes, he even brought Frankie and Marie's dirty dishes up from the basement and rinsed them.

"What, Aaron? Is he taking chances? You can tell me. You know I don't judge."

"There've been some . . . disputes. Guys moving in. But meth isn't as territorial as crack, so you don't have to worry."

Meth. Right, she had nothing to worry about. If Frankie didn't get her arrested, he would blow her sky high. "So he is—?"

"Yeah," Aaron admitted.

So not only selling it and storing it, but making it in her house.

"I don't like it," she said, catching Aaron's eye. "I wish I could make him stop."

"It's hard for anyone to tell Frankie anything."

"Yeah. I'm scared of him, you know." She had never said that out loud to anyone. It didn't sound so bad.

"He wouldn't hurt you."

"He might."

"No, I wouldn't let him."

And that was as far as she let it go, that time. Lenore resolved not to discuss Frankie again with Aaron, not unless Aaron brought up the subject.

She started taking a little more care with her appearance. Small things, like lipstick in the morning, before she came downstairs to put the coffee on. A new peach robe, modest in cut, but silkier and more close fitting than the old terry-cloth one, and with a matching nightie. She got a pedicure, although now fall was coming on and the kitchen floor was cool beneath her feet as she padded about. Marie asked Lenore why she had bothered. "Pink toenails on an old lady like you? Who cares? Who sees your feet?"

"I'm only forty-two," Lenore said. "I'm not on the shelf. Some women have babies at my age."

"Gross," Marie said, and Frankie nodded. Aaron didn't say anything. Lenore poured him a glass of juice and passed him the plate of muffins—from a box mix, but still fresh and hot. "What about me?" Frankie asked and she slid the plate across the table to him—but only after Aaron had made his choice.

And this was how the days went by, fall fading into winter, Aaron sleeping in the spare bedroom more often than not, Lenore taking ever more care with her appearance—looking younger day by day, even as she behaved far more maternally than she ever had. She cut back on drinking and joined the local Curves. She splurged on lotions and moisturizers, choosing those with the most luxurious smells. Alone with Aaron, she confided in him, but always in a maternal way. How she worried about Frankie, how she wished he would just say no to drugs, how she was nervous about him getting busted. How she wished she could save him from himself, but wasn't sure that anything would work for Frankie, even the forced sobriety of prison.

The only problem was Marie, who was turning out to have sharp eyes in that pudgy little face.

"Flirting with a boy your son's age," she said one night, peeved because Lenore had forgotten to buy Lucky Charms, Marie and Frankie's new favorite, although she had remembered Aaron's Mueslix. "You're pathetic."

"I'm just being nice," Lenore said. "Besides, a young kid like that could never be interested in an old broad like me."

"Got that right," Marie said, stomping downstairs to the basement. Soon, Lenore heard her laughing with Frankie, and their laughter was as ugly and acrid as the smells that rose from the floor below. Aaron was down there too, but he wasn't laughing with them. Lenore was sure of that much. She was also sure that she was going to have to sleep with him, eventually. The only question in her mind was whether it would be before or after.

It turned out to be after, and it was Frankie, in his way, who made it happen. The four of them had been sharing another late breakfast—this one with cinnamon rolls, the kind that you baked at home, then coated with sticky white frosting. There were eight in a carton, two apiece, but Lenore had decided she wanted only one and passed her extra to Aaron.

"I wanted that," Frankie objected.

"I'm sorry," Lenore said, not the least bit sorry.

"You act as if he were your son," Frankie said. "Or your boyfriend. Just like when I was younger."

"I never had boyfriends when you were a boy," Lenore said, upset by the unfairness of it all. She might not have been a good mother to Frankie, but she had never been a slutty one. "I was strict about that."

"Oh, you didn't let guys move in or have breakfast with us, but you still brought them home sometimes, did them up in your room and sent them on their way before I woke up. If I didn't have a step-daddy, it wasn't for the lack of free samples. You just never could seal the deal."

"Who wants the cow when you already have the milk?" said Marie, clearly unaware of how much milk she had given away in her young life.

"I wasn't that way." Lenore realized her voice was trembling. "I did the best I could, under the circumstances."

"You were a shit mom. You chased away Dad, then you just sat back and let them take me to juvie, didn't even spring for a decent lawyer when I got into trouble."

"I did the best—"

"You didn't do shit." Frankie banged his fists on the table. "You were a shitty mom and now you're a stupid cunt, mooning over some young guy. It's disgusting."

He stomped out of the kitchen, followed by Marie. Lenore began to clear the kitchen table, only to drop the dishes in the sink, her shoulders shaking with sobs that she didn't really have to fake.

"He didn't mean that." Aaron came over and started patting her shoulder awkwardly.

"He did," she said. "And he was right. I wasn't a very good mother. I should have found him a stepfather when his own father left, or at least put him in some program. Like Big Brother, or whatever it's called. I failed Frankie. I failed him over and over again."

"It will be okay," Aaron said, but it was more a question than a statement.

"How? He's either going to get arrested or killed. If he gets arrested—well, that'll be even worse for me, once he tells the police he was dealing here. They take your house for that, Aaron. Even if you can prove you didn't know, or couldn't stop it, they take your house."

"Frankie's pretty careful—"

"You said there was some quarrel over his territory?"

"Not so much now." She turned then, and the hand that was patting her shoulder passed briefly over her breast, then dropped in embarrassment. "A little."

"He could be killed. Some guys who want his corner could just open fire one night, and the police wouldn't even care. You know how they do. You *know*."

"Naw—" He met her gaze. "I guess so. Maybe."

"Killed, and no one would care. No one."

Two nights later, Aaron woke her at three AM to tell her that Frankie had been shot on the corner, gunned down. He was dead.

"Were you there?" she asked.

"I had gone to the 7-Eleven to buy smokes," he said, very convincingly. "When I started back, I saw all the cop cars, the lights, and decided not to get too close. Marie was shot too."

"So she's a witness."

"Maybe. I don't know. What should we do?"

"What should we do?" She hugged him in a perfectly appropriate way, a maternal way. Her son was dead, his friend was dead. It made sense to hold him, to comfort each other. It also made sense when he kissed her, and when he reached under the peach gown that matched her silky robe. It made even more sense to crawl on top of him and stay there most of the night. Lenore had not been with a man for a long time, but that had only increased her stamina, and her longing. And, besides, she was very grateful to this young man, who had done what she needed him to do, and without her ever having to ask straight out.

In the morning, after the police called to ask if they could swing by before she went to work—Frankie didn't have a current ID on him, so it had taken them a while to sort out where he lived, if he had next of kin—she told Aaron that he should probably move on, go somewhere else, maybe back home to Colorado.

"Marie is conscious," she told him. "And saying she thinks it was a white guy who fired the shots at them."

She could see Aaron thinking about that.

"She's also saying it was a robbery, that she and Frankie were just walking home from a club. Still . . ."

"I've got a friend in New Mexico," he said.

"That's supposed to be nice."

"But not much saved up," he said, a little sheepish. "Even with you giving me a free place to stay, I never did put much away."

"That's okay," she said, reaching deep into a cupboard, behind layers of pots and pans, one place Frankie and Marie would never have meddled. "I have some."

She gave him the amount she had stashed away without admitting why she was saving it, a thousand dollars in all.

"I didn't—" he said.

"I know."

"I even thought—"

"Me too. But I want you to be safe."

"I could come back. If things cool down."

"But they probably won't."

He looked confused, hurt even, but Lenore knew he would get over that. Perhaps he felt used, but he would get over that too.

The police were on their way. She would have to get ready for that, be prepared to cry for the loss of her boy. She would think about Frankie as a child, the boy she had in fact lost all those years ago. She would think about the boy she was losing now. Somehow, she would manage to cry.

And then, when the police were gone, leaving her to the business of burying her own boy—she would go down in the basement and begin the business of reclaiming her own house, washing sheets and throwing open the tiny windows in spite of the wintry chill. Her house was hers again, and no one would ever take it from her.

LUSTING FOR JENNY, INVERTED

Elizabeth George

When Marion Mance dropped dead in her bathroom on April
Fool's Day, she was unclothed, a circumstance she would not have
greatly appreciated. Even less would she have appreciated having
her body discovered some three days later by a young couple who,
having enjoyed each other's fleshly company on the hooked rug in
the Mance living room, were seeking a place to perform some necessary postcoital ablutions. These individuals were Karen Prince
and Troy O'Hallahan, sixteen and eighteen respectively, but the
reader need not take the time to remember them as they do not
loom large in this tale. They were present on the scene because
Karen's mother—being the postmistress in Port Quinn, a matter
which the reader may also pass by without serious effort at mem-
orization—had sent them there to check upon Mrs. Mance since
she had not picked up her mail in those three days and she was
generally quite regular about her habits. As Mrs. Mance had not
spoken about her intentions of leaving Crawford Island for any
length of time, as a careful questioning of the ferry boat operator had revealed no departure of Mrs. Mance that might have
gone unmentioned by the woman, and as the postmistress had
long considered the elder islanders her personal responsibility, she

dispatched her daughter to the cottage on West Bluff Road where, tucked into a forest of alders, cedars, hemlocks, and dogwoods, Mrs. Mance had lived for forty-two years, six months, and exactly three weeks. Not rousing Mrs. Mance with a hearty knock on the door and not seeing her by means of peeping through windows—which were fairly obscured by curtains, anyway—and finding her front door unlocked, the young couple seized what they saw as a carnal opportunity that fortune had placed before them. This was not their first physical encounter nor would it be their last. It would all end in tears when Karen found Troy in an obviously compromising position with Sandy Jackson in the backseat of his father's 1962 Dodge Dart down by Miller Creek some six months later, but that's a tale for another time.

Considering the lapse in time between death and discovery, Mrs. Mance was not in a condition that could be called comforting in appearance. Between rigor mortis, a moderate rise in temperature, and the lividity attendant to *post obitum* inertia, her body—alas, clad only in pink chenille mules—was startling, to say the least. For a young girl stumbling in on it after a satisfying tryst on a hooked rug less than thirty feet away, it was a terrifying sight, as if the jaws of hell had opened so that she could glimpse those wages she had to look forward to should she sin again with Troy O'Hallahan. Karen Prince got over this horror, of course. But at the moment, she screamed. The scream brought Troy on the run.

The youngsters thought murder, first. They thought evidence, second. They thought of the hooked rug, third. They thought of hightailing it out of there, fourth. But as the postmistress had sent them to see if Mrs. Mance was, perhaps, in some sort of trouble and as they had come upon rather clear evidence of just that fact, there was in reality nothing else for them to do but to phone the sheriff, who soon appeared in the person of Deputy Martin Behr. They threw themselves upon his mercy and told a somewhat modified version of their engagement with each other on the hooked rug. Deputy Behr said, "Damn fool kids," and "Where is she, then?" and had a look for himself, upon which look he blanched decidedly. He asked them didn't they notice the smell, for the love of God? What were they, blockheads? They said they hadn't or maybe they had but it had seemed like bad fruit in the cottage or something and anyway they called out and looked through the windows, which made them think no one was home and actually no one *had* been home in the true sense of the word since one couldn't really call a corpse someone and during their cursory peeks through the windows they saw the hooked rug and since the front door was unlocked, they didn't break in and they definitely didn't touch anything except a few doorknobs and a lamp that got knocked over when Karen got a bit more enthusiastic than she should have gotten when they rolled about and—

That, Deputy Behr told then, was more than enough information. They could wait outside.

So wait they did. Wait everyone did. It wasn't long before the word came down: No murderous beast wandered the early springtime lanes of pretty Port Quinn. Sudden heart failure and not homicide had taken Marion Mance from them. Her next of kin would need to know. And that was how Jenny Kent, forty-nine years old, mother of five, and a first-time grandmother, found herself on the auto ferry, making the two-hour passage from the mainland to Crawford Island, some three weeks later.

Jenny hadn't been close to her aunt Marion, either by proximity or by blood. She lived in Long Beach, California, amid the pleasures of sunshine, ocean, sand, palm trees, freeways, traffic jams, unbridled housing construction, and offshore oil derricks, while her aunt lived off the coast of Washington State, on a distant Puget Sound island inhabited by a mere two thousand people. Beyond that, Marion Mance was her aunt only by marriage, having been wed to Jenny's maternal uncle for more than fifty years. There had been no issue of that happy union, however, and since Marion had, prior to her death, harbored a fond and extremely distant memory of Jenny's First Communion some forty years prior to drawing up her fifteenth and, her attorney fervently hoped, final testament, she chose Jenny—one grain from the sands of her time—to act as executrix of her will. Its main beneficiary would be Port Quinn itself.

Had this information come to Jenny Kent at another time in her life, she might well have passed the job on to a local attorney hired for the purpose of settling her aunt's affairs. But coming as it did shortly on the heels of the Kent empty nest being filled once again by the return of the eldest Kent child with toddler in tow and possessed of the mistaken expectation that Jenny would nurture and rear grandchild much as she had done five children of her own, Jenny decided that a period of reflection was called for. The fact that her husband disagreed with her need to consider her options at this point merely spurred more firmly her intent to be gone. Aunt Marion's affairs needed seeing to—whatever those affairs might be—and she would do it.

"Are you seriously leaving me alone with . . . with *them*?" Howard Kent had demanded, as if his daughter's flight from what had turned out to be a chronically unfaithful husband had rendered her an alien species with a miniature alien attached to the hemline of her denim skirt, nose running and thumb plugged into mouth. "What if they keep me *up* at night? What if I've got *surgery* in the morning? You can't *do* this, Jen."

Ah, but she could. The surgery-in-the-morning line had worked for more than twenty-five years, but the last nine months with the final child gone had opened Jenny's eyes to what she'd done with her life and she didn't like the sight presented. So she booked her airline ticket, flew away, rented a car, took herself northward to a ferry dock, and chugged off to Crawford Island for the period of reflection that fate had handed to her.

Now, one might argue that life had been good for Jenny Kent in Long Beach, California. She had not been a trophy wife—no woman having the needs of five children to meet could be said to be any gentleman's trophy—but she'd had placed within her grasp the sort of assistance that made her job in the family home and among the various Kent offspring easier than it would have been had she been asked to manage everything on her own. There were gardeners for the large Kent property, on a leafy street in the east part of town; there was a housekeeper who did just that; there was a cook who applied herself to whatever diet-of-the-month was being pursued; there were au pairs—always two of them—to sort out the children's various affairs. If a child had difficulty in one school subject or another, a tutor was hired. If he or she wished to engage in a sport, a coach was sought. If music was an interest, lessons were provided. Jenny's main labor was thus akin to directing traffic within the household and writing checks as well. For all of this was rather expensive, so it was indeed a blessing that Howard's reputation as a cardiologist was one of the highest in the state of California, cemented into place once he performed open-heart surgery on a long-ago governor at the tender age of twenty-nine. Howard, that is, not the governor.

Since he was a busy man much in demand and because his profession was a taxing one, Howard asked only for peace, quiet, and two glasses of cream sherry when he returned to the bosom of his family at night. It was Jenny's job to provide this, and for the years of their marriage, she did the job with grace, pleasure, and as little reflection as possible upon the fact that she could have been something far different than a wife, a mother, and a director of familial traffic in Long Beach, California. For the truth of the matter in this modern day is that rare is the woman who finds the myriad needs of her complex psyche met through uxorial and maternal activities.

In Jenny's case, what loomed large in her history was what she had fled in her youth and why she had fled it. The *what* was Olympic downhill racing. The *why* was impatience, lack of drive, and the temptations of a life made easier by ready money. Born to two ski instructors whose sole ambition was to follow the snow and whose pecuniary condition certainly reflected this fact, Jenny had tired of living in straitened circumstances by the time she was thirteen years old. No matter the athletic gifts that nature and exposure had bestowed upon her, she wanted a different sort of life than the one her parents dreamed for and urged upon her, and she understood at an intuitive level that her parents' real desire was for a vicarious experience of gold medals and glory. This, she decided, had nothing to do with *her* per se, and while she cooperated with them during her high school years—anything to get out of having to take physical education classes was fine with her—by the time she was nineteen, she decided that having only achieved replacement status on the U.S. ski team was not a sufficient harbinger of good things to come. In short, she dropped the entire endeavor, began to ski only when she felt the urge to do so, and otherwise waited on tables in Park City, Utah, where she fortuitously met a young resident physician on holiday and was married to him before her twenty-third birthday, producing the first of their children before her twenty-fourth. In the meantime, it was her younger sister who went on to fulfill their parents' dreams of Olympic gold, afterward becoming a television sports broadcaster, a position from which she rose to the height of national news anchor with all its attendant fame, fortune, and glory.

It cannot be said that Jenny Kent was not proud of her sister, for she was. But such sororial success tends to instill in the heart of a sibling a certain degree of envy, not to mention regret, and this was the case for Jenny. She suffered from the knowledge that what could have been was certainly *not* to be now that she was forty-nine years old. This suffering brought with it the discontent of a woman who finds herself with too much time to reflect upon it. While the advent of eldest-child-with-grandchild-in-tow might have mitigated the disgruntlement of a woman having had little youthful potential for glory, that was not the case for Jenny Kent. She'd *had* the potential, as we have seen. In her mind, she'd squandered it, and the day of reckoning for such squandering had come.

So it mattered little to her that Howard might be inconvenienced by her absence from Long Beach. She would go to Crawford Island, she decided, and there she would manage the final disposition of her aunt's affairs and, if she was lucky, she would also find herself in the position of having another chance in life to make her mark . . . in something, she hoped.

She knew absolutely nothing of the island, having never been there. So she was unprepared for the great contrast it provided to Long Beach. There, the environment was dominated by a massive port, by oil derricks insufficiently camouflaged to look like towers of modern art, by no fewer than three freeways trisecting the city, by large houses sitting on minuscule squares of land, by small and historic bungalows relentlessly torn down and replaced by condominiums. But Crawford Island was none of this. It was fragrant forest and twisting lane. It was rolling field of green populated by sheep, by llama, by cow. It was craggy coastline and crystal bay. It was beach and driftwood, fishing and boating, planting and harvesting, stream and trail.

Crawford Island possessed one town only, and this was Port Quinn. Passengers debouched from the ferry here, at the end of a street called Coastal Promenade, where a grassy park offered picnic tables, benches, and sites for lawn bowling and croquet. Climbing a hillside from this point, three streets curved languidly in the direction of the local monument, a peg-legged man with spyglass to his eye: Josiah Quinn, founder of the eponymous town. Other streets ran perpendicular to Coastal Promenade, and it was on one of these that Jenny Kent found the office of Lawrence Davis, longtime attorney of Marion Mance.

He provided Jenny with the key to Cedar Dreams, for such was the name of the Mance cottage. He offered her advice as to where to stay in town and told her that, following an initial look at her aunt's situation out at Cedar Dreams, he and Jenny could meet and lay their plans.

At first Jenny thought, ridiculously, that he was referring to Marion Mance's corpse when he used the term "aunt's situation."

But of course, she realized that could hardly be the case since Marion had been, at this point, blessedly in the ground for three weeks. So she told him she would prefer to lodge at the cottage itself rather than at the recommended hotel, and when he began to protest this idea, she firmly informed him that while his suggestion was kind, it was also unnecessary and where could she find a map of the island as well as a market to pick up what she might need to enhance her stay, such as food.

Lawrence Davis was not a man who wasted effort on people who were determined to be what his elderly mother called "pig minded." He made a rather charming antique bow from the waist, handed over a map that he'd already purchased in anticipation of her arrival, and told her where she might find the market. The phone in Cedar Dreams was in working order, he said in conclusion to their meeting, so she should call him when she was ready to discuss the manner in which she wished to proceed.

He gave Jenny a commiserating smile as she left, which should have told her not everything was as might be imagined in a cottage called Cedar Dreams. But she was already enchanted by Crawford Island, and she took no note of this, so much in a hurry was she to be out on one of the lanes she had spied from the ferry.

She found Cedar Dreams with very little trouble since the five wrong turns she took had exposed her to more visual delights than she'd had in twenty-six years in Long Beach. For spring is excruciatingly beautiful on Crawford Island, offering juvenile bald eagles soaring from cedars, bluebells nodding in the shade of forest and glen, new green leaves so fresh they look edible, fawns and their mothers lifting cautious heads from holly bushes and, alas, from newly planted gardens. Indeed, spring on Crawford Island is capable of making one quite forget November through March on Crawford Island, when the rain, the wind, the sleet, the snow, the toppling trees, and the inability of the town council to deal with these yearly manifestations of climate make the place not only inhospitable but also virtually unlivable: a land fit only for those possessing pioneer spirit and the funds for a generator to cope with the continual losses of power.

But Jenny knew about none of this when she found Cedar Dreams in its little glen of trees. What she knew was that she'd somehow come upon a slice of heaven, a place of balm for her discontented spirit, and an opportunity to consider how to alter her life.

She was at least partially disabused of these notions when she stepped inside her aunt's abode. There, she quickly discovered why Lawrence Davis had made his suggestion about accommodation in town. For to call Marion Mance a collector would be putting too polite an appellation on the matter. She'd been instead a hoarder, and her late husband had not been any different. Indeed, the only spot that was unencumbered of a collection, a stack, a pile, a heap, or a mound was the very spot that—unbeknownst to Jenny Kent— the two teenagers at the opening of our tale had experienced carnal knowledge of each other prior to finding poor Marion's corpse.

Now understanding that look of commiseration that Lawrence Davis had offered her upon her departure, Jenny made her way through rooms containing everything from ancient newspapers to unopened packages from mail-order catalogs. Had there been pictures on the walls—and there probably were, all things considered, since this *was* an abode—she could not have seen them, so obscured were they by the stacks and piles before them. Each room had, over time, been reduced only to pathways leading to relevant objects like a chair in which to sit, a television or a radio or a bed.

Jenny Kent had to cope with all of this. Not only that, she had to sift through it. For settling her aunt's affairs was going to mean dealing with years of mail that had been left unopened, not to mention somehow finding whatever paperwork related to the cottage itself, the land upon which it sat, and such details as bank accounts, retirement accounts, investments, insurance policies, and the like. But Jenny was not a woman who engaged in this sort of endeavor unassisted. So despite that parting smile of his—which Jenny was beginning to see more as maliciously knowing than commiserating—Lawrence Davis was going to have to be pressed into service.

This wasn't a conclusion she reached at once, though. First, she spent two days engaged with the newspapers, magazines, catalogs, brochures, five hundred offers for credit cards, and three hundred and twenty-one suggestions that the recipient join the AARP, at which point she fled to town and threw herself upon the attorney's mercy. She didn't cry uncle to him. She was too proud for that. Instead she asked him if, since she'd never been an executrix before, he could recommend a course of action and someone to help her take it.

Lawrence Davis being an attorney, he was only too happy to offer sage advice. The wheat definitely needed to be separated from the chaff out there at Cedar Dreams, he agreed expansively, and he knew just the man who could help her do it. This would be Donald McCloud of Port Quinn Estate Sales and Antiques. She would find his establishment on Fourth Street.

"McCloud's the man you need," Lawrence Davis told her. "Donald McCloud. *Don*ald."

The strange emphasis that the attorney gave to the man's Christian name did not escape Jenny, but she assumed—quite wrongly as things turned out—that Lawrence Davis was dwelling upon this identifying detail due to his own mistaken belief that Jenny was incapable of remembering it. She was, after all, a blonde, and Lawrence Davis was, after all, a man fully capable of leaping to inaccurate conclusions when faced with a female who was manicured, pedicured, coiffed, and stylishly garbed. Thus, Jenny Kent went on her way and found Port Quinn Estate Sales and Antiques not only with very little trouble but also with very little thought as to the connotation behind that emphatic repetition of the business owner's name.

The day was one of a long string of glorious days on Crawford

Island, and the sun streamed into the shop in such a way that dust motes glittered in the air and the furry patina they formed upon every visible surface was actually soothing, rendering objects with an air of permanence and solidity and giving the appearance of a business long held and hence completely trustworthy. This same sun caused Jenny's eyes to need a period of adjustment once she entered the establishment, and an intriguing and pleasant masculine voice was saying, "Hello, there. May I help you?" before she was able to see who the speaker was. To her, he was merely a shadowy form in a creaking desk chair from which he was rising to a decent height of at least six feet. When she asked if he was Mr. McCloud, he told her that he was indeed and if he could be of some assistance to her . . . ?

"McCloud" was the key. That was what remained in Jenny's mind from her talk with Lawrence Davis. This was not because lack of mental exercise had rendered her incapable of recollecting such a simple thing as the name Donald. Rather, it was because her natural impatience—that quality which had defined her youth and eliminated the possibility of Olympic glory—caused her to want to get on with things and the main thing she wanted to get on with was the clearing of her aunt's cottage so that she herself could enjoy it and the springtime that surrounded it. Hence, "McCloud" told her she'd found the man she sought. The fact that he was Ian and not Donald did not concern her.

It must also be said that once her eyes adjusted to the ambient gloom of the shop, Jenny Kent was rather taken with Ian McCloud, as would have been any woman who was not blind, deaf, and mute. For Ian comprised the stuff of Romance in every aspect: He was dark of hair and swarthy of skin but, surprisingly, blue of eye. And the flecks of gray in his Vulcan locks—which neither Jenny nor any other woman could have known he put in himself to add an air of both maturity and distinction to his overall appearance—made him seem simultaneously worldly and ready. And, as has been wisely noted, "the readiness is all," which remains a compelling

fact to women who, like Jenny Kent, find themselves at a cross-
roads in their lives.

As Jenny explained the circumstances of her visit to Port Quinn
Estate Sales and Antiques, she couldn't help taking in other salient
details of Ian McCloud's appearance. His clothes were paint spattered, his shirt was open at the neck, and he wore a gold chain.
While this final sartorial element might have caused her concern—
she had never cared for men adorning themselves with necklaces
and even less had she cared for men who felt it necessary to display their chest hair—she saw that a gold wedding band hung
from this chain and that Ian McCloud fingered it as he talked.
After a moment and with an appealing smile that demonstrated
what years of orthodontia and consistent teeth bleaching can do
to one's dental gifts, Ian revealed that this ring had belonged to
his beloved grandmother and he wore it as a talisman, day and
night.

Jenny Kent blushed when he said this, not because the mention of talismans and grandmothers was in any way embarrassing,
but rather because she understood he was mentioning the ring's
provenance because she had been staring at his chest as she talked
about her aunt's estate. She hastened to tell him that she hoped
Port Quinn Estate Sales and Antiques might be pressed into service
to assist her in the ultimate disposition of Marion Mance's belongings.

"Is this the sort of thing you do?" was how she put it.

The correct answer to this question was that Ian McCloud did as
little as possible, which was why Lawrence Davis had emphasized
Donald as the man to match the mountain of labor Jenny Kent had
described to him. Ian was the only child of said Donald and the
adult apple of every female eye in his family, being the only male
born to the women of his mother's generation and *her* mother's
generation and *her* mother's generation as well. So he'd grown up
admired, coddled, adored, and undisciplined, which anyone knows
is a fatal combination of suffocating love and outright indifference.

As a result of what might be called far too much positive reinforcement directed at his mere existence, Ian had entered adulthood adhering to the belief that somehow life owed him something for the simple reason that he deigned to live it. This sense of entitlement, however, united with a natural charm. These two elements in conjunction with Ian's good looks had served him well.

Yes, indeed, this was exactly what Port Quinn Estate Sales and Antiques did, Ian McCloud told her. "So you're Marion's niece," he added and he flashed a smile that had melted hearts for every one of Ian's thirty-three years. "It's nice to meet you. Can I call you Jenny, or do you prefer Mrs. Kent?"

"Jenny's fine," she replied, and as she spoke, she unconsciously twisted her wedding band and the five-carat diamond that Howard had bestowed upon her for their twenty-fifth anniversary.

Ian was no stranger to this gesture, having seen it often. He read it for what it generally was: that moment in which a woman wishes for things that weren't, at least at present. He also took note of the ring itself. The diamond ring, that is.

He had no intention of stealing it. Ian was not and had never been a thief. He merely saw it, wondered about the man who had given it to her, and wished he himself had the means to buy such an adornment for a woman. Not that he would have used the money to do that, however. He would instead have used the money to finance the achievement of his latest ambition, which was to own and operate a winery that produced—naturally—gold-medal wines. This was the latest of a long line of plans that Ian McCloud had possessed for himself and his future. At the present time, however, he was caretaker of a lovely estate on the south end of Crawford Island, a domicile owned as a blissful getaway by a Hollywood film editor and his wife. As they were seldom able to make the journey north, Ian usually lived there in solitude, paid for looking after their horses, seeing to the general upkeep of the house, and guarding against the marauding hordes that someone from Hollywood is likely to believe might at any moment pour over the electrified fences of a property on a peaceful and idyllic island of two thousand utterly indifferent souls.

One well might wonder, at this point, what Ian was actually doing in Port Quinn Estate Sales and Antiques on this day when Jenny Kent made her fateful appearance in the shop. The truth of the matter is that he *was* actually there to work, since his father was off on a lengthy anniversary cruise and since Ian shared not only shop responsibility with his father—although he put forth little enough effort to make a success of this endeavor—but also Donald McCloud's adherence to that eternal optimism of Mr. Micawber: Sooner or later, something was bound to turn up. In Donald's mind that something was going to be the ultimate jackpot of a Winslow Homer or an Andrew Wyeth hanging forgotten behind a dining room door in a house whose possessions had to be sold. In Ian's mind, that something was going to be the free lunch he'd so far lived his life in the hope of consuming.

Jenny Kent personified the possibility of both.

The fact that there was a sixteen-year gap in their ages gave Jenny pause and slowed things down to a simple flirtation at first, what might be called a testing of the waters between them. She found Ian breathtakingly attractive, but she wasn't about to make a fool of herself if he had no interest in her. Besides, she had no intention of actually being unfaithful to Howard. So when Ian came to Cedar Dreams in his paint-spattered clothing, his open-necked shirt—with the sleeves rolled up most appealingly to show manly forearms—his gold chain, and his gray-flecked hair, she attended to the business of the cottage, brushing past him when the opportunity presented itself, placing a hand on his arm when she had a question. For his part, Ian took this in, knew what it meant, and considered whether, at thirty-three years old, he wanted a fling with a woman approaching her sixth decade. She was, after all, the executrix of Marion Mance's estate, not its chief beneficiary.

So they were both cautious, although Ian McCloud was cautious about more than one thing. He was also cautious in his approach to cleaning out the detritus of Marion Mance's past, having been schooled over the years by his father that something could turn up in the most unexpected place.

That happened, eventually, although neither Jenny nor Ian knew this at first. What they did know was that a catalog of Items of Interest had to be amassed prior to the sale of said items, and this was a catalog of some considerable length. For after the mountain of debris had been meticulously looked over and disposed of, filed, paid off, burnt, bundled up, and otherwise handled, what remained in the cottage was furniture, clothing, china, utensils, pottery, books, letters, statuary, knickknacks, coins, stamps, tools, bells, buttons, and bows. . . . In short, what remained was a lifetime of items with which an elderly couple had not been able to part.

"We're lucky this place isn't any bigger," was Jenny's reaction to the mass of possessions they found in every closet, under every bed and other piece of furniture, in the attic, in the basement, and outside in the two sheds on the property. "This could take forever."

Ian said, "I don't mind that. Do you?" and the smile he gave her told her that her flirtation had not gone unnoticed.

Neither had some very curious postage stamps.

This part of our tale begins with a simple, "Look at this," which was voiced by Jenny on a sunny morning in which their endeavors had taken her and Ian into one of the cottage's three tiny bedrooms. She was at a desk that sat beneath one of the room's two windows—Marion Mance having been a stickler for cross ventilation at the time of the cottage's design—and at her feet she'd placed two boxes. Into one she'd been depositing the obvious discards from this piece of furniture. Into the other she'd been placing items she had entered into her catalog. From the bottom drawer of the desk, she'd drawn a dented strongbox minus its key. This box was not locked, however, and what she found within it was a stack of what appeared to be old love letters mailed to Jenny's uncle Walter—this would be Marion's husband—during the time of the Korean War. These letters were bound together nicely with an old red ribbon, and it looked as if it had not been untied since first being tied decades ago.

Now, for her faults, Jenny was a respectful woman, and she had no wish to pry into the love life of two souls now gone to eternity. She showed the letters to Ian and said, "Sweet, aren't they? You know, I don't have a single letter from my husband. He always sent cards just signed with an *H*."

"Not a *single* love letter?" Ian asked. "Why, that's too bad."

Jenny took this to mean that in the same position, Ian would have sent a thousand letters, and her heart stirred at this. It beat light and fast, and she continued to browse through the rest of the tin box in something of a flutter. It was in this flutter that she came upon another envelope, this one not containing a letter at all. Into it, instead, had been stuffed postage stamps, with no particular regard for the care of them. As there was also stationery in this drawer from which the box had been drawn, Jenny thought nothing much of the stamps at first, assuming they'd been placed in the box to be used on letters and subsequently forgotten. Nonetheless, she drew them out of the envelope and gazed upon them, for some of them looked foreign and all of them looked old.

Out of duty as executrix of Marion Mance's estate, she began to catalog them, but she got no further than jotting down the details of the first six she picked up when Ian came to join her. He said, "Now *these* look interesting, Jenny," and the emphasis on the second word indicated that nothing else they'd come upon in the endless job of sorting through belongings had amounted to much.

In his quick assessment of the stamps, Ian McCloud was correct. They *were* interesting. For the sixth stamp that Jenny Kent held in her fingers was Canadian, a #387 as it was called, and it celebrated the St. Lawrence Seaway. What made it notable was its central image of leaf and eagle. These, along with the numeral indicating the stamp's worth, were printed wrong side up.

The very fact that the stamp was worth a mere five cents indicated its age, for who could mail a letter for five cents any longer? The additional fact that its image was inverted indicated it probably had value. What Ian McCloud would find out that evening in a search of the Internet—on which he had recently spent considerable time communicating with a widow in New York City whose financial position he'd been endeavoring to discover—was that this tiny bit of misprinted paper was worth approximately $15,000, depending upon its condition. At the moment, though, he knew only that it was unusual. As was the previous stamp, which Jenny had already cataloged.

This was American in origin, a tiny thing with a printed value of twenty-four cents. Like the other, its image was inverted. Unlike the other, as Ian would discover, its worth was considerably more than $15,000. For this little bit of postal blundering featured a World War I biplane. It had long been called the Inverted Jenny, and any philatelist worth his salt would have given his right arm to possess one. The fact that Walter Mance had stuffed it into an envelope and placed it in a tin box in his desk was due not to indifference or disrespect, but to ignorance and a faulty memory on the part of more than one of his progenitors. The stamp had come to him via his paternal grandfather who'd been given it by *his* uncle who'd been given it by *his* brother who'd been given it by a girl he was courting who had thought it "sweet and curious" when she found it in her father's underwear drawer while tucking his freshly laundered shorts into place. Being something of a collector, Walter's grandfather had put it into a Luden's cough drop box with several other stamps. Not given to passionate curiosity, organizational skills, or studious habits, Walter's grandfather had gotten no further than passing along the cough drop box to his grandson when at nine years old Walter had come upon it—out of a desire to play mumblety-peg—while looking for a pocketknife among his grandfather's handkerchiefs. In short, no one knew what they had for several generations, and the stamp had lain unmolested and perfect in every way among a few others for decades.

It must be said that Ian McCloud had no immediate thought to put his hands on either one of these stamps. In his time assisting his father, the McClouds had never come across anything of greater value than a $5,000 silver tea service so badly tarnished it was deemed to be pewter. But as we've seen, Something Is Bound to Turn Up was rather a family motto and Ian's dream of a winery and awards and recognition for such little effort as he presumed a winery to require of its owner caused him to delve into the arena of philatelic research that very evening. One can easily imagine first the surprise and then the temptation presented to a man with dreams—*and* with a sense of entitlement—when he first realizes that he is within inches and degrees of possessing the world's most famous postage stamp. Its value: $200,000 and climbing with every passing year. How could a man learn that and not be tempted?

The problem for Ian was the other Jenny, the *un*inverted, human one. Not only did she know about the stamp—being the one who found it—she also had already cataloged the damn thing. That catalog had to be presented to his own father prior to the estate sale so that an evaluation of articles within it could be made. Because of this, Ian had to get the human Jenny on his side of the philatelic fence, which meant he had to woo her, win her, and then convince her that appropriating one of the curious little stamps for themselves was a small matter only, requiring a simple recataloging of dear Aunt Marion's possessions. And wouldn't it be romantic to appropriate the stamp that had long been referred to as a Jenny? Surely, Providence itself had placed such an article among everything else in Cedar Dreams.

Of course, Ian couldn't go directly to this matter. He had to woo and win his human Jenny first.

This wooing and winning began with an invitation to dine at Blackberry Point, the estate owned by the aforementioned Hollywood film editor and his wife, the very same place of which Ian was caretaker and inhabitant of a small single-room domicile not far from the stables. But Jenny was not to know of this particular detail regarding Ian's habitation at Blackberry Point. As he had the key to the house and because the film editor and his wife were not due to put in an appearance on Crawford Island until the Fourth of July, it was no difficult feat for Ian to remove the superficial signs of their ownership—such as family photographs and an enormous album of their wedding pictures—and establish himself as lord of the manor, the better to impress poor Jenny.

His paint-stained clothing was helpful in his general dissembling. He'd been wearing it when Jenny first met him because he'd been painting the six bathrooms of the house in advance of the owners' return to the island. But now, as a means of casually explaining how he happened to possess such a magnificent estate while being ostensibly employed only as an occasional assistant to his father, he became a painter of the artistic ilk, a present-day Jackson Pollock whose studio was conveniently off-limits to Jenny's eyes since his genius was of a delicate nature, easily quashed by anyone's viewing of his masterpieces before they were completed.

"My God," Jenny breathed. "I had no idea . . . Ian, why haven't you ever *said* . . . ?"

Of course, he'd never *said* because he'd never thought of it until the Inverted Jenny caused him to lay his wooing and winning plans. But he couldn't tell her that, so he shuffled his feet and hung his head in what he assumed would communicate humility. "It didn't seem like . . . well, you know . . . ," was his reply.

That this remark was apropos of absolutely nothing was a fine point Jenny overlooked. For she was seeing him through eyes that were dazzled by the myriad facts she was quickly amassing about Ian McCloud.

First among these was what he ostensibly possessed: thirty-two acres of waterfront land on a heavenly isle, seven of what *definitely* appeared to be Arabian horses grazing in a verdant meadow, an expansive house with even more expansive views—not to mention a sunken spa bathtub overlooking Puget Sound where orcas could be daily seen doing their orca thing out in the water—a barn, a stable, a studio in which museum-quality art was being created . . . To a woman used to living in a situation in which money was no particular object, a change in position to one in which money was *also* no particular object was infinitely preferable to marginal poverty no matter which way one looked at the matter. Not that Jenny was *thinking* about making a change. Not yet, at least.

Second among the dazzling facts that Jenny thought she was gathering was what Ian had ostensibly done with his life: *He* had lived the dream, succeeded on his own terms as every artist must do, fulfilled the potential given him by the gods or by fate or by whatever. How impressive.

Third among these facts was the singular fact of Ian himself: intelligent, articulate, amusing, in possession of those excellent teeth and a copious amount of hair—Jenny's Howard, alas, had been completely bald for the last fourteen years—companionable, and potentially romantic and attentive. To a woman who'd spent more than twenty-five years as a wife and mother while all the time *knowing* she could have been more, Ian McCloud was not only Jackson Pollock. He was James Bond. He was Mr. Darcy. He was Marc Antony to her Cleopatra, Romeo to her Juliet. He was, in short, what she had always wanted: Possibility without Effort, the answer to the question about what she was supposed to be doing with her life instead of raising a grandchild.

They didn't become lovers at once. To Ian, that would have been too obvious. To Jenny, that would have been too easy. Because of the difference in their ages—those sixteen years yawned between them as the great unmentionable—Ian knew that his apparent love for her had to have the appearance of coming upon him in a Saint Paul moment, illuminating the utter rightness, complete goodness, and absolute godliness of a miracle of fate: that they had *somehow* been thrown into each other's path. And Jenny knew that her very real and growing desire for him had to look like the walls of Jericho tumbling, one reluctant stone at a time. This was adultery after all. Big sins ought to require big effort. *Oh I can't* and *I mustn't* had to be rejected in favor of *I can* and *I will*, but not so quickly as to make her seem cheap or to imply her desperation.

The entire matter took four nights. That they weren't *consecutive* nights and that they were divided by several days of nurturing that inchoate spark—always present between an attractive man and woman thrust into close proximity—into a palpable current gave the affair the necessary imprimatur of This Being Bigger Than Both of Us. When at last they consummated their desire, this consummation—it must be stressed—was something craved by both of them: Ian may have wanted to put his hands on the Inverted Jenny, but at the end he wanted to do the same to the uninverted one as well. As for Jenny herself . . . it was glorious to be so desired by a man. It was even more glorious to be so desired by a man of means. And to be led to a bedroom whose window framed a breathtaking sunset which itself was framed by magnificent fir trees and a landscaping job the expense of which had to have been astronomical. . . . This was metaphorical icing on a cake beyond Jenny's wildest imaginings.

"Good for you, darling?" Ian murmured afterward.

"Lord," was Jenny's trembling reply. And then came tears, for not only were they called for by the situation, but they were also true to her feelings. She had never been unfaithful to Howard, and she needed reassurance now she'd crossed the line.

Ian was only too ready to give it, and he gave it by uttering the sole word that a woman in Jenny's position longs to hear spoken by the man sixteen years her junior to whom she's just given her virtue: *us.*

There followed a period of rapturous daily lovemaking, along with angst, reflection, discussion, guilt, desire, and more rapturous daily lovemaking. *What are we doing we can't we can't* transformed, as these things generally do, to *It was destined by God we must we must* and that, as these things also do, finally transformed to *What's next for us, my love?*

In the meantime, of course, nothing much was getting done in the way of cataloging Marion Mance's belongings. Ian was too intent upon positioning Jenny and Jenny was too intent upon being positioned.

A month went by before two events supervened upon this amorous interlude in the lives of Jenny and Ian. The first event was Lawrence Davis's phone call, pleasantly but nonetheless pointedly inquiring as to how Jenny was coming along with her duties as executrix. "The city council's got a plan for the cottage and the land," he told her. "As soon as you're finished, they'll be turning the whole place into a park, named for Mrs. Mance. Did I mention the city council's been informed that Port Quinn is chief beneficiary, Mrs. Kent? How are you finding Mr. McCloud? Helpful, I hope?"

Ever so, she told him. There were, however, reams and reams of documents, oodles of bills, pages and pages of this's and that's, cupboards and drawers and closets and boxes just filled to the brim . . .

"Need more help?"

Oh no, she told him. She and Ian were making good headway, Mr. Lawrence.

"Ian? *Ian?* Where's his dad?"

By this time, Jenny had forgotten all about Ian's dad. She'd forgotten he even *had* a dad. She'd forgotten to ask why Ian wasn't ever going into the shop on Fourth Street, why he wasn't painting, why he wasn't, in fact, doing much of anything but nibbling on her ear, running his tongue along her collarbone, and sliding his hands—those terribly manly attractive hands—beneath the lovely silk blouses she wore. "Ian's been helping me," she told Lawrence Davis. "He's been a marvel, really, Mr. Davis."

"I expect he has," Lawrence Davis said. "Perhaps I need to come out and see how you're doing."

As lovers will do, Jenny shared this information with Ian, along with information pertaining to the second event that interrupted the bliss they were sharing. This was Howard. He didn't appear on the doorstep. Nor did he phone. He was far too busy for either of these activities. But he did send a note via their eldest daughter: a card with a photo of the grandchild tucked inside, along with the single sentence, "Dad wants to know when you're coming home and so do I."

These two incidents, falling so closely one on the heels of the other, stirred our two lovers into action. Ian saw from Lawrence Davis's words that the jig was perilously close to being up. Jenny saw from her daughter's note and her husband's message what the future held if she returned home. There was nothing for it but for her to encourage Ian's advances and for Ian to make a declaration of love, permanence, lifelong allegiance and all the et ceteras as soon as possible.

"Leave him," was how Ian put it. There are times when succinctness is called for and this was one of those times. "Stay here."

"But, Ian," Jenny said, "this cottage isn't mine. It's the town's now. So it's only a matter of time—"

"Be with me. Come to me. Live with me."

"Are you saying . . . ?"

"I'm saying."

What he wasn't saying, naturally, was that he had less than a month at Blackberry Point before the owners showed up, which meant he had less than a month to win Jenny over not only to the winery but also to the means of funding it. She was steps away from finding out—courtesy of Lawrence Davis—that he was a lowly caretaker and to keep her from finding out before he was ready to confess all to her and throw himself on her infinite mercy, he had to secure her in the only way he knew.

"Leave him, for God's sake," he told her. "What d'you have to go back to compared to . . . us?"

There it was. That word.

"What shall I tell him?" she said.

"Tell him the truth."

"About you?"

"About . . . us."

So that's exactly what she did. In a fever and that very night, she penned a letter and in that letter, she told Howard all. She gave him every chapter and every verse, foolishly pouring out every passionate detail and with enough lubricious accompanying descriptions to seal her fate. She used the word "divorce" and—foolish girl—she told Howard to keep everything they had amassed together. For what she had now was worth more than jewels. She had love in its purest manifestation. Of course, this generous means of severing ties with her husband was also prompted by weeks of often thrice-daily sex, not to mention by Blackberry Point, six bathrooms, orcas viewed from the window behind the spa bathtub, Arabian horses, and Jackson Pollock. But she didn't want to reflect on that. She just wanted to get the letter written, get the letter mailed, and get on with her life.

When she'd completed her missive, it was long after midnight. But she could not wait for the morning to mail it, so fearful was she of losing her nerve. So she drove to the post office in the darkness, dropped it in the slot, said good-bye to her past, and embraced her future. The letter, she saw, would depart with the first ferry. Good-bye, she thought. Good-bye, good-bye.

In the meantime, Ian was doing what he could to make Blackberry Point ready for Jenny's arrival while at the same time rendering upon the house and the property no permanent alteration. By his reckoning he had one week before he had to get the place back in original order for its owners. What he didn't count on was a Hollywood wife's sudden pique during a cocktail party, which sent her northward in a state of high dudgeon, which sent her Hollywood husband hot on her tail, intent upon avoiding a costly divorce.

Mr. and Mrs. Hollywood arrived on Crawford Island via float plane some two weeks into Ian and Jenny's adventure in cohabitation at Blackberry Point. The Hollywoods had patched things up on their lengthy journey, and they were ready to grit their teeth and enjoy each other's company until one of them decamped to California again. They entered the house at 9:27 in the morning, whereupon they received the first hint that something was wrong. This was the dining table, littered with dishes from a meal *à deux* on the previous night. The Hollywoods quickly saw a trail of discarded clothing leading from the table to the stairs, and in no short order they followed this trail to find their caretaker in a somewhat acrobatic sexual act with a woman in the beautiful spa bathtub.

Mrs. Hollywood screamed. She would later say this was due to the fact that she thought Ian McCloud was murdering someone. Her husband, on the other hand, would counter with the sardonic comment that *no one* gets murdered in that fashion, babe, and he would go on to reveal that her scream had less to do with murder and more to do with how much water was sloshing from the spa tub onto the previously pristine windows and the bamboo floor. Then *she* would ask how he expected her to react when their home and their privacy were being invaded by Ian McCloud and some unknown woman. And *he* would say if any invading of privacy was going on, *they* were invading *his* and how would *she* like it if someone caught *her* with one leg hooked over . . . and another leg stretched out . . . and . . . One of them was definitely a contortionist, he declared.

But all that was later. At the moment, Ian and Jenny were caught, and Jenny's screams joined Mrs. Hollywood's screams while Ian scrambled for the bath sheets and flung them mindlessly into the water.

Can there be any doubt that Ian's employment at Blackberry Point met a precipitate end? For so it did. "Sent him packing" puts the matter too nicely. He had virtually nothing to pack anyway. But in doing what limited packing was necessary, he led Jenny to his painter's studio, where she discovered neither a single canvas nor one tube of paint.

Oh my God, she thought. What have I done?

Damn the timing, he thought. Well, all's not lost.

He fell to his knees. "I lied for your love," he said to Jenny Kent. "How could I make you love me if you knew . . . *this*?" *This* was his dwelling, a sad contrast with the manse in which he and Jenny had been romping.

"You're not a painter," Jenny said, stupidly.

"I'm a painter, just not *that* sort of painter," Ian replied. "But what I said about you, about us . . . all of that was real, Jenny."

She looked around, dazed. Since he'd been summarily thrown from his job, she didn't need to spend time evaluating his circumstances. There *were* no circumstances. He was, effectively, homeless. So, for that matter, was she.

"What will I do?" she said, more to herself than to him. She hadn't heard from Howard yet. There was a chance, she thought desperately, that he'd not gotten her letter. On the other hand, it wasn't like Howard to let weeks go by without phoning her with a plaintive hello, so chances were very good that he'd indeed received it. On the *other* other hand, perhaps their daughter had taken it from the mail, read it, decided her mother was suffering a bout of temporary insanity, and destroyed the letter without letting Howard see it. But if *that* had happened, if he *hadn't* seen it, then either he would have called with that plaintive aforementioned hello, or their daughter would have called demanding to know if Jenny had lost her mind, yes? Or perhaps someone *else* would have . . .

"Jenny, Jenny," Ian said, for he could read the battle going on within her. "I'm not going to let you sink. I've got plans for us."

"Plans?" she said. "You mean that all along you've had plans?"

"What? You think I'm a good-for-nothing? You think I don't have a *future* in mind? Of course I've got plans. Come here. Let me tell you." He led her to the camping cot that served as his bed, and there they sat. He took her hand in his and kissed her palm and he told her about his winery. Not here, he said, not on Crawford Island. There was too much rain and the soil wasn't right. But east of the mountains the land was cheaper and with a nest egg of a couple hundred thousand, they'd be ready to start on a brand-new life, just the two of them, the grapes, and the wine.

"Making love in the vineyard," was how he put it. "At sunset, Jenny. At dawn. At noon."

She didn't ask when the work would be done. She had a larger and more important question. "What couple hundred grand?" she asked. "Do you have a nest egg you haven't told me about?"

Now they'd come to the tricky bit, but Ian was confident he'd win the day. She was, after all, in the same position as he at this point. Homeless and fundless. She'd see reason.

So he told her what he knew about the Inverted Jenny they'd found among her aunt's possessions. A single postage stamp, he told her, one of just one hundred that had gone out to the public on the day of issue. People had spent entire lifetimes trying to track down an Inverted Jenny, and they—he and *his* Jenny—had one that they could offer for sale.

She stared at him for a moment. Then she laughed.

He said, "Look, I know what you're thinking: It isn't ours."

"You're right," she said.

"But it *can* be ours because only you and I know we have it. All we need to do is to rewrite the catalog of your aunt's belongings, leave out the stamps, and we're home free. How tough is that?"

"Impossible," she said.

"Don't *be* that way, Jenny. This is our chance."

But they'd had their chances, and both of them had blown them off their palms like fine, dry sand. Which was, essentially, what Jenny told him although in language far less metaphorical than one might expect.

She'd written to Howard the very night she'd decided to leave him for Ian McCloud, she explained. She was all in a lather to have a new life, so she'd taken the letter to the post office that night and there she'd mailed it before she lost her nerve.

"So?" Ian said, which was the first indication Jenny Kent had that Ian McCloud might not be as shiny a coin as she'd originally thought he was. "So you mailed the letter. So what, Jenny?"

"The stamp, Ian."

He began to see. But it was too impossible, too horrible to contemplate because, if it was true, they were sunk indeed. "The stamp?" he repeated. "That stamp?"

"Yes. The stamp. *All* of the stamps. I used them on the letter. It was long and heavy and . . . and . . . I don't have a single one of them any longer."

Thus Ian McCloud and Jenny Kent found themselves faced with one of life's bitter lessons, and this lesson dealt with the ephemeral nature of a love that blooms from one's baser instincts. For such a love is not love at all but merely a tortuous path that leads time and again to an unanticipated and often unpleasant destination.

As Marc and Cleo and Romeo and Juliet only too readily could have told them.

OTHER PEOPLE'S CLOTHING

Susan Wiggs

For a good many years, Laney McMullin had been wearing other people's clothes. She did so secretly and not without shame, but a girl from her circumstances didn't have many options. As a young woman with no money, she had to take advantage where she could.

McMullin's Kleen & Brite, founded by her parents thirty years before, lay two blocks east of respectability, on the fringes of Las Vegas. It was here that people from the high-rises and luxury vacation homes sent their couture gowns and Italian suits to be cleaned and pressed after a show, a gallery opening, or a black-tie affair. At any given time, the never-ending automated rack might be crammed with gorgeous, one-of-a-kind fashions from the appointment-only boutiques along the strip.

From the age of thirteen, Laney had worked in the shop. Her father, always so certain Easy Street was just around the next corner, had promised her the hard times were only temporary. Even when her mother left in disgust, running off with a postman because even he outearned the cleaners, Laney's father swore everything was on the verge of a major turnaround, and for a long time Laney believed him.

Instead of going to college, she labored over the luminous satin and sequined gowns of other girls preparing for sorority rush. She treated stains, sewed on buttons, pressed creases into sumptuous fabrics.

Over time, though, imagining her most privileged clients engendered a deep resentment in Laney. She grew to hate everything about her job: the long hours, the smell of human musk that pervaded the clothes, the reek of benzine and perc used in processing, the heavy heat of the pressing machines, and most especially the knowledge that each month's receipts would barely cover the store's overhead.

The borrowing had begun back when she was in tenth grade, and a new boy at school asked her to a dance. At first she'd demurred, protesting that she had nothing to wear . . . until her gaze fell upon a rich Jessica McClintock satin dress on the pickup rack, sealed in its thin clear cocoon of plastic wrap, looking better than new.

Discontent lodged around her heart and turned it hard, and sometimes Laney thought she'd go crazy. Day after day she stood behind the counter, and after ten hours there, she headed home once the worst of the Las Vegas heat had faded. She passed neighborhoods where she could never afford to live. She wandered among luxurious houses and mirror-sided condos, where the sidewalks appeared to be miraculously free of oily stains, flattened wads of gum, and dog shit. Trees with their own watering systems wore stiff skirts of wrought iron and people walked around in thousand-dollar shoes without a care in the world.

Customers from these neighborhoods sent their help to drop off or pick up their cleaning. People around here could afford to do that.

Before sending a garment for processing, Laney had to check all the pockets. It was remarkable how careless people were about leaving things in their pockets. Unfortunately, there was rarely anything of value, the most common items being claim checks and ticket stubs. Today, the search yielded a disposable lighter, an ATM receipt, and an errant phone number scribbled on the back of a sticky note.

Then she came to an overcoat of dove-gray superfine. There was a peculiar crackling in one inside breast pocket. Reaching in, she found an engraved invitation on thick card stock: "You are cordially invited to attend a reception to benefit the Field's End Literary Foundation. The Vista Ballroom, Regency Plaza Hotel. Formal attire." The event was scheduled for that evening at eight o'clock.

Laney knew instantly that she would go. She slipped the envelope into her pocketbook. Then she went looking for something to wear.

Joey Costello, the delivery-van driver, came whistling in through the back, at the same time each afternoon, having finished his rounds. Laney tried scowling him into silence. He was sexy in a coarse way that she didn't like to admit she found attractive.

"What?" he asked, turning his hands palms up in innocence. "Can't a guy be happy?"

"Working here? Gimme a break," she said.

"Hey, it's a living. What more do you want?"

Everything, she thought. Anything.

"I'm getting out of here," she said, thinking of the invitation she'd found. "For good."

"You don't want to do that. You'll miss me too much."

"I won't miss anything about this place, you included."

"When are you going to quit thinking you're too good for this place? For this work? Get over yourself, Laney. Quit trying to be someone you're not."

"Shut up. Can I help it if I think this is no kind of life?"

"You're right. It's only work," he went on. "What we do after—

that's life. You know what your problem is? You haven't figured out how to like the life you've got."

"If I learned to like this life, I'd shoot myself. You know what *your* problem is? You haven't figured out how to think big."

"Thinking gives me a headache. Hang out with me tonight. I know how to show you a good time. You'll see." His standard line. Joey invited her to do something at least once a week.

"I don't need to see. You go bowling, you drink beer, you go home, and you fool around."

"Not unless you come with me, I don't. C'mon, Laney. Whaddya say?"

He had a kind of goofy charm that actually tempted her for about two seconds. She reeled herself in with three simple words: "And then what? Then we get up the next morning and drag ourselves into work again?"

"Or maybe we hold each other and watch the sun come up and feel fantastic."

"Forget it." She turned her back on him and switched on the automated sorting rack, watching the finished clothing whir past.

Laney wanted to meet a man who would take her away from all this. Not a guy like Joey. And not some flaccid, self-important businessman or fast-talking gambler, but someone young, exciting, and handsome. The only way to do that was to find the places these people congregated—like tonight's gala at the Regency.

After work, she took the bus to downtown and reconnoitered the place like an army scout, noting the location of the ballroom and the restrooms, the public and service entrances. Then she headed home to get ready.

She had her looks. She knew this without vanity. She checked her appearance the way other people checked their bank balances. Wiping a circle in the steam-fogged bathroom mirror after her shower, she gave a curt nod of approval. She was still in the black.

For the gala fund-raiser, she'd chosen a red-and-silver gown of beaded silk with an Escada label inside. She had learned to recognize all the couture labels by reading glossy fashion magazines. Joey often teased her, saying if she had studied at school as hard as she studied those magazines, she could've gone to college.

Yeah, sure.

The dress, heavy on its padded hanger, belonged to one Amelia Barclay, a regular at McMullin's for years. Laney had never met Mrs. Barclay, who always sent the help to pick up and drop off her cleaning, but even so, Laney knew plenty about her. She knew when Mrs. Barclay came home from a cruise or a ski trip or a vacation to the tropics. She suspected Mrs. Barclay was single; there were never any men's clothes mixed in with hers. The address indicated money, maybe from an ex-husband. Maybe more than one.

Sometimes Laney made a game of constructing a person's life out of their cleaning. It didn't take much to imagine the wearer of a tuxedo redolent of cigar smoke and expensive aftershave, riding around town in a limo while sipping brandy, perhaps spilling a drop or two on the lapel. Or a debutante in her layers of crinoline and lace, poised in the doorway of the ballroom at the MGM Grand. Or the implication of an illicit smear of lipstick in a place it didn't belong.

She slipped the dress on over her Kmart lingerie. What did it matter what she wore underneath? It was the look on the outside that counted. She copied a hairstyle she'd seen in a magazine and slid her feet into strappy sandals that would be a dead giveaway if someone looked at them closely. But she would have to risk it. She took only one other item that properly belonged to her—a small satin evening clutch she'd been given on her eighteenth birthday. It hardly matched the luxury of the gown; she only hoped no one would look too closely. She slipped her ID, along with cab fare, a tube of lipstick, and the engraved invitation, into the clutch, and she was on her way.

Laney's heart sped up as the vehicle headed into town. She'd splurged on a taxi, not wanting to risk being seen driving herself in her secondhand Vega. Her palms were clammy, but she didn't let herself wipe them on the dress. To distract herself, she watched the flow of traffic and pedestrians outside. Taxis clogged the freeway interchange in a bright yellow surge, interrupted by the occasional panel van or tourist bus. Hired cars, like shiny black beetles, lined up at the portes-cochère of casino hotels, which sprouted like theme parks at each intersection. Laney was more interested in the private cars, glittering like jewels as they sped past. She pictured the intrepid drivers, exuding confidence as they navigated the freeways and busy streets.

You could tell a lot about a person by the car he drove, and Laney had made a study of this, much the way she had of clothing labels. A station wagon guy—forget it. He was like Joey, all about having fun and going nowhere. The sporty rides, like Jeeps, belonged to guys who were worried about taking risks but didn't want people to know it. A flashy red convertible? All style and no substance. Hybrids? Boring guys who thought they were saving the earth.

Laney herself was always on the lookout for cars like the Maybach, rare as a four-leaf clover. Or something from Italy, like a Ferrari that seemed as if it might sprout wings and take off flying with the push of a button. Men who drove those cars: They were the ones who intrigued her. A car like that belonged to a guy who could have anything he wanted.

The thought bolstered her determination to make the most of this evening. She *could* pull this off. She was determined to meet someone fabulous, someone rich.

At the hotel, she stood for a moment on the sidewalk, composing herself. She'd learned that the best policy was to walk into a place as though you owned it.

She couldn't help noticing the doorman's livery, which bore the glossy sheen of too much processing. Some people were such amateurs.

Posture was everything. She squared her shoulders, lifted her chin, and glided across the lobby toward a wide, carpeted staircase that swept upward to the mezzanine. At the base of the stairs was a sign pointing the way to the Vista Ballroom.

"Miss, excuse me," someone called, just as she was about to enter the room.

Laney's blood ran cold, but she kept her face expressionless as she turned. "Yes?"

"I think you dropped something." A waiter held out the white card with the invitation.

She nearly slumped with relief as she took it from him. "It must have slipped out of my purse."

He held her gaze for a moment. "Be careful, now."

The evening was everything Laney had hoped it would be—almost. She met people who talked jovially of the places they'd traveled and the people they'd met. When asked about herself, Laney gave vague answers; then she'd deflect the questions by asking some of her own. She felt so far away from her real life, from long hours at work and bills that needed paying. This, she thought, was something she wouldn't mind getting used to.

Waiters in crisp white coats circulated with trays full of fussily prepared hors d'oeuvres. She sampled a bite here and there, but found she didn't much care for the food. It never tasted as good as it looked. Besides, none of the other women appeared to be eating at all.

Men invited her to dance, and one of them, whose name was Grayson St. George, said he'd like to see her again. His suit was Armani or Baroni in a silk and viscose blend, and it had been tailored to fit. His body—thickly indulged but not unattractive—had the look of a guy who had once been athletic.

There was strolling and mingling through the ballroom. She eavesdropped on conversations about things that sounded foreign and exotic to her, the things classy people talked about, like travel (they never said "vacations") and the universities they had gone to, the condos and weekend places they had bought, or intended to buy. They smiled, but their laughter came in only brief, polite murmurs. Nobody burst into a belly laugh the way she and Joey did at work sometimes.

She went to the ladies' room—Ladies *Lounge*, it said on the door—as much to check it out as to use the facilities. Restrooms at classy places were often luxurious and interesting, and this one was no exception. There was a lounge area with mirrors and banquettes and an old-fashioned fringed fainting couch. Music piped softly through speakers in the ceiling. Laney set her clutch on the sink and washed her hands, then helped herself to a pristine, folded linen towel.

She leaned toward the mirror and fixed her lipstick. As she did, two women came in. "I've forgotten a comb," said the dark-haired one. "Amelia, can I borrow yours?"

The woman called Amelia handed a beaded evening bag to her friend. "Help yourself," she said, then smoothed a hand over her sleek blond hair, which she wore pulled back in a chignon. She did a double take when she noticed Laney.

"I'm sorry," she said, "I don't mean to stare, but that dress . . ."

Laney's heart skipped a beat. *Amelia.* Dear God. Was this Amelia *Barclay*? Laney had no choice but to brazen it out. "Do you like it?"

"Like it? I have the exact same gown."

Laney smiled, dying inside. "Then we have something in common."

The other woman didn't smile back. "I was told it was one of a kind."

"Really? So was I. It makes me wonder how many others were told the same thing." She tried not to rush through blotting her lipstick. "Have a nice evening," she said, and left—not too quickly, but she didn't waste any time either. Once outside the ladies' room, she decided it would be a good time to leave. She told herself she wasn't worried about Amelia Barclay putting two and two together. Still, she didn't want to hang around and risk it.

She descended the staircase with a vague sense of disappointment. It had been a lovely evening, but she hadn't encountered someone who could change her life. Grayson St. George had shown a tiny bit of promise, but she kept thinking about the fact that during the entire time she'd danced with him, she'd had to remind herself to smile.

A guy stood at the bottom of the stairs, watching her hurry down to the lobby. When she noticed him, Laney nearly tripped over the hem of her dress. As though summoned by her discontent and her yearning, he simply stood there, as if waiting for her. He flashed a smile that felt like a caress.

He was perfect, she thought, deliberately slowing down. The tux pants and white shirt he wore weren't new, hinting that he was a regular at this kind of social scene. He held his jacket negligently by one finger, slung over his shoulder, and his sleeves were rolled back to reveal forearms boasting a Saint-Tropez tan. He was as slender and handsome as a storybook prince, and he was looking right at her.

Laney was possessed by an instant sensation of . . . she couldn't quite put her finger on it. Recognition. *Possibility*. Here, finally, might be the answer to everything. In the space of a heartbeat, she could picture herself with this stranger, swept into a life she'd only ever dreamed about. And she didn't have to remind herself to smile.

"Leaving the party so soon?"

She eyed the shirt, loosened at the throat, the tie missing. "You've already left."

"Did you have a nice time?"

"Yes, thanks."

"You look great in that dress," he added. The sweep of his gaze warmed her—a turn-on. Some guys just had a knack for saying a lot with their eyes.

"Thanks," she said again, trying not to feel too nervous about Amelia Barclay, up in the ballroom. "I need to find a cab."

He hesitated, but only for a moment. "Let me give you a ride," he said. Another beat of hesitation. "I've got my car."

Now it was Laney's turn to hesitate. She felt the cold blast of the air-conditioning on her neck and heard the distant ding and clatter of slot machines in another part of the hotel. "I don't get in cars with strange men," she told him.

"Trevor Greenway," he said. "And you're . . . ?"

"Laney McMullin."

He walked with her across the lobby. Out on the sidewalk, there was a line for taxis, and even though it was dark, heat still pulsated in the air. "So we're not strangers anymore. My car's just down here." He led the way down a side street to a lot marked VALET ONLY. He saw her looking at the sign and said, "The valets take forever. It's quicker just to get the car myself." He took a key from his pocket. A moment later, one of the cars winked at them.

Laney couldn't stifle a gasp. A car she'd only seen pictures of was beckoning them. It was a Bentley Azure, long and sleek, rounded on the ends like an exotic carapace. It was every bit as much a sculpture as an automobile. She knew from her glossy magazines that only a few hundred were sold each year. It wasn't flashy; it didn't scream for attention. It was simply the most luxurious car in existence.

She sank into the leather embrace of the passenger seat. Trevor put the top down with the push of a button. She glanced over at him, watching the way his chiseled profile seemed etched against the false glow of the neon sky.

As if he felt her watching him, he turned to her. "I have a confession to make."

Married, she thought with a sinking heart. Because a guy like this was too good to be true.

"I confess that I don't want to take you home." That smile again. "We just met, Laney, but there's something about you. Something special. I'd love to spend more time with you."

"What did you have in mind?"

"How about a drive in the desert. Just a drive, Laney, with the music playing. What do you say?"

"I say I'm about to do something crazy," she admitted.

"That's my girl."

When he grinned at her, the last of her reservations melted away. She clicked her seat belt into place and off they went, gliding through the streets, onto the freeway, past the shadowy, tumble-weed-choked wildlife fences at the edge of the desert. The drive seemed to take only minutes, the Bentley sweeping along like a yacht. Her hair swirled back from her face. Sexy jazz slid from the stereo, and Laney smiled at her companion. Trevor. She'd wished for someone to take her away, and here he was. She'd found him.

There was no other explanation for this feeling that possessed her. It was like a drug, but utterly genuine, something she had never felt before. Something strong enough to last a lifetime.

He saw her looking at him, and lifted one side of his mouth in a grin. "You seem happy."

"I am. I'm glad I met you, Trevor."

He stopped at a dark overlook facing the amber glow of the city, in the distance. The desert smelled of piñon and purple sage, and a light wind offered a tease of relief from the heat. "How glad?" he asked, reclining his seat back.

Oh, those eyes of his. That smile. With exquisite gentleness, he took her hand, held it against his chest. Then he winnowed his fingers into her hair, skimming the pad of his thumb across her cheekbone as he leaned forward. Just that, and she began to forget who she was.

His kiss was soft, yet she could feel the subtle bite of his teeth on her lower lip, and with that, she knew the night was his.

She was careful with the gown as she slipped off her shoes and climbed over the console to straddle him.

Laney rode back to the city in a haze of contentment. It wasn't like her to go driving into the desert with a strange man. And it absolutely wasn't like her to have sex on the first date, and this wasn't even a date. But she had a feeling about Trevor Greenway. The moment she'd seen him in the hotel lobby, she'd imagined a future, one in which the cleaners was just an unpleasant memory.

As if reading her mind, he reached over and toyed with her hair, caressing her neck. "Ever feel like doing something totally crazy?"

"Didn't we just do that?" she asked with a laugh.

"I mean *totally* crazy."

Intrigued, she said, "What did you have in mind?"

"You got an ID on you?"

She held up her handbag. With a nod, he wheeled into the parking lot of a neon-lit building. A blazing sign read, SUDDENLY MARRIED WEDDING CHAPEL. MARRIAGE INFORMATION. OPEN 24 HRS.

He shut off the ignition and turned to her. "This is what I had in mind. This kind of crazy." He jerked his head toward the chapel. "So, Laney MacMullin. Are you game?"

Her mouth dried and her pulse bolted into overdrive. She looked at him, felt the deep cushiony embrace of the Bentley's passenger seat. "Why not?" she said.

She felt giddy as they drove away from the chapel. This *was* crazy. It was also a dream come true.

Trevor guzzled champagne from the bottle that came in the wedding package they'd bought at the chapel. "Where to, Mrs. Greenway?" he asked.

For a moment, she was speechless with the thrill of hearing him call her that. "To our future together," she replied, the roof of stars sliding overhead like a meteor shower.

He punched the accelerator, then threw back his head and laughed, the sound riding the night wind in their wake. A high, clear note unfurled from the stereo.

She saw him flick a glance into the rearview mirror. That sound wasn't coming from the stereo after all. The flashing lights of the police cruiser turned the night an eerie shade of blue. The light imbued his face with chilly calculation.

"Trevor?"

The car's big engine surged as he accelerated again. Dear God, was he going to make the police chase him?

Apparently thinking better of it, he signaled, gliding across the lanes to the shoulder of the freeway. With his free hand, he passed her the champagne bottle. "Ditch this if you can." Then he handed her a cell phone. "You got a lawyer?"

"What?"

"Call him. Call your lawyer. Tell him your husband's in a bind."

For a wild moment, Laney panicked. Maybe Amelia Barclay had somehow realized the truth about her dress. She whipped a glance back to see a state trooper striding toward them, a clipboard in one hand, his other hand on his holster. Oh God, thought Laney. Ohgodohgod . . .

"I need you to step out of the car, sir," the trooper said. He barely looked at Laney.

Jerky with nerves, Trevor obeyed. Laney felt affronted on his behalf. He'd done nothing wrong. He'd had a little champagne, but he wasn't drunk. How dare the trooper treat him like a criminal?

Call your lawyer. He couldn't know that Laney didn't have a lawyer. She worked at the Kleen & Brite; why on earth would she have a lawyer? Trevor couldn't know that either.

Surely Trevor had a lawyer, she thought. Guys like him always had a lawyer on Speed Dial. The thought struck a spark of hope. That was it, she thought, flipping open the phone he'd handed her. His lawyer would be on his list of contacts.

She frowned down at the screen. Was she reading the display correctly?

"This can't be your phone," she said, though he wasn't close enough to hear. She wanted to be confused about this. Oh, how she wanted to.

Clutching the back of the seat, she turned around to look. The trooper had him spread-eagled over the squad car, hands cuffed behind his back.

Laney pressed herself back against the seat, noticing that a line of sequins had come loose on the dress. A sinking feeling weighted her stomach. She checked the screen of the phone again, just to make sure.

The palm-size screen read ACME VALET PARKING.

Bump in the Night

Stephanie Bond

Don't ask me why I let my ex-boyfriend in at two AM. I knew better. But he woke me from a dead sleep, pounding on my apartment door, yelling like Marlon Brando. With a groan I realized that he'd used my code to get into the building. I guess I should've been glad he hadn't used the key I'd given him a long time ago and simply walked in.

Two of my neighbors—Mr. McFelty and Mrs. Bingham—had stuck their heads out in the hall bellowing for him to shut the *bleep* up. He had returned with a *bleepity-bleep* of his own. When the obscenities escalated to the point of insulting ancestry, I peeled my eye from the peephole that rendered Daniel Hale's face bulbous (but still handsome, god*bleep*it) and unlocked the dead bolt.

"Daniel, it's late and I have to be at the office early," I said through a crack. "What are you doing here?"

My neighbors shouted parting expletives and slammed their doors.

Daniel, looking lethal in a rumpled tuxedo, gave me one of those heart-bending smiles that used to make my underwear fly off. "I was missing you, Renni."

That's me, Renni Greenfield, dressed in pajamas with penguins on them, my sexuality having been shelved for months. "Daniel, you need to go home."

"I'm drunk," he slurred. "You don't want me to kill myself or someone else driving home, do you?"

"No."

"Then let me spend the night. I'll crash on the couch and be gone before you wake up. Please?"

I sighed, my resolve crumbling like the wall of a gingerbread house. I hated Daniel for cheating on me with Leora, the legs-for-days paralegal in our office, but I truly didn't want to see his Jag accordianed into a Peachtree Street telephone pole on the morning news while Atlanta commuters honked at the delay caused by extracting his body. And even though I wouldn't have minded inheriting one or two of his big-money clients, I knew I couldn't handle the extra workload I'd get if something happened to the cad.

So . . . I let him in and diverted him from my bedroom, reminding him of the way to the couch. He pouted, but staggered toward my tiny living room, shedding clothes along the way. By the time I'd fetched linens from the bathroom, he was naked and sprawled on my sofa. Then he curled his hand around my wrist, and before I knew it, I was naked too.

I reasoned that he owed me.

Unlike most men, Daniel's performance seemed to improve under the influence of alcohol, but afterward he was asleep instantly. It made for an awkward dismount, but I managed. He was too far gone to move, and curling up next to him in the five inches left on the couch was unappealing, so I simply went back to my bed and fell into an exhausted sleep, postponing regret until the morning.

When my alarm went off at 6:30 AM, I hit the SNOOZE button twice. I hadn't heard Daniel leave, but then I was a notoriously sound sleeper. I dragged myself out of bed and headed toward the kitchen in pursuit of coffee. When I rounded the corner and saw Daniel's arm hanging over the edge of the couch, I frowned—so much for his being gone by the time I woke up.

Then I saw the bloody knife sticking out of his bare chest.

It wasn't the kind of "gone" I'd expected.

Forget law school. I'd learned *from* TV trials that guilt or innocence was usually decided by the jury on the basis of the 911 call, which, of course, would be taped. So when I called, I spared no emotion—not a stretch because I was only a couple of short breaths away from full-blown hysteria. When the operator asked if the stabbed man on my couch was dead, I assured her he was. When she asked if I knew who'd stabbed him, I said no. When she asked whose residence it was, I said mine. When she asked if an intruder could still be there, I panicked.

Why hadn't I thought of that?

"I don't know. I didn't look." And at the moment I was riveted to my penguin pj's lying on the floor, next to the couch, spattered with Daniel's blood in an arterial pattern. I glanced toward the front door, which was closed, the dead bolt locked. While my mind raced for an explanation, my gaze bounced around the apartment to places where a murderer might be hiding. Under the desk, in the pantry, in the shower. "I don't see anyone," I said into the phone.

"Is there somewhere safe you can go until the police arrive? Maybe to a neighbor's?"

"I have to get dressed," I murmured, then flinched when I realized that I was saying every wrong thing.

The operator agreed that I should get dressed, but warned me not to touch anything and to stay on the line until the police arrived. I pulled on sweats with the cordless phone crooked between ear and shoulder, breathing like a sprinter. My normally well-ordered mind was operating like a Roomba vacuum cleaner, pinging off every barrier and heading in another direction. The operator continued to ask questions—How did I know the deceased? What was his full name? Where was I when the stabbing occurred?—but I didn't answer. I was already thinking like a criminal, reviewing my alibi (sleeping), and brainstorming about how I could shore it up before the uniforms arrived. I unlocked the dead bolt and cracked open the window in my bedroom even though it was on the second floor and the only way anyone could have reached it was with a ladder. Ditto for the window in the living room.

"Ma'am, don't touch anything," the operator repeated, and I realized that the sounds of all my movements had been caught on tape. I could picture a prosecutor re-creating the noises for a jury. *Here she's unlocking the door, here she's opening a window.* I heard sirens, so I disconnected the call before I incriminated myself further.

The next two hours brought a flurry of bodies through the door—police, EMTs, a medical examiner. A slender black female detective sat with me in the bathroom—me on the lid of the commode and her on a chair draped with the white shirt I'd worn to work yesterday. Her name was Detective Salyers.

"Miss Greenfield, you had sex with the victim?"

"I told you, yes." I was growing irritated with the repetitive questioning, primarily because I was paranoid about saying something wrong. The reason I'd opted for real estate law versus criminal law was my lousy public-speaking skills. "Like I said, Daniel knocked on my door around two in the morning. He was drunk and asked if he could crash on the couch. He was disturbing my neighbors, so I decided it was easier to let him in than to try to get him to leave."

"Had this happened before?"

I nodded. Daniel had been fond of late-night episodes in which he'd banged on the door as a prelude to banging *me*. "But not for months." Not since he'd dumped me.

"So you let him in, and then you had sex?"

"Yes. Then he passed out and I went back to bed. When my alarm went off, I got up and found him, dead."

"You didn't hear anything after you went to bed?"

"No."

"And nothing is missing."

"That I know of. Of course, Daniel could've had something valuable on him."

"His wallet, cash, and gold watch are intact."

Damn—so much for robbery.

"So after you went to bed, someone entered your apartment and stabbed Mr. Hale to death for no apparent reason?"

"It appears so."

"How did they get in?"

"Like I said, I left the door unlocked." The lie was getting easier, sounding more plausible.

"Someone intent on doing harm entered your apartment through a door that you happened to leave unlocked, walked right past you sleeping in your bedroom, killed Mr. Hale on the living room couch, and left?"

"They could've gotten in through a window," I offered.

"Both windows raise only a few inches, for safety. An adult couldn't have squeezed through."

"Oh. Right."

The detective blinked slowly. "Miss Greenfield, the knife in his chest matches the other knives in your kitchen."

"So the murderer used one of my knives."

"Are we going to find your fingerprints on the knife?"

"Possibly, if it came from my kitchen." I pushed to my feet. "I'd really like to take a shower."

Detective Salyers stood too. "I'm afraid I can't let you do that. You're going to have to come to the station with me, Miss Greenfield."

I closed my eyes and sighed. "I need to make a call first."

She extended her cell phone. "Use mine."

"I came as soon as I could."

I lifted my head from a sticky wood table scarred with key-carved initials to see Grant Bellamy standing in the doorway. I had maintained my composure to this point, but when I saw that Grant was wearing the navy blue crested blazer I had bought him for one of our two wedding anniversaries, I melted into a big gobbet of goo. Gentle brown eyes, severely clipped hair, and triple-pleated chinos that I had once found so wearisome suddenly embodied strength and security.

"There, there," he said, rubbing my back as I clung to him. "We'll get this all straightened out."

And even though I'd heard—and seen—him say the same thing to serial killers that he'd defended, I believed him.

"Let's sit," Grant said, guiding me back to the chair.

I was overcome with humiliation that the first time I'd talked to Grant in the three years since we'd divorced was to ask for his help to ward off an imminent charge for murdering my ex-lover. I felt compelled to make some kind of small talk.

"Thanks for coming," I said. "How have you been?"

He smiled. "The same—fine."

That was Grant, a constant term in the nonlinear equation of life. "And your folks?" His father had had a cancer scare when Grant and I were married. I felt petty for not having stayed in touch.

"They're fine. Now tell me what happened, Renni."

With excruciating unease, I relayed the sordid details of Daniel's arrival, our coupling, and his murder just as I'd recited them to the detective (including the lie about the unlocked door). But if I thought that my postdivorce coital activities would upset Grant, I was wrong. His expression remained concerned, but untouched, as if I'd called to ask for his help with a flat tire. With jarring clarity I realized that my law school sweetheart, the man who'd loved me more than I'd deserved, was over me. It was salt on my selfish open wound.

"What's going to happen to me?" I murmured, clasping his hand. I knew, but I wanted to hear his comforting spin.

"You'll probably be questioned again, then released. You don't have a record, and you're an officer of the court. No charges will be filed until the forensics are processed, which will take a day or two."

Until the forensics are processed. Then it hit me—Grant actually thought I'd killed Daniel.

"That will give us time to get our ducks in a row," he said, patting my hand, the one that had once worn his wedding ring. I was still too stunned to speak. If Grant thought I was capable of murder, I didn't stand a chance convincing anyone else I was innocent.

"I'd recommend that you go back to work tomorrow," he continued. "It's important that you maintain some kind of routine."

A knock on the door sounded. The detective was back, with two bottles of water, which she offered to me and to Grant. We both declined. My head was spinning.

"When can my . . . client go home?" Grant asked, and I had the strangest feeling he'd had to stop himself from saying "wife."

"Soon," Detective Salyers said. "Miss Greenfield's apartment has been processed, but I'd like to ask her a few more questions."

"Go ahead," Grant said. "Renni has nothing to hide."

Salyers looked doubtful, then turned to me. "Mr. Hale was wearing a tux when he arrived at your place. Did he say where he'd been?"

"He didn't say, but there was a charity dinner at the Ritz last night that the partners of the firm attended."

Salyers looked puzzled. "You weren't invited?"

"I'm not a partner."

"I meant as a date. I assume guests were allowed."

"No, I wasn't invited."

"Who did Mr. Hale take as his date?"

I shrugged. "You'll have to ask someone who attended the event."

"We did. Mr. Hale took a paralegal in your office." The detective looked at her notes. "Leora Painter. The same woman he began dating when the two of you broke up, I'm told."

So they'd already interviewed her coworkers. "Actually, Daniel was dating Leora before he and I broke up," I supplied.

"Your cheating ex-boyfriend shows up on your doorstep fresh from a date with the woman he cheated on you with, wanting to spend the night with you. Must've stung."

I wasn't sure what would make me look worse—saying I'd been angry over the late-night booty call or saying I'd been pleased that Daniel had chosen to spend the night with me versus Leora. I said nothing.

"Your theory cuts both ways," Grant pointed out. To me he sounded amiable, as if he were offering Salyers a piece of apple pie. "Maybe the Painter woman followed Hale to Renni's and stabbed him out of jealousy."

I perked up.

Salyers acknowledged his remark with a nod. "We've already questioned Miss Painter, but we didn't see a reason to hold her."

I deflated.

"Miss Greenfield, can you think of anyone who'd want to hurt Mr. Hale?"

"No. But Daniel and I haven't been seeing each other for a while, so I wouldn't know everything going on in his life."

"To your knowledge, was he involved in anything illegal—drugs or gambling?"

I wracked my brain for a bone to toss her way, but as far as I knew, Daniel's only vice was blondes. And redheads. And brunettes. "No."

Salyers studied me for a long time, then pushed away from the table. "We're done here, but don't leave town. How can I reach you?"

Grant extended a card to the detective. "She'll be staying with me."

Even though it was out of character for Grant to speak for me, I didn't argue with him because I'd been at the police station all afternoon and still hadn't had a shower. I could smell Daniel's cologne on my skin, and the cloying stench of it had driven me to gnawing my nails down to the quick, a habit I'd kicked in grade school. I was grateful—giddy, even—for Grant's offer of hospitality. I couldn't bear the thought of staying in my apartment tonight, and a hotel seemed too sterile.

Grant took me back to my place to pack a bag and grab my briefcase. Someone had turned off the air conditioner, leaving my apartment stifling and pungent with the odors of garbage that needed to be emptied and other, more foreign smells. While I gathered my things, Grant studied the crime scene. I couldn't bring myself to walk into the living room—the bloodstains alone were burned into my brain. I wondered if I'd be able to live here again . . . assuming I didn't get sent to prison.

One of my fears was allayed rather quickly—I met both Mrs. Bingham and Mr. McFelty, the neighbors who'd exchanged expletives with Daniel, as we were leaving. Mr. McFelty looked bleary-eyed, but kindly asked how I was handling things. I felt a pang of regret because the man worked three jobs and last night hadn't been the first time that Daniel had awakened my neighbors. On top of everything else, I felt as if I'd unwittingly exposed them to a criminal element. Mrs. Bingham, the resident cook, patted my arm with an oven-mitted hand and managed to pass the card of her cousin in Marietta who specialized in crime scene cleanup. "Vivian did a terrific job when Roy in the apartment upstairs shot himself last year. The new renter says she can't even tell where the drywall was repaired and painted."

I winced. Roy had been a troubled young man who'd blasted heavy metal music and apparently had taken the violent lyrics to heart. It was the music, looping over and over, that had led the superintendent to his grisly discovery. If Vivian had extricated brain matter from the ceiling, a little blood on the upholstery and carpet would be a cinch.

"Free air freshener," Mrs. Bingham added cheerfully.

"Er, thanks. I'll call."

Grant walked up and saw the business card in my hand. "That can wait. I need to get our own forensics person in here."

That made sense, of course. I marveled over how all of my training and know-how seemed to have moved to the recesses of my mind in the wake of needing legal advice rather than doling it out. I informed Mrs. Bingham of where I was staying and told her she could have my daily *Atlanta Journal-Constitution* for the time being.

"If that friend of yours stops by," Mrs. Bingham said, "I'll let her know that you're going to be gone for a while."

"Friend?"

"The pretty blonde," the older woman offered. "She was here yesterday asking which apartment was yours. She didn't give her name, but she said she was supposed to meet you for lunch and had gotten delayed in traffic. Said she wanted to slide a message under your door."

I froze. There was no blonde friend, no lunch, no message. But I had an inkling of who it could have been. "Was the woman tall?" As in long, lethal legs.

"Why yes, she was quite tall. And slender, like a model."

Leora Painter. "What time was that, Mrs. Bingham?"

"Around noon. I remember because I was coming back from checking the mail."

I said good-bye, then rushed to fill Grant in on the presumed identity of the woman. "It must have happened like you said—she followed Daniel here after the charity dinner and killed him! And framed *me*!"

Unfortunately, Grant didn't share my excitement. "But the detective said the Painter woman didn't raise their suspicions."

"So she's a good actress. It's too much of a coincidence that Leora is *at* my apartment the same day that Daniel is murdered *in* my apartment."

He lifted his hand and rubbed my jawline with his thumb in a comforting gesture that I realized I'd missed since our split. "Let's let the police handle it, okay, Renni?"

"You'll tell the detective to look into it?"

"You know I will."

I climbed into my car and followed Grant to the small house in Virginia Highland that we'd once shared. As I parked in the driveway behind him, a wave of nostalgia swept over me. The daylilies I'd planted around the mailbox had multiplied and were well maintained. The tarnished birdbath that Grant had hated from the day I'd dragged it home from an antiques market was filled with seed on one side, fresh water on the other. He'd even painted the shutters the bright yellow I'd always wanted.

I was suddenly nervous standing behind him as he unlocked the front door. I felt small and selfish, my heart burning over the way I'd abruptly ended our marriage mid-sentence and for no tangible reason, leaving him openmouthed and broken. It wasn't him, I'd said, it was me. I couldn't admit that I'd found his fastidiousness suffocating, his organization unnerving. I'd known those things about him when we dated, but after the wedding, his compulsive behavior seemed to intensify. I found myself watching him and watching myself . . . and found him watching me as well, silently disapproving every time I opened a box of crackers on the wrong end or snorted when I laughed. The affection I'd once felt for him had withered under the tension. I had begun to understand how husbands and wives could snap and murder the other in his or her sleep. I'd had to get out of there.

"Welcome back," Grant said, swinging open the door.

I stepped inside, to see the same leather furniture situated the same way, the same silk floral arrangements on the same end tables, the same botanical prints hanging on the same walls. I half-expected to see a pair of my sandals tucked under the chair where I used to sit watching Grant watch me.

"I love what you've done with the place," I joked, and he laughed, an unbridled noise that surprised me.

"I'll sleep in the guest room," I said, then added, "if it's still a guest room."

"Everything is pretty much the same as when you were here before," he said, as if I'd been a visitor then too.

"Do you mind if I take a shower?"

"Go ahead. The soap you like is in the vanity."

I didn't ask why that was—it seemed perfectly natural that Grant would anticipate my needs. Besides, I was single-mindedly focused on getting to the shower. Once there, frothy with ginger-orange soap, I lost it and cried like a little girl. For whatever reason—sex, companionship, or sheer laziness—Daniel Hale had been compelled to visit me last night . . . and was dead because of it.

"Be careful about what you say at work today," Grant told me over morning oatmeal. I wondered if his cholesterol was still high, his arteries clogged with the stress of a disorderly world.

I set down my spoon. "Grant, I didn't kill Daniel."

"Of course you didn't," he replied easily, then took a drink from his coffee cup. "But until you're cleared, anything you say can be misconstrued. The important thing is that people see you getting back to normal."

I squinted at him. "I can't simply behave as if nothing has happened. A coworker, a man I also used to date, was murdered in my apartment. Don't you think everyone would expect me to be traumatized?"

"I didn't realize you got that attached to people," Grant murmured.

A direct hit. It felt good, actually. I'd often regretted not giving Grant the chance to tell me what he'd thought of me for walking out—it would have hurt less than living with the fact that I'd robbed him of even that satisfaction. "I wasn't in love with Daniel," I said evenly, "but it's not every day that someone gets murdered on my couch."

"I saw you and him together once."

I blinked. "When?"

"A few months ago, in a restaurant. You looked happy."

I wiped my mouth with one of the cloth napkins that Grant preferred—I was more of a paper-towel girl myself. "Grant . . . I'm sorry."

"For what?"

"For leaving you with no explanation. You deserved better."

He shrugged. "Water under the bridge. Right now let's concentrate on getting through this mess."

That you created. His unspoken words hung in the air, next to the light fixture with the little shades that had tiny, uniform ducks circling the edge. It was true. If I hadn't been so susceptible to Daniel's charms even after he'd cheated on me, I wouldn't be sitting here eating steel-cut oats with my former husband in my former breakfast nook. The surprising thing was . . . it wasn't so bad. Well, except for Daniel being dead. But the knowledge that Grant could forgive me, to the point of defending me, made me feel humble and philosophical, and gave me the strength to face my boss and my coworkers.

Unfortunately, Leora Painter was the first coworker I saw walking in from the parking garage. The woman did a double take before falling into stride slightly in front of me.

"I'm surprised to see you here," she said, then stabbed the button for the elevator.

"Maybe we can have that missed lunch," I suggested sweetly.

"My neighbor said you stopped by my apartment the day before yesterday. Funny, but I don't remember us making plans."

She turned narrowed eyes on me. "Nice try. But I gave the police the text message I got from you to meet you there because you wanted to tell me something about Daniel. Little did I know it was a ploy to get me out of the way so you two could have a quickie rendezvous."

I gaped at her as the elevator doors opened. "I didn't send you a text message. There was no rendezvous."

"Whatever." She stepped into the elevator, then held up her arm to prevent my entry. "I think you'd better wait for the next one."

I did, if only to digest the information that I had allegedly sent Leora a text message to meet me. I pulled out my PDA and, to my horror, found that message in my sent folder amid other business and personal messages. In a panic, I deleted the message while my mind churned for an explanation. The device typically sat on my desk in my doorless office, accessible to anyone who happened by. And hadn't I read somewhere that anyone with a gadget from the cable company could hack into someone's PDA within a half-mile radius?

I was sweating copiously as I made my way to my tiny office. I tried to meet everyone's cagey eye contact with a mournful—and innocent—smile while scrutinizing the foot-traffic patterns in the vicinity. Out of about fifty employees, I deduced that half of them could have been in or around my office without raising suspicion: everyone from Daniel's two partners in the firm to the roving coed intern whose eyes were red rimmed. Julie had been crushing on Daniel, I recalled, and made a mental note to tell Detective Salyers when I next spoke to her.

The mood was solemn but busy as everyone tried to recover from the office being closed most of the day before after hearing the news of Daniel's demise. I tensed when I saw Sarah Finn, Daniel's secretary, heading my way. She was an unmarried, scrupulous woman approaching fifty, and the only fool she suffered was Daniel. I exhaled when she handed me one of the two cups of hot green tea that she carried.

"I thought you could use this," she soothed. "How are you holding up?"

I sipped. "Still trying to absorb everything. I didn't know what kind of reception to expect here."

"Mr. Wallace called us together yesterday morning before he closed the office and reminded everyone that you were presumed innocent until proven otherwise."

Nice of him, I conceded. "Sarah, did Daniel have any enemies?"

She dunked her teabag up and down. "Like I told the police, from knowing Daniel, I'd say his murder had to have been motivated by lust. It's no secret that he was a whoremonger."

The tea scalded my tongue. I waited for the prim woman to burst into flames for using such raw language.

She gave me a contrite little smile. "No offense."

"None thaken," I murmured thickly.

Rick Wallace, one of the remaining two partners, rapped on the glass wall of my office and stuck his graying head inside. "Good morning, Renni."

"There've been better," I returned.

He inclined his head, but it was clear he didn't want to engage in small talk or assurances. "We're having a memorial service for Daniel tomorrow morning in the chapel at the church across the street. Sarah, I need to talk to you as soon as possible about reassigning Daniel's cases to Eric."

"I'd be happy to help pick up the slack," I offered.

"We'll see," he said without looking at me. Sarah followed him out.

I tried to pretend it was any other workday, but it was impossible not to think about Daniel at every turn. In my desk drawers were matchbooks from restaurants we'd gone to. In the break room, by the coffee machine, sat his Vanderbilt University mug. I walked by his office once. Eric North, the attorney who presumably had inherited Daniel's cases, was inside with Leora Painter, their heads and hips close. But when they looked up, Leora pinned me with a glare.

When I got back to my office, my phone was ringing. I sank into my chair and picked up the receiver, hoping to be immersed in a hairy real estate legal issue, something that would bend my mind away from the murder matter. But it was Grant.

"How's it going?" he asked.

"It's awkward, but I'm hanging in." Then I remembered the damning text message that I'd stupidly deleted. "I have some information . . . and a confession to make."

A shadow fell across my desk. I looked up to see Detective Salyers standing there holding a document that I recognized as a search warrant. And from the pointed look she gave me, I knew she'd overheard my last comment.

"Standard procedure," Grant assured me over a dinner of grilled fish and mixed vegetables. Grant could stoke a mean grill and had done all the cooking when we were married. "I would expect the police to search your office, and Hale's too."

"They took my PDA. I shouldn't have erased that text message."

"Probably not," he agreed. "But don't worry."

Nice try. I lay awake that night in the guest bedroom reliving all the mistakes I'd made in my life, including abandoning my marriage. I hadn't been wholly happy here with Grant, but I'd wanted to be. He had loved me, and wasn't that worth something? Maybe a counselor could have helped us . . . or maybe if I'd been honest with Grant about how claustrophobic I'd felt. . . .

I wiped my eyes. I realized now that the sense of freedom I'd felt after the divorce, like a balloon being cut from a child's too-tight grasp, was actually the sensation of being afloat and bumping along the horizon, lost.

I heard a noise at the door and when the knob turned, my heart catapulted to my throat. Grant stuck his head inside, his glasses askew and his hair ruffled.

"Is something wrong?" I asked, sitting up.

"Just checking on you," he said softly. "I didn't mean to wake you."

"You didn't. I can't sleep."

"Try to rest, you need your strength." He started to retreat.

"Grant? Stay with me?"

He walked over to the bed and sat down, stretched his legs out on the mattress, next to me, and leaned against the headboard. He sandwiched my hand between his. "I'll stay until you fall asleep."

I'd been a fool to run from this man's love, and I was ashamed that it had taken something so sordid to bring me to my senses. I deserved to be tossed in the clink for stupidity alone. I exhaled against Grant's pajamas' leg, repentant.

When I woke the next morning, I felt more rested than I had in months. The spot next to me was cool, but I heard Grant in the kitchen.

When I shuffled in, he was whistling under his breath.

"You're in a good mood," I ventured behind him.

He turned and smiled. "It's nice to have you here." Then he sobered. "Even under these circumstances. Do you want me to go to the memorial service with you?"

I shook my head. After last night's revelation, I was feeling too vulnerable to ask anything more of Grant.

"The police will be there," he warned.

"Surely they won't arrest me at a funeral," I said with a little laugh.

"Probably not," he agreed, although by the tone of his voice I could tell that he was more worried than he'd previously revealed.

"Did your forensics people go through my apartment?"

"Yes. Other than one unidentified fingerprint, it's all you, Renni."

At the church, the laser stares of my coworkers penetrated my skin as the minister talked about justice in the afterlife even as justice on earth seemed elusive. Guilt oozed out of my pores. Instead of reflecting on Daniel's life and his good deeds, which were ticked off as if Saint Peter himself were taking notes, all I could think of was how Daniel had manipulated so many people, and the law, for his own selfish ends. How he had plowed through hearts and beds with no regard for the outcome.

And what kind of person did it make me that I'd gone back for seconds?

I started to cry, great guffawing sobs for the random senselessness of his death and of my life. Faces turned to glare. Only Sarah Finn, Daniel's assistant, was kind, taking my arm and leading me out of the church and into the parking lot where she lent me a tissue purse pack.

"Nice performance," a voice behind us said.

I turned to see Detective Salyers standing there.

"Will you excuse us?" she asked Sarah. After Sarah was out of earshot, I steeled myself for the handcuffs. Instead Salyers removed her sunglasses. "Feeling guilty, Miss Greenfield?"

"Feeling sad."

"Sad enough to make a confession?"

"No. Have you questioned everyone in the office?"

"Finishing up today."

"You might want to ask Leora Painter about the message she told my neighbor she was going to slip under my door as a ruse to find out which apartment was mine."

"I will." Then she angled her head. "The intern at the office, Julie Sun, told me that you and Miss Painter used to be friends."

"I thought so. I was wrong."

"Has Miss Painter ever been inside your apartment?"

"No."

"So you can't explain why her fingerprints would be on a book-end in your living room?"

I felt my mouth open, then close. "She was there. She killed him."

"Maybe. Or maybe you brought home something from the office that she touched and planted it. Or maybe you and Miss Painter are still friends, thinking that if you point the finger at each other, that you'll both get away with murder."

I heard my inner lawyer's voice whisper to stop talking now.

"Miss Greenfield, are you still staying with your ex-husband?"

"I was thinking I might go back to my apartment tonight."

"Just so I know where to find you." Salyers walked away.

The others were emerging from the church, heads down and hands in pockets as they headed for their vehicles. Julie the red-eyed intern watched me nervously. The partners kept their gazes averted, but their body language told me that I should be looking for another job. Leora Painter and Eric North hadn't sat together during the service but now their bodies converged. I stood there until they passed me. Haughtiness twisted Leora's face: She was glad Daniel was dead. I wanted to tackle her, press my thumbs against her eyeballs until she confessed. Or had Eric killed Daniel so that he could have Daniel's clients *and* Leora?

Crazily, I felt a pang of jealously. What would it feel like to have someone so madly in love with you that they would commit murder? The idea pinged a chord in my subconscious . . . as if I'd once humored that very thought, the thought of killing someone for love—for lust—but had buried it in a grave of unwanted memories.

A sudden headache bloomed . . . foggy sensations of a violent scene unfolding . . . a dream? A remembered scene from a disturbing movie? Had I heard Daniel being killed?

Or had I done it?

I walked to my car on elastic legs and drove to the office, trying on, as I would a hat, the idea of murdering Daniel, moving it from side to side and ultimately deciding that it was all wrong.

Still, the possibility rendered me numb. I kept picturing Daniel lying on my couch, blood everywhere, but it was like sorting through childhood memories. Did I remember it because I'd been there when it happened, or did I *think* I remembered it because I'd seen a picture after the fact?

Breathless, I called Mrs. Bingham's cousin (The Crime Scene Clean Queen, Refer Us and Get Some Green!). Cousin Vivian was the chatty sort, with a vivacious voice that had me imagining a woman in white Capri pants and a tiara removing blood from my upholstery while she yakked with her kids on her cell phone. She'd been expecting me to call, she said, and went over the options. She could visit the "site" and give me an estimate, or if it was just a matter of blood, she could go ahead and clean it on the spot. My dwellers' insurance would pay for it. She would get the key from the superintendent and be finished before I got home. The only question was what kind of free air freshener I wanted.

I opted for "ocean breeze," in honor of all the times that Daniel had promised to take me somewhere exotic. (Strangely, she didn't offer "parfum de takeout and sleepover.")

I spent the rest of the day walking into corners of furniture and moving papers around on my desk. Detective Salyers moved in and out of my line of vision, talking to everyone who sat in the vicinity of my office, while scrupulously avoiding me. She spent an inordinate amount of time with Julie the intern, the woman who had inferred that Leora and I were friends. Grant called me twice. I didn't answer because I was afraid I might confess, and he didn't leave a message. I was still sifting through the images in my head, hoping to explain them away. I wanted to wait until I saw my apartment before deciding whether or not to go back to Grant's. Maybe returning to the scene of the crime would help to reconcile some of these jagged feelings.

Then I frowned. . . . Didn't psychopaths feel compelled to return to the scene of the crime?

If not for the ocean breeze air freshener, one wouldn't have known that anything gruesome had taken place in my living room. I stood looking down at the striped sofa and patterned area rug, trying to find shadows of Daniel's blood, like a gruesome game. All traces of him had been removed. I wondered vaguely as I stared at Vivian's business card on my kitchen counter if she could somehow remove the ugly images from my head. I sprawled on my bed and closed my eyes, trying to remember someone sneaking past my bedroom. Leora? Eric?

Or was I repressing memories of doing something so horrible that I couldn't bring myself to remember it? I had the capacity to hurt people—take Grant, for instance.

My doorbell rang, and when I looked through the peephole, I had a sense of déjà vu. The last time I'd looked through the peephole, Daniel had been standing on the other side.

This time it was Grant.

Had I conjured him up simply by thinking about him?

I swung open the door and knew instantly that something was wrong. His pallor was gray, his mouth pinched.

"Grant? How did you know I was here?"

"I took a chance and saw your car in the parking lot."

"What's wrong?"

"Leora Painter has been arrested and charged with Hale's murder."

I went limp and leaned into him. "But that's great news."

"Not really. She admits she was in your apartment the night before last, but insists that Daniel was dead when she got here. She passed a polygraph, and . . ."

"And?"

"And the police are on their way. They're going to arrest you too Renni."

I leaned harder. *"No."*

"I'm here for you," he murmured into my hair. I could feel his hands shaking on my shoulders. "I didn't mean for this to happen."

I froze. Something in the tone of his voice, in his body language, set off sirens in my head. Disparate events converged: the fact that Grant had seen me with Daniel . . . had been so quick to come to my defense . . . that the house had been eerily ready for my return . . . that I'd been shown the error of leaving him.

I pulled back, alarmed that he'd somehow maneuvered his way inside the doorway. "How did you get into the building just now?"

Grant frowned. "I followed one of your neighbors inside."

Had he been following me? Watching me? "How did you know that the man you saw me with at the restaurant was Daniel, the same man who was killed?"

"I just assumed it was the same man."

The knives . . . one of the few household things I'd taken with me when I'd left Grant. Had he found it especially ironic to use one of them to kill Daniel? I'd wondered what it would feel like to have someone commit murder for me, and the prospect stalled my vital signs.

"Renni, are you okay?"

"Get away from me!" I stumbled backward, into the hallway, panic choking me. Mrs. Bingham was emerging from her apartment, holding a steaming covered casserole dish and heading for Mr. McFelty's door. I flung myself in her direction. When she saw me, she lit up like a marquee.

"How are you, dear? Vivian said your place cleaned up beautifully."

"Mrs. Bingham, I know who killed Daniel. The police are on their way."

She patted me with her free hand. "Don't worry, dear. The man deserved to die."

Grant rushed up behind me and I positioned myself between them, equally confused and repelled. "What?"

"A jury will never convict me," Mrs. Bingham said matter-of-factly. "The man was a nuisance, just like the fellow who lived upstairs, blasting his music at all hours. Poor Mr. McFelty works three jobs and he needs his sleep. I thought you got rid of him, but then he showed up again, shouting like a maniac. Young people have no respect, but a jury will understand."

"How . . . how did you get inside my apartment?" I asked.

"I lifted a master key from the super once when I delivered a green bean casserole."

While I processed her inexplicable confession, Grant stepped in front of me and eyed Mrs. Bingham's casserole as if it contained a grenade. "You killed Daniel Hale *because he made too much noise?*"

"And the man who lived upstairs," I added, horrified. "She shot him."

Mrs. Bingham made a face. "That was ugly, though. I used a knife this time. Less mess."

"For the cleaning service," I murmured.

She smiled. "Vivian gives me a two-hundred-dollar referral fee. That's a lot of money for someone on a fixed income."

After the police led Mrs. Bingham away, Detective Salyers filled in the holes. The intern Julie had confessed to using my PDA to send Leora the message to keep both of us busy while she and Daniel went to a hotel for "lunch." Leora suspected he was cheating on her, and followed him when he dropped her off after the charity dinner. Poised for a confrontation, she'd used Daniel's key to enter my apartment, found him on the couch, and picked up the bookend to kill him. When she realized he was already dead, she left in a panic, knowing she couldn't report it without incriminating herself.

It seemed that Daniel had been doomed to die that night.

After Salyers left, I sat in the hallway cradling Mrs. Bingham's casserole in the woman's perennial oven mitts—the reason she hadn't left fingerprints in my apartment. Grant sat down next to me, and I burst into tears.

"It's okay now," he soothed, putting his arm around my shoulders.

"I'm sorry I even thought you could commit murder, Grant."

"I'm sorry I thought the same about you. Besides, you were right to be suspicious. I was acting . . . strange." He made a rueful noise in his throat. "I'm going to sell the house. That's why I finally did all the things to it that you'd always wanted me to do."

"You're moving?"

"Moving, and moving on. I gave my notice at the firm."

I was suddenly concerned. "Are you dying?"

He laughed. "No. I owe you an apology, Renni. I let you shoulder the blame for ending our marriage, when I was the one who didn't have the guts to tell you how trapped I felt."

"You too?"

Grant nodded. "I loved you. I still do. But the pressure of being a husband, it changed me. Suffocated me."

It was my turn to laugh. "Me too."

He smiled and shook his head. "What a pair we are."

"What did you mean by moving on?"

"I bought a sailboat. She's seaworthy. I was thinking of taking a few months to explore the East Coast."

I looked up at him with new eyes. "Did I ever tell you that I used to sail with my dad?"

"No," he said, picking up a lock of my hair. "One of many conversations we should've had."

And would.

INVASION

Julie Barrett

The arrival of Miss Merlinda McCrane would have caused quite a stir had it not been for the fact that Pecan Blossom, Texas, was in the grip of Martian mania. Orson Welles's little Halloween "prank" had caused quite a stir among the farmers and ranchers in the county, and those of us who worked at KPB radio were run off our feet tracking down sightings. Personally, I thought the sightings were another prank cooked up by Mark Truett, the local high school quarterback, a boy with less brains than talent.

I would have had an enormous laugh over the entire thing had it not been for the fact that Ma Jenks was dead serious. Ma—excuse me, Mrs. Henrietta Jenks—runs radio station KPB with all the grace and twice the stubbornness of a mule at the living Nativity scene down at the church. Come to think of it, she was the one who had the bright idea of making a halo for the baby Jesus out of a gelatin mold—with the carrot salad still inside. Well, at least she bought a new doll for little Peggy Jo Pritchett.

KPB served the rural area up toward the Texas border with information and educational programs from sunrise to sunset. Information and education in those parts consisted mainly of farm reports, weather forecasts, planting and harvesting tips, all courtesy of farm-implement and seed manufacturers. Homemaking programs were sponsored by food companies and home-appliance manufacturers. The remaining hours were filled with music and dramas, all morally "improving" fare selected by Ma Jenks herself.

Mrs. Jenks didn't own the station, even though she liked to think that she did. Her husband, William, had taken over ownership after his dad threw himself in front of the interurban train. The rumor was, he'd invested heavily in the very agricultural companies that kept the station afloat, and when the dust storms rolled out from West Texas, the entire farming economy nearly collapsed. Half our population up and left for Dallas then. I had a suspicion that Gloria might drive the rest out in due time.

Gloria was Gloria Rivers, the title character of KPB's own locally produced soap opera, *For the Love of Gloria*, and Miss Merlinda McCrane was coming in from Dallas to take the lead role for five episodes. Ma Jenks was furious, but William held the firm belief that this would be the biggest thing to hit our town in years. He might have been right if it hadn't been for Orson Welles and the Martians.

We were all pretty well convinced that Henrietta wasn't quite right in the head, and she'd only gotten worse since William started taking trips into Dallas to line up new sponsors. She had always felt that our programs needed to be up to a "certain standard," as she put it. The agricultural and homemaking programs were important, but the balance of airtime had to be given over to what she called "improving" programming. In other words, she firmly believed that her mission in life was to keep the residents of Pecan Blossom on the straight and narrow. Even Reverend Butcher thought she was a bit overzealous.

So when Mrs. Jenks announced that Gloria was going to "improve" the Martians, I couldn't put up much of a fuss. That was, until her husband announced that Miss Merlinda McCrane was coming to town. Then the fur began to fly.

Monday morning I walked the four blocks from my house to the station, a folder full of scripts pressed against my chest. The wind had picked up and the sky was tinged with the familiar rust-colored West Texas dust that preceded a cold front. Elm Street was deserted save for a few stray leaves tumbling across the street. Main Street was unusually quiet—even for November. People tended not to go outside during a dust storm if they could, and even the birds had the good sense to flee the approaching cloud.

The local Farm Service director greeted me as I slipped inside the door of the station—or rather his voice did. Every couple of weeks they sent up a batch of programs from Austin on sixteen-inch records. Today he was prattling on about garden nematodes. Through the double-paned window in the lobby I could see Jerry Simpson, half asleep at the control board, a cigarette dangling from his lips. The curtain to the window on the opposite side of the control room was open, and I could make out the shadows of microphones on stands in the darkened recording studio beyond. I knocked on the glass to let Jerry know I was there, then went to answer the telephone at the front desk. It was Thelma Burris, the voice of Gloria—when she wasn't teaching English at the high school. "I've been fired," she announced.

"Fired? From the school? What—"

"No, from the show. He's got another Gloria." I could hear her sobbing on the other end of the line.

"All right, calm down."

"I can't go to school. It's too humiliating."

This was not good at all. "What happened?"

"You don't know?"

"It's the first I've heard, Miss Burris." It did come as quite a surprise. Thelma's no Shakespearean actress, but she could read her lines and Mrs. Jenks was happy with her—or so I had thought.

"He told me that he's bringing someone else in to play Gloria—an actress from Dallas. An *actress*. I thought I was good enough."

"You're fine," I reassured her. "I think you may have misheard." Then the front door opened with a bang.

"You are NOT putting that hussy on the air!" Henrietta Jenks stormed through the door, her husband following. He tipped his hat at me and I covered the mouthpiece on the phone and let them know that Miss Burris was on the line, and that she was upset.

Ma Jenks went on with her tirade as they walked into the adjoining office. She closed the door with an authoritative "bang" that was loud enough to make Jerry Simpson start. I turned my attention back to the panicked Thelma Burris.

Five minutes later, I walked down the hall to the room I called an office, in the back of the building. It was really a mail room, sound-effects storage room, and record library. An old wooden table shoved up against the wall held a typewriter with a bent *g* key. Stacked near the edge of a nearby table were three freshly cut acetate transcription discs. Miss Burris brought a group of her students by every couple of weeks to record poetry for broadcast. That's part of our educational programming. At least I assumed that's what was on the recordings, because Bobby, KPB's engineer, had forgotten to mark the discs with a grease pencil. He should have left a run sheet listing the contents of each disc on my desk, but he seemed to have forgotten that as well. I had no choice but to take them into the recording studio and listen to them one by one. It wouldn't do to mix up a Shakespearean sonnet with "The Charge of the Light Brigade"—not that anyone could tell the difference the way those kids read.

Technically speaking, we had only two types of programs— live and transcribed. "Transcribe" was essentially a fancy word for "recording." Like other programming we recorded at the station, they were "cut" to blank acetate discs using a turntable with a special needle, though I could play them back using an ordinary turntable. I preferred the term "record," but since they came in a box marked "transcription discs," that's what they were called. Unlike the prerecorded pressed vinyl discs that came from the Farm Service and various sponsors, these discs were quite fragile. If one was dropped, it would shatter like Grandma's best china plate.

I reached over my desk and turned up the volume on the control-room monitor, which carried whatever went out over the air. It was about time for the news, such as it was. Jerry took the latest headlines from the news wire, plus a smattering of items culled from the newspaper and announcements provided by local groups.

" . . . and the sheriff's office says that the latest Martian sighting was, in fact, Ed Ferris burning trash. I know he looks scary, especially when he hasn't shaved in a few days, but he's no Martian." That did it. I heard the door to the adjoining office open and close, and the slow, measured footsteps of William Jenks as he walked across the hall to the control room. Jokes were one thing, but one overriding rule at KPB was to respect our listeners. Lord knows some people around Pecan Blossom seemed to have targets painted on their backs, but small-town gossip was bad enough without us getting involved. This was one of the few "improving" rules I happened to agree with.

The sweet tones of "How Great Thou Art" emanated from the loudspeaker. Our morning religious block was under way. I could only imagine the conversation going on in the control room right now. I reached up to lower the volume on the monitor speaker so I could work in relative peace.

"Leave it up, Barbara." Mrs. Jenks stood in the doorway. "I do love the uplifting programs." I sighed and sat down at my desk. This might have been the perfect time of day for farmers and housewives to take a break and pray, but I had to get to work. I suspect God just may have understood that I had a "morally improving" script to finish. I rushed forward as she pulled a chair across the room, her large hips bumping the stack of transcriptions on a nearby table.

"Oopsie," she exclaimed with a little squeak as I just missed catching the topmost disc before it fell to the floor and shattered. I reached for the broom and busied myself with sweeping up the shards. She didn't even think to ask which program lay on the floor in pieces. Normally, she would have shown some concern, but that particular morning she was rather preoccupied with *Gloria*.

So was I. "I had a call from Miss Burris this morning. She was in tears."

Mrs. Jenks pulled a handkerchief from her dress pocket and began to twist one end with her fingers. "You've heard about Merlinda McCrane."

"Yes." I sensed that the last thing I needed to do right now was to get her all excited. "But honestly, I didn't know what to think. Neither you nor Mr. Jenks has told me firsthand, so . . ." Truthfully, Mr. Jenks had told me something vague in passing, but that was best left unsaid.

"Well, I'll *tell* you what to think: That woman is a no-good, two-bit hussy with designs on my poor William. No radio station in Dallas will hire her, so she's hitched herself to his wagon."

"Let me guess: pretty, but not talented?"

"In a nutshell." I wondered if she'd ever seen the "hussy" in question and asked her as much. "I've seen a picture. Of course, it's all fancy lighting and expensive clothes, but I can tell she's up to no good."

Naturally, it crossed my mind that being up to no good ran two ways. I didn't have much time to dwell on it, as the conversation suddenly pulled back to the matter of the Martians. Again, I had to tread lightly, but I was very much afraid that this particular story line would do *For the Love of Gloria* in for good. As the writer, it was my duty to at least make an attempt at defending Gloria's honor, which, when you boiled it down, was *my* honor. Gloria may have been Henrietta Jenks's baby, but it was my name on the credits.

"Perhaps I'm missing something," I said, "but I still don't understand why we need Martians in the program. We just brought Jake Dermott's character into the show, and judging from what I've heard around town, he's popular with the listeners. If you're going to the trouble and expense of bringing an actress in from Dallas to attract sponsors, wouldn't it make sense to use her in this story line rather than bring in the Martians?"

Boy, did I say the wrong thing. Ma Jenks resumed twisting her handkerchief in her hands as some preacher from South Texas droned on over the monitor about loving thy neighbor—unless they neighbor was a sinner, in which case he was going straight to the hot place. Mrs. Jenks muttered "Amen!" under her breath. I said a silent prayer for help.

I heard a door open down the hall, followed by the sound of heavy footsteps. Ma Jenks stiffened in her chair as her husband entered the room. He had removed his suit coat and rolled up his shirt sleeves. In his right hand was a half-smoked cigar, which he twirled nervously between his fingers and thumb.

"Ah, there you are," he said with a nod to me and a forced smile to his wife. She ignored him, concentrating instead on her handkerchief. "I'm sorry to interrupt, but we—I mean, Miss McCrane—has had a change in plans. Another engagement for next week. You know how it is in show business. I'm afraid this means she's arriving later today."

If I hadn't known Mr. Jenks better, I'd have sworn he looked smug as he delivered the news. As it was, I simply thought that he was happy to see his plans were still in place. After all, he had put a lot of time and effort into securing Miss McCrane's services.

The news did not seem to go over well with his wife. She gave her handkerchief a final twist, then gave him a look that made me glad I wasn't standing between them. If looks really *could* kill, her gaze would have been positively lethal.

They stared at each other for what seemed like ages until Mrs. Jenks shifted her gaze in my direction and made her best attempt to smile. "I'm afraid we need those scripts a little sooner than we thought."

Mr. Jenks stuffed his cigar in his mouth and chewed on the end a bit. "Well, then. I'll leave you ladies to it." With that he returned to his office, his footsteps lighter than they had been beforehand.

Mrs. Jenks simply smiled as she heard his office door close.

"How are next week's scripts coming along?" By that she meant the Martian story.

I turned to my desk and pulled a folder from the tray. "Here's the batch we were going to record on Friday. They're all ready to duplicate." I had no hope of getting her brain off that Martian story, but I had to try.

To my surprise, she thumbed through the thick stack of mimeograph stencils and returned them to me with that smile still plastered on her face. "You know, I was thinking. With Thanksgiving so near, why don't we bring the entire cast in and record two sets of shows? That will give everyone more time to spend with their families during the holidays."

How could I not agree with such a sensible plan? Still, I took a risk and gave her one extra nudge. "If I work late I can get a batch of scripts together for the Martian story line, but I honestly don't think I can have them ready before the afternoon."

Ma Jenks gave my proposal some thought. It was quite apparent to me that she wanted Miss McCrane to record the Martian programs out of spite. I could understand that, and I could also see that if Miss McCrane did record that set of shows, any potential sponsors would laugh Mr. Jenks all the way back to Pecan Blossom. But times were tough, and I had my job to think about. On the other hand, it seemed to me that the notion of getting Miss McCrane out of the studio and on the first train back to Dallas had a strong appeal for Mrs. Jenks.

"Well then," she said as that odd smile spread across her face, "I guess Miss McCrane will have to record next week's episodes."

The four thirty interurban train screeched to a stop at the station. I was on my way to the drugstore to get some headache powder, but truth be told, my headache made for a good excuse to be walking in the direction of the station. The dust storm had rolled through, followed by a crisp wind out of the northwest. A few anemic-looking clouds drifted overhead, carried by the wind. I passed a group of farmers arguing over whether or not those punky clouds meant that rain was on the way. After the brief exchange of words, they decided it would be best to head into the Blossom Diner for a cup of their strong coffee. Margaret Truett rushed by with a bag of groceries, her head bent against the wind. I supposed that I should have worn a scarf, but a little mussed hair was a small price to pay for the sight of Miss Merlinda McCrane alighting from the car.

She wore a sable coat over an expensive suit, her blond hair mostly hidden under a hat. William Jenks was there to help her off the train. Miss Merlinda McCrane smiled and dropped her white fur muff to the ground. I'm no fashion plate, but a white fur muff with a sable coat seemed just a bit much. I didn't know whether to be relieved or appalled when the muff let out a high-pitched bark, sprouted four legs, and took off at a run down the platform.

"Tootsie!"

I suppose it wouldn't be fair to judge another person based on only one word, but nails on a chalkboard might not be an unkind description. Thelma Burris had nothing to fear.

Several men scrambled to retrieve the poodle before it ran under the train. Freddy Shackleford cornered the pooch and presented it to its owner. I don't think he was expecting anything more than thanks for his efforts, but the way she gingerly reached out and plucked the dog from his hands, as though she was afraid of catching a deadly disease, was criminal. At least Mr. Jenks had the good sense to thank poor Freddy for his efforts.

In all the commotion no one seemed to notice a man wearing a slick black suit follow Miss McCrane off of the train. Clearly he was with her, but he didn't seem to be her class at all. Where she was all flashy jewelry and sable, he simply had an aura of wealth. His suit was expensive but tasteful. William Jenks grinned broadly and shook his hand. I had a funny feeling that Mrs. Jenks didn't know about this development.

I rushed down to the drugstore and was out with my headache powder before the trio had left the train station. Pulling my collar up against the wind, I rushed back to KPB while Mr. Jenks made a big show of pointing out the sights downtown. I hung my coat up on the rack and watched through the picture window as they ambled in the direction of the station. The stranger seemed genuinely interested; Miss McCrane appeared bored. She clamped one hand to the hat on her head and clutched her poodle to her coat with the other as she resolutely walked down the street.

The red light over the control room was off, and I pushed the heavy wooden door open. Gerald Moore lifted his coffee cup in salute and looked down to cue up a disc. It was pushing five o'clock, and we'd soon be shutting down the transmitter for the day.

As the afternoon farm report wound down, Gerald placed the headphones over his ears and flicked the microphone switch. The red glow of the ON THE AIR light was visible through the porthole window. "This is KPB, 560, the voice of Pecan Blossom, Texas. It's time for the afternoon poem, read by students of Pecan County High School." With a practiced move Gerald released his fingers from the turntable, turned down his microphone volume, then flipped the switch. Some poor child was struggling valiantly with Keats. I think the poet was winning.

Gerald shook his head and handed me a sheet of paper. "Another one from the sheriff. This is starting to look like something out of *Amazing Stories*."

"I wondered who was buying the drugstore out of copies," I quipped. Gerald laughed and took a swig of his coffee as I read about the latest apparent Martian sighting. "You realize," I said as I returned the paper, "the more vigorously they deny that little green spacemen have invaded, the more some people will believe it."

"I'm not showing it to Mrs. Jenks."

"No, but she'll hear the announcement when you read it."

"Maybe I'll just forget to read it."

"Not if you value your job."

The door swung open and Miss Merlinda McCrane stepped through. She clutched her dog to her chest and appraised the studio for all of five seconds.

"How quaint."

I made quick introductions and escorted our starlet out so Gerald could do his job. She certainly didn't seem happy to be unceremoniously shepherded out of the control room, but I had no choice. Gently I steered her out to the lobby where Mr. Jenks stood in low-voiced conversation with the man who had accompanied Miss McCrane to town.

"Barbara, I'm glad you're here. I'd like you to meet Mr. Harland Johnson. He's buying KPB."

I tried not to act completely shocked, not with Miss Merlinda McCrane standing there, tapping the toe of her expensive pump with an air of impatience. "A pleasure to meet you, sir," I stammered.

"The offer was a bit unexpected, but I think I'm ready to retire." The little dog started to growl. My opinion of that poodle was getting better by the minute.

"Tootsie needs a break," cooed Miss McCrane. "Excuse us."

That was my cue to take my own leave back into the control room. I found Gerald furiously scribbling away at log sheets. We were required to keep a list of everything that went out over the air—all subject to government inspection. I felt a brief pang of pity for the inspector who would have to decipher Gerald's hieroglyphics. "Wouldn't it be easier if you took care of all that during the shift?"

"Where's the fun in that?" He glanced at the clock and started another transcription—an evening prayer from Reverend Butcher—while he slapped his headphones back on and looked over a script. He flicked the microphone switch and read, "KPB broadcasts from sunrise to sunset on a frequency of five hundred and sixty kilohertz. We now conclude our broadcasting day. Good night." Over the monitor speaker I heard the buzz indicating that Bobby had shut the transmitter down from the adobe shack behind our building. We could hear a faint signal from out west over the static. Gerald dropped the monitor volume.

I waited for him to take another sip of his coffee and finish sleeving the transcription and place it on the shelf. I didn't want another broken record on my hands today. "Uh, Gerald."

"Yeah?"

"Have you heard any odd rumors about the station?"

"As in why Miss Big City has deigned to darken our dusty door?"

"For a start."

Gerald took a deep breath and grabbed my shoulders. "Sit," he said as he gently pushed me into the old leather chair behind the console. "You don't get out of Pecan Blossom much, do you?"

"I've been to college," I said defensively. Commerce isn't exactly the big city, but I'd like to think I had a pretty good education.

Gerald chuckled. "Let's just say that the reason she can't get on the radio in Dallas is that her act is visual." I wasn't terribly sure what to say. "Well, she's not a mime, if that's what you're thinking. She does do amazing things with feathers and balloons—or so I'm told."

The idea of William Jenks—a deacon in the church—watching that sort of performance certainly didn't seem right, and I told Gerald as much. He simply swept up the last of the log sheets, dropped them in my lap, and told me that if I thought that was all Mr. Jenks was up to on his trips to Dallas, then perhaps I was in need of some education that college didn't provide. Just because I'd attended a women's college didn't mean that I was naïve. Still, the thought of someone as old as Mr. Jenks with someone like Miss McCrane sent a shudder up my back.

"Ah," was the best I could bring myself to say. That certainly put it all in a different light—except for Mrs. Jenks. I was fairly certain she was as much in the dark about this as the rest of us had been.

As Gerald readied the studio for the morning shift, I filled him in on the latest news that didn't involve Martians in Pecan Blossom. I left him checking over a stack of blank transcription discs for cracks and scratches, and I went down the hall to button up my desk for the night. Not that there was much to button up, but I liked to at least toss a dust cover over the typewriter and clean my coffee mug. On top of my neat stack of scripts for *The Love of Gloria* lay three pieces of notepaper—Bobby's idea of a run sheet for the transcriptions he'd cut yesterday. I typed up a set of labels and carried the two unmarked discs to our recording studio so I could listen.

The recording studio was a large, soundproofed room next to the master control room and across the hall from Mr. Jenks's office. It had its own small control room where an engineer oversaw production and recording. It also doubled as an auxiliary on-air control room, just as the main control room could function as a studio control. We couldn't afford to lose any airtime due to equipment problems.

A light was on, and through the porthole window I could see that Mr. Jenks was showing Mr. Johnson around the studio. Miss McCrane and dog had returned; she stepped up to a microphone and idly tapped at the grill. I saw Gerald cringe. If that microphone had been hot, she might have damaged the ribbon. Mr. Jenks stepped over and took her hand. Better him to explain microphone etiquette than me. I might have wrung her neck.

In fact, I decided that the discs could wait a day. I stacked them back on the table in the back room, well away from the edge this time, and turned out the light.

The lobby phone was ringing as I unlocked the front door the next morning. It was Thelma Burris. I apologized for not calling her and explained the plan to record two weeks' worth of shows today. Could she possibly come to the studio after school let out? And yes, Miss McCrane would be recording, and no, she wasn't going to take over the role permanently. It was, as far as I knew, a publicity stunt for the station. That was mostly the truth. I really didn't think it was my place to tell Thelma Burris that the station was being sold. Even if it was, I knew the news would upset her. It upset *me*. There was a very real possibility that I'd lose my job. It wasn't just me: The local programming was the beating heart of this community. Being on the radio didn't pay much, but it was a source of pride for people to be able to say that they played the banjo or read a part in a program. As silly as it might sound to someone from the city, this was important.

I could have been completely wrong. The new owner might have decided to keep things around here just as they were. Somehow I didn't think that would be the case.

The first item on the agenda was to get labels on those discs. I picked up the stack of three recordings and—hold on. There had been only two discs on the table last night. I checked my desk. There was no new run sheet to go with the disc, and no markings to tell me what might be on the recording. We hadn't been scheduled to record anything the previous night, but it was not unusual for Reverend Butcher to drop by when he had a few minutes and record a week's worth of prayers. That must have been it.

My efforts to get the discs labeled were thwarted by the arrival of Ma Jenks. This time I made it a point to position myself between her and the discs. She sat down at my desk and stared at the stack of scripts.

"Anything I can do, Mrs. Jenks?"

"Oh, Barbara. The most awful thing has happened."

I backed up and sat down in the other chair. Mrs. Jenks's face was pale, her eyes red and puffy. I couldn't help wondering if, in a fit of righteous indignation, she hadn't poisoned the casserole and now three people lay dead at her house. Perhaps I had been reading too many pulp novels.

Of course, she probably didn't know that I knew about the sale of the station. And, perhaps, other things she still might not have known about. Unless three people really *were* laying dead at her table.

No. That was just too bizarre to contemplate.

Definitely no more pulp novels for me.

I let her tell me about the sale and hoped that I acted appropriately surprised and shocked and whatever other emotions she expected me to show. Then she dropped the bombshell.

"That . . . Miss McCrane will not be staying for long. She will be recording one episode of *Gloria* at eleven o'clock. I wouldn't have her do that except for the fact that we've been making announcements on the station for the past week." She dabbed at the corner of one eye with her handkerchief. "As much as it pains me to do so, I have to keep my end of the bargain, even if I do enter into an arrangement with the devil."

The plan was for us to make two recordings of Monday's episode of *Gloria*. Miss McCrane would be taking one back to Dallas with her, presumably as proof that she could act her way out of a paper bag. We would air our copy on Monday and be rid of her.

Mr. Jenks spent the morning in meetings with Mr. Johnson while Mrs. Jenks paced the building, wringing her handkerchief. Our diva finally showed up at ten thirty, poodle in hand, going on nonstop about her horrid room down at the hotel. The bath was cold, the breakfast was not served in bed, and poor little Tootsie spent the night shivering on the floor. I was surprised that the mutt didn't sleep with her.

She sniffed at the cup of coffee I handed her and set it aside as though she expected bugs to crawl out of it. I dropped the script on the table. "We have one hour to rehearse and record. I'd appreciate it if you'd do us the courtesy of reading through your lines before we get started."

Miss McCrane bristled at the affront to her apparent stardom, and then gave me a look as though I were simply not worth her contempt. With an air of indifference she picked up the script and flipped through the pages. "Who wrote this drivel?"

She knew perfectly well who had written it. My name was at the top of the script. "A *real* actress could make any drivel come across like Shakespeare."

"Well!" Miss Merlinda McCrane turned on her well-heeled foot and plopped into a chair. I swear, she looked just like a little child who had been sent to the corner to think about her sins. I left her to it and walked down the hall to the studio to do a final check on sound effects.

We gathered in the studio—dog and all—for the rehearsal. Miss McCrane refused to watch for her cues, and then, after much prompting, began to read. Each episode would begin with a monologue during which Gloria recounts the story so far, just in case anyone missed an episode—or cared about the story line. The words didn't match my script. Judging from the panicked looks in the control room, her words weren't on any script. She'd rewritten the monologue during those twenty minutes she'd had with the script, and it was terrible. I cringed. Ma Jenks actually smiled.

Somehow, we muddled through the recording. Our one hour of studio time had stretched into four, during which Miss McCrane alternately fluffed lines and tended to her dog. Finally, Mr. Jenks declared that we had a decent recording.

I tidied up the sound-effects area while the men congratulated Miss McCrane on her original interpretation of the role. Someone tapped my shoulder and coughed quietly. Mr. Johnson stood on the other side of the effects table. "If we can have our copy of the show, we'll be going. We have a train to catch."

I walked next door to the control room and found Bobby changing the needle on one of the transcription cutters. He informed me that he had passed the discs along to Ma Jenks.

"You did *what*?" Handing Mrs. Jenks an acetate transcription disc was like asking the Marx Brothers to guard a piece of valuable china. There would be many pieces to clean up in the end.

I found Mrs. Jenks at the worktable, ready to affix a label to a disc. "Let me do that for you."

"I've got it all under control. Look." She spread her arm over the table to show that each disc had a label. "I needed something to do." She handed me a freshly labeled recording. "Here. Get them out of my hair."

With pleasure.

I returned to the back room to find Mrs. Jenks seated in the rickety chair next to the worktable. "I'm going to miss this place. Oh, well." She placed a hand on the worktable to steady herself as she stood. I sprinted across the room and managed to save the discs. "I nearly killed Gloria. Oopsie." With that she waddled out of the room.

With all the excitement I'd nearly forgotten that we were supposed to record more episodes of *Gloria* this afternoon. I was very tempted to rerecord today's disaster just so we'd have a little insurance. This could very well be one of my last scripts to see air. After the hatchet job on today's script, I'd be lucky to get a job typing invoices down at the grain elevator. I started a fresh pot of coffee and walked down to the recording studio to prepare it for the next round of recording. At this rate we wouldn't get started until after five.

A tapping sound on the window brought me out of my funk. Gerald had pressed his log sheet to the window and pointed at the time slot for the poem. In all the fuss today I'd forgotten to pull the disc. I waved my acknowledgment and ran down the hall.

The disc lay on top of the stack, neatly labeled. I must admit that I felt a twinge of guilt as I ran back down to the control room. I had to trust that Mrs. Jenks had put the labels on the right discs. In fact, I did briefly consider repeating a poem from last week so I would have the time to check the record before air. I had just two minutes, but it was enough time to swap discs. As I considered that option, Mrs. Jenks stepped out from her office. "Is that today's poem, dear? I'm sure we'll all find it most improving. I certainly did."

Gerald pulled open the control-room door. "You want dead air? Or should I read from the phone book?"

"Hurry," Ma Jenks prodded. I had a feeling of impending doom as I rushed the disc into the control room. Mrs. Jenks followed close on my heels. We watched Gerald cue up the transcription and introduce today's special poem. A series of clicks were followed by a few seconds of silence. Gerald reached for the fill music. Mrs. Jenks simply smiled.

"Merlinda, dear, don't do that." The sound of William Jenks's voice filled the tiny control room. "It's not good for the microphone ribbon."

Gerald let out a word he shouldn't have spoken in front of his employer and reached for the volume knob. "I was just testing out the equipment," he stammered. "I threw the disc in the trash."

"Keep it going," Henrietta Jenks ordered.

"Just a few more days," her husband's voice implored. "Once the sale goes through, we'll have all the money we need. Henrietta can play with her Martians for a couple of weeks and she won't be any wiser."

I hated to admit it, but this was compelling stuff.

Merlinda McCrane spoke. "Sweetums." Gerald and I exchanged a glance. "I can't wait forever. Come to my room tonight."

Mr. Jenks cleared his throat. "I can't. Henrietta's already suspicious. Just be patient. Then we'll be off to New York . . . Hollywood! Wherever you want. . . ."

"I think today's reading is over, Gerald." Mrs. Jenks pulled the needle across the transcription. The high-pitched screech of the needle moving over the grooves put Merlinda McCrane's voice to shame. "Oopsie."

We did not record the Martian programs.

That little broadcast was the talk of the town for a week, during which time no one saw hide nor hair of Mr. Jenks, and very little of his wife. She would arrive at the station early, make sure everything was in order, and then take the interurban into Dallas. I decided that it was time to start looking for another job.

The day before Thanksgiving another dust storm moved through. I made my way down Main Street holding a scarf to my face so I could breathe. By the time I got down to the dry-goods store two doors from the station, I felt a cold gust of wind followed by something wet on my cheek. Large, dirty drops of rain had begun to fall from the sky. By the time I made it to the front door of the station, it was coming down hard.

I found Reverend Butcher huddled underneath the green canopy that covered the entrance to the station. "This is such a blessing," he declared as I unlocked the door. I had to agree. As I closed the glass door behind us, I looked out onto the street. Among the early morning shoppers dashing from store to store I noticed more than one person standing with their arms outstretched, as if they were trying to catch the precious drops before they hit the ground. It had been a good long while since we had seen a downpour.

Mrs. Jenks was waiting in the lobby, grinning broadly. This wasn't the same odd smile of a week ago; this morning she seemed genuinely happy. "I wanted you to be the first to know. KBP has a new owner."

While I'd prepared myself for this, I hadn't expected her to be so cheerful about it. KPB had been her life.

"It's me!" She was positively giddy. Reverend Butcher and I exchanged a glance. I suspected he was thinking the same thing that was going through my mind: The woman had finally cracked. "The government, you see, is very reluctant to give a broadcasting license to someone who is not of good moral character. My attorney was able to convince William that I was better suited to own the station."

Reverend Butcher cleared his throat. "You'll be needing a new deacon," she said. "Mr. Jenks will not be returning to Pecan Blossom, Texas."

Ma Jenks shooed me off down the hall. I had another week of *For the Love of Gloria* to write. As I walked away I could hear her chattering to the reverend. "Now about the Nativity scene. In the spirit of welcoming our neighbors, I think we ought to replace one of the shepherds with a Martian . . ."

Cold, Hard Facts

S. J. Rozan

Hey, Danny. Good to see you, man. Thanks for coming, getting here so fast. Sorry to wake you up in the middle of the night, make you drive all the way here, but there's no lawyer in this town I'd want, no one I could count on, in a mess like this.

Yeah, I'm fine, I'm okay, but jeez, can you get me out of here?

What, they can't do, what is that, arraignments, they can't do that overnight? Oh, for God's sake, I know it's not New York City, why do you think I live here? No, sorry, Danny, didn't mean to snap at you. Listen, what about the husband? I told the cops about the husband, have they found him?

You try calming down, being shut up in here! Yeah, no, it's okay, it's okay, I'm sorry, it's just, being here . . . But hell, I couldn't call the bank until morning anyway, right? How much bail, bond, whatever you call it, how much do you think they'll want?

What do you mean, they might not? How can they—*I didn't kill that girl,* Danny! I don't care what Cecilia says, that's not what happened!

Cecilia. The blonde, for God's sake, the one who—no, of course not, not *my* Cecilia. Oh, Jesus—does she know? Oh, Christ, Danny, does Ceecee know about this?

No, no, of course you wouldn't. I'm not thinking straight. I just—no, I guarantee I'm sobered up. It's just, I can hardly believe it, what happened, and then, being in here, Danny, in here, it's like I'm different from the rest of you, like I'm solid and these walls are solid but the rest of you, you're ghosts, you're not real somehow and you can come and go, in and out of this place, and I'm solid and I can't.

Unreal? What are you talking about? No, that's not how I felt about her! Of course I knew she was real! Damn, Danny, it's a metaphor! I'm a writer, it's what I do. I know what's real and what isn't, you know that. I'm not one of these writers who gets lost in my own head.

Because it *is* her name. Cecilia. Um, wait—a color, Brown, Green—White! Cecilia White, and the dress was silver, that dress she had on, God, that silk dress . . .

Annette? What are you talking about, Annette?

I swear to God, Danny, she said her name was Cecilia. That was the first thing she said to me at the bar, she came up next to me and she even said, "Excuse me," you know no one says that? They just say, "You're Jack Frank," like I don't know that, for God's sake! Yeah, I'm sorry, it's just, I can't believe this whole thing, Danny. In my worst nightmare I couldn't have come up with something like this. In my worst novel! Damn, this would make a pretty bad one, huh? No, of course I don't think it's funny, Jesus, Danny, cut me some slack! I'm just trying to get a handle on what's happening.

Okay. Yeah. So she said excuse me, she was sorry to intrude. Well, Jesus, intrude? I'm sitting there trying to smudge the photo in my mind, pour enough scotch on it so the hard lines and jagged edges of that hypersharp shot, Ceecee in the doorway saying good-bye, so the damn photo could finally start to blur and waver. And suddenly next to me, it's all softness, it's pale and smoky . . . Even her voice, husky, whispery. Intrude? That silver dress rippled like music, Danny. Debussy, everything hint, suggestion, nothing hard, nothing solid. Nothing hard about her, anywhere. Her hair was this pale cloud, I thought if I touched it my hand might go right through, it would be too soft to even feel. And her eyes, huge, blue, but a gray blue, like mist, you could fall into them and disappear, float away and you wanted to, Danny, you wanted to!

Blue. Yes.

Well, shit, isn't that just perfect. Her name is Annette and her eyes are green, that's what you're saying? Yes, I'm sure! Jesus, you think I could forget eyes like that?

No, *not* the same blue as Ceecee's eyes! Hers had this gray, I'm telling you, this mist thing going on, I've never seen anything like it. But not green. Definitely not green.

Well, obviously they were contacts. Because she was setting me up! From the beginning! Look what happened! She's crazy, Danny! What the hell do you want from me?

I know. I know. I'm sorry. But, Danny, I'm just telling you what happened.

Yes, I know you're listening. The way you sit there, like a stone, who could miss it? Solid, Danny, you're one solid guy.

So, so she said, "Excuse me," and she said she recognized me, and she'd read all my books and she loved them. And I thanked her and then she said, except *Nightswitch*. She was mad at me about that. So I asked her why. Partly to keep her talking, her sitting there all soft, that shimmery silver dress . . . and partly because I wanted to know, I really did. When someone gets mad at you for something you wrote, it means it hit a deep place in them, and that's kind of great, you know? So I really wanted to know.

She said what was wrong was, she recognized the loneliness, the lostness, the woman's fear of cracking up after her boyfriend leaves her. Her husband had walked out on her, she said. Cecilia said. Annette, whatever! Dumped her for someone else. It made her feel like in my book: lost, invisible, like everything was solid and real but her. Like she had no weight and might float, drift right through the walls and disappear. She said she thought that was her own feeling, only hers, and she kept it a secret from everyone. Especially her husband, she didn't let him know. Well, who would? But then that's what the girlfriend feels like in my book. It surprised her and it made her mad, she told me that, it made her furious that I would give away her secret like that. She said when she read that book she felt like I knew her, and betrayed her.

No! I never saw her before, Danny, I swear.

Lane said that? Well, I don't give a damn what Lane says. For God's sake, Lane's crazy, he's always got all kinds of stories. It's one of the reasons I drink at his place, everyone knows that, especially now, it was in that damn *New Yorker* profile last month, even which shifts Lane works. I was a little pissed off about that, I felt like I'd been outted, where I live, what I do, a little too close, you know? I thought I might have to do the hermit thing for a while, way down the end of my dirt road there, but there wasn't all that much fallout, just a few tourists, I could handle it. Lane loved it, made his bar famous, he said. And I kept going there, even though lately the place got more crowded, too close, you know, the music's too loud? But most places have, it's a hard feeling to describe, but since Ceecee left, there's too much weight, too many edges . . .

Sorry, Danny, sure, sure, what happened. Where was I? Lane's. I kept going because he's a great source for stuff too crazy to make up. Oh, come on, Danny, for *me* to make up! *He's* making it up right and left. Three-quarters of what he says can't be true. No, I'm not saying he's *lying* about this, Jesus, Mary, and Joseph! Maybe it seemed to him like we knew each other. The way she was looking at me. And maybe how I was looking at her. Because I was thinking how much, right then, I wanted to know her. But we didn't, Danny. I swear.

Yeah. Okay. So she's sitting there telling me she loves my books, but she's mad at me about *Nightswitch*, about telling her secret. I said I was sorry, and could I buy her a drink to make up because I sure didn't want her mad at me—*of course* I was putting the moves on her, Danny, have you *seen* her? Girl like that sits down next to you, in that perfect time about two drinks down when the whole place is starting to soften, girl sits down and she has eyes like that, who wouldn't—blue, yes, dammit, blue!

Maybe that's a good idea, coffee. It's cold in here, right? Thanks. And maybe when you're out there, check with them, see if they found the husband yet. Why are you looking at me like that? He's the key, I know he is.

Thanks. Okay, so I bought her a drink—a cosmo, I think. Yeah, that's Cecilia's drink, but a lot of girls drink cosmos, so what? A martini? Why would I have bought her a cosmo if she asked for a martini? I don't care what she says now! She asked for a cosmo! My God, I don't believe this.

Okay. Okay. So I bought her the damn *cosmo* and I said that feeling, the one you get when someone leaves you, like you're invisible and weightless and you can't hold on to anything, she shouldn't feel like I was telling her secret about that because it's pretty universal, it's the way lots of people feel. And her eyes flashed and I thought she was going to snap the stem of her glass. She said no, other people didn't feel that way, it was private and I shouldn't have told. Because her husband called, he read the book too and he called and mocked her. Was that how she felt, he wanted to know? Like the girl in Jack Frank's best seller that everyone was reading, everyone everywhere? Is that how he made her feel when he dumped her? And he laughed at her, that's what she said.

I said I was sorry, really sorry. But it wasn't something to be ashamed of, that feeling. It wasn't just her. Lots of people felt like that. And she asked me if that's how I felt when Cecilia left me.

Well, you know I don't talk about it much, you know that, Danny. But to her . . . I felt I wanted to explain it, like she had a right to ask. Because that rippling dress, the cloud of curls, the whispery voice, it was like she was making space for me, moving the weight and the hard edges away—okay, I was drunk! I'm not denying that. But it's not a crime.

So I told her. I said, no, that wasn't how I felt. I felt the opposite. Like I feel in here, Danny. Ceecee, she was soft, gentle, she was my spring breeze. When she left, it was like gravity changed, everything got heavier and pressed on me, got sharper, got louder, more solid and more real.

Nothing, at first she didn't say anything. Just stared at me for a long time with those misty eyes. Then she said, if I felt the opposite, why did I write it the way I did? Why did I tell her secret? But she didn't wait for an answer. She said oh, never mind, and she drank her drink, and she said she'd read about my breakup with Cecilia and knew it was none of her business but that was why she'd come over in the first place, to say how sorry she was. And that was why she'd had the nerve to come over, she said, to walk up to the famous Jack Frank in a bar. Because she thought maybe I wouldn't mind, maybe it would be okay for her to talk to me, because her name was Cecilia too. That's what she *told* me! That her name was Cecilia.

That made me smile. Most people just walk up into my face, too close, and touch me, and get loud, like they're *hoping* I'll take a swing at them or something, like it's what they want. But here's a soft vision, and she's keeping a distance, and she's saying "excuse me" and explaining how she hoped I wouldn't mind because her name's Cecilia. So I told her her name could be whatever she wanted it to be, I would never mind someone like her talking to me, or sitting quietly next to me, whatever she wanted to do. I *know* it sounds cheesy now, Danny, but it's what I meant. And I told her again I was sorry about her husband. She looked down, and finally she smiled too, then lifted her head, gave the smile to me. Like that glow you see, the sun in the mist. It made me feel like we had a secret together, like we'd known each other forever and had a lot of secrets together. Maybe that was what Lane saw, I don't know. If he did, I can't blame him for believing it. I almost believed it myself.

And she said she was over the husband. He was gone and that was that.

I don't know. But, Danny, you need to find him! Because he

knows about her, that she's crazy! That she was upset over *Night-switch*, that she had a thing about me—what do you mean? Of course she did! That's what this was all about!

I am. I'm trying. Just the way it happened.

It didn't matter anymore, the husband, she said. And the funny thing, the other woman? They were friends now. That woman, her name was Linda, she'd gone ahead and dumped the husband, served him right, and they were friends now and she was here too, at a table, did I want to meet her? Damn, Danny, if she'd said she was in Timbuktu, did I want to meet her, I'd have been on a plane in a minute. To see what kind of woman any man could have left Cecilia for.

And to stay close to Cecilia, that would have been my other reason.

Danny, for God's sake, of course not! Are you listening? How long have you known me? You think I can't tell one Cecilia from another? You think I'm crazy?

You do. Oh, Jesus, you do, don't you?

What do you mean, just consider it? Temporary *what*? *Cop* to this? You can't be serious. No way I would consider it! For God's sake, Danny. I wasn't temporarily or any other kind of insane when I killed that girl! Jesus, no! Because *I didn't kill that girl*!

No, Danny, I know you are. But how does that help, for you to think I'm crazy?

Don't patronize me. You do. My God, I can see it. Look, I know I haven't been myself since Ceecee left, and I haven't been writing, and okay, I've been drinking—no, I don't think it's something to be proud of! But the point is, it's not news either. And I've never lost touch with reality and I've never goddamn killed anyone!

Yeah. Okay. You want to hear the story. Though what the point is, if all you think it is, is a story . . .

So I bought us all another round—cosmos, for both of them! Me? Fourth, I think, maybe my fifth, what's the difference? You know I can hold it, Danny! Yeah. I bought them and followed her to the table. Well, Jesus, Danny. It was like mist and marble sitting there together. Cecilia pale and soft and lit from the inside, in that shimmery silver dress. Linda all angles, that razor-edged black hair, that top with those glittery sequins—you going to tell me that's not her name too? Linda? Well, thank God for small favors.

Dammit, Danny, I know she's dead! I stood there and watched that lunatic kill her! Oh, Jesus. Oh, Jesus. I think I'm going to be sick again. No. No, I'm okay, just give me a minute. My God. My God. I can't believe this is happening. You've got to find that husband, Danny. You've got to get me out of here.

Right. Uh-huh. I'll try. Swear to God, Danny. I'll try.

What happened next, what happened next . . . We drank, we sat for a while and drank, talked, you know how it goes. Then they said, the two of them, they both said maybe we should go somewhere quieter, we could get to know each other better. Cecilia—all right, Annette, whatever her name was!—she said how about her place, but it was kind of a mess, and Linda said hers was neat and clean, she had even just changed her sheets.

Danny, I never did that kind of thing before! No, I'm not saying I never picked up a girl in a bar, of course I did. But I never did a three-way, and here were these two knockouts, absolute knockouts, and they were talking about sheets. What was I supposed to do? They grabbed up their things and we left, Jack Frank walking out of Lane's with mist on one arm and marble on the other. Linda drove, we went back to her place, a condo over—oh, right, of course you do. I guess it's pretty famous right now, that condo. Bright lights, yellow tape, every crime scene tech in the county must be there, huh? No? Why, they have another big crime tonight?

No, you're right, what do I care? I don't, I don't. Sorry. I guess I thought maybe I could distract myself.

Linda's place, what happened . . . We had another drink, then Linda asked did we want to look around, see the place. Well, for God's sake, I knew what that meant. She showed us this and that, me and Cecilia making polite noises like we gave a damn about the Danish modern furniture or the stainless-steel kitchen. Finally we headed upstairs. We were all pretty wasted. Next thing I knew there we all were on those clean white sheets. All three of us, in all the ways . . . After a while I was, I was done. You know. I could've fallen asleep right there. I could've gone home. God, don't I wish I had! But I didn't. I lay there, wiped out. And Cecilia said she and Linda wanted more, they were both laughing, she said they weren't done and they needed me to get interested again. I didn't think I could, but she said she knew just how. She went to the closet and took the belt off Linda's bathrobe. Linda was lying on those rumpled sheets, just watching, a little glassy-eyed and thinking slow, you know, we were so drunk, but you could see she was intrigued. Cecilia jumped on top of her, grabbed her hands and tied her to the bed. Linda gasped and then was laughing, giggling, squirming— yes, laughing! And yes, dammit, Cecilia tied her! It wasn't me! I never did that kind of thing, Danny! Never in my life!

But I got to tell you, I got to say she was right. Cecilia. It worked. Linda lying there like that, Cecilia teasing her a little . . . I got, like she said, interested again. I was ready for more. I know how that makes me sound, Danny, but it wasn't like that. No one was getting hurt. Linda was into it.

Then Cecilia said we should go ahead, have fun, she'd be right back. Nude and everything, she headed downstairs, I didn't know why, but honestly, I didn't care. We did, me and Linda, we had fun, and she was tied up but I didn't hurt her, Danny, I swear I didn't hurt her! She was into it as much as I was. And then when I was done, and this time I thought I really was done, my God, for like a month, there was Cecilia again, smiling and saying I should get up for a minute. So I did, I rolled out of bed, I was saying something about whatever she had in mind next I didn't think I could, and she took this knife out from behind her back and gave it to me and said, "Kill her."

And she was still smiling. And I thought I heard her wrong, I was so wasted, and I thought the knife was to cut the belt but I could untie it no problem and I started to give her back the knife so I could do that.

Danny, she was wearing gloves.

And I still didn't get it. I stood there like an idiot holding the knife out to her and she kept smiling and she said the bitch, she pointed at Linda, the bitch stole her husband and she wanted me to kill her. It was unreal, Danny. Like she was speaking a fucking foreign language! What the hell was she talking about? I didn't know. I didn't know and I didn't move and I didn't know until she took the knife from me, and stopped smiling. She climbed on the bed again, on top of Linda like before. And Linda, her face, she was thinking slow but light glinted hard off the knife and suddenly she started to scream. And she's struggling, thrashing, screaming, and then there was blood, Jesus, everywhere, and I'm still standing there like an idiot, I can't move at all.

I don't know. God in heaven, I don't know. A dozen times, maybe?

Fifty-eight?

That lunatic stabbed her *fifty-eight times*?

No, I'm okay. Yeah, thanks, water would be good. It's so hot in here, so close.

Thanks. Then—I am, Danny, I've been trying to be careful all along, as accurate as I can. But it's all blurry, Jesus! No, I'm not snapping at you. I appreciate what you're doing for me. I really do.

Then. So then Cecilia, she's naked and she's all covered in blood, and I am too, everything is, I mean, if you're telling me fifty-eight times . . . She jumps up, off the bed, and stands there looking at . . . looking at . . . Jesus, Danny. And I can't move, and she just stands there for a minute, and then she turns to me and smiles the same secret smile from the bar. And whispers that Linda should never have done that, stolen her husband.

And her husband should never have made fun of her.

And I should never have written about how it felt.

And then she put the knife in my hand. She closed my fingers around it, gently, like it was a gift. I stared at her, and she smiled again.

Then she opened her mouth, like in slow motion, it took forever, it just got wider and wider. And then she screamed. Screamed, and screamed, and ran down the stairs, outside, into the snow, pale and naked and covered in blood and screaming out there . . .

I ran too. To get out, to get away. The walls were crushing me, I couldn't breathe in there, I had to get out. I wasn't chasing her, I didn't even know which way she went! I was just running and running, running . . .

Because it was in my hand! She'd put it in my hand!

Yeah. Yeah, I think I do need a minute.

Okay, I'm okay, let's go on. But I don't really know, Danny. It's a blur, after that. Until I was in that cop car, wrapped in that blanket, it was a soft blanket . . . I guess by then I was half frozen, I don't know. I don't know where she was, I don't remember the screaming ending or the cops coming. But what she says, Danny, the story she's telling now, that's not what happened. What happened, she set us up, me and Linda, she killed Linda and set me up to take the fall.

Of course it was all part of it! The name, the blue contacts, are you kidding? She's trying to make me look like I'm nuts, like I was obsessing on Cecilia and—what do you mean, how do I know I wasn't? *Because I wasn't!* She, this Cecilia, Annette, whatever her name is, *she* was obsessing on *me*! Because of the book. Because of *Nightswitch*, and me telling her "secret." Who does she think she is, the only one to ever feel that way?

Hostile? Of course I sound fucking hostile! The woman set me up on a murder rap, you expect me not to be hostile?

Jesus, Danny. Jesus, I'm exhausted. I'm wired and exhausted and I can't believe any of this is real. But swear to God, Danny, what I just told you, it's the truth. It's the facts.

But can you see now? You see why you need to find the husband? Because he can tell you about the book, about her and *Nightswitch*, about how he made fun of her about it and how crazy she is. You have to find him, Danny.

What?

Give me a break, Danny! After everything I just told you, you're springing that on me again? I don't *care* how short a nuthouse stay you can get me, I don't *care* what a nice place you can arrange for! I didn't crack up over Ceecee, Danny. I'm not insane, I didn't kill Linda! That lunatic did and I'm not copping a plea!

What do you mean?

You're serious? You're goddamn serious?

Oh, but, Jesus, Danny, why didn't you tell me that? Why are you sitting here letting me tie myself up in knots? Why didn't you *tell* me? No, I know, you needed to hear the whole story first, and okay, but Danny, this is great! So he'll tell them, right, he'll tell them she was fixated on me, on the book. He'll tell them, and her whole story, her whole crazy story will . . .

Sure he will. Why wouldn't he? What's he got to lose?

Because he can't? What does that mean?

No.

Not dead. Tell me he's not dead, Danny. That's not what you said, I didn't hear you say that. Oh, Jesus. Oh, Jesus God. What am I going to do?

Worse? How could it possibly get worse?

That's not true. That can't be true, Danny, someone's lying. *My* yard? In *my* yard? That's not true!

Calm down? How the hell am I supposed to calm down? Okay, okay, I don't know, I don't go down there much, where you're saying, down by the streambed, in weather like this, all those jagged rocks in the ice. But she did this. You know she did, Danny. It's a lonely road, you know how isolated it is where I live. No one would have seen her.

And then, yes, came to the bar, found me, set me up! Killed him, double-crossed Linda, framed me. She was obsessed, Danny, with the book, that I told her secret. She was getting back at us, at all of us.

With *me*. *She* was obsessed with *me*.

Danny, Danny, I told you, I swear to you, I never even met her!

What are you talking about? No, Danny, don't go! Don't leave me here, man, don't just disappear! These walls, it's airless in here, it's cold! Everything's pressing down on me!

Unless I tell you the truth? But I am! I did! Everything I just told you, Danny, every word! It's what happened, Danny.

Danny, man, please? Come back? What I told you, it's what happened. I know what it sounds like, what it looks like. But what I'm telling you—I swear to you, man, it's true.

Please, Danny, you've got to believe me. I'm not blowing smoke here. These are the facts, Danny.

The cold, hard facts.

Catch Your Death

Linda Barnes

Tracey and Phil were a steamy topic before they married. They were still a hot item on the spectacular fall day they wed and long after the deed was done. The gossip hummed along, an undercurrent to the Boston social scene, occasionally bursting into the newspaper columns with a little levity and a touch of envy. Tracey, with her impeccable breeding and long-legged style, oozed nonchalant elegance. Phil was masculinity personified: great bones, big hands, and down-to-earth aw-shucks humility. As a twosome, they were so breathtakingly good looking they could have tangoed off a Hollywood movie screen.

"Oooh, please, tell me it's true looove," you might hear at the Oak Bar on Friday night or at a Park Plaza soirée on Saturday.

"You mean it might not be? Sweetie, grab me another margarita off that tray."

"I think it's more like a prolonged roll in the gutter—for her."

"And for him?"

"Can you hum a few bars of 'Tiptoe Through the Greenbacks'?"

Tracey had money. She was also my friend, so I failed to contribute to the gossip. Scathing words died on parted lips as I approached, although I didn't go to half the parties Grandmère, my only living relation, urged me to attend. Recovering from a brief and disastrous marriage, mostly I hid out in my childhood bedroom and tried to imagine the next phase of my life. I considered having calling cards printed: formerly well-fixed socialite, currently penniless divorcée. I ate pizza and the occasional Ding Dong and watched late-night TV.

I generally despise television, but that summer and fall I made an exception for anything having to do with Sherlock Holmes. Channel 44 came in poorly, the color oddly greenish and the sound scratchy, but they were doing a rerun of one of those marvelous Jeremy Brett Holmeses. I was cozily ensconced under a warm comforter and less than halfway through *A Scandal in Bohemia* when the doorbell rang.

How many thrilling Holmes adventures begin with a knock at the door, a young woman requiring the master's aid. My mind filling with copper beeches and speckled bands, I wrapped the belt of my robe more tightly around my waist and peered out the peephole.

Tracey Miles and I were roommates at school, a strangely matched duo. At Milton Academy, I was the standoffish, defensive orphan, she, the universally acknowledged queen of our year. I was small, tough, and excellent at anything that allowed a girl to get sweaty, fencing in particular. Tracey, on the other hand, wouldn't have known a rapier from a broomstick. Grandmère always declared I had too much energy and too little grasp of etiquette. Tracey, even as a girl, had the manners of an angel. She gave her corn silk hair a quick flick each morning, while I wrestled a steel comb through my dark curly mane. I was never able to sit quietly at my desk and behave like a good girl, but Tracey was, and her friendship spread a special aura that protected me from the nastiness some of the other oddities were forced to endure.

My eyes sought the twelve-year-old Tracey I had known behind the soigné adult mask I was looking at. Her long, golden hair was pinned back with a tortoiseshell clip. She wore glasses rather than her customary contacts. I opened the door at once.

"Can I come in?" She smelled faintly of cigarettes.

"What's wrong?" A gust of cool air entered with her. Rain battered down on Commonwealth Avenue outside the gated entryway of my grandmother's brownstone.

"Oh, Franny," was her reply. She said it with a shiver.

"Let me get you a towel—and some tea."

"Is your grandmother—"

"Asleep." Grandmère would sleep through the Apocalypse, let alone the doorbell. "Don't worry." I tossed the comforter in Tracey's direction and made off downstairs for the kitchen.

When I got back, carrying both towels and tea, she was where I had been, curled under the comforter on the deep red sofa, watching Jeremy Brett, in the guise of a clergyman, as he endeavored to fool the immortal Irene Adler, "of dubious and questionable memory," into revealing the whereabouts of her prized royal photograph.

"That wouldn't work," Tracey said thoughtfully, "would it?"

"Holmes always works," I replied.

"So you think that would be a good way to locate a hiding place?"

I turned my attention to the greenish screen. Following Holmes's instructions, the faithful Watson was tossing a smoke bomb through the French doors of Miss Adler's rented villa.

"Crying fire? I've never tried it. What's up, Trace?"

"Would Jack's Joke Shop carry those phony smoke bombs?"

"Home Depot, more likely; plumbers use them to find sewer gas leaks—or they used to. When I was a kid, Grandmère had to have all these ancient pipes replaced; I remember the smell. What's bothering you, Trace?" She hadn't smoked in months.

"Oh—I don't know—"

"Please don't tell me you just decided to go for an hours-long walk in the rain on a whim."

She glanced at her Rolex and her eyes widened. "It *has* been hours."

From the state of her shoes, the duration of her trek was obvious. She certainly hadn't made any mad two-minute dash from her place on nearby Marlborough Street. "Tracey, seriously, this is not the best time to wander the area at night."

"The BBR, you mean?" She tossed her head and shot me her goofiest smile. "Like he's going to pick on little ol' me?"

Tracey was tall, I'll give her that. She measured almost six feet, but she was tall in the way that models are tall; willowy, rather than stocky or muscular. In my opinion, she had little reason to believe, as she always seemed to, that evil would pass her by and select a shorter victim. I felt she assumed a rationality in bad guys that in actuality they rarely possessed.

The so-called Back Bay Rapist was no paragon of rationality, except insofar as territory was concerned. He had started his string of crimes on the banks of the Charles River, working the paths of the Esplanade. The police believed he had ventured farther into the Back Bay only because women were no longer running the Esplanade late at night.

The rapist was moving steadily inland, across Beacon Street to staid Commonwealth Avenue and fashionable Newbury Street. But what worried the police and the female population even more than his steady encroachment was his increasing level of violence. The last woman he'd attacked, a tourist apparently unaware of the postmidnight threat, was still unconscious at Mass General.

"Tracey, it isn't like you're Superwoman. You're not even mildly athletic."

"But I look athletic," she said complacently. "That's what counts. Don't I look like I could deck a guy?"

Tracey had never needed a roundhouse punch to knock men out, a little eyelash fluttering being generally sufficient. "Still, not the best night to wander," I said.

"On the 'catch your death' scale?"

I smiled, the way I always did when Tracey slipped into our old school jargon. "You'll catch your death in that," was something

Grandmère used to say when she caught me wearing a revealing outfit. If an outfit didn't earn a "catch your death" rating, it was hardly worth wearing.

"Tracey," I said, "be a dear, drink your tea, and tell me why you're not in bed with the handsomest man in Boston. Is he working late tonight?" Part of the reason for the gossip about their marriage was the fact that Tracey's Phil was not one of us, not a Brahmin, not even a black-sheep Brahmin like me. He was working class, a gem of the meritocracy, actually a policeman, an honest-to-God cop, although far above and past the uniformed man-on-the-beat phase. "Is he out hunting the BBR?"

She was staring at the TV like it was a fireplace, her gaze faraway and unfocused.

"Trace?"

"If you give someone a present," she said slowly, "that's it, right? You can't take it back."

"Usually." The query fit the story on the screen: The king of Bohemia had given his mistress, the divine Irene, a cabinet portrait of the two of them together. Now that he was about to be married, the noble cad desperately wanted the portrait back before his holier-than-thou father-in-law-to-be found out about their affair and called off the wedding.

"Even if you thought they were going to, say, give your present away?"

That didn't fit with the Holmes story. "Like regifting, you mean?"

"Or if they were going to sell it."

"Sell your present, something you had given them, to the highest bidder?"

"Yes."

"Tracey, what the hell are you talking about?"

"I thought Sherlock Holmes hated women."

"Shall I turn it off, so we can talk?"

"No. She's really gorgeous."

"The actress playing Irene?"

"Sometimes gorgeous people, they're not . . ." She seemed to drift away from me.

"Tracey? Go on." When she hesitated, I spoke her name a second time.

She smiled and shook her head, then gazed at her teacup as though wondering how it had gotten into her hand. "Do you have anything stronger than tea?" she said. "Do you ever hide any of Grandmère's brandy bottles down here?"

"She's tipping back martinis this week." When my grandmother drinks, she drinks. When she does martinis, she starts with a pitcher. When she moves on to brandy, entire bottles disappear, even when I forget to hide them.

I unearthed a half-empty bottle of Armagnac from under the sofa, dumped the remains of the tea into a nearby potted plant, and poured.

"That's better," my guest said with a sigh. "I've been thinking of going back to work at the museum."

A quiver in the set of her jaw told me it wasn't what she had intended to say, but I let that pass, eager to hear more. Prior to her marriage, Tracey had been an administrative assistant at the Museum of Fine Arts, a high-powered whiz, an up-and-comer. I'd often wondered why she had left a job for which she'd seemed so well suited, a job she had obviously enjoyed.

Far from being the dumb blonde some assumed her to be, Tracey had advanced degrees in art history as well as finance, and had practically lived in European museums when she hadn't been at school. Not that she would have needed to visit museums to admire artwork. The paintings on her mother's walls were legendary, especially the exquisite Picasso sketches Tracey had received on the occasion of her wedding.

"Howell would kill to have you back," I said. "Would you work with him again?"

"I don't know. Alan is such a fastidious pain in the ass. The only person more anal than I am."

When I roomed with Tracey, she folded her underwear like origami.

She shifted under the comforter. "And if I do give in and go back, then as soon as I get pregnant, he'll fire my sweetly rounded ass."

"So you're trying?" I couldn't help it; I felt a twinge of jealousy.

"I wish Phil were half as eager to be a daddy as I am to be a mom."

"And you've been talking to Alan? About working with him again?" I said lightly.

She said nothing.

"Well, he can't fire you if you get pregnant. It's against the law."

"He'd make me unwelcome; he sees pregnant women as unesthetic."

"What? With all those Madonnas?"

"They have the child, not the belly."

"So fight him in court."

"I'm not good at making waves, Franny. I need you for that."

It's true; if wave making were a craft, I'd have a dozen merit badges: I do most of my drinking at working-class bars rather than secretly like Grandmère; I sport an indiscreet tattoo, and I once dyed my hair purple on a dare.

"Tracey, are you in some kind of trouble?" I asked her.

"How does living at home again suit you? Is Grandmère making herself totally unbearable?"

I let her change the subject. I regret that now. We discussed my thus far futile attempts to recover the bulk of my estate from the con artist I'd married, while she kept her eyes on the TV screen as though it were an oracle. If you need an oracle, you can do far worse than Holmes, so I left the program on for her enlightenment.

"Is everything okay with Phil?" I finally asked her.

"Oh, sure. Phil is Phil, you know? He's thinking of quitting the force."

I'd already heard as much through the grapevine, and it was only to be expected. Why would anyone keep working undercover vice, putting in brutal hours at a brutal job, when they had the Miles pile to draw on?

I nodded sagely. "So you'll be able to travel more? Do you have any plans in the works? Tuscany? The Greek isles?"

"Franny, I wish he'd keep working. I love that he works. I mean, I ask myself, is so much money good for anybody?"

I almost said, "I wouldn't mind some."

She read my mind. "I'm sorry. I always say the wrong— Are things very dreadful? With the ex?"

"He's a wonderful liar."

"We all thought you were the luckiest woman in the world. Such a hottie, and a med student to boot."

I didn't want to go into the grim details, so I simply quoted from "The Adventures of the Speckled Band": "'When a doctor goes bad, he is the worst of criminals.'"

"You don't blame me for introducing the two of you, do you, Franny? If I'd had any idea—" She gave a faint laugh and broke off. "But just think, it could have been worse; you could have married Henry."

Henry is Tracey's ne'er-do-well big brother. When I dated him, he was the bass player in a drug-addled punk-rock band. He'd had occasional spurts of employment since, none of the gilt-edged-banker variety.

"Henry's still not married, is he?" I asked.

"Believe me," Tracey said, "you do not want to go there. Oh, if you just intended to use him for casual sex, that would be fine. I mean, he'd love it and . . . You're not dating anyone, are you, Fran?"

"I'm not desperate enough for Henry yet, but who knows? Maybe next week."

Tracey had been tactfully yawning for some time, the wings of her nostrils delicately flaring, and I realized I was yawning too.

"How awful of me," she said contritely. "You want to go to sleep."

I glanced out the window; the rain was still bucketing down. "Stay the night," I said.

"No. Really, I should get back."

"Please. You shouldn't walk home alone."

"I'll be fine. Don't be ridiculous."

"I am not being ridiculous."

"Yes, you are," she said. "Don't worry."

"But I didn't do anything to help. You didn't even—"

"Henry," she said softly. "My own brother. Of course."

"What?"

"I don't need your help after all. It's elementary, my dear Watson." With that parting shot, Tracey tossed her blond head, closed the door, and disappeared into the rainy darkness.

Holmes never says that in the entire canon, but I didn't get the chance to tax Tracey with her error because I never saw her again. Two nights later, her body was discovered in an alleyway off Clarendon Street and the newspapers went berserk with the story: beautiful, privileged Tracey Miles, the first of the Back Bay Rapist's victims to die.

Trinity Church was filled with arum lilies, tall stems bunched and tied with ropy beach grass, just as they had been at the wedding. Same church, same flowers. A heavy coffin instead of a happy couple. Guests in rustling black instead of party clothes. The smell of lilies was overwhelming, the overheated sanctuary stifling.

I couldn't recall a single funeral in Holmes. In *A Study in Scarlet,* Jefferson Hope makes an appearance at the deathbed of his beloved, Lucy Ferrier, and rips the wedding ring of his detested rival from her hand. "She shall not be buried in that," he thunders.

"Faites attention!" Grandmère whispered sharply. "You will step on my poor feet!"

The more she drinks—and she drinks plenty—the clumsier I become.

"Your dress is disgraceful," she said. "You'll catch your death in that!"

I shared a secret laugh with Tracey, who'd helped me pick out the short black dress, admittedly for another occasion.

Phil, surrounded by men—by their attire and demeanor, fellow officers of the law—looked gaunt and pinched, as dreadful as a man with his enviable bone structure could appear. I was glad his friends shielded him from the pressing crowd and relieved that he had his own people present. As Grandmère offered the widower our condolences, Tracey's brother, Henry Miles, elegant and ravaged, approached. Grasping my hand, he begged me to sit with him in the front pew. I felt initially uncomfortable at the breach of etiquette; I was hardly family. But it was a way to rid myself of Grandmère, who seemed thrilled that Henry had chosen me from the masses and who would likely spend the day informing her claque of elderly busybodies how close the two of us young people were, implying that a marriage with the wealthy Mileses was surely a certainty.

Lay and religious leaders spoke movingly about Tracey's talent and spirit. Afterward, I joined Henry in the back of a limousine for the endless ride to Mount Auburn Cemetery where more flowers were heaped on the pile of raw earth. Hydrangeas and roses, this time, and the sky was a perfect blue.

Tracey's mother invited me for tea after the funeral. I was longing to get away, but she and Henry both implored me to stay, and I allowed myself to be persuaded. In the scarlet-and-ivory dining room, so familiar from long school weekends, I poured myself a cup of steaming liquid from a vintage silver pot, and longed for fortification from one of Grandmère's many hidden bottles. I felt a hand on my shoulder and turned to find Phil.

"Why on earth would she have gone out of the house so late at night? Didn't she know the danger?"

I wondered whether he had asked each person in the room the same two questions. I wasn't sure from the look on his face that he realized he was speaking out loud.

"Who could she have possibly been going to see?"

His face looked frozen, almost frightening, and somehow I couldn't bring myself to tell him that Tracey might have been on her way to visit me. Again.

"I blame myself. I've been working the late shift so long. I'll kill the bastard when I catch him. She was so worried about me, that something would happen to me on the job. And now this."

I half-opened my mouth, but failed to come up with a single comforting word to say.

"You don't think she was having an affair, do you?"

My teacup rattled against the saucer. "What? Why would you think I—"

"She told you things, Franny, didn't she?"

"Are you drunk?"

"God, I wish I were. Why did she go out? Where was she going?" He moved away and for a moment I thought I might have hallucinated the entire encounter.

Henry Miles was everywhere, hanging on to my hand, flirting, moaning, downing aspirin, nervous and shaky. Whenever he'd release me, to shake hands or wipe his eyes with his handkerchief, I'd move away. Five minutes later, he'd catch up with me again.

I sought refuge in talking to a dark man with watchful eyes.

"You must work with Phil," I said.

"How did you guess?"

"I never guess." I decided against mentioning the wrinkled suit, the bulge of the holster beneath the armpit. Nor did I add that I was quite certain, from his age, habitual squint, and military bearing, that he had served in the first Iraq war.

"The shoes, right?" he said. "They're a giveaway, but even if I wasn't a cop, I'd need 'em, I guess. Flat feet need lace-up shoes. Although flat feet, that's a cop disease right there. Maybe if I wasn't a cop, I'd wear better shoes." He smiled. He had an engaging smile.

"Max," he said, offering his hand.

"Frances." I asked him why the police seemed so certain that the Back Bay Rapist was in fact Tracey's killer. The man had never killed before.

"Oh, it's the same guy," he said. "Same MO."

"But surely someone could have copied him."

"We don't tell the newspapers everything."

"The missing locks of hair?"

"How do you know about that?"

"Common gossip." Several acquaintances had mentioned that the rapist snipped a souvenir from the head of each victim. "People talk."

"Too much."

"Was Tracey's hair—"

"I can't say."

"I hope that's not the fact you're holding back."

"Don't worry. It was the Back Bay Rapist. We can prove it and we'll catch the bastard."

Oddly comforted by the encounter, almost convinced I might be able to eat something for the first time since I'd heard of Tracey's death, I moved on. At a linen-swathed table in the front parlor, Alan Howell was selecting finger sandwiches and tiny pastries from an assortment of silver trays. He seemed untouched by the tragedy, removed, but then Howell always maintained a surface shine. It was almost impossible to imagine him grieving. He was more like one of the paintings in the museum than a real person.

I watched as he studied a portrait of Tracey that hung in a shaded alcove. She had been barely a teenager, the artist undistinguished, but Alan gave it careful scrutiny, as though he were considering making an offer, having it reframed, and hanging it in his office. I eavesdropped shamelessly as he spoke to Tracey's mother and uncle. He seemed to be trying to inspire commemorative donations to the MFA's building fund.

I noted the warm gleam of his shoes, the well-cut Brioni suit, and I wondered if Tracey might have indulged in an extramarital fling with her former boss.

Henry, growing increasingly tedious, took to keeping a possessive hand on my arm, using me as a shield to ward off certain disapproving relatives. He'd obviously been drinking, but on the whole, he seemed to be holding his liquor fairly well. I smiled and nodded occasionally, rarely following the entirety of a conversation as I watched Alan Howell work the room.

Then, clear as a crystal bell, I heard it. Brother Henry, in response to a former classmate's query, was saying how long it had been since he'd seen Tracey, how much he'd wanted to see her, and how devastated he'd been on discovering that she'd come to visit him on the very day before her death. She hadn't waited, had just left a brief note and taken what she'd wanted. So like a little sister, that was.

"What did she take?" If Henry's balding fraternity brother hadn't asked, I would have interjected the question myself.

"I don't . . . I still can't figure out why she wanted it. You know, I'm producing now, but when I was still performing, I wrote this weird, sort of spooky song. I wanted a fog effect for performance, so I bought a smoke machine secondhand. I showed it to Tracey once; I think she might have borrowed it for a party." He turned to me. "Was she planning another party, Fran?"

I swallowed suddenly, feeling abruptly light-headed. I made my excuses to Henry and the rest of the family and walked the mile and a half to Grandmère's to clear my head. In the familiar kitchen, I brewed coffee. The clock ticked loudly as I sat at the long wooden table and attempted to organize my thoughts.

"I can't make bricks without clay," Holmes insists in "The

Adventure of the Copper Beeches." Bricks are theories. So what were my facts, my troubling lumps of clay?

Tracey had been worried when she came to see me; I had no doubt of that. She had been smoking. She had speculated about how one would go about getting a gift back. She had watched *A Scandal in Bohemia,* and seemed quite taken by the method Holmes had employed to find Irene Adler's hiding place. She had been killed.

All separate and isolated facts—until paired with the vision of Tracey making off with brother Henry's smoke machine.

The next day, dressed in a demure and ladylike suit, I set off for lunch at the Museum of Fine Art, timing my arrival for Alan Howell's fashionably late 2:35 lunch break. Tracey always said you could set your watch by him. He never brought a brown-bag lunch or sank to the level of the cafeteria. He lunched at the posh restaurant on the second floor, presiding over a round table to which certain members of the staff were invited along with a variety of wealthy contributors. I was confident that Grandmère's money, which she periodically threatens to leave to a home for cats, would guarantee my place, and indeed, when I caught his eye, he motioned for me to join him.

We were five at table. We discussed the new Hopper exhibit and what effect its popularity might have on property values in Truro. The two art conservators left first, called back to chemical pursuits that left telltale stains on their fingers. The docent left for her tour groups fifteen minutes later—surely no one who spent that kind of money on shoes and clothing had need of paid employment—and I simply outlasted the other potential donor. Once left alone with Howell, it was not difficult to lead the conversation in the direction I wished it to go.

"I don't know what I'll do without her," he said at the first mention of Tracey's name.

"She spoke to you about coming back to work?"

"Never. If she had, I'd have hired her in a flash. I've had three people in that position since she left and none of them do half what she did. Oh, I can't believe . . . I just can't believe she's gone. I keep . . . She wasn't a jogger. What was she doing out? Why didn't she . . ."

"Why didn't she what?"

He expelled a deep breath. "I wanted to marry Tracey. I don't know if she ever mentioned that to you? Oh, it was years ago, but I don't think I ever got over her. And now . . ."

"Now?"

"I don't know if you've heard—I mean, I just heard, so you probably haven't. She left us a bequest. Not to me, personally, to the MFA."

Tracey would have had a will. The truly well off, those with too much at stake to leave to chance, are always hand in glove with estate attorneys.

If she hadn't had a will, Massachusetts would have peremptorily divided her estate, with the first $200,000 going to her husband outright. Phil would have gotten half the remainder of the estate as well.

"Did she leave art?" I asked.

"Money."

The bequest to the museum couldn't be the gift she wanted to take back. If Tracey had decided against a bequest, she needed only to speak to her attorney to have it altered.

"A very generous amount. But not her little Picassos," Howell added with a sigh of regret.

"She couldn't have left you those, Alan. She sold them several months ago."

"Sold them? Who told you that?"

"Well, I'm quite sure I heard it somewhere," I said, retrieving my napkin before it slid to the floor. "I'd rather assumed she'd discussed the sale with you."

"She would never have sold them."

"I heard she got a phenomenal offer."

"I don't believe it. I know she was thinking of donating them to us. She'd mentioned it recently. Oh, damn those sketches anyway."

"I thought you adored them."

"Oh, I do. They're superb. But I think Tracey believed that I . . . that I fell in love with her in the hope of someday owning those drawings. And while I admit to my share—maybe more than my share—of art lust, it wasn't true. I loved her, but she never—" He stopped and straightened his silverware, carefully repositioning knife and fork.

"Did she happen to visit you last Wednesday? The day before—"

"No. No. I only wish she had."

I thanked him for lunch, took the escalator to the first floor, and stopped at the West Wing coat-check stand. The tall student on duty had an unfortunate case of acne and a straggly mustache.

"Were you working on Wednesday?" I asked him.

He squinted in an effort to remember, finally bobbed his head yes.

"Right through the fire alarm?"

"Last Wednesday? There was no fire alarm."

"The bomb threat, then?"

"What are you talking about, lady? No bomb threats, no fire alarms. Biggest thing happened last week, I misplaced some dude's umbrella."

Deep in thought, I strolled through the Japanese garden. In his heyday, Holmes kept hidey-holes filled with the elements of his disguises all over London, rented rooms festooned with racks of clerical garb, wigs, and theatrical makeup. I was forced to retreat to Grandmère's and endure a squall of her bad temper while I changed into a mannish white blouse, dark trousers, and an aged pair of flat-heeled walking shoes.

"But where will you go dressed *comme ça*?"

"Out," I said firmly, suiting action to word.

I walked, grateful for my comfortable footwear, as far as Howell's South End apartment building, where I rang a bell in the foyer. Not Howell's bell. Any bell. Several bells. I was there to test the smoke detectors, I informed a woman whose raspy voice finally erupted from the squawk box. Had I been a man, she might, fearing the Back Bay Rapist, have called the police. My voice was undeniably female, high, light, and unthreatening, so she buzzed me right in.

I ascended to the fourth floor and knocked on the doors of Alan Howell's closest neighbors. After no replies at the first three apartments, I worried that I would find no one at home, but at my very next target, a man who looked like he drank for a living hauled the door ajar and seemed gratified to answer any and all queries. He hadn't been awakened by any fire alarms for two and a half years, easy. His wife, who worked the day shift, would have screamed bloody murder if the smoke detectors or the fire alarm had gone off Wednesday night.

I walked down Marlborough Street on my way home. How Tracey had loved her building. It lacked the magnolia trees that adorned the front garden of her mother's house, but she had planned to take cuttings from the mature trees and reroot them in new soil. I gazed up at the windows of the penthouse. If she hadn't sold her Picassos, they would still be hanging on the bedroom walls.

My testing-the-smoke-detectors tale gained me easy access here as well. By this time I was beginning to feel mildly foolish. Perhaps Henry had made a mistake. He had drunk so much, and who knew what other substances he might have downed to improve his mood? His tale of the missing smoke machine might have been part of a fog of his own invention.

Tracey's next-door neighbor was eager to divulge all the details of the scare her family had experienced late Wednesday night when, from out of the blue, the hallway smoke detector had gone berserk and begun to wail.

As Holmes clearly states in "The Adventure of Silver Blaze," "One true inference invariably suggests another."

When the evil Vincent Spaulding of "The Red-headed League" needs uninterrupted access to the cellar of Jabez Wilson's pawnshop, he invents a ruse that will absent Mr. Wilson from his place of business for days on end. I needed only a few hours.

I called Phil at work, disguising my voice, avoiding caller ID, and made an appointment for him to interview an attorney in Portsmouth, Maine. Tracey's family has a summerhouse in Maine; various parcels of surrounding land belonged to Tracey. I made it a matter of some urgency. Tomorrow at three fifteen.

By three o'clock I was back in Tracey's building, armed with the key she had given me to use in case of emergencies. Tracey and I had always given each other keys to our respective homes. The previous "emergencies" had usually involved articles of clothing. "God, Franny, can you bring my black moiré sandals to the Ritz tonight; these pumps are killing me." Once, Tracey had required a bra and panties, in a discreet shopping bag, delivered to her office at the museum. I tried and failed to remember whether that was before or after she had met Phil.

Until the moment I opened the hall closet in Tracey and Phil's condo and saw the smoke machine on the floor, I thought that the chain of facts I had built into an assumption of guilt might yet be proved wrong. But there it sat, solid and square, a power cord trailing from its underside like a thin black snake. I sank to my knees on the carpeting and played my tiny flashlight across the pile. Tracey had worn kitten heels, her usual footgear. No other footprints marred the surface. I stood and made my way carefully, quietly, into the master bedroom, only to discover that someone had run a Hoover across the silver broadloom.

The bed was a canopied four-poster heaped with lacy white pillows, the furniture antique cherry. One of Tracey's scarves was draped across the corner of a gilt-framed mirror. The emptiness of the far wall brought my eyes to a halt. I examined the wallpaper, noting the faint outlines where the Picasso sketches had hung.

They'd had an iron-clad prenuptial agreement, Tracey and Phil. Cleverer than I, Tracey would have been able to walk away from her marriage with her fortune intact. Unless, of course, she had seriously compromised her net worth by giving the Picassos to Phil.

It was Phil, dear Phil, who had told me she'd sold the Picassos. And I'd believed him.

My theory: When Tracey used the ruse of fire to get Phil to betray his hiding place, to indicate where he had hidden the Picassos, the gift she now wanted back, Phil realized for the first time that Tracey was thinking of leaving him. He knew that if she found and reclaimed the Picassos, he would walk away with nothing.

I believed he'd killed her in a fit of rage, then escaped detection by moving the body and staging the crime scene to throw blame on the Back Bay Rapist. Phil, a former homicide detective, would know whatever the police knew about the BBR.

I was determined that he should not profit from his crime.

What would Holmes do?

I sat cross-legged on the floor and considered hiding places. "A Scandal in Bohemia" features a "recess behind a sliding panel just above the right bell-pull." In "The Adventure of the Musgrave Ritual," a seemingly meaningless recitation guides Holmes "west by one and one, and so under."

The nature of a hiding place is often determined by the thing to be hidden. I visualized the five Picasso sketches. Framed. Flat, eight by six, small eloquent sketches.

Oh, Tracey, I thought, why give them away? Why give them to a man, to *any* man?

Hiding places. Hiding places. The Six Napoleons? No. Irrelevant. In "The Adventure of the Second Stain," the hiding place is underneath the rug. I'd already moved the small bedside Oriental and there were no stains to be found. In "The Adventure of Charles Augustus Milverton," the vile society blackmailer keeps his compromising letters in the safe.

Did the brownstone run to a safe? I pried artwork away from the walls.

These old brownstones were so alike, all built at the same time, as soon as the landfill that made up the Back Bay settled sufficiently to permit residential construction. The layout of this place was almost identical to Grandmère's, and at the back of Grandmère's closet there used to be a fur-storage vault, a cedar closet tucked behind the regular closet, hidden so no thief would think to look inside.

In the closet of the master bedroom, Tracey's scent was overwhelming, her perfume everywhere. I sank to my knees and began the hunt for the mechanism. I went by memory, the memory of a small child who used to hide in Grandmère's closet, who liked to pat the "bunnies" in the secret closet, who learned the movement, the motion, the magic click that would release the spring and reveal the hanging furs.

The click when it came seemed terribly loud and the panel fell away into darkness. Grandmère's secret closet had a pull chain, a tiptoe reach for a child. I aimed my keychain flash, located a similar pull chain, and yanked.

The framed sketches glowed against the paneled walls. But what held my horrified eyes, what must have held Tracey's eyes, were the coils of hair, the ribbon-tied locks of hair, each pinned at eye level to the far wall. Beneath each horrid souvenir was a collection of newspaper articles, roughly clipped from the *Globe* and the *Herald*. I didn't need to examine them to know that here was every detail ever published about the Back Bay Rapist. A wooden crutch leaned against the wall and I wondered whether it had been abandoned by some previous owner or whether it was part of the BBR's MO, a harmless man with a broken leg taking a late-night stroll.

No, I thought. Not Phil.

No, I thought again, when I heard the unmistakable sound of footsteps behind me.

I whirled to face him, fastening what must have been a ghastly smile on my face. "Phil! Tracey told me she'd leave me her pearls and I dropped by to pick them up. I know I should have called but—"

"I should never have given you a key."

"You didn't. Remember? You didn't have to. You said I could always use the one Tracey gave me."

"You greedy little tramp. She trusted you. She never imagined you would—"

"Don't give me that. She trusted you too."

"You told her about us, didn't you? Bragged about us?"

"No!"

"That's why she went back to that creep Howell."

"No, she didn't—"

"That's why she wanted the Picassos back. Because you told her about the two of us."

"No. I didn't. Why would I—"

His voice dropped half an octave, lowering in volume as well. "And now you want her pearls, darling? Is that really all you want?"

"Yes." I measured the distance to the pull chain, knew I couldn't reach it to suddenly kill the light.

"And have you seen everything you came to see?"

"I don't know what you mean." The crutch was the only defensive weapon available. If I moved quickly.

"Oh, I think you do."

I seized the crutch by the cross brace, spun without thinking, attacked, grimly aware that here was no *piste*, no formal playing ground, no umpire to shout, *"Allez! En garde."*

With little room to lunge, parry, or riposte, the match, I feared, would be brief. The crutch, far heavier even than the épée, was unwieldy within the confines of the closet. My opponent was stronger, heavier.

Holmes never screams. Not once in the entire canon, not once in the four novels or fifty-six adventures, does the master cry out. Watson, his devoted sidekick, maintains a stoic silence as well.

I, despite their example, screamed because I knew that soon I would be unable to make any sound at all. Phil had his big hands on the crutch. He was winning the battle for its control. Once he wrested it from my grip, his hands would close around my throat, as they must have closed around Tracey's throat. I screamed again, louder, and the sound echoed off the walls of the closet behind the closet, the small room I was certain would become my death chamber.

There was a crash and a rush of heavy feet. Phil started, turned, and the crutch came loose, skittering to the floor. A voice yelled, "Get down!" and I obeyed, cowering, my knees giving way, my head seeking shelter beneath my shaking arms.

The dark-eyed policeman from the funeral tea, Max of the regrettable shoes, was the first to approach. "You should have trusted us to do the job, Frances," he said severely. "We were watching him."

"Phil was the—"

"Back Bay Rapist, yeah."

Had Holmes ever made such an egregious series of errors? I'd assumed Phil had killed Tracey for her money, killed her and used the serial rapist's increasing violence to account for the death, but now I saw the sequence of events far differently. Tracey, growing increasingly uneasy about her marriage, perhaps suspecting our affair, had determined to dissolve her marriage, but was equally determined to leave with the Picasso sketches.

Phil must have hidden them, told her possession was nine-tenths of the law, hinted that he'd never give them back. She must have suspected they were still in the house.

How horrified she must have been to discover not only the hidden sketches, but the trophies of Phil's crimes as well. Had he found her in the fur vault? Or had she foolishly tried to confront him, to urge him to turn himself in?

Max was speaking. I made an effort and focused on his words.

He said, "Who knows what makes a guy like that tick? Married to a beautiful woman? Having affairs, left and right? It sure wasn't about the sex."

"And I would have thought he'd have had his fill of power as a cop."

"Yeah, I just don't get it. Terrorizing his own neighborhood like that." Max shook his head sadly. " 'But improbable as it is, all other explanations are more improbable still.' "

"What did you say?"

He repeated himself. "It's a quotation from—"

"From Sherlock Holmes," I said. " 'The Adventure of Silver Blaze,' isn't it?"

"Yes, but Holmes uses it, in slightly different words, in no less than six of the stories. I know he says something quite similar in 'The Adventure of the Beryl Coronet.' "

"And again, in *The Sign of Four*."

"My favorite of the novels," the policeman said.

"Don't most readers favor *The Hound of the Baskervilles*?"

" 'An exception disproves the rule.' "

I gave my lashes a flutter Tracey might have envied, and smiled up at him. "I have to admit, I'm not familiar with that quotation."

"Holmes again. From *The Sign of Four*, the one you just mentioned." Max returned my smile with interest. "Are you feeling better now?"

"Much."

"I'll have one of my men drive you home, Frances. Or—"

"Or?"

"If you wouldn't mind waiting while I tidy up a few loose ends, there's an interesting concert at the conservatory later this evening."

"A violinist, I presume."

"I've heard he has a very light touch with Chopin."

"That would be splendid, Max."

INTRODUCING . . .

THE RUNAWAY CAMEL

Barbara Fryer

My fellow partners at Budde, Schmidt, Jackson, and Hesketh think it is a sleazy public relations nightmare. Harold Schmidt is the one exception. He understands as I do that one man's ceiling is another man's floor.

At sixty-one and with a predilection for ascots, pipes, poetry, and esoteric facts, Harold comes from another generation, more romantic and less selfish than my own. He is as close to a mentor as I need or can handle, which is to say he hired me and later recommended me for partner. Harold is a good man to have in your corner. Sometimes he turns up in court. I see him in the back row, watching and weighing. He is a meticulous litigator who loses very few cases, which accounts for the corner office from which he can see all of downtown Philadelphia.

Today he sees a crew from *Extra* lurking near the fountain at the front of the building. I know why they are there. The cameraman wants a picture of me, and the blond cutie with a mike is looking to lob a few hardball questions my way. *Are you covering up for Dijon Roosevelt? Are the two of you an item?* Harold suggests I leave via the Chestnut Street exit unless I want to see myself on the front page of the *Inquirer* in the morning. I do as he suggests.

When I was nine years old, I jumped off the roof of the St. Ignatius Elementary School auditorium because my brother Bill said, *I bet you can't.* I broke my right leg in three places and was in a cast for twelve weeks. But when I think back to the experience, I don't remember the pain—only the exhilaration of falling; the flash of tiny stars; the gasp of sudden air; the radiating quiver; the unstoppable, insatiable tumbling. That was how I felt the first time I saw Dijon Roosevelt, a year ago at Arena Stadium at the Serpents' opening game. He was black, beautiful, and unshaven, with high cheekbones and thick, dark brows. At seven feet he was bigger than life and certainly better proportioned. He wore the same blue-and-silver warm-ups as the rest of his team but he stood apart, an original museum piece among cheap, back-alley knockoffs.

"Who is that?" I asked my date.

"Dijon," he said. "Dijon Roosevelt. He leads the league in scoring." I smiled, not doubting that fact for a minute, knowing that if he reached his long arms into row G, seat 7, I would have let him take me in front of a sellout crowd of twenty thousand. I could not take my eyes from him the entire game. He moved with the grace of a cougar, sure and sudden, attacking the rim again and again.

In the days that followed, I read everything about Dijon Roosevelt that I could get my hands on. I learned that he spoke three languages, four if you counted street; that his biceps measured nineteen inches; that he himself had sketched the tattoo of planets orbiting his right bicep; that he had anger issues; that he spent two semesters at Temple University, which was long enough to impregnate the coach's daughter, a high school senior at Saint Maria Goretti. And I also knew, as did everyone in the city, that he was the Serpents' key to an NBA ring, if not this year then certainly next.

I went to a second and third game. I bought a jersey with Dijon's number seven on it, and wore it to bed at night. I read about a charity event he was sponsoring. I went, hoping to run into him. I didn't see Dijon, but I saw his wife, Tara, a tiny brunette in a black Prada cashmere cardigan, who wore a gold necklace with a diamond-studded number seven dangling from it. Her toddler son sat on a booster chair at one of the back tables, crayons and coloring book in front of him and a nanny beside him. He was a miniature of his father. Anyone could see that even without the name tag—Dijon Junior—attached to his tiny jersey. I stooped to pick up a crayon he had dropped, but the nanny took it from me before I could return it to him.

I loved the relentlessness of basketball season, the sheer stamina required of the players who had only a day or two to recover between games. But even more I loved the frequency of the games because it satisfied my insatiable need to be with Dijon Roosevelt. I bought a season ticket on the Internet, which positioned me center line, five rows back. I came early to watch Dijon warm up. He was loose then, stretching, joking, shooting from half-court. But when the game started, his brow furrowed, his focus intensified, and he went to work.

Despite the noise that rumbled through the stadium and vibrated the seats, despite the drone of an organ and the screams of D-fense! D-fense! D-fense! the drama on the floor narrowed to a single body as far as I was concerned. With the intensity of a medical student, I studied the bulge of his deltoid, the quiver of his bicep, the pivot of his foot encased in silver-and-black athletic shoes, size sixteen. With the eye of an artist I memorized the way his tongue flicked in and out whenever he made a difficult shot; the way he skipped up court on a fast break; the intricate dance of his pump fakes. And with the wonder of the besotted, I imagined his tongue playing on the hard court of my body.

Off court I steeped myself in this foreign culture of his. I devoured the daily sports pages, picked up *Sports Illustrated* on a regular basis, listened to call-in radio where fans vetted their after-game blues; and, of course, I drilled the experts, who included my apartment super, the security guard at our law firm, and just about every bartender in the city.

In the beginning I went only to the home games, but soon I was traveling out of state. Newark. Chicago. Miami. Detroit. Orlando. Twice I went to Texas, first Dallas and then Houston. I found out where the team stayed and booked rooms there. I sat in strange lobbies with my BlackBerry, conducting business, ever vigilant for a single glimpse. I saw Dijon's teammates, his posse, his coach, but never him.

It was in January, after the Serpents beat the Celtics, that one of Dijon's guys approached me in the lobby of a Boston hotel. "You around a lot," he said. "What's your story?"

I was relieved to know that Dijon's friends kept an eye out for strangers who might want to stalk him. "I'm here on business." I handed him my card.

"Whoa. A lawyer." He commandeered a winged chair next to mine, his eyes patrolling the lobby.

"What about you?" I asked. "What do you do?"

"A little of this. A little of that." He rapped my knuckle with his. "Tee," he said. "D and me go back a ways."

"Are you his bodyguard or something?"

Tee shrugged.

"I bet you know all his secrets."

"Ain't nobody know everybody's secrets."

I let it drop.

Our conversation, what little there was, halted when Tee spotted a young blonde in the hotel doorway. "Got to go to work," he said. He ambled in the direction of the door, said something to the blonde, and then walked her toward the bank of elevators. They both boarded one.

A few minutes later Tee returned and headed to the bar. I waited around for a long time, but the young woman never came down.

I spent a lot of time daydreaming at the office, but since spring was in the air, along with other pollutants, my inattentiveness was overlooked by everyone. Except Harold Schmidt.

"Why so pale and wan?" he asked, stopping at my open office door on his way out one evening. "I thought you would be walking on air after the legal coup d'état you pulled off in court this morning. That look on the opposing attorney's face was priceless."

"You were there?"

"You didn't see me?"

I said I hadn't. I wasn't sure why I lied. Perhaps I was embarrassed to admit that I got off on being observed by a senior partner at the top of my game.

"You were unyielding," he said. "Magnificently unyielding."

"Thank you." I bowed and smiled.

He looked over the spectacles sliding down his broad nose. There was a flicker of something I couldn't read in his dark eyes. "Is everything all right?" he asked.

"I always look this way when I mull."

"Personally, I find moving, pacing, that sort of thing, an effective way to mull," he said.

"I may try that next."

"Do, and let me know the results." He nodded and left me. My way of mulling wasn't working, so I decided to try Harold's method. I stood and paced from desk to bookcase. Three steps. Not enough stimulation for a single thought. I walked toward the door. Then back to my desk. I kept thinking about the one encounter I'd had with Dijon's friend Tee. There was something about it that didn't ring true. I didn't look like a groupie nor did I appear threatening. Why then had Tee approached me that evening in the hotel lobby? It came to me in a rush. I stopped pacing. Tee wasn't the one who had noticed me. He was only the messenger, an emissary sent to take a street version of a deposition. Yes, that was it. Dijon had seen in me a challenge, a mirror reflection of himself. He had dispatched Tee to see if he was reading me correctly, to see if I wanted what he wanted. And I did. I wanted to leave the social niceties on the bench. I wanted to execute under pressure. I wanted to win. I understood that the giggling adoration of his adolescent groupies bored him. Possibly his wife was beginning to have the same effect.

Now I knew how Dijon felt waiting at the officials' table to go into the game. Adrenaline coursed up and down my arms; my legs twitched and my head buzzed. I was focused. My eyes were on the prize.

Five games remained. The Serpents had to win three of them, which they did, to go into the postseason play-offs. City pride oozed blue and silver. The NBA store couldn't keep Dijon's number seven jersey in stock. TV sports analyst and Hall of Famer Charles Barkley picked Dijon to be that season's MVP.

The Serpents went on to win game four, but they lost their last regular-season game to the New Jersey Nets after two overtimes, which meant their momentum going into the postseason had been compromised.

I stayed in the hotel lobby a little longer than usual that night in case I could be of solace to Dijon, so I wasn't surprised when Tee tapped my shoulder. "He needs you," he said.

I shut down my BlackBerry, stood, and followed him into the elevator. He inserted a card, pushed *P* for penthouse, and we started our ascent. We did not speak then or as we walked down a carpeted hallway, which dead-ended at a pair of thick, wooden doors. Tee rapped three times.

The door opened. Dijon Roosevelt stood there in a pair of green sweats with a loose body shirt. I stepped back. I may have gasped.

He was even more beautiful close up. He waved Tee away and guided me toward the couch in the front room. I sat.

"We don't have much time," he said.

My breath caught. The room smelled of cigarettes and sex. A half-eaten orange spilled from a fruit basket on the coffee table. "Help yourself," Dijon said when he noticed I was staring at it.

I demurred. A piece of fruit was not what I wanted.

He set a dog-eared business card on the table in front of me. It was one of mine.

"I had Tee run a check on you," he said.

I smiled. "I take it I passed."

"You're clean, all right."

What I was thinking was not.

"That means whatever I say stays between us," he said. "Right?"

"Only if you're talking attorney-client privilege."

"That's what I'm trying to tell you. I want to hire you."

"You brought me up here to hire me?" I sounded angry. I was angry.

"I'll pay you." He sank down on the couch beside me. His leg brushed mine. A bolt of electricity shot through me. For a moment I lost all power. He gnawed on his index fingernail and waited for me to say something.

I wanted to get up and leave, but his scent pinned me to the sofa. My foot tapped the floor. I debated my next move. If I got up and left, I could kiss good-bye any chance I had with Dijon Roosevelt. On the other hand, if I were to agree to his proposition I would have access, means, and opportunity.

"Okay. All right," I said. "Tell me everything."

"I shouldn't have let her in," he said. "I was feeling low about the loss tonight and, well, one thing led to another. Two consenting adults. You know what I'm saying?"

"Go on," I said.

"She wanted to call her ex afterward. She got it in her head that telling him about me would make him want her back. When I told her it wasn't going to happen, she started screaming stuff like how all men were alike, how they covered for one another, shit like that. She threatened to go to the cops."

"Consensual sex isn't a crime," I said.

"But rape is. She was going to say I raped her."

My chest tightened at the ugly images the word evoked. I took a deep breath. Then another. My head cleared. I shifted into legal mode. "Did you use anything when you had sex with her?"

"Damn right. I was wearing something. I got Tara to think about."

"How rough was the sex?"

He gave me a funny look.

"If there are any tears or injuries, it could corroborate her claim."

He shook his head. "The timing sucks with play-offs in a week. What if she goes to the press and does a Kobe Bryant number on me? What if I end up in jail?"

"You're jumping the gun."

"I can't afford to let down my team."

"Does anyone else know about what happened?" I asked.

"Tee. He got rid of her."

"Get him in here."

Dijon opened the door to the suite. Tee stood, arms crossed, in the hallway, a sentry, cradling a bottle of Rolling Rock beer instead of a gun.

As it turned out, he was the shortcut to collusion.

"I could be your witness," he told Dijon. "I could say she was one crazy bitch."

"No offense," I said, "but the cops will think you're covering for your friend. We need somebody who is . . ." I paused, looking for a kinder, gentler phrase than "more upstanding." "We need someone unbiased."

"Right," Tee said. "And where you gonna find 'em?"

My heart pumped. My head buzzed. Tiny gold stars flickered in front of my eyes. Dijon was tumbling. He was going down. Unless . . .

"It's a Hail Mary shot," I said. Then I diagrammed the play.

Tee's knee jiggled. "Are you sure, D?" he asked.

"Hey, what have we got to lose?" Dijon said.

I said, "Everything."

A smile slid slowly from the corner of Dijon's mouth. He looked at me. I felt myself listing. "Baby," he said, "I like those stakes."

Anyone who has watched basketball knows about "big minutes," those crucial seconds that determine the outcome of a game. Only special players—the Spurs' Big Shot Rob is one—can be counted on to rise to the occasion.

It was Dijon's turn to prove that he had it in him, that he could run the floor, that at the last second he could bounce-pass to me, his trailer, and that I could finish it off.

I knew how to work the system. You had to give something to get something. Gone were the days when you could "Deny, Deny, Deny." The crooked CEOs of this country had seen to that. The plan was simple, with splinters of truth. Yes, Dijon would say, the accuser had come to the suite. She had gotten past his personal security. But nothing had happened. Dijon had told her to beat it. He had a special lady with him that night. A threesome was not on his agenda. His bodyguard Tee had escorted the angry intruder from the building. Dijon's lady friend had witnessed the whole thing. When asked if he could produce this lady friend, Dijon would stall. He would tell the authorities he was a married man. He would say his witness was a big-shot corporate attorney who didn't need to be dragged through the media mud. Dijon would be the gallant lover, the concerned husband caught between a rock and a hard place by a spurned woman determined to make trouble. He would acknowledge his wrongdoing. He was weak. He was sorry. But it was lonely on the road. The sordid, titillating details of a professional athlete's life would seep out. Slowly, gradually, begrudgingly, Dijon's interrogators would find themselves feeling sorry for the poor, dumb bastard, who was suddenly one of the boys. It would be a blend of gallantry and guilt that would set Dijon free. Not the truth.

Then I would turn up, apologetic and tearful. I would give my statement, which would support what Dijon had already told them. Who were they going to believe, a twenty-something groupie who'd tried to push her way into Dijon's room for the sole purpose of having sex with him, or a woman who was a valued member of the legal community and, as such, was attempting to do the right thing, no matter the personal cost? I didn't have to mention the Duke University lacrosse team case and what had happened to the district attorney who rushed to prosecute three players, falsely accused of rape. It was on everybody's mind, including the assistant DA, who'd told police they did not have much of a case. The authorities decided not to file charges against Dijon. No harm, no foul, I said when I phoned him with the good news. "The only loose end is the girl, who might go to the tabloids."

"I got that covered," he said. "Meanwhile, baby, tell me what I can do to thank you. You name it. Diamond studs. A tennis bracelet."

"Forty-eight minutes," I said. "Alone. With you."

For a second he said nothing. Then I heard his familiar chuckle. "Just so you know, I only average about forty-three minutes a game. Coach pulls me for a rest at the end of each quarter."

"Is that because you don't have the stamina to go the whole game?"

"Let's see who needs a time-out first."

At forty-three, I had to consider presentation. Angles, best sides, packaging, camouflage. I dabbed miracle creams around my eyes, which had once collected accolades like "smoky" and "dangerous" although not recently. I colored the silver in my hair, which fell blunt and blue-black on my shoulders. I lathered my olive complexion with magical formulas and worked out twice a week with a personal trainer.

And it was worth it. There I was, an acolyte, making a sacred pilgrimage, trekking over the cliffs of his hips, down the narrows of his abdomen, and through the steamy jungles of his tiny, black curls to his holy place. With fingers, tongue, breast, I bowed my head and worshipped. I saw the pride of entitlement in the arch of his body as he displayed his exquisite wares. I felt a whiff of nostalgia for all things hard and young.

Dijon lifted me. I felt light, almost dainty, a rare experience for a woman of my height, which was just three inches short of six feet. I straddled him. My breasts leaned into the palms of his hands.

"I never did a lawyer before," he said.

Sexual commentary wasn't something that I ordinarily needed or liked, but the timbre of his voice hardened my nipples. "What are you waiting for?"

His nineteen-inch bicep stretched across the bed. I heard the crackle of cellophane.

"Let me," I said.

He watched me shield his organ. And I watched him watch me. Teasingly, he slipped inside me. Then out. Then back in. Then we were bucking and fucking. The smack of skin. The hunger of more. The need to break the barrier of flesh. The frenzy. The panting. The moaning. The pain of enough. Enough. Enough.

We took a time-out. We sipped Cristal champagne. I snacked on a bag of cashews, in the refrigerated bar. Dijon listened to Jay-Z on his iPod while he watched Reggie Miller narrate the ten-best moments in sports history. Twenty minutes later we were back in the game.

Afterward Dijon ran his finger across my lip. "We're good. Right?"

"More than good," I told him.

It wasn't until he sat up that I realized exactly what he'd meant: The team was heading to the locker room. A debt had been paid.

"Are you hungry?" I asked. "We could order room service."

"You can, baby. Put it on my tab. I can't stay. Coach called a mandatory meeting. First round starts tomorrow, y' know." He walked across the room to a chair where he had hung his trousers. He stepped into them.

The bag with the rest of the cashews sat on the end table. I put a handful in my mouth. They tasted bland.

He came to stand beside me. He picked up my blouse, toyed with its top button. "Hey, it's not like I want to go."

"What if you were late?"

"Coach could fine me. Or keep me out of the starting lineup."

"He wouldn't do that."

He withdrew a box from his pocket and flipped it open. A diamond tennis bracelet sparkled against a black velvet background. "This is for you," he said. "Call it a retainer."

Never had a legal term brought such orgasmic joy. I held out my wrist. Dijon fastened the bracelet. I allowed myself to smile. This game, baby, was far from over.

There were whispers about Dijon. About something that had happened with a young blonde in a New Jersey hotel room in March. But nobody in an official capacity was talking. And the fact that the Serpents had made it out of the first round and were three-three in the second round overshadowed everything else.

The city was on edge. I was too, but for a different reason. Four weeks had passed since Dijon and I had gone one-on-one with each other. Seeing him on court was no longer enough. I wanted him up close and personal. I found myself screaming D-jon! D-jon! D-jon! with more passion than anyone else in the stadium. I saw Dijon glance into the stands once, holding his hand behind his ear and smiling. I knew he had plucked my voice from the mass chant.

The Serpents took game seven, but not without a fight, sending the city into a frenzy, which manifested itself in parades of vandalism and rowdy drunkenness. I carried my cell phone with me everywhere that night, but the only call I got came from my brother, who wanted to talk about matchups when the East faced the West in the finals. Kenny and Charles predicted San Antonio would win in five. Local sportswriters were banking on another seven-game series.

I wanted a sweep, and I didn't care which team won. I wanted Dijon's undivided attention.

I ran into Tee in the lobby of a San Antonio hotel after game three, which the Serpents lost. The series stood at two–one, Spurs' favor.

"How is he holding up?" I asked.

"Tara's with him."

"Is she here for the rest of the series?"

Tee rubbed his chin with his fist. "I think so."

I heard what he was saying. He was telling me to hold on until things got back to normal.

I held on. So did the Serpents for three more games. But in the end they lost.

Their season was over.

I didn't know it then, but so was mine.

There was a picture in the Inquirer a week after the finals showing Dijon running to catch an early morning flight to Korea to train for the Olympics. There was a second photo when the U.S. team won its first game a month later. Another photo op when the team returned from abroad.

But there were no calls from Dijon to me.

I left messages for him at the facility where the Serpents practiced. I drove by his home on the Main Line.

Late one fall afternoon when I left the office, there was Tee, in baggy jeans and backward cap, waiting for me. He linked his arm in mine and steered me toward the square on the other side of the street.

"You don't want to be harassing D," Tee said.

"Harassing?" I tried to read the expression on his face.

"D's got that ADD thing when it comes to ladies. You know what I mean?"

"Did he send you?" I asked.

"Don't matter. It is what it is."

I nodded, but I knew nothing was what it seemed to be.

"Look, girl, he play smart ball. That all-defense shit. You know what I'm saying?"

I didn't answer. A pack of pigeons in the square pecked at the remnants of a doughnut.

"We're good then?" he said.

"You and I were always good," I said.

He tapped my knuckles with his. When I turned away I saw Harold Schmidt running toward me from across the street. His face was flushed, his hair askew. "Are you all right?" he asked.

"Why wouldn't I be?"

He nodded toward Tee, who stood about ten feet away, palming something shiny.

I called out to Tee, "It's okay. I know him."

Then I turned back to Harold. "Were you following us?"

"Well, of course. I was not about to allow anything bad to happen to you." He cupped my arm while his hooded gray eyes took inventory. "Did that hood threaten you? Do you want me to file a restraining order?"

"No. And no," I said.

He stepped away. He was wearing brass knuckles.

When I asked what he intended to do with them, he told me whatever was necessary. I lifted his hand and asked, "Where did you find these things, Harold?"

"Sotheby's. They are beautiful, aren't they?" His hands caressed the brass. "So seldom is beauty functional. And for the record, I could have taken him without the artificial knuckles. I lettered in wrestling in college, you know."

I smiled. "Wrestling, huh?"

"Hey, my college record of take-down points still stands." He combed his fingers through his hair. A strand of brown fell onto his forehead. He looked at me, a disheveled portrait of confidence.

What else could I do but offer to buy him a drink for coming to my rescue?

I spent a week of otherwise billable hours making lists of adjectives describing Dijon Roosevelt. Mythical. Arrogant. Parlous. Provocative. Magnetic. Egotistical. Luminescent. Addictive. Indelible. Exquisite. Young. Dumb.

I spent another week treating the nagging ache in my stomach. Tums and Rolaids. After that I turned to a prescription that had always worked for me in the past: other men.

Then it was late October. Training camp for the Serpents was scheduled to begin. I sat in my office, trying to outline an opening statement in the Tantum case, but I was uninspired.

"Gloom does not become a beautiful woman," Harold said to me. He lounged in the doorway, a tan overcoat slung over his arm. "I have just the antidote. Get your wrap."

He took me to his club. He ordered us dry martinis, declaring them America's only gift to the world.

"What about democracy?" I asked.

He lifted his glass. "This, my dear, is what wins hearts and minds." Harold held forth on a number of topics that evening.

Contract law. British poets. The moral asterisks that punctuate lives. This segued into survival tactics, which, after martini number three, led to a serious discussion about how to stop a runaway camel.

"There is a tendency to pull hard on a camel's reins, but you must resist it. You could tear the camel's nose." Harold leaned back, assuming a professorial pose and drew on his pipe before continuing. "You must remember to use the reins for balance and grip the camel with your legs. Do not fight him. If you can get him to run in a circle, all to the good. Simply hold on until the camel stops."

"And what if he doesn't stop?" I inquired.

Harold smiled. "Camels are not like us," he said. "They have no staying power. They will run for only so long before they tire and sit down."

November was the cruelest month.

I hated being a fan. The chants of D-jon, D-jon, D-jon mocked me. I thought about selling my season ticket, but I couldn't do it. I couldn't sacrifice my only contact with Dijon.

Right before Thanksgiving I traded places with a spectator whose seat was adjacent to the path players took to and from the locker rooms. After the game I leaned over the railing as the players left the court, high-fiving the fans. My hand reached out when Dijon passed. His hand brushed my palm. A series of explosions ripped through me, the static electricity that lingered a palatable impersonation of what had once been. I sank onto the bench behind me, feeling wobbly. By the time I rose, I had a plan.

The rumors started slowly. Just a certain NBA player and a prominent attorney. They grew, as rumors tend to, until there were names and speculations about a particular March night in a particular New Jersey hotel. The press began to dig. There were whispers of a rape, a cover-up, special treatment. Dijon was going to need me again.

I knew it wouldn't be long before the phone rang. Dijon would beg to see me. We would have to meet to synchronize our stories. We would pick up where we left off.

"Not to worry," I would say to him. "I have your back covered."

I played with the diamond bracelet at my wrist, comfortably satisfied no one would have thought to pull a more cunning tactical maneuver. It was basic Law 101. And I knew how it would end.

I waited for the phone to ring.

Each time it did I thought it would be Dijon, but it was the media or a client wanting to know if the rumors were true.

"What rumors?" I would ask, determined to squeeze what orgasmic pleasure I could from the juxtaposition of my name with his.

Then Dijon did the unthinkable. He issued a statement denying the rumors of any cover-up. He said the incident in question had been blown out of proportion. True, a crazed fan had accused him of rape, but he'd said he was with an old friend at the time the accuser said the alleged crime occurred. Was I crazy or did he seem to emphasize old? He identified me as that friend although by this time it was common knowledge. He said the press owed me an apology for maligning my reputation. He said he owed me a debt of gratitude for saving his marriage. Saving his marriage. I wanted to gag.

I tossed the newspaper into my circular file. Then I retrieved the newspaper, sat, and reread the story. I was still staring at it when the phone on my desk rang. It was Harold, summoning me to his office. "Well, the ballyhoo is finally over," he said. "Dijon Roosevelt did the right thing. You can tell me about this young man who is named after a mustard when we celebrate this evening."

There was little to celebrate, but Harold didn't know that. So I agreed to join him for dinner at his place. He had, after all, been so steadfast throughout the last couple of weeks.

So here is how it is. His hands are steady and strong. They graze my breast and hold me in place as securely as chains.

An hundred years should go to praise / Thine eyes and on thy forehead gaze / two hundred to adore each breast. Poetry? Do I hear it or think it?

"You taste good," he whispers. His hands slide down my body. I spread my legs and melt into the adulation of a single finger.

"You *are* good," I say. "Or do I mean bad?"

He looks at me. The longing in his eyes takes me back in time. I am young, desirable, and blinded by his idolization to the blasphemy of my body.

He holds me at the wrist. My tennis bracelet pinches skin. His tongue explores my neck, my breasts, my stomach. I close my eyes. I do not see that his face is lined, his shoulders thick and strong, a mix of silver and black hair.

I lie there, reined in place by the seductive power of memory, beholden to Harold for the splendor of the moment, resisting the slide into the soft sands of sensation.

A Madness of Two

Peggy Hesketh

So, where to start? With Aunt Daphne, she of the beautiful, albeit artificially bobbed nose and side of the head blown off? Or Harry Honda, the vaguely handsome yet unassuming entomologist? Of course, I'm assuming Harry was unassuming only because, while it took me forever to meet him, I'm sure I would have forgotten him in a day if it weren't for what he'd had to say about sad women and Ziploc bags full of imaginary bugs.

I'd set up the appointment to meet Harry because I'd nearly run out of feature-story ideas for the suburban newspaper where I was working at the time. I was a reporter back then. And just by coincidence, I'd been assigned to do a feature story about a guy who worked for the county as a bug expert. It was the sort of thing you did when you worked for a newspaper in those days. You found people in the community who had interesting jobs, and you talked to them, and if you were lucky, they were interesting. And if they were lucky, you cared enough about their strange little slice of life to write a thirty-inch story that they could photocopy and send to whatever family member cared enough to say: "That's nice, dear."

Which is to say, I'd already written far too kindly about the balding, doughy-faced man-child who lived with his mother and spent his days and nights wearing flip-down machinist's magnifying glasses while painting tiny replica Civil War soldiers; about the steely-haired woman who lived behind a second-run movie theater and who rescued opossums from neighborhood backyards and kept their pickled offspring in mason jars lined up according to fetal age in her back-bedroom closet; and about Sue the Traveling Insect Zoo Lady, recently divorced, whose living room was stacked from floor to ceiling with *National Geographic* magazines and whose kitchen shelves were equally crammed with GladWare containers, holes poked in their plastic lids and housing a horrifying assortment of emperor scorpions, six-inch-long centipedes, and hissing cockroaches from Madagascar, among other insect exotica. Did I mention that these, unlike the opossum lady's collection, were not dead specimens? That these deadly creatures paced around the plastic perimeters of their lives waiting for someone to innocently lift the lid off their containment, while they gathered their little insect legs in one last angry leap aimed at sinking their venomous fangs, stingers, or god knows what into the unsuspecting hack unfortunate enough to be the lid lifter?

"Oops," Sue said.

"Holy shit!" I said.

Sue, clearly offended by my off-color language, still desired the potential publicity. And me? I'll admit I'm a tad skittish when it comes to the unexpected lunging of poisonous eight-inch-long arthropods, but I still needed to file my damn story by five PM. We more or less called it a draw.

"So, what drew you to collecting and exhibiting exotic insects?"

"Divorce."

Sue was a little fuzzy on the distinction between cause and effect, but *All the President's Men* this was not. No need to press the issue. Sue got her ink, and I met my deadline.

"Nice job," my editor said. "Fun story."

"Loads of fun."

I guess that made me Senior Bug Correspondent, because my

editor next suggested I write a personality profile on the man who ran the Vector Control agency for the county of Orange.

I had a set of questions all prepared as I walked into the somewhat disappointing Quonset hut that served as his office. By that, I think what I mean to say is that I was expecting a real office with hallways and handicapped bathrooms and air-conditioning. Heck, even a paved parking lot with a sign that told me which way to go. I have directional issues.

Luckily, my directional confusion at Vector Control was relatively short lived. After executing a few dusty doughnuts around the mostly beat-up Toyotas and Chevys clustered near the entrance of one of the unmarked Quonsets, I settled on the most likely suspect.

I parked, locked my car, and knocked on a door marked E. I hoped that meant entomology and was not a letter-based code for five. Bureaucracy often works in mysterious ways. After no response, I knocked again.

"It's open," a somewhat testy voice responded.

I twisted the knob and walked into what could only generously be called the "foyer" of the field office for the county entomologist. Inside I found a gunmetal desk with a tired-looking woman of about sixty sitting behind it. The desktop was, for someone like me, a person who grew up in and has learned to embrace controlled clutter, disturbingly bare: There was a standard-issue touch-tone beige phone with two lines and a translucent red Hold button, and an institutional desktop calendar, the one with the big metal U rings over which this clearly dedicated public servant marked each day by flipping its duly marked page. Behind the woman behind the desk was a portable, padded, beige-weave wall, upon which were tacked several fliers announcing the upcoming fire-ant eradication schedule; mosquito-fish distribution program (the fish are free, bring your own plastic bags); the times and places for low-cost spaying and neutering services for pets; and three snapshots of dutifully smiling budding bureaucrats. Missing was the standard-issue, brown with white lettering, six-inch-by-two-inch nameplate.

I gave Ms. Anonymous my name. She told me to take a seat and nodded at the green Naugahyde chair opposite her desk. I complied. She walked around the padded wall and I pulled out my reporter's notebook and began going over my prepared questions.

I wanted to know, for example, what to do about fruit rats. I'd written a story about rats once, earlier in my journalistic career, so I knew that avocados contained vitamin K, a natural coagulant, and as such, a natural antidote to most common rat poisons that cause rats to bleed internally when ingested. I had rats in my backyard. So I thought: two birds, one stone. I get my story, and I get to get rid of my rats, which scurry across the telephone wires, about four feet above the concrete-block wall that delineates our property line and about two feet below the avocado and bottle-brush treeline in our neighbor's yard that shades the telephone wires.

"I just read that most fruit rats' bodies are eight inches long, but their tails are nine inches long," my neighbor's wife informed me just the other day. She's a high school chemistry teacher, but she used to be a biology teacher, so she is both rather distressed by the rats that gird our neighborhood, and fascinated by their physiology, and thus aware of their avocado weakness.

But I digress. I keep wanting to talk about me, when there is a story that's really not about me. It's about Aunt Daphne.

What I know, or what I think I know, is that my aunt Daphne was killed by my uncle Willie. It was laundry related. He was a troubled man. She was a wife who'd had the end of her nose snipped off and the bridge of it broken to appear less Italian for the one boy of seven in my extended Italian family who didn't look Italian himself. Sandy hair. Blue eyes. Even the name, when Americanized, didn't sound Italian. So, of course her dark-haired, Sophia Loren beauty, or at least as close as an Italian girl in a terribly depressed town skirting Pittsburgh could come to that ideal, wasn't enough for Uncle Willie. At least that's what I initially concluded. Of course, I'll never know for sure. The only one who might know is my aunt Maud, but she's tight lipped these days. She's ninety-two years old and still holding on to secrets. But then, so am I.

What I do know for sure is what I heard from Aunt Maud about Aunt Daphne's so-called suicide. My aunt Daphne had called my uncle Willie, who'd been separated from her for a good while. Uncle Willie was supposed to be helping her carry her laundry up from the car to her bedroom, when, according to Uncle Willie, he heard a gunshot. He dropped the stack of folded sheets, ran upstairs, and found his wife head-fricking-blown-off dead. And so he called the police. And gosh, who should show up but his and Aunt Daphne's son, the straight-and-narrow state trooper Will Jr.

When Aunt Maud called to tell me the news, all I could think to say was, "Uncle Willie was helping Aunt Daphne with the laundry? Are you kidding me?"

But I'm getting ahead of the story here. I was talking about Harry. Or Harry's office, to be more exact. I knew that entomologists were, by definition, concerned with insects, not rodents. Still, I knew that Vector Control was at least tangentially concerned with the interrelation between insects and higher-level species because I'd once received a free plastic bag full of mosquito fish from Vector Control's main office to prevent mosquitoes from laying their larvae in the small koi pond that my husband had dug in our backyard.

And I'd visited another Vector Control office—*Who knew there were so many, with so many specializations?*—on another occasion, to have a spider the size of my palm, which I'd caught squatting on my living room wall, analyzed to make sure it wasn't something deadly. Once the VC office secretary had quit shrieking rather unprofessionally after she insisted I open the GladWare lid (thanks for the tip, Sue), she'd called someone other than Harry to come and identify the troubling arachnid, which I suspected had hitched a ride on some furniture we'd ordered from a factory in South Carolina, back when South Carolina was still making furniture. But again, another office. Another digression. Rats were on my mind when I met Harry.

I thought Harry might have gleaned some practical knowledge on rodent eradication from his colleagues. Turns out he wasn't much help with our rats. Or our arachnid infestation either. It was the curse of specialization, I suppose.

But Harry had an inadvertent insight into Aunt Daphne's death. Not that I'd asked about what had been ailing Aunt Daphne before her untimely demise. And certainly not that Aunt Daphne cared much anymore, her being long dead. I thought Aunt Maud still might care, though, since she'd soaked herself in ammonia baths for months to get rid of the bugs, which she'd gotten from Aunt Daphne, until they disappeared the week after Aunt Daphne died.

Aunt Daphne, according to Aunt Maud, claimed that invisible bugs had invaded her bedroom. So much so that Aunt Daphne had started sleeping on top of her dresser because she was convinced the bugs were coming up through the baseboards in her bedroom and that they'd found their way into her bed. She'd stripped the sheets and blankets and boiled them in bleach every morning for three months straight. She'd duct-taped the cracks between the baseboards and the floor and walls. She'd sprayed the room with every bug spray known to man, and she'd bought a new mattress and box springs, but the bugs were relentless.

"That woman's nuts," my aunt Maud proclaimed the first time she told me about the bugs. "She says they're coming out of her toothpaste tube."

Then, three or four months after that telephone call, Aunt Maud started feeling itchy. Just a little bit at first. Mostly when she came back from lunch with Aunt Daphne. They usually got together once a month to go to this Chinese buffet off Highway 22. Sort of a wild choice for them, given their meat-and-potatoes backgrounds.

At first Aunt Maud thought that maybe she was allergic to Chinese food. So they moved their little lunch get-togethers to the Italian Club, ordering their hottest fried banana peppers and garlic linguine on the Old World assumption that the spicy food might somehow make their blood less appetizing to their microscopic tormentors. But whatever these bugs were, they weren't vampire bugs, as they only seemed to grow more insidious, garlic be damned.

That's when Aunt Maud started thinking that Aunt Daphne's bugs had invaded her own husband's car.

"It has to be how I got the bugs," she told me when I called to wish her a happy Thanksgiving.

Aunt Maud didn't drive. So her husband usually dropped her and Aunt Daphne off wherever they wanted to go to lunch and then he came back an hour or two later to pick them up and drive them home. Sometimes I think the only reason Aunt Maud stayed married was so that when she had to travel farther than the three-mile circuit she walked to get around her very small world, she had a ride. But sometimes I think hers was a great love affair that lasted too long. That she and my uncle, despite their seeming indifference to each other by the time I was old enough to observe them, started their life together in a state of forbidden passion. I'd like to think so anyway, but then I'd like to think that about just about anybody, except maybe Uncle Willie and Aunt Daphne. I think these two were drawn to each other like a mosquito to a throbbing vein and I'm not sure which was which.

Once Aunt Maud had become convinced that Aunt Daphne's bugs had slipped invasively into the upholstery of Uncle Charlie's late-model Buick, I started receiving phone calls late at night from Aunt Maud telling me about the ammonia baths that were the only thing that helped relieve the itch.

"What itch?

"From the bugs."

"What bugs?"

"Daphne's bugs. I can't sleep. I don't know what else to do."

"You're taking baths in *ammonia* every night?"

"Every night except Tuesdays," Aunt Maud corrected. "That's

when they hold the drawing down at the VFW. It's too late to take a bath by the time I get home."

"So what do you do?"

"I take it first thing Wednesday morning. I don't want to keep Charlie up, so I take my bath as soon as I get Charlie off to work. But I don't sleep a wink Tuesdays."

I suppose I could have suggested she not worry so much about disturbing Uncle Charlie's sleep. My experience was that by two in the morning, and anything past six or seven shots of Jim Beam, Uncle Charlie wasn't going to be bothered by the whisper of water running in a bathtub in the next room. But that's in retrospect. At the time I was just trying to figure out what the hell was going on. As far as I could see, the only real ties between my aunts were the bugs that no one could see and the brothers they were married to. But I had a theory. Daphne's estranged husband, my uncle Willie, was a bastard, and somehow the bugs were all his fault.

Still, I didn't know how. Aunt Daphne had already kicked him out of their house. And from what I'd heard, he'd left her pretty much alone. So I couldn't exactly accuse him of planting mind-fucking bugs in her bedroom and in my aunt Maud's car.

"There's a name for what you guys had," I told her. Aunt Maud, that is, quite some time after Aunt Daphne's death.

"It's called 'Delusory Parasitosis,'" I told her. Or at least that's what I think I told her. I might not have told her the official name. That would have made me sound too educated. "Don't want to put on the dog," my father used to say by way of explanation when he dumbed down a technical term, which he pretty much always did. My family's not all that forthcoming when it comes to intellectual issues, let alone emotional ones. Nature or nurture. Take your pick.

"I met this guy," I think I may have said. "He's an expert on insects, and he says that . . ."

Okay. It got kind of tricky here. How to say that, as Harry Honda explained, what she and Aunt Daphne had been experiencing is essentially a mental disorder associated with middle-aged women coping unsuccessfully with feelings of loss often tied to marital difficulties.

". . . he's seen lots of cases like yours and Aunt Daphne's."

I think what I wanted to convey to Aunt Maud was that she wasn't alone without making her think she was crazy because she so often felt alone in a roomful of family, because Aunt Maud is a lot of things, but she's not crazy. As for Aunt Daphne, I had no idea. The fact that she married Uncle Willie didn't exactly testify to her sanity.

And it didn't help her case, or then again, maybe it did, that Aunt Daphne's death was investigated—or at least responded to, and written off in the official report as a suicide—by the Pennsylvania state trooper who happened to be her son, and may be my half brother. But that's another story. Or maybe it's really *the* story.

You see, part of the trouble between Aunt Daphne and her husband, Uncle Willie, had to do with my father, which was what I was led to believe on the day of my father's funeral when Aunt Maud explained in whispered tones in the limousine ride to the cemetery why Uncle Willie had threatened to kill me the month before my father died.

I thought it was simply because I threw him out of our house when I overheard him on the phone telling Aunt Daphne to pack her bags, and come on out to California. "The house is ours," he practically crowed into the phone, not knowing, or perhaps simply not caring, that I'd just walked into the house.

"The house" being my mother and father's house that I'd mostly lived in since my parents had packed their bags, separately, since they were separated at the time and had only arranged to get back together if my father moved away from all the bad influences in their hometown and got a good job and found a decent place to live, which to his credit he did. He sent for my mother and me six months after moving to California, finding a promising job as a machinist in the aerospace industry and renting a decent little apartment in Anaheim, not far from Disneyland. Two years later we all moved into the house my father was able to purchase with the savings from his first steady job in all the years he and my mother had been married. It seemed pretty storybook to me (especially the part about the name of the housing development he moved us into, which was called Cinderella Homes—and you could tell they were Cinderella Homes because of the gingerbread trim in the front of the houses and the four little bathroom tiles in the shower that depicted a magic wand, a pumpkin, a glass slipper, and a magical carriage), except for the part about leaving my dog and my grandfather and my cousins and aunts and uncles and my other grandmother's fried chicken and rigatoni Sunday dinners and lightning bugs and Kennywood Park and moving to California where I suddenly realized I was an only child. That part was kind of sad and lonely, but at least there was no one to make me feel even worse, like when I still lived back in Pittsburgh, and I used to wonder why I hadn't seen my father for months at a time.

"Your mom won't let him in the house, not since he got drunk and knocked down those twenty-seven mailboxes on Old Monroeville Road," my cousin Jimmy said. "I'll bet he was with Audrey again."

"He's in jail now," his sister Marie was only too happy to add.

"Don't worry about it. He's an asshole," Cousin Louie would reassure.

"They're all assholes," Cousin Ed would say later. "Compared to most of them, your dad's not so bad."

To be clear, most of the men in my dad's family gambled and drank too much, and most of them even ran numbers for a few extra bucks. They got into bar fights, and okay, Uncle Lennie, who worked for the railroad, had derailed a freight train or two when he wanted an extra-long weekend off. But it was all small-change stuff. Nothing malicious. Out of all my dad's brothers, Uncle Willie was the only one I'd heard rumors about spending time in a mental hospital. And there were whispers about the *real* reason Aunt Daphne had gotten her nose fixed.

I first heard those rumors the day of my father's funeral.

I was sitting in the lead limousine with Aunt Maud, Uncle Charlie, and my cousin Ed. I'd asked my aunt why Uncle Willie hated me so much, and why so much of the family had taken his side when he'd threatened to kill me.

"You remember when your grandpap died?" she said.

"Sort of."

"Remember your dad came back to the funeral alone."

That much I remembered. I was only ten years old at the time. We'd moved to California the year before and there wasn't a whole lot of extra money, so after my grandfather's heart attack, my dad flew back to Pittsburgh by himself. I don't know about my mother, but I didn't much mind staying home. My grandfather was not a pleasant man, which is probably why my grandmother stipulated in her will that she be buried with her first husband when she died fifteen years later. That caused a real rift in the family. My dad and Uncle Charlie, and Uncle Virgil, who was her only son from her first marriage, sided with her. The other four sons saw it as an insult to their dead father, and by extension, them. That caused another twenty years of general bad blood between the brothers, and an extended probate fight. But once again, another story. Another blood feud. On the day of my father's funeral I was most interested in my uncle Willie's long-standing, particular animosity toward my father, and by extension, toward me.

Aunt Maud leaned in real close so Uncle Charlie couldn't hear. Charlie was sitting in the front seat with the driver. Cousin Ed was in the seat behind. He'd promised to watch my back in case Uncle Willie caused any trouble at the funeral, and he'd taken his promise seriously.

"Nine months after your grandfather's funeral, your cousin

Willie Junior was born," Aunt Maud said. Her tone was meaningful.

My twenty-six-year-old cousin, "Little Willie." It took me half a minute to do the math and make the leap. I had known that prior to my father's final illness, my uncle Willie hadn't spoken to my father for twenty-six years, but I'd never known why. When Uncle Willie first arrived in California, unannounced, to visit my father after word got out that he was dying, my father reacted with an odd mix of surprise and uneasy elation. My mother had died the year before, and my dad wasn't handling her loss well. After a few awkward days and nights sitting at the kitchen table talking with Uncle Willie into the wee hours, things seemed to thaw out between the two of them and my dad seemed to draw some comfort from his presence. But unlike all the other family members who'd come out to visit for a week or two and helped sober him up after my mother's death, Uncle Willie's agenda didn't seem to include returning home.

Or in keeping Dad on the wagon. Before long Willie had persuaded my father to sign over his car to him and he kept the vodka flowing. After my father was hospitalized and he'd lapsed into a coma, Uncle Willie called Aunt Daphne and told her it was done. To get on out to California.

"Hell, I don't know, Daphne. Summer clothes. And maybe a sweater. It gets chilly here in the evenings."

That's when I'd walked in.

That's when I told Uncle Willie to get the hell out of our house, and he clenched his fists tight.

"I *deserve* this," he told me.

"No you don't."

"I could kill you right here."

"Get out of our house."

"Okay," he said, smiling sweetly.

I smiled back. He underestimated me. After he was gone, I took a quick inventory and found the TV in my dad's room missing, along with all his country and western albums. So I changed the locks on the house and had taken out a restraining order by the end of the business day. I think that surprised Uncle Willie. After sleeping outside the house in my dad's old Cadillac for a couple of days, and getting rousted by the police more than once, Willie decided to cut his losses and head home. He made it back to Pittsburgh just in time for my father's funeral.

Home and family are powerful draws. Even though my parents had lived the last fifteen years of their lives in California, made friends, and built a decent life for themselves here, both made it clear they wanted to be taken "back home" to be buried in their family plot. I try to visit their graves when I can, but I live three thousand miles away.

But once again, I digress. All that family history. It's only tangentially germane to the story. Harry Honda knew nothing about my family or me. What he knew had to do with bugs, especially the ones that plagued Aunt Daphne.

We were walking through his Quonset hut, lined with gray industrial tables and shelves stacked with plastic boxes. I'd been following Harry from table to table, shelf to shelf, nodding and uttering the appropriate "uh-huhs" and "oh reallys" for each specimen, meticulously soaked in formaldehyde, pinned to acid-free poster board, labeled, and alphabetically filed according to genus and phylum, without a hissing cockroach in sight.

This is where I generally probed beneath the "professional" veneer of a subject. Where I asked what he did when he wasn't identifying and cataloguing indigenous bugs. Despite his day job, or maybe because of it, I was pretty sure Harry didn't paint tiny Civil War figurines in the evenings, or keep a collection of fetal marsupials in his spare bedroom.

"I play softball. We have a Vector Control team in a Santa Ana league."

I told him I played in a city league too. Mostly newspaper staffers.

"I hate softball," Harry said.

"I hate to shop." I thought we might be making a connection here. I decided to open up to Harry. "Every time I go shopping, I think I'm the only woman in Orange County who wasn't born with the shopping gene."

"So why shop?" Harry said.

"Necessity," I rejoindered. "Why do you play softball?"

"Camaraderie."

Harry had a wry streak. I sensed we were bonding.

"Do you want to see something funny?" Harry handed me a sealed Ziploc bag.

I raised my eyebrow. The bag was empty. It had been a long day of bugs.

"At least once a month, I get one of these," Harry said.

"A Baggie?" I said. I had lots of practice asking open-ended questions.

"Mostly from women," Harry said. "Mostly married. Mostly middle-aged."

Harry seemed sheepish. Maybe because he sensed I was married and middle-aged. He seemed like he didn't want to offend. He led me to what passed for his desk, which was more of a table with lots of meticulously labeled boxes stacked neatly under and on the metal shelves behind it. He reached up to the second shelf, and pulled down a shoebox-size box marked CL.

CL?

"Crazy Ladies." Harry Honda lifted the lid off the box. No leaping scorpions, just a slippery stack of fifty or more empty Ziplocs stashed inside. Each one was labeled with a name and a date that spanned about a decade. All but three names were female.

"The exceptions that prove the rule," Harry said.

And to be exact, not all of the Baggies were entirely empty. A handful appeared to contain small lumps of lint. A few more held flakey little bits of what looked like dandruff, dust, scabs, pet hair, and who knows what other bits of dried detritus. But most of the Baggies seemed to hold nothing more or less exotic than stale air.

Harry swore to me that he got at least one EZB (Empty Ziploc Bag) every other month or so from some woman who'd claim it was full of unseen bugs that had invaded her house and caused unbearable torment. The first time this happened, Harry said he told the woman what was clearly the case.

"I'm sorry, but there's nothing here," he had said after dipping a glass slide into the bag and scooping out a big dollop of nothing and placing it under the microscope to prove his point. When the woman grabbed her Baggie in a huff and lodged a complaint with his supervisor, Harry said he was given some advice.

"Humor them, boy," his boss said. "The bugs aren't real, but what they feel is."

"And what exactly do they feel?" I wondered aloud.

"Nothing," he said. "Nothing at all. That's their problem, see?"

It isn't about Harry, this story, by the way. And it's definitely not about Harry and me. Despite our little softball and shopping chitchat, we never really made a connection. I'll bet if you asked him the next day what color my hair was (*reddish-brown with gray streaks*) or what I was wearing (*posthippie chic: sandals, jeans, and a tapestry blouse*), he'd shrug and say he hadn't noticed.

And that's the point Harry was inadvertently making. It was about not seeing someone. I think I understand now what my aunts were going through. Not the direct abuse or benign indifference from their husbands. But the invisibility. The idea that once you've lost your ability to spawn children you somehow fade into that corner of the universe reserved for thick-waisted ciphers, pert nosed, or not. Single or married. Good marriage or bad. After all the years of fawning and fumbling and falling down and stumbling back to your feet, you start to feel like you're starting to crack the nut of your sexuality in all its weird glory, and that's when you find yourself in a nation of one while everyone else has gone off to

Aruba for a fling with flat-bellied bikini girls. It's that sort of loss of possibility that I think killed Aunt Daphne. And whether by her own hand or Uncle Willie's, I'm starting to think that part is beside the point.

That day in his tidy little Quonset hut, Harry had explained to me that there had been a lot of studies written up in both psychological and entomological journals about women and their Baggies full of invisible bugs. The scientific name for the syndrome is "delusory parasitosis."

Harry said his supervisor advised him to listen dispassionately to whatever the women had to say, to prepare a glass slide from whatever "bagged specimen" was presented, and without agreeing that there was something there, per se, to offer some sympathetic concern. He said suicide was an extreme, though not entirely uncommon, outcome. He said the only real treatment was psychiatric.

"But you're not a psychiatrist."

"No. But I can be sympathetic."

Harry told me that it was standard office procedure—not just at the OC Vector Control office but throughout most government entomology offices to give these sad women a tube of anti-itch lotion and a referral to a psychologist familiar with this syndrome.

"We don't tell them it's all in their heads, though," Harry explained. "We tell them the lotion will help with the immediate symptoms, and the psychologist will be able to help them work through the trauma of their bug infestation."

"You mean you just flat-out lie to them?"

"Well, not exactly," Harry said, taking the empty Baggie labeled "Martinez, L.; Nov. 1997" from my hands. "Okay. Yeah. We lie to them a little. But I think it helps them."

"Lying to them?"

"Listening to them."

I remembered all those crazy-ass calls from my aunt Maud. Harry returned L. Martinez's Baggie to the CL box and closed the lid.

"You know, I had an aunt once who thought she had a bug infestation, and then another one of my aunts thought she got it from her," I said.

"That's not all that surprising. This kind of obsession gets passed on to susceptible family members," Harry explained. "There's a name for that too: *Folie à deux*."

"It sounds like some sort of dance," I said. A waltz, I thought, where two people, oblivious to the rest of the world, move step by step to the rhythm of music only they can hear.

A madness shared by two.

"Oh, here's something you'll like," Harry said, moving on to the next table. "Have you ever seen a Jerusalem beetle in all its developmental stages?"

Against my better judgment, I went to a family reunion this summer. It was organized by Aunt Maud, who milked the "I'm ninety-two years old. I don't think I'm going to be around much longer . . ." canard that she's been rolling out since she hit seventy-five. And as usual, it worked. There must have been seventy blood relatives and their families milling around her backyard at one point in the evening, and because I lived farthest away, she'd dubbed me guest of honor.

I'd flown a red-eye into Pittsburgh and I hadn't had time to do much more than wash my face and change my shirt before cousins upon cousins and their kids and grandkids started piling out of an armada of SUVs and the digital cameras came out along with the rigatoni and fried banana peppers and potato salad and baked beans and macaroni and cucumber salad and linguine and Iron City beers.

I leaned over to my cousin Ed.

"You know what's missing? Your dad and my dad sitting out there under the apple trees sipping whiskey. And then a little later, everybody breaking out the guitars and singing."

Ed laughed. "Yeah, and right after that, a couple fistfights breaking out."

"Those were the days, eh?"

Aunt Maud bustled in and out of the kitchen every now and then to do a head count.

"Where's Caroline and her brood?"

"They're driving up from Atlantic City."

"What the hell are they doing there?"

"She had a coupon for a complimentary room for the week," one of Caroline's sisters said. Caroline loved to gamble. Sometimes she won and sometimes she lost. But she was a familiar enough face at the tables that her rooms were generally comped.

"What about Will?"

"I don't know. Wasn't he down in Mexico?"

"Yeah, but he said he'd be here."

Will hadn't come to my father's funeral. I hadn't seen him since he was maybe five years old and his nickname was "Festus" after the lame deputy sheriff in *Gunsmoke*. From what Aunt Maud told me, he'd grown up to be a pretty good guy. So I started thinking that maybe there was some sort of cosmic plan to the world, that this reunion was designed to tie up all the loose ends. It was my chance to ask all the questions I had about him and me, and in return, I could explain to him what I knew about his mother and her bugs, courtesy of Harry Honda.

Then someone handed me a vodka tonic. And I got into a long conversation with my cousin Leroy, who had gone to my father's funeral but who I hadn't seen since. He asked me whether I believed in evolution. He didn't. I did. Mercifully, the long-awaited cousin Caroline's brood of five children, nine grandchildren, one great-grandchild, and their sundry spouses broke up our little Scopes trial redux. In all the commotion, I didn't notice that my cousin Will and his wife, Bettina, had arrived.

". . . so when the hurricane warnings started coming in, we figured we'd better get the heck out of Dodge."

The voice came from a ramrod-tall man. Next to him stood a willowy brunette. Their summer clothes were crisp and clean. Unlike me, they didn't look like they'd spent half the night and all the rest of the day traveling. They were brown eyed, tanned, and their short-cropped hair was perfect.

"We probably could have gotten a flight out tomorrow," Bettina said.

"Chipper" came to mind as the perfect word to describe her voice, her smile, her posture. Everything was perfect, except for her eyes. There was a black-hole tiredness behind them.

"But then we would have missed the party," Will said, wrapping his arm around her shoulders.

Aunt Maud came scurrying out from the kitchen to welcome the latest arrivals.

"Grab yourselves a plate. We got plenty of food."

Will let go of Bettina to stoop down and give Aunt Maud a hug. He finished explaining about the chaos in the Cancún airport as tourists packed the ticket counters, fighting for flights once the hurricane warnings were issued. "Thank goodness Bettina works for the airline."

"I'm a flight attendant," Bettina said, waving off an offer of fried peppers and Italian sausage.

"We were really lucky."

"We really weren't in any danger."

"But we needed to go."

"No we didn't."

"Yes we did, honey." Will recounted how, even with Bettina's connections, they hadn't been able to get a flight to Pittsburgh, so they flew into Cleveland, rented a car, and drove straight to the party.

"Made it from Cleveland in a little over two hours," he said, sipping his cola.

"Looks like the storm's followed you here," Cousin Ed said, nodding at the darkening clouds that were blowing in from the south. "Hey, Mum. Let me help you with that tray."

And suddenly, there among the stew of family genes, it was just Will and Bettina and me. We stood quietly, face-to-face for a minute, maybe two, Will sipping his cola, me nursing my vodka tonic, Bettina smiling.

"Your hair was red the last time I saw you."

"Your hair was curly."

"My dad's hair was curly."

"So was your dad's."

Will ran his hand over the spikes of his meticulously trimmed flattop.

"Regulation."

"You've gotten taller."

"We come from a tall family."

I noticed Will had brown eyes, not blue like his dad's. Deep. Wide set. We had the exact same eyes. But so do Ed and I. And all but two of the rest of my twenty-seven cousins. We call them the Andriotti eyes. Eyes mean nothing, really.

"Hey, Will." Ed leaned in between us with a couple of Iron Citys hooked in his fingers. "Did you get something to drink?"

Bettina started to respond. Will shook his head.

"That's okay. But Bett and I'll take another couple Diet Cokes if you've got 'em."

You're not a drinker, I thought to say but didn't. That's a dominant Andriotti gene he didn't inherit.

"So you're still a state trooper?" I did manage to cough up, reaching in to my old journalist's bag of conversational tricks. "What's the most interesting case you ever had?"

"Mostly I just write speeding tickets. Nothing much interesting about that."

I wondered about responding to his mother's shooting. How much more interesting could that be? I thought. I said: "And how about you, Bettina? What airline do you work for?"

"She works for American."

That's nice. Kids? Two. You? None. Dogs? Two Aussies. We've got a Great Dane. How did you like Cancún? Fine. Me too. I was there two years ago. Just before the last hurricane hit. And so it went. We danced around the unspoken elephant in the backyard for at least forty minutes, me gliding through my best Ginger to Will's light-stepping Fred.

Folie à deux.

"Honey, it's getting pretty late," she said at last, scratching absently at the back of her neck. She looked exhausted. Will smiled stiffly. "Remember, we've still got a long drive home."

"Yeah, okay."

"Good seeing you."

"Good talking to you too."

"Nice meeting you, Bettina. If you two are ever out in California . . ."

"Of course. I'll give you a call."

"Please do," I said, even as the skin on the back of my neck started to tingle.

ANYTHING HELPS

Z. Kelley

The news fell like a hammer. One morning, Louisa Escamilla had a good job (not a great job but a good job) and by noon, she did not—through no fault of her own.

Perhaps she should have paid closer attention, or recognized that the rumors abounding had carried a whiff of the truth. But Louisa Escamilla, who supported her mother and a disabled son named Eduardo, had little time for gossip. So she ignored some obvious indicators that clearly showed her employer to be on the downhill side of a slippery slope called gambling and cocaine.

Louisa placed great store in a solid work ethic. Unmarried, she was raising Eduardo with her mother's help. He'd broken his leg badly when he was five and, since they could not afford proper medical care, a wanna-be doctor at the urgent care clinic had set the bone improperly. Now, as Eduardo grew faster and taller, so did the bone. Only it wasn't growing well and so the boy was often in pain. He used a wheelchair sometimes, and soon he'd need surgery.

"If you don't have this fixed before he's ten, he might not be able to walk at all," a doctor told them when Eduardo turned eight. Now, he *was* ten and Louisa saw clearly—time was running out. She and her mother struggled to put away $50 a month, but all they'd saved was $650. Louisa planned to ask her employer for health benefits when, on that day in April, several corporate-looking men and women in business attire appeared on the factory floor and called together all the hourly wage workers at Taylor Made Novelties. The professionals then broke the news. "The factory is now closed. You will receive a severance payment along with your paycheck, so if you'll each come up when we call your name, we'll move this along."

No one protested or asked questions as they went up to get their final checks, though a few of the women who'd been there the longest cried.

"Thank you for your service," said the woman who gave out the paperwork. But after the first ten or twelve employees, her comment became rote and unfeeling.

Louisa was equally numb as she took her pay. She'd been there nine years, had been promoted just a month before. She opened her envelope in the parking lot and saw that her severance amount was $125. There was no anger within Louisa, only shock as she waited for the bus home.

But Louisa had never taken the bus that early in the day. So overwhelmed was she by her sudden predicament that it was several miles before she realized she was on the wrong one.

The driver kindly let her off at a transfer point, and Louisa found herself standing on the corner of Luxuria and Avaritia streets, at the frayed outskirts of Las Vegas. Beyond all the tumbledown housing and mercantile excess stretched the impenetrable desert. Louisa stood there blinking, not feeling the heat at first since she'd grown cold to the core with fear and anxiety.

"What am I going to tell them? What will we live on? Deep breaths," she told herself. "Take deep breaths." Louisa Escamilla had to get home before she was altogether lost, so she gathered herself up and took stock of her immediate situation.

"I will get another job." She said it out loud. There was no one around to hear her. Louisa was standing in front of a casino / gift shop called Mor Slots 4 U and she desperately needed reassurance. She'd go in, buy a soda, but forgo the snack, she decided. There was time, fifteen minutes before the next bus—so the driver had informed her.

But even as her hand reached to open the door to Mor Slots 4 U, an offer was given to her despairing mind. Help Wanted it said, Gift Shop Cashier. Must Work Nights. And though she was not a superstitious person by nature, Louisa took it as a different kind of sign.

I can work nights, she thought, and she went in. The store portion of Mor Slots 4 U was surprisingly clean and organized. Food and beer coolers combined with the cheap trinkets, T-shirts, and gifts in some indescribably rational way, as if they were alphabetical or arranged by size. Red Doritos, orange Cheetos, yellow Funyuns blended with stacks of green, blue, or purple T-shirts, as if to satisfy one's desire for color by using the entire spectrum.

The casino in the rear, however, was a windowless cavern filled with a cacophony of beeps and clangs and rings. A mantle of smoke overhung the room like a dark, neon-lit corner of hell.

Louisa Escamilla was not a gambler and could not grasp the wastefulness of it. She explained this to the two owners, brothers who introduced themselves as Mr. Hosn. No first names, each was to be called Mr. Hosn.

The Hosn brothers liked Louisa Escamilla. They liked her face, which was calm, with dark-tipped eyes. They also liked the extra forty-five pounds she carried on her five-foot, three-inch frame because the weight implied that Louisa might be insecure in her own self-estimation, and that could, possibly, make her a more amenable employee. So Louisa Escamilla was hired on the spot.

She went home to tell her family.

"All right, good news and bad news," she said, closing the door of their small apartment. Her mother and son were already sitting down. "I lost my job," Louisa said. Their faces crumpled. "But I found another one right away." Their faces brightened. Then

Louisa saw her mother's frown when she described Mor Slots 4 U.

"It's just for a little while, Mama, just until we get enough to buy a car and move to Los Angeles to be near Aunt Rosa. Then, I'll get a better job." Louisa did not mention the surgery. They never talked about the surgery in front of Eduardo.

"I don't like it, *mija*." Her mother shook her head. "A casino?"

"No, they have a store too, Mama. I work in the store."

"And *cerveza*? They sell the *cerveza*?"

"Mama, please. They sell food and gifts." Louisa sighed and got busy gathering up the laundry. Focusing on something, anything, so she wouldn't have to look at her mother, an uncanny woman who could read faces and the headlines written there. Louisa Escamilla did not want her mother reading her face about some of the other items sold at the Mor Slots 4 U gift shop and casino. She did not want her mother even to guess at what the Hosn brothers dubbed one section of the gift shop / food mart: the Blue Room. A video library, they had called it, as though it contained an important film collection rather than a room full of pornography.

That night, the three slept on the couch bed while the drunken drama of the Las Vegas ghetto appeared outside their windows, as it did nearly every night. No flashy fountains for the residents of this strip. No headline acts or grand entrances aglow with a quadrillion lights. Here, people stayed inside after dark, away from the windows. Streetlights were shot out but weren't replaced with any municipal haste, for who'd complain? The Escamillas and their neighbors lived the hand they'd been dealt and the game was simple: survival.

The old woman could not sleep that night and so, she got up and went into the bedroom where they rarely slumbered because only one floor below, outdoor gunplay had once perforated their drywall.

The moon was full. It poured a tiny cascade of light on the chrome of Eduardo's wheelchair, like blue water emptying across the floor and into the home where the three Escamillas lived cheek by jowl. The old woman was emboldened by that moonbeam. Driven by intuition, she knelt and prayed with a ferocity she had never before expressed in a lifetime of devotion.

"We the faithful, we your servants, now we need you." She talked directly to the moon. "*Necessitamos milagro. Ahora mismo.*" Send us the miracle, she told the moon, a celestial body that might carry the message to another, unseen, celestial body. She wasn't asking. She never once said, "Please." She was telling, describing, laying it out. "*Milagro ahora,*" she repeated and repeated until the sun pulled up behind the moon and the sky was a painted blue ceiling. "Miracle. Now," she called after the moon.

Louisa Escamilla began training at Mor Slots 4 U on the early morning shift, a calmer prelude to the chaos at night. "Easier you learn," a Hosn brother told her. But barely two minutes into the shift, the "gimme-gimme machines," as Louisa secretly called them, would start to intrude with their endless chatter.

All day, cars would pull into Mor Slots 4 U, dispensing people laden with fresh hope. Later, the cars would pull out, the people and their pockets depleted. But back they'd come the following day or the following week because "You can't win if you don't play," they'd say, all the while thinking that strips of paper and little metal disks would somehow save them. They came for money. They left with none, and Louisa began to see in their eyes something that reminded her of a slot machine. A customer would see the slots or the pornography or the alcohol, and somewhere back in the brain's neural tangle, bells went off, lights popped on, and the person would suddenly have the vacant mechanical look of unrequited want.

Louisa was surprised to find that she was invisible in this place. Customers would take their purchases from her hand with eyes that couldn't begin to recognize another human. Unless.

Unless, that is, they wanted something from the Blue Room.

Then they looked at Louisa, all right, and then she wished they wouldn't.

"Can ya buzz me in back here?" Men would leer at her, then lurch against the door when the buzzer sounded.

"Whatcha got that's good?" they'd call out, seeing her discomfiture. "What's YOUR favorite?" Or they'd hold up a DVD—"Betcha like watchin' this one, huh?" That was when she tried to practice being truly invisible, but the best Louisa could muster was indifference. She would withhold eye contact, small good that it did.

The worst part, though, was the touching. She was repulsed by their hands outstretched to drop money into her palm. She hated handling the sordid and sad movies and magazines, which she slipped into black plastic bags reserved specifically for that inventory.

In her first week on the day shift, a bearded man came out of the Blue Room with what was called a motorcycle magazine. He had unwrapped the cover it came in and held it open to the centerfold—a woman with large breasts bared, her leather vest askew, her lace panties hanging off one leg. She languished on the seat of a motorcycle, fingers splayed across her exposed red crotch.

Louisa looked away.

"You could look like that, dahlin', you drop a couple of them pounds," the man said to her, oblivious to his own pork roll hanging over a western belt buckle. "You got a right pretty face, chiquita."

One of the Mr. Hosns was on duty in his office. The office had a window that overlooked the checkout counter and he hurried out to offer protection. "Hey! Hey! You put that away!" he yelled. "Do it again we not sell to you anymore."

"Ah, fuck you. No need to get up on your high horse there, Abdullah." The man continued to leer his way out the door.

"You don't come back here, asshole," the brother shouted but it was too late. Another particle of Louisa's soul had withered beneath the exchange—a soul's slow murder, happening too often. She knew, someday, she'd weep for the loss.

Moments later, watching as Louisa reached up to stock ciga-rettes on the top shelf, the brother said quietly, "That man's an ass-hole, yes, but he was right about one thing. You have very pretty face. You lose weight, be a very pretty girl."

What could she say? Louisa hated that he was looking at her backside. Her face was hot with mortification.

Later that day, a coworker named Clarisse teased Louisa into putting money into one of the slots. "Come on. It's fun. When was the last time you really had fun?"

"Are we allowed?" Louisa asked.

"Sure, the brothers let us play as long as we don't drink or come back late from break."

"I don't know." This was uncharted territory for Louisa.

"Oh, c'mon. We all do it. Just play a dollar, for chrissakes. Nobody gives a shit," Clarisse said. "Here, I'll even give you the dollar." But Louisa shook her head.

"I don't like the gambling."

"Are you kidding? For a dollar, you could win, like six hundred. Don't tell me you don't need six hundred dollars."

So Louisa agreed, but she played using her own money and won three dollars on the first try. She looked into the flashing lights. She heard the rhythmic call and all was revealed to her in that instant; what could happen, what could be. Clarisse said, "See? Ain't this fun? Go for it."

Louisa put in another dollar and another and soon the two women were laughing the way girlfriends do. The slot machine chuckled and flashed, urging them on, and sometimes, money dropped into their hands. There was an exhilaration that was so new and so welcome that Louisa wanted to stay in that lunch break forever. The feeling. The joy. Louisa would lose, lose again, and then she'd win. Lose, lose, win, and Louisa thinking, "I can still win." Until, suddenly, time was up. The inevitable end of the hour came, and Clarisse said, "Time to get back."

There was no chance to win any more unless she kept playing

and Louisa had to go back to work. She always went back to work. But, suddenly, with nothing to show for it, she'd lost $20 and this was devastating. That money was supposed to last for the rest of the week. It was money for the laundromat or a new T-shirt for Eduardo or a fast-food dinner for three. Gone now. There'd be no more until next payday. The reminder of her financial fragility was like a punch in the gut to Louisa. Plus, she'd have to explain the loss to her mother.

"I dropped it," she said when she got home. "I don't know where it is, Mama, it fell out of my pocket." This was unlike Louisa and her mother asked, "Did you check your other pockets?" until Louisa got angry. Uncharacteristically angry. Her mother kept quiet, watching her daughter with silent speculation.

That night, Louisa washed their clothes in the bathtub while her mother and Eduardo watched videos of funny Americans and dogs and weddings gone awry, though they'd already seen that particular show. Louisa wasn't laughing. Eduardo twisted around in his wheelchair to call to her as she bent over the tub. "Look, did you see it, Mommy? That was so funny!"

"What?"

"The man fell down the hill and he was holding the leash and he pulled the dog with him."

"I've seen it," Louisa answered.

The boy stopped laughing. His grandmother silently repeated her mantra, "*Milago. Ahora. Milagro. Ahora.*"

Later, when Eduardo was asleep, they made tamales in the kitchen. Her mother suggested an outing they might enjoy, a trip to a municipal pool that cost nothing. Louisa said, "I can't. I have to work a double."

"A double shift, *mija?* Why?"

Louisa burst out angrily, "Because in case you haven't noticed, the rent is going up and bus passes are seventy-five dollars a month. And Eddie needs that surgery now. We need the money."

"We go to Los Angeles. Rosa will help us." It was an old refrain.

Louisa had heard it time and again and she answered with her own refrain.

"We can't go to Los Angeles without money. *No dinero, no Los Angeles para nos.*"

It was not an easy night in the Escamilla household. The old woman was awake long before dawn. The moon in its declination seemed to ignore her, but call she would. "Send us our miracle now," as though there were one particular miracle waiting just for them and she intended to claim it.

The next morning, Louisa noticed a homeless man standing in the shade of the tall electronic sign outside the Mor Slots 4 U. He was holding a piece of cardboard that was folded over and thickly duct-taped around the edges. There was something written on the front of it, she assumed, though from her place behind the register, she couldn't see what it said. When Louisa went to the bus stop that evening, he was still there, holding the sign. It was handwritten, the way a child might make a sign with a ballpoint pen. ANYTHING HELPS, it said. Its holder was of average height, but stooped. His clothes were either beige or filthy white and far too warm for that time of year. His hair and his beard were both dark and unkempt.

Louisa avoided looking at the man, fearing he'd ask her for money. But he made no overture toward her. He simply stood in the orange light that marked the dying coals of a desert sunset. While Louisa waited, a car full of teenagers stopped at the light. When it changed to green, they rolled down a window and threw a cup of some frothy white beverage at the homeless man. It doused him as they drove off. The whole thing, quick and dirty. What, Louisa thought, could be gained by mocking the hardship of someone already reduced to soliciting by cardboard? The man smiled when Louisa looked at him. He wiped what appeared to be milk shake off his dirt-colored clothes.

He wiggled the sign a little and then gave an elaborate shrug as if to say, "Anything Helps . . . except that."

She laughed. She laughed with him. Then she looked away. The bus arrived and the two of them resumed their places, she returning to her tiny apartment and family, the homeless man staring down the street, motionless behind his sign.

It was a week later when the older Hosn brother remarked to Louisa, "Who is that guy out there, your boyfriend? He's only out there when you work. He leaves when you leave and is never here on your day off." With that, the brother went off to count the register. Louisa, with that never-ending chorus of chinka chinka! bing! chinka chinka bing! behind her and the omnipresent smoke encasing her, found a weird solace in studying the man on the corner of Luxuria and Avaritia. He always stood exactly where she could see him. The shade from the towering sign circled around him, but he did not move.

She grew fascinated with the vagrant. Who was he? How had he ended up like that? What drew him to that corner, when surely there were better, more lucrative intersections in Las Vegas? Heat did not seem to affect him. He never appeared drunk or high in a city where drunk and high passed for normal. Each day, he came in to buy something from the store, and it was always water or soda or candy. Never beer or cigarettes. He never put a dollar or even a penny in the slots, though they beckoned and everyone else responded to their siren song.

Louisa noticed that he seemed . . . what? She couldn't find the word. Aware, maybe. He only came inside when the brothers weren't there or were occupied elsewhere. Louisa knew, as he must have known, they'd kick him out. They would not tolerate a homeless dirty beggar in their place of business. Regardless of the porn, the gambling, and the smoking, the Hosns had their standards. They ran a very hygienic operation. If the homeless man hadn't been standing on city property each day, they'd certainly have run him off.

Louisa was glad the brothers were sticklers for cleanliness. She, herself, began to feel a disgust for many of the customers. She developed a trick for taking their money and giving them change without making physical contact with them. She'd leave her hand on the register an instant longer than necessary or she'd fiddle with items on the counter, as though oblivious to the person standing there with a hand full of money. Arranging and rearranging, sometimes even humming as she did it until the customer grew tired and put the money down on the counter. Then she would pull it in, make change, pile the change on top of the paper receipt, and push it back at them. No touching, no talking.

But the homeless man seemed to catch on to Louisa's little trick. That night, she told her mother about it.

"I just can't bring myself to touch people, you know?" she said as they folded clothes. "I don't care, I just don't wanna touch them And then this homeless man who's been standing outside for a couple weeks—you know, my bosses say he's only there when I'm there—well, he came in to buy a bottle of water. It must have been a hundred degrees outside. So when he gave me the money, I waited for him to put it on the counter. I straightened out some lighters and some other stuff, you know, waiting for him to put the money down. But he didn't. He stood there, with his hand out, holding the money like he'd wait all day for me to take it. So, finally I had to take it and he put the money in my hand and . . ." She stopped.

"And what?"

"It felt weird."

Her mother stopped as well. "What do you mean? How did it feel?"

"I don't know. It's stupid, really."

"No. It's not stupid, *mija*. It's important." Her mother was intense, leaning in.

"Well, for the first time since I've been in this job I felt . . . I don't know how to describe it. When his hand touched me, I felt like everything was going to be all right."

The old woman sat back. She said nothing. Louisa shook her head at the memory of the exchange.

"Weird, huh?" she said.

Her mother didn't answer.

The Blue Room continued to be a great source of discomfort for Louisa. She dreaded buzzing someone into the pornographic depths of the "video / magazine library," and she'd wear a thousand-mile stare for the duration of any transaction arising out of the Blue Room. Louisa feared the craving that drove men, and only men, into that place. Emerging, they seemed to look at her as something to be used and discarded, and their wanting spoke to her of every rejection, every slight, every insult and abandonment that had left her single, still young, and living with her mother and her damaged son in a desert. Layers of fat did not protect her. Every other propensity of mankind—the drinking, the gambling, even the drugs—seemed almost harmless sport compared to what lay behind that blue door.

But as Louisa found out, there were some behaviors worse than lust.

On an evening in her third week, she worked the night shift. The brothers had gone off the premises to have dinner. Louisa was left to oversee Mor Slots 4 U with Clarisse, who took a cigarette break out back by the Dumpster the moment the Hosns' car was out of the parking lot.

A group of men pulled up near the front door in a big white SUV. There were five of them. They came into the store, one of them nodding coldly at Louisa. He perused the newspaper rack near the front door. The other four circulated among the carefully ordered shelves of candy, chips, and gifts. None of them entered the casino. After a minute, Louisa looked up at the round convex mirror above the beer cooler to see where each was located. One was in the candy aisle, one was reading magazines, and, in front of the beer cooler, staring right back at her in the mirror, was a third. It was a shock, suddenly catching his eye. His look was deliberate.

An ancient fear burst through Louisa's heart. Where was the fifth man? Her stomach plummeted in a rush of panic.

No other customer had noticed the men. They were captivated by more and more slots for them. No one but the man in the mirror looking back felt Louisa's fear. She knew what was about to happen, and she edged toward a silent alarm button under the counter.

Just then another one of the men dumped an armload of junk on the counter and began asking loudly, "How much is this? How much is that? And this?"

Louisa stuttered. She felt encased in a rapidly hardening cement of panic as the man lifted his arm so that she could see the butt of a very large gun in his waistband.

A movement to the left and the fifth man was behind the counter, six feet away from her. His gun was out. "Open the register, bitch." A quiet, lethal voice, pure in its darkness.

I'm dead now. Louisa heard the thought as if it had been spoken aloud by someone else.

And suddenly—a shout. "Hey!"

The homeless man stood inside the door.

Everything froze in its place. Louisa was watching, apart from her real self. The five men looked at the homeless man. All he did was nod at their car. There, outside, a tendril of white smoke was meandering out of the engine compartment of the SUV.

Louisa saw the five men struggle with an instantaneous and unspoken conversation.

Grab and run?

Just run?

Is this guy fucking with us?

Louisa could see them look one to the other. Then they all looked at the man behind the counter, now two steps from Louisa with the gun aimed at her head. They looked back at the car. Back at him. The small spindle of rising smoke showed no visible flames. Maybe there was still time. All this was silent, considered as mere seconds ticked past.

The homeless man finally decided for them. He held up a hand as if to say "Listen," though he said nothing. As if in answer, a faint siren sounded blocks away.

And, to a man, they sprinted, all five of them, out the door, into the SUV, smoke be damned, and away, screeching away from Mor Slots 4 U.

Louisa had to open her mouth wide to breathe.

The homeless man stood in front of her.

"He had a gun," she said and gripped the counter for support.

He turned and went to the coffee service on the end of the counter and came back with a cup of coffee. "He had a gun," Louisa took the coffee from him, starting to shake. It was bitter, black. One hot gulp brought tears. She started to shake. "Oh, thank you. Oh, thank you, oh God." Relief poured through her in a torrent. She felt faint and carefully placed the coffee on the counter where she held on, her head down.

The homeless man put one of his hands on top of hers and there it was. That feeling, the one without words.

Louisa looked at his hand and at her own beneath it as some sensation pulsed between the two.

"Who are you?" she whispered.

He smiled and, forgetting the moment, the horror, the fear, she saw that his teeth were clean and straight.

A fire engine pulled up in front.

Louisa didn't move as the homeless man went back out to his corner. Much later, after all the talking and describing, she was done. Louisa went to wait on the bus bench. The homeless man wasn't under his sign. But the bus carried her home through peach-colored light and the soft hot air. Everything felt different, like gliding, like taking an opiate after hours of pain.

Louisa kept seeing that hand on hers.

The next day she brought him a bag of tamales.

"They're for you," she said, "they're a thank-you. Sort of." He said nothing. His silence left her filling in the blanks with wrong answers. "They had a gun," she said, "and I was so scared and so I appreciate what you did. I mean it was cool the way they didn't know what to do. . . ." She felt confused and she giggled nervously when she handed over the grocery bag. "Anyway, these are for you."

He smiled. The skin on his face, she thought, was not really a homeless person's skin. Not sun leathered and pocked by alcohol like so many.

"I better go . . . ," Louisa said.

He nodded as he held the bag close. It was the most she would get from him, she thought.

The Hosn brothers were watching through the window. They cleared their throats as she put her things away and came back to the cash register.

"Did you just give that guy something?" they said.

"Some tamales."

"Tamales? No, no. Don't feed him. Don't encourage him. There's something not right about him." Elder Brother was especially upset.

Younger Brother merely rolled his eyes. "He just like all the rest of homeless. He just a beggar."

"No! This one's different. I see him sometimes. People throw coins out the car window and he leaves them on the ground. He just leaves money on the ground. Doesn't even pick it up. I found four dollars last week, just lying there. Why he beg for money and then not take it, huh? You tell me, smart man."

Louisa smothered a question that burned on her tongue, but the other brother asked it instead.

"You greedy bastard. You go out and pick up the beggar's money?"

"Hey, four dollars is four dollars. It not growing on cactuses, you know."

Back and forth they went.

Louisa hadn't told her mother about the attempted robbery. It would worry her, she'd thought, and lately her mother had seemed worried enough. They'd had to dip into their $650 savings to pay the last doctor's bill, and his news wasn't good. Surgery now or crippled for life. He'd suggested they investigate possible loans. He asked if they had family who could help, and Louisa waited for her mother to mention Rosa, Los Angeles, Rosa, Los Angeles.

But the old woman never said a word about anything, for she wasn't sure if the miracle she'd ordered was on its way. It was a new-moon night, the darkest phase, and this was the time when doubts could hatch. Doubts were toxic to miracles. *Milagro ahora.* Time was running out. No. No. *Milagro ahora.*

That night, after Eduardo took his medication and sat, docile, in front of the TV, the women stood outside, leaning on the balcony railing, watching their neighbors come home from work or from the bar. "Maybe I should look for another job," Louisa sighed.

Surprisingly, her mother did not jump to agree. "Wait and see," she told Louisa, and the next morning, her mother gave her another bag of food for the homeless man.

Louisa said, "No, Mama. The boss told me no."

"You give him this, Louisa. *Es muy importante.*" Her mother rarely used her given name and Louisa could not defy her.

She got to work early and saw him again with his duct-taped sign—"Anything Helps." Louisa made a surreptitious gesture. She put the white plastic bag on the end of the bus bench where she always sat.

"For you," she said softly as she passed him. He nodded very slightly and pointed to his sign. Yes. Anything Helps.

Louisa went into Mor Slots 4 U with a lighter heart, knowing there was someone in this wasted desert who didn't care about the money people threw at him, but who would graciously accept her mother's tamales.

For the rest of the afternoon, she planned ways to speak to the homeless man. But when she had her break and started outside, she saw him talking to two other people, a man and a woman. They looked homeless too. All three were laughing and Louisa felt glad, for it meant he might talk to her. Later though. He had friends with him now. But later maybe he'd tell her what he and his friends were laughing about out there and she'd laugh too. Anticipating laughter felt good, normal.

But the problem was that Louisa didn't understand the way things were with the homeless: how they worked the corners, who worked where, and what happened if you worked someone else's spot. She especially didn't understand what happened when you wanted someone else's corner, that place where so much money was thrown at you that you could just let it fall.

On her day off, they took Eduardo on the bus to the mall where it was air-conditioned and they could eat in a food court. Louisa told her mother, "I'm going crazy." She told her about the pink cloud of feeling that she now associated with a homeless man who told the world, "Anything Helps." She said, "I mean, I don't like, *like* him, you know what I mean? Not the way you'd like a boyfriend. I'm just glad he's out there. It makes me feel better while I'm working if I can see him on the corner."

Her mother said cautiously, "Well, maybe he was sent there," and Louisa thought her mother was a little crazy too.

By the time they got home, Eduardo was pale with pain, so Louisa bathed him, then gave him the extra-strength pain pills that made him snore like a little bear. Louisa fell asleep next to him on the couch and the old woman went to her post at the window. The moon was waxing now. It would be full again soon. The cycle was almost complete. She felt her message answered. As yet, she had no proof, but now the old woman repeated only this, "Thank you," she told the moon. "Thank you."

Louisa wasn't concerned at first when she got off the bus and didn't see her man with his sign. The heat had melted gum on the sidewalk and it stuck to her shoes and distracted her so she didn't notice the caution tape that marked off the rear portion of Mor Slots 4 U until she was almost inside the door.

Then she stared at the bright yellow tape—a line of demarcation behind Mor Slots 4 U, some Dumpsters, a row of flimsy apartments, and beyond them the endless desert, brown, sere, lifeless.

Inside the casino, two Las Vegas cops were talking to one of the Hosn brothers in the office.

"What happened?" Louisa asked Clarisse, who was going off shift. The slot machines tolled in the background, but Louisa was inured to the sound.

"You know that homeless guy used to hang out on the corner?" Clarisse lit a cigarette and closed one eye against the smoke.

"What about him?" Louisa's voice lost its strength.

"Well, they caught the guys who did it, actually a guy and a woman, piece a trash both of 'em, homeless people anyway. They somehow got him back behind the place last night, I don't know when, and they beat the living crap out of him. Blood all over the fucking place. They took his money, but I heard he didn't have that much even though you'd think he'd make like two grand a day standin' on that corner. . . . Hey, you didn't see this, okay?" Clarisse stopped her rapid speech and glanced surreptitiously from the Hosn brother and the cops to the beer cooler where she and Louisa stood. In one swift motion, she opened the door, extracted a bottle of beer, and stuck it in her purse.

Louisa said faintly, "But I didn't see blood."

"Oho, it's there. Fuckin' gross."

"Is he all right?"

"Who?"

"The man. That man with the sign."

"I dunno. He wasn't looking too good when they took him away, but that was hours ago. I think that's what the cops are talking to dickhead about." She shrugged toward the office. "I gotta go. Remember, you didn't see nuthin'."

In truth, Louisa hadn't seen anything, only the backs of two police officers standing in front of the Hosn brothers' desk. He was staring up at the police with a look on his face that was a combination of shock, horror, and annoyance that Mor Slots 4 You should be the scene of such human depravity.

Louisa approached and overheard a piece of the conversation. She stopped.

". . . so, it's homicide now," the cop was saying. "Passed away about an hour ago at the hospital. Which means we'll have our forensics people on your property for at least—"

Then, the Hosn brother saw Louisa. He held up a hand. All three men turned to look at her.

"You. You're late." The brother was angered by the circumstances and by his own powerlessness more than by any tardiness on Louisa's part. "Get on your register. Go. Go."

She did not go. "Is he dead?" she asked bluntly.

"Hey, none of your biz—"

One of the cops was older and recognized that particular look on Louisa's face. He put a hand out to stop the brother. "Did you know him, ma'am?"

Louisa suddenly felt as though she were staring at the three men from a great distance and the question "Did you know him?" hung between them, stretched out like a long scroll to be read and considered. When she finally answered, "No, I never knew him," she felt a sense of loss that was too much to bear. She turned, went to the register. No one stopped her. She counted her drawer, every scrap of paper, every metal disk. She felt the men staring at her. She felt raw.

That shift was the busiest she'd ever worked. The slot machines called and cajoled with empty ringing promises and the smoke from cigarettes made her eyes sting. A drunk man wanted entrance to the Blue Room, and she buzzed him in absentmindedly until he cried out, "It ain't fucking opening," so she went to the door herself with the key. But when she got there, he stood too close and as she unlocked the door he said, "Well, aren't you a sweetheart," and rubbed his erection against her backside until she screamed as though her own son had died.

Both brothers came running. They threw the man out. They gave her tissues and said, "Okay, okay, now." But she couldn't stop weeping and one brother said, "Look, you go outside. Go pull yourself together. Go out front."

As Louisa was walking out the door, the brother said in passing, as though it was a normal everyday thing to do, "Louisa, while you're out there, check the ground. Bring back all the change you find."

Louisa stopped. The brother continued on into his office. He didn't see her go back and get her purse. It was all she could do to keep from shouting, but there were no words for the uselessness of people always wanting more. No one at Mor Slots 4 U ever had enough of anything. They were in constant need of things they didn't have, or things they already had but not enough of. Never enough. She could not stay. She could not become them. She would lose her son, her mother, herself, and she knew it.

Had they looked, the Hosn brothers might have seen Louisa standing where the homeless man had stood under the electronic sign. They would not have seen that she stood on a boulevard that was a virtual forest of neon come-hither signs. *Buy this. Come in here. Nude Girls! Gamble! Wager! Win!*

Louisa saw the bus many blocks down the street. She saw silver coins glittering on the cement, but she didn't pick them up. She merely waited.

When the bus arrived, she was starting to board when she saw the sign. There, propped up in the place where she always sat and waited for the bus, she saw it. It was his duct-taped, folded cardboard sign, ANYTHING HELPS.

"Wait!" she told the driver and he just had time to shout, "Lady, I ain't waitin' for—" before she was back on, flashing her pass and taking a seat on her last trip home from Mor Slots 4 U, clutching a dirty piece of cardboard to her chest.

Her mother saw the cardboard sign. She knew the instant Louisa walked in. "What happened?"

"I quit. I'll tell you later."

Louisa left the sign on the top surface of a bureau, the one small space she could call her own in those cramped quarters. She cleared off the hair clips and cheap jewelry to make room for that piece of cardboard, bent and taped, and she placed it as reverently as an offering.

The three of them went to McDonald's for dinner, normally a special occasion. Eduardo was happy, leaning forward in his wheelchair telling kid jokes. The women laughed, but only Eduardo was fooled by the gaiety. They walked there and back, talking little, listening to the street, feeling the heat of day become the swelter of night. Louisa's mother linked her arm through her daughter's. Her girl, now a woman, a beautiful woman, pushed the wheelchair and her mother held on to her arm. The moon came up, full and red, like eyes that had been crying.

"Can I watch SpongeBob, Mommy?"

"Yes. I'll watch him with you," Louisa said.

Eduardo was ecstatic at the way the night had turned out. The special dinner, a long walk, his mother watching his favorite cartoon with him. There had been no arguing, no harsh talk about money, no whispering, no worried faces. Just a strange quiet that, to an innocent ten-year-old boy, felt remarkably like peace.

At bedtime, Louisa gave him a back rub and her son fell asleep with his mother on one side and his grandmother on the other. The old woman feigned sleep for a long time. Then it started—a gentle shuddering of the bed as Louisa let her grief leak out. It was soundless but no less potent. Finally, around dawn, the old woman checked. Both the boy and Louisa were asleep. Outside the window, the full moon was clear—a pale, pitted white rock in a powder blue vastness. The mother took the battered sign off Louisa's bureau.

At 6:05 AM, Louisa had a pure joyous moment of the unremembering that comes in the first instant of waking. All too brief, the split second was gone and Louisa remembered why her eyes felt hot and swollen. She had no job to go to. And there was confusion too. She'd lost something, but what?

A homeless man whose name she never knew.

Her mother was sitting at the kitchen table. A dishcloth covered its surface. Louisa sat. No coffee was ready. Unusual.

"It's here," her mother said.

"What is."

"*El milagro.*"

A rose-colored light behind her mother came from the sunrise. Louisa did not recall seeing her in that light before. There was beauty in her mother's face. There was knowledge in each line and soft plane.

Louisa lifted the dishcloth. She saw that the duct tape had been cut. The cardboard sign had been unfolded.

And on the small kitchen table, sitting upon the unfolded sign, was money.

Money in stacks. Money in bills. Large bills, hundred-dollar bills.

"Mama?" she whispered. A dream might be disturbed by speaking too loudly.

Louisa's mother didn't answer.

"Where did this come from?"

Her mother held out her hand like an offering. "He left it for you."

"It was in there?"

"Yes," her mother said.

There were ten stacks. Ten $100 bills in each stack. "Ten thousand dollars," Louisa whispered. "Mama, we have to give this back."

The old woman pulled her chair up to her daughter and began, gently, to push the hair off her girl's face. "To who, *mija*?"

Louisa was silenced by the thought.

"Maybe he had family . . . maybe, a child, I—"

"No," The old woman put a hand on her daughter's arm as they both stared down.

Louisa started to speak. Her mother turned her forcefully to look—face-to-face.

"Listen." Louisa's mother spoke from a center as dense and ancient as desert stones. "How do you know this man was not sent to you, as your guardian? Why do you think you were glad of his presence? I asked for our miracle and here it is. He was sent to help us."

"Oh my God. I don't know." Louisa pressed her fingertips against her mouth.

"Look. This sign, 'Anything Helps.' It's not a sign for begging, *mija*. That's why he didn't pick up the coins. He came to tell people that anything helps, and you, Louisa, you heard him. You helped him. He left this sign on the bench for you to find. No one else took it. All the people who took the bus that day, before you got there. None of them took this sign. We cannot give away our miracle, *mija*."

"He's dead."

"No, he is home now. We all go there someday."

For a moment they were silent. Then Louisa knelt before her mother on the cracked linoleum floor. Mother held daughter and Louisa Escamilla wept in torrents. Her tears were like healing rain on a dry and dusty world and the world was suddenly green, and Louisa learned what her mother already knew: Every life has immortality and, having that, it has enough.

BACK TO SCHOOL ESSAY

Patricia Fogarty

"MY SUMMER OF LUST"
Harlan Dudek
Period 4

(Mrs. Funkhauser, please do not read out loud to the rest of the class. Thank you.)

Before the phone call that started the whole thing, my uncle Eddie didn't know me from shit. So when he's all Why doesn't your boy come out and spend the summer with me and the family in Huntington Beach? I should have guessed right then that something was up. He might have said something about working. I don't know because it was my mom who did all the talking. No surprise there.

She sure as shit didn't say anything about a job. So there I am, telling my buds about how I'm going to be surfing all day and making the scene all night. California girls, parties. That kind of shit. Instead, it's dirty clothes and hot dryers all the time because it turns out that what Uncle Eddie needed was a day manager for one of his laundrymats. That's right, laundrymats. You'd think he could read the sign in fucking three-foot letters over the door maybe just once in the last fifteen years and notice that there is no *y* in laundromat. Tells you how fucked up I'm getting when I start thinking about how maybe Eddie's got it right and there ought to be. A *y* that is. What the fuck is up with "laundro," like it's all high class and everything? Like people are bringing in white shirts and hankies and shit like that.

Which they aren't. It shouldn't be a surprise or anything, this laundrymat being so close to the beach and all, that there's sand in the bottoms of the machines. I'm thinking how the fuck am I supposed to get that out of there? But turns out no one cares. Well, once in a while someone does, but I just look at them like who the fuck are you and what do you think this is, a laundromat? Chill out, lady. It's the beach.

For all the fucking good it does me. The beach, that is. One thing about the laundrymat business is that it's 24/7. My shift is eight in the morning until four in the afternoon. You got to understand, kid, says Eddie. Your cousin Eddie Jr. has prospects, and he'll pull his weight as long as it doesn't interfere with his schoolwork. Pull his weight means that Eddie Jr.—I call him Fuckwad Jr.—works a four-hour shift between me and the night guy. Oh, did I say works? Because I should have said is supposed to work. So let's just be up front about it and say that I work from seven in the morning until seven at night. Fun fun fun, huh?

So like I said, it's the beach and all, and there's a ton of shit going on at night, but it's not like I'm going to leave this shit hole and hit the clubs with my hair all flat and melted-gel tracks down the back of my neck because there's a wall of dryers pumping out hot air all day and no AC. I'm like Why don't you get AC in here, Eddie? And he's all Are you kidding? You got ocean breezes here. You don't like it I can transfer you to Garden Grove, okay, kid?

Whatever.

So I'm thinking how this is the worst summer of my life so far and maybe ever, when all of a sudden in comes this chick and right away it hits me. She's it, man. The One.

My dad used to try and say deep shit he thought I'd remember for a while since it would have to last me all week until the next visit. Like I've got some kind of shortage of adults telling me what to think. Like I could be sitting in my room sometime and my head comes up empty. Anyway, one of the things he used to say to me was something about a door closing and another opening. I remember thinking at the time What the fuck? But maybe I wasn't ready to hear that one at that particular time in my life.

Which brings me to the point about how I'm thinking the summer is completely fucked and how it would be so much finer to be back in Red Bluff with my crew. The door had like closed on the summer when in she walks through the door of the laundrymat. In this case that door thing my dad said was literally true. Cool.

It's not like she was all that fine. If you want to know the truth I'd had it with the hot chicks. The hotter the bitchier I'd kind of decided. There were these three chicks—roommates—who came in together on Sunday afternoons. In bikinis. The first time it happened I'm like have I died and gone to heaven or what? But they're all ignoring me except when the change machine is out of order and they want me to make change. Then they'd leave and not come back in time and then chew out my ass because someone had emptied their shit out of the machines and left it on the folding table. And yeah, if you leave your thong underwear out where pervs can see it it may not be there when you get back.

The worst part was they'd usually come back wasted with a few guys. And then the guys would chew out my ass after the chicks did. Wanting to know what kind of place am I running here. Oh wait let me give that some thought. Where do they come up with this shit? So then they all sit around while the shit is drying and you can tell these guys are working it out. Who is going to do which one of the chicks when they get back to the skanks' place. And if there are moms in the laundrymat while this shit is going down then *they* chew out my ass. What kind of place am I running here all over again.

So when *she* walked in and *wasn't* all hot, I was ready for her.

Don't get me wrong. It's not like she was a dog or anything. What she had going for her was really shiny hair and a wicked smile. Her hair was long and straight and it kind of moved like a wave all down her back. Her smile was like some kind of beam pointed right at you. I was like me? You're smiling at me? What could have used some work was her outfit. And I guess she was carrying a few extra pounds here and there, which was probably why she was a little more covered up and frumpy than most of the other chicks that you saw walking around.

She came in every other day or so with a little kid. Her brother. He was much better behaved than any of the other brats I'd seen. Which may have been because he was retarded. He didn't look funny or anything. It's just that he never talked or played or even ran around. Just sat there. You got the feeling she was kind of embarrassed about that. Personally, I thought it was a welcome change, but I could see as how it was likely to cause trouble in some other areas of his life.

She had to do the wash for her whole family, so she was there for a while when she came in. The first time she threw me that smile I thought okay—what does she want? But nothing. She just went back to staring out the window. Which was probably her way of keeping the kid company. Then I started thinking maybe she's not the sharpest knife in the drawer either.

Which had kind of been my pattern in love so far. I guess chicks who don't talk much let you fill in the blanks. Which would be cool if you got it right. But you never do. Like when I tried to give my old girlfriend from ninth grade a present. I mean, what's wrong with a book about the history of horses when she tells you she likes them? *Liked. When I was like ten or so. And who wants a fucking book anyway?* Well, for one thing, Indians didn't even have horses in this country until the Spanish brought them here. Ever think about how weird it would be to see all those Indians running around without horses? You need books for that shit.

So I decided to test this chick in the laundrymat. I waited until the joint was empty and I sat down across from her and said all casual, "I guess there's someone having a worse summer than me, huh?"

At first she's all what? Then the smile. And then she said, "How come?"

"Oh, this place and all." I hadn't worked out what I was going to say back.

"I kind of like it. Chance to get away by myself. And you're okay." Then the smile. The kid was giving me the fish eye though. "What's your name?"

This is going to sound really weird and all, but when she said that I started to get a little excited. Sexually that is. *What's your name?* It couldn't have been the words. I'm like not going to get a hard-on when some old teacher (not you!) finds me smoking behind a portable and says it. It's like she wanted to know who I really am.

So I told her and every time after that when she came in she said it. So I'm like getting excited when I hear my own name. Is that fucked up or what?

It was getting to where I only had three more weeks before summer was over and time to go home. I had to do something to get with her. Another saying from dad about how you always regret the shit you didn't do more than the shit you did. That one bites, or as they say on the History Channel, subsequent events would prove otherwise.

But I was all young and inexperienced and hot to hear her say my name, so one day I grab one of the carts and take it over to where she's sitting with the kid. "The wheels don't crap out on this one," I say.

After that smooth come-on I'm waiting for her to jump my bones and drag me into the back office. In my dreams. I'm really waiting for her to think of something to say that wouldn't make me feel like a complete shithead. She's got to be good at shit like that what with her brother and all.

Anyway, she's stalling for time pretending to look at the wheels of the cart and shit and finally she says, "Thanks, Harlan."

I'm wanting her worse than I ever wanted anything in my whole life, and since she said my name and all I've got a major hard-on. So I move the basket in front of my crotch. She's all throwing clothes into the basket and I'm thinking she's got to see what's going on unless she's looking really hard at those dirty jeans she just threw in. Which she might have been. They were wicked dirty. Next thing I know there's tighty not so whities going into the basket and I figure she's all embarrassed about that. But instead she looks straight into my eyes and kind of pushes up against the basket. Shi-it.

So I'm telling her how I've got to go back home in three weeks and she's all sad about it. "I wish we could've met before," she says.

Which got me to thinking about how fine it would have been to have had her to IM last spring when that asshole ran into the Taurus and my mom told me how I was nothing but trouble and how different life would have been for her if she hadn't had me to fuck around with for the last sixteen years. None of it was my fault. The asshole. Being born.

"It's not like I have to go home." That may have been the woody talking, but when you really think about it, it's not like there was anything I really had to go back to in Red Bluff. My mom most of all.

And then she says the words I'd been waiting to hear all my life. "Want to do something later on?"

She was supposed to meet me in front of this candy store down on Main Street at eight thirty. Which meant that if Fuckwad Jr. started his shift on time at four o'clock, then I would have plenty of time to shower and grab a burger. And maybe pigs would fly out of my ass.

I would be lucky if he showed up at all. Especially on a Friday. Which meant that I would have to wait until Rudy the night manager showed up late for his eight o'clock shift. No shower, no burger. No chick.

As it turned out, none of it happened the way I expected. At seven thirty Fuckwad Jr. showed up. "That joint in your sock drawer says my dad thinks I got here at four o'clock."

Like I'm some kind of rat or something. Whatever.

Turns out Uncle Eddie wanted to catch Rudy getting here late so he could fire his ass, and so he gets here a few minutes after Fuckwad Jr.. "What're you doing still here?" he says to me. But he doesn't wait for an answer. Instead he starts going off on me about how I hadn't filled the detergent dispensers and what is he paying me for anyway? So he grabs Fuckwad Jr. and goes to the back to get the boxes of tiny detergents, going on about how he's got to do everything around here himself and support his sister's lazy-ass boy on top of it.

While this is going on, Zeke, one of the guys who comes into the laundrymat to scavenge bottles and cans out of the trash comes into the joint dragging a pillowcase full of dirty clothes. He dumps the stuff from the case in one of the washers, and then, real quick he takes off the T-shirt he's wearing and dumps that in too. Considering that it's the beach and all, I didn't think anyone would care that much. Except that when he sits down across from this mom, she looks at him and picks up her kid and all her stuff and comes over to where I'm standing. She's all you've got to get him out of here I don't want my little girl looking at that. And I'm all oh great Zeke is exposing himself now what do I do call the cops?

But when I get over there, turns out Zeke is all zipped up and minding his own business except that he's all inked on one side of his stomach. Which some people are going to object to no matter what, even if it's a plain old tribal tat. But Zeke's tat was you might say kind of different. It was a chick stretched out on this red velvet couch thing with carved wood and little buttons all over the cushions. She's got this long hair and these righteous boobs and she's naked except for this long high-heeled boot that laced all the way up to her knee. Probably one on the other leg too except it ended just above the knee where Zeke's stomach hair began. And she's got her eyes closed and her arms up over her head holding onto the chair behind her and her legs are completely spread and you can see all of her parts. And since the rest of it was really realistic I just have to assume that her parts were too.

The mom is looking over at me like what are you going to do about this? So I tell Zeke he's got to cover the tat or else leave. And he's all with what? To tell you the truth, I should have come up with something, but honest to god all I could do was stare at Zeke's stomach. At how ugly it was. How this chick is spread out across Zeke's fat hairy belly and how there's this yellow brown mole right over the top of her head. And he's got these long white scars all over like he'd been stabbed or something and two of them run right through the tat. Through the chick.

And Zeke is like suit yourself maybe I'll hit the street for a while and I'm like okay you do that you ugly perv. Only when he gets up to leave he turns around and aims the tat at the mom and Fuckwad Jr., who's come out of the back with the tiny detergents and asks if Fuckwad wants to see his girlfriend.

Which he did. Fuckwad is like Awesome! Whose work is that?

And Zeke tells him go to Fredo at Fresh Ink down the street. And you can copy the design, only you're going to have to use your own girlfriend ha ha ha. And Fuckwad is all laughing like he's even got a girlfriend to use.

So Zeke splits and the mom takes her little girl and goes over to where her clothes are going around in the dryer and opens it. The stuff looks a little damp, but she dumps it into her laundry basket anyway and takes off. Except on her way out she stops and says to me Do you think that's what it's all about between men and women? And I just shrug. Because I don't know. Not because I'm some kind of smart ass. I mean do I look like someone you'd go to to ask what it's all about between men and women? I'm the guy who gets hard hearing my own name. But she's acting like I'm the one with the horny chick on my gut just because I don't know what I'm supposed to say.

Turned out Rudy the night manager didn't even bother to show. Fuckwad Jr. told his dad he couldn't stay because he had to study for his SATs , so Uncle Eddie said he'd do it except first he had to drive to Garden Grove and empty the coin boxes. Which left yours truly. "Here's twenty for you, kid. It'll only be an hour tops and you can use the dough, right?" So he takes off.

It's not like I can pretend I have SATs to study for. Whatever.

So I'm probably going to be twenty minutes late to meet the chick, whose name I should tell you: Mary. It's supposed to be a common name, but I never knew anybody who had it. Trouble is, she never gave me her cell number. Come to think of it, I'd never seen her with a phone. I knew there was something different about her, but I just couldn't think what it was at the time.

Along about this time Zeke comes back to put his stuff in the dryer. He was acting like nothing had happened, probably because his memory's shot for one reason or another, most having to do with things you put into a pipe and smoke. Another example of this is that he forgot to put detergent in the wash load judging by the look on his face when he pops the lid and gets a whiff of his wet clothes.

He must have been short of funds too, because he stood there thinking it over for way too long, like if he runs another wash cycle he won't have money for the dryer. All of which got me to thinking. "What'd you have to pay for that tat, Zeke?"

He looks at me like what tat? And then like he remembers that he just happens to have a nude chick with her one and a half legs spread open across his ugly gut. "Nothing. Guy wanted to see what it would look like and did it for free."

"So that's not your girlfriend?" Like I needed to ask. As if a chick like that really existed, and if she did she'd want Zeke for a boyfriend.

He'd already gone back to stewing over his financial affairs and for a minute I thought he was ignoring me. "Nah," he finally says. "I think it's *his* ex-girlfriend. Fredo's. The guy who did it. She works at the Dry Dock, that chick. Looks just like her too."

As if he knew. "She seen it?"

"Shit yeah. Fredo gives me money to go to the Dock and have a few beers so she can look at it. Really pisses her ass off too. She tells me I got to put on a shirt except the manager thinks it's funny and tells me I don't have to. Wouldn't be right, anyway. Fredo ain't paying me to cover this up."

I'd thought about giving him four quarters to redo his wash, but I didn't want him to get the idea I was paying him to come in here, so I didn't. He went ahead and put his dirty wet laundry into one of the dryers, and we both pretended not to smell it when he took it out with all the filth and stink baked in and stuffed it back into the grimy pillowcase. Didn't bother to fold it.

By this time I was already a half hour late and no sign of Uncle Eddie. Good thing too because he probably would have chewed me out for letting Zeke do laundry here in the first place, Eddie being a Catholic and all.

Ten more seconds and Zeke would have been out the door, but just then in walks Mary and wouldn't you know she ends up staring straight down at Fredo the tattoo artist's ex-girlfriend the cocktail waitress's crotch. I couldn't make this shit up.

I was pretty embarrassed about it, and it seemed to take Zeke forever to throw the pillowcase full of clothes over his shoulder and split, but he did and there we were. Mary and me. Alone.

"I kinda wondered if you were going to show up," she finally says.

And now I can't figure out where to start, or what to say. The deal is she's dressed different. Cause she's on a date dickhead! I mean I should have been exfuckingstatic about it right? Because she's got on this low-cut top and these low-cut tight jeans. But nothing. Maybe after Zeke and all, it was kind of fucking with my head to see her that way. Maybe later on she would say my name and things would start to perk up, if you get my drift.

"I'm sorry about Zeke—that guy—that you had to look at that."

"It's no big deal. Anyway, I've seen it before. Everyone has. That guy walks around town like that all the time."

I tell her about how Uncle Eddie's coming to take over for me and she's happy to sit in her usual seat and stare at the people on the sidewalk outside. All the traffic is one way now with everyone headed downtown. Mostly kids our age dressed to impress. The other chicks are in tight jeans and low-cut tops too. All the guys who haven't got shaved heads have their hair styled and gelled, unlike yours truly.

There's no one else in the laundrymat, so I take the seat next to hers where her brother usually sits. She's her usual quiet self, and so I get to thinking. If I were back home in Red Bluff I'd probably be at the river, lying on an old blanket and looking up at the stars between the cottonwood branches. You park your car along Highway 92 next to where there's a path cut through the woods to the riverbank and you're there. Maybe you know that already from when you were my age. My oldest friend Justin Kepler (period five) had told me they'd been building fires at night and the chicks were going with them. I was kind of sorry to have to miss that action. No cicadas singing at night in Huntington Beach either. My mom actually held the phone out the window once so I could hear them. I didn't, but I lied and said I had. There's the ocean and all, but the tide going in and out makes me lonely. When you really think about it my mom's had it pretty hard raising me all by herself and she does her best. I hope Justin and them used protection.

"I wonder if anyone will ever put me in a tat?" Mary finally says.

I'm thinking it's that thing where you say the opposite of what you really mean, but that doesn't strike me as the kind of thing she's likely to do, so I don't laugh. "You want that?"

"Yeah! It would be kind of a tribute. Like how all those artists back in the day painted their girlfriends naked and made them famous and all."

She had a point there. Either way you're putting your girlfriend out there naked for everyone to see. Just not on a wino crackhead, I tell her. And maybe not stretched out on a red velvet couch. And with her legs together. Besides that, tats fade in the sun and people get old and shriveled up and when they die the tat goes with them.

"Yeah, I know all that. It's just that it's hard to know when someone really loves you these days. Someone puts you in a tat, at least you know where you stand."

Tell me about it. At least she was half right.

I should have explained to her about Fredo and how he put his ex-girlfriend on Zeke's gut just to disrespect her, but if Mary couldn't guess that for herself just by looking at the tat, then I don't think there's much hope for her, you know? And even though I'd been fantasizing all day about us going out on the pier and her leaning up against the railing and me leaning up against her with my hands up her blouse . . . I guess I just didn't want to be that guy after all. I sure as hell didn't have any plans to get her inked onto my stomach.

Turns out, Mary wasn't really that into me anyway. After Uncle Eddie got back we walked around and stuff. And I told her about my mom and the deal with the Taurus and the asshole and her holding the phone out the window, but she wasn't really listening. When we got to the DQ she went to the can and one of her friends told me there was this guy who'd made it with Mary and then dumped her and she was kind of hoping he'd see her with me and get all jealous and stuff.

About midnight she told me she was going to sleep over at one of her friends' and so they were going to take off. "You're a really nice guy, Harlan," she told me, and then she gave me a big hug like you give your friends. Her smile was still beautiful, and I'll always remember how pretty her hair was. And while there was a bit of a stirring down there, it wasn't like it had been that day in the laundrymat.

That never happened again. After that night, she came into the laundrymat with her little brother just like before, and when three weeks were over she wrote down my cell number and said she'd give me a call sometime, but I'm not holding my breath. Turns out all that looking out the laundrymat window was just her hoping to spot that guy who dumped her. Maybe for a little while she thought she had it for me. But I don't think so. Turns out she wasn't The One after all, which means the chick who is is still out there somewhere. Maybe she'll turn up when I'm ready for her.

Just to wrap things up, here's what I learned this summer: First, I don't know what it's all about between men and women, and second, I can't trust my pecker to help me out with that. Which really *is* that thing when something is the opposite of what it's supposed to be. We'll probably study that again this year.

But I'm only a junior and there's a whole year ahead of me to figure it out. The stuff between men and women I mean. Like that's going to happen. But you never know. So maybe you'll have us write about what we learned at the end of the school year and I can tell you all about it. Ha ha! Don't hold your breath!

(I hope you don't take points off for language.)

PADDY O'GRADY'S THIGH

Lisa Alber

On an April afternoon with steel-tipped clouds whipping by overhead, Teresa Ahern angled for a view of the disinterred body of Paddy O'Grady and fretted over her boyfriend. Gavin had been acting suspiciously attentive of late, as if he were having it off with another woman. Either that, or he wanted to marry Teresa herself. Honestly, Teresa couldn't decide which possibility was worse given that she was torn between affection for Gavin, and, increasingly, irritation.

She stifled a yawn. That morning she'd woken disoriented, almost woozy, which was odd because she'd drunk but two pints at the pub on the previous evening. She'd also slept harder than usual, so she had no idea what time Gavin had slunk off to his mum's house. He'd left a note that stated the obvious fact that he'd dozed awhile before leaving.

True, she usually wakened enough to kiss him good-bye, but still, why the silly note that included *I miss you already!* and a dozen Xs and Os standing in for love and kisses? Never mind what anyone else might say, this behavior was uncalled for, in Teresa's opinion. After all, Teresa needed little reminding that Gavin's mum brought the wrath of God down on him when he stumbled home just in time for breakfast.

A gust off the Atlantic slapped hair into Teresa's face and returned her to the task at hand: furthering her journalistic career. The breeze wiped the air clean of its usual scents of cow and marshy grazing land, and riffled the tent the guards had erected over poor Paddy O'Grady, buried only the previous week, poor soul.

Teresa hadn't known Paddy, he being from Doolin and she a recent transplant from Limerick with her first real newspaper job. Not that the *Clare Challenger* won the prize for brilliant coverage, but it was a step toward bigger and better bylines—starting with Paddy O'Grady. Since Teresa had reported Paddy's funeral, she'd begged for the chance to follow up on his disinterment. Her editor had rolled his eyes at her request until she dropped her uncle's name: Detective Sergeant Danny Ahern, thank you very much.

"Detective Sergeant, give us a look, can you?" she called, but the tall man otherwise known as Uncle Danny continued to ignore her.

A woman with a tatty black shawl and frazzled gray hair sidled closer to Teresa along the yellow crime scene tape. "Could be I fancy a peek, as well," she said. "Just to see, you know."

The woman spoke so fast and in such terse fashion, Teresa barely understood her. "Have a personal interest, do you?" Teresa said.

"Could be I do."

Teresa always recognized the rare voice raised on Irish, but this old troll didn't carry the lilt of that language on her tongue. Yet she was no foreigner, not with her freckles. Therefore, she was a tinker, one of the indigenous Traveler folk. Like the Romany gypsies, they lived for the most part in caravan communities, let their horses graze along the roadsides, and weren't known for their work ethic. Most of all, they kept to themselves and as far away as possible from law enforcement officials.

Teresa's story-sniffing radar went on full alert. She asked the woman's name and was awarded with a grunted, "Just Mary to you."

"Mary, so, I could help you with a nod to the DS over there."

Another grunt.

"Uncle Danny!" Teresa yelled. "Come along, do us the favor, then."

Later, after the wind-driven rain beat a rash into her cheeks, Teresa loitered in her crusty Volkswagen with her notebook on her lap. Her car sat on an embankment across from the cemetery, and her view included dozens of towering Celtic crosses and lone Mary, who stared toward the open grave still hidden by a tent. The woman looked like a pagan queen lurking there, all in black and as immovable as a statue.

Despite his irritation, her uncle had eventually arrived at her side. "Jesus, Terry," he had said, "quit with the *uncle* in front of my men."

Mary flapped a hand in Teresa's face to forestall her. "Uncle," Mary said, and Danny raised two slow eyebrows, like he did when yoking his impatience. He stooped closer, and Mary stood taller. "Uncle, my book's gone the way of my youth. Poof."

"How's that?"

"Charms and potions and other cures; I earn money from them. You can't be expecting me to remember all the recipes without my book, can you?"

Danny turned his eyebrows toward Teresa, who shook her head, nonplussed.

"And if you'd be letting me see yonder dead man," Mary continued, "I could perhaps find my book."

"You lost your book in this cemetery? When?"

"No, you blasted—" Mary caught herself. "Someone nicked my book, you see, and perhaps it's here."

Teresa could tell her uncle had now written Mary off as a nutter. His tone turned distantly polite. "I'll send a guard over to take a statement, and we'll notify you if we find your stolen book. Now, if you'll excuse me."

"Detective Sergeant," Teresa called after his retreating back.

"Not now, you," came the response.

Frustration caused Teresa to turn on the old gnome. "Grand. Now I have zero to report, and there you were, going on about some book as if that would get you into the crime scene tent."

Mary squinted at Teresa. "Why, you're Gavin's girl. Fancy that." She turned pensive, then, before Teresa knew what was what, the old bat cackled. "Christ in heaven, aren't you the lucky lass?"

Teresa had been so flustered by her boyfriend's entrée into the conversation that she'd blundered through a few questions with no finesse whatsoever. How did Mary know Gavin? How did she recognize Teresa? What was so blasted funny anyhow? Never mind Teresa's current state of ambivalence toward Gavin, no one best mock her choice in men.

In the end, Teresa lost her objectivity. In other words, she cocked up the interview. Canny Mary had sidelined Teresa's questions and refused to reveal how her recipe book connected to poor Paddy O'Grady.

Now, rain drummed against the car roof while Teresa jotted a few particulars, including a comment Mary had mumbled just before Teresa stomped back to her car. Something about a *first* unburied body.

No, Mary wasn't canny, after all; barking mad more to the point. And, come to that, she was burly enough to have shoveled up poor Paddy herself.

Teresa sat with this thought for a full minute. Then she rang Gavin, who had to be acquainted with Mary somehow. Gavin cooed with delight that she'd chosen to ring him first for once. She let him think the call turned around him because she wanted off the funeral-and-wedding circuit and on to real stories. She arranged to meet Gavin for dinner back in Ennis then rang off, all the while imagining herself with award-winning bylines. If truth be told, she planned to gather a decent portfolio and get her bum to Dublin and the *Irish Times*.

Across the narrow lane lined with hawthorn, her uncle still muttered about the scene. He was like her, eager for promotion, and to support his cause, he insisted on shooting a set of unofficial crime scene photos with his own camera. Teresa wasn't sure playing the photographer would help his career, but then again, what did she know? Here she sat with an empty fecking notebook.

Teresa watched Uncle Danny pause at the tent's threshold and snuggle his digital camera into a waterproof bag. Once completed, he let the wind propel him toward a decrepit Peugeot that he'd parked in the next pasture alongside a bathtub that doubled as a water trough. Just as he dropped the camera onto the passenger seat, one of the crime scene lads hailed him. He dashed back toward the tent with trousers already soaked to his skin.

Teresa perked up, and in less than a minute she was hopping from tussock to tussock on her way to Uncle Danny's car. She tripped ankle deep into boggy puddles and stooped low behind a drystone wall lest her uncle catch sight of her. She arrived at the Peugeot with a kinked back to find the car unlocked, no surprise, this being the end of everywhere in County Clare.

She hunkered down in the backseat and turned on the camera. Then, she hesitated. Uncle Danny could get suspended, or worse, if she published facts not meant to be revealed yet. Bollocks to that, she told herself. She was a journalist now. Besides, everyone knew her uncle never gave anything away. He'd be fine.

Guilt at sneaking one past her uncle disappeared quickly enough when she cycled through the photos of the body. She'd best forget her initial theory about a grave robbery—unless she counted the strip of skin that some deviant had cut clean away from poor Paddy O'Grady's thigh. She pictured the headline, *her* headline: *Corpse Desecration in Liscannor Cemetery!*

Dear pathetic Gavin, sniffing the cork as if he knew a merlot from grape soda. His dainty nostrils quivered before he positioned the cork next to his soup spoon. His voice always turned squeaky with excitement, and now it positively squealed as he toasted the turnabout in their relationship. Teresa tipped her glass against his and avoided his hopeful gaze. What turnabout? she wondered. Because *she* had called *him* this afternoon?

She sipped—the house red, whatever it was, tasted fine to her—and considered telling Gavin that he reminded her of a puppy that pissed the carpet yet remained too adorable to give up. For now, at least. Deep down, she felt the end coming like an alarm set to go off inside her head.

"This place is a bit posh, don't you think?" she said. "I meant a bite at the pub, to talk."

"To talk, of course I heard you." Gavin grabbed her hand from across the table. "To talk."

Teresa maneuvered her hand out from under Gavin's squeezing fingers. She fiddled with a wildflower bouquet that lay on the table between them. Gavin was too sweet, desperate really, the way he named each bloom he'd brought her—early purple orchids, violets, and primroses—then settled back with a contented smile. In fact, he'd come off bloody odd for an Irishman when she'd met him two months earlier. At first, she'd written him off as bent, but his ever-ready willy had proved her wrong. Soon enough, she'd found herself telling her friends that his was the most endearing face, what with its chin dimple and impossibly blue eyes. These days she couldn't help thinking that sweetness was one thing; desperation, however, quite another.

"Yes, to talk," she said. "I'll be needing your help with a story."

The light in Gavin's eyes dimmed as she detailed poor Paddy's flayed thigh. "This is our talk?" he said.

She waited for him to recover his eagerness. She predicted that within thirty seconds, he'd start tripping over himself to please her. Unfortunately, instead of his usual compliancy, he frowned.

Teresa tickled one of his fingertips that poked through a plaster and wondered if he'd bandaged it himself. But of course not, silly her for the thought; Gavin turned green at the mere mention of blood, so much so that he'd elected out of working alongside his father at the butcher shop in favor of apprenticing as an electrician.

"The flowers are lovely," Teresa said. "Truly. I hope you didn't injure yourself on my account. While picking them, I mean."

"On your account," he echoed. "I pine for a real relationship. If you only knew."

"How could I not?" She swallowed her impatience. He was such a girl sometimes, the way he sulked and mooned about. *Pine for.* Christ in heaven.

Their meals arrived. Gavin asked for extra water in which to tuck the bouquet in hopes it would remain fresh until they returned to her basement flat.

"The flowers will look nice beside the bed," she said. Gavin ventured a smile, which was a good enough go-ahead signal for Teresa. "So, today I met a woman who apparently knows you. A Traveler who goes by Mary—sound familiar?"

"Oh hell," Gavin said. "Not her. Can't we have a nice dinner?"

As they ate their lamb and potatoes au gratin, Teresa cajoled Gavin into revealing that Mary's son worked at his father's butchery. The son went by Wally the way Mary went by Mary. They kept their real names hidden within their extended Traveler family. According to Gavin, Wally wasn't to be trusted, but at least he was more modern than his batty mother, who dropped in each Friday to collect the raw drippings that Wally saved for her fertility brews. Wally insisted the concoctions worked for barren women.

Teresa could have done without Gavin's tone—as if he pondered her prospects for carrying a child—and interrupted his monologue with, "Have I met Wally?"

"I'd say so," Gavin said. "He's the one who hops to when you come around to fetch me from the office."

Right, the office where Gavin volunteered time helping his da with the paperwork. Apparently, Mary had given birth to the wall-eyed bloke who spoke with what Teresa had believed was a speech impediment.

"Him? Never did catch his name, did I?" Teresa said. "Wally can't be that bad if he suffers to work a regular job."

"So you say, but how else to fetch in customers for his mum than mingle with us settlers? I'll lay a wager he steals meat when he can, the thieving bastard."

It seemed that stealing meat was just one of Wally's many sins. He also either scared the customers or flirted without shame; handed out leaflets for everything from recycled goods to bare-knuckle boxing tournaments; and sold his family's Traveler music CDs. He was a one-man sideshow with no care given to Gavin's father's reputation.

"Okay, okay," Teresa said to halt Gavin's tirade. "I get it. He's an all-around untrustworthy tosser. Now, can we get back to Mary?"

"You can't be trusting her either."

"Humor me, please. This is my career we're talking about. Have you ever seen her with a book filled with voodoo recipes?"

Gavin gulped his wine. A flush settled deep into his skin. "The thing is, this conversation's not what I expected. I feel—"

"Gavin, please. What about the book?"

"—like you're neglecting me, that's what I feel."

"What's got you wound? And you'd better not say *Wally*. You're mental if you think I'm keen on your father's counter boy."

Gavin jerked against the table. The flowers tipped onto the bread basket, and Teresa ground her teeth as water soaked into the hard rolls. "I need to talk to Mary," she said. "Since tomorrow is Friday, I'll pop around the shop from work. What time does Mary retrieve her drippings?"

Mac's Five-Star Meats sat off O'Connell Square, a short walk from the *Challenger* office. It was a modern establishment with track lighting aimed at rows of glistening flesh. Despite his tetchy stomach, Gavin took pride in his father's upscale reputation, and he'd given Teresa a tour of the place on their second date. Meat lockers, silver counters large enough to lay out whole cows, floors that sloped toward drains, electric saws—the entire unsettling operation.

Teresa stood on the threshold and remembered why she bought her chicken breasts at the Spar. Here there was no masking the aroma of an abattoir. Blood weighted the air enough that she tasted it on her tongue. This smell was too real, too much a reminder of the carnage the human species got up to on a daily basis.

Hold on there, she reminded herself. Carnage landed journalists on the front page, therefore, carnage was her best mate. She stepped toward the meat displays.

Gavin pushed in behind her with an 'allo called out to his father. His head swiveled between Mary's son, who waited behind the counter, and Teresa. "Oh, all right then," Gavin said in response to Teresa's head jerk. "Your mum come around yet, Wally?"

Wally had inherited his mother's burly physique but without the troll-like side effect since he was tall. Teresa smiled into his wandering eye and ignored Gavin's bristling. Wally's limber fingers cradled a knife that looked sharp enough to create sparks. A beef slab waited before him, ready for cutting. To Teresa's relief, Gavin's queasy nature outstripped his pettiness; he fled to his father's office.

Wally glared after him, then returned to studying Teresa. "That old mum of mine said you had an interest," he said.

"She seems to know what's what."

"Can't help herself, being psychic," Wally said. He placed his blade along the line between fat and what Teresa guessed was a loin cut. With wrist flicks, he sculpted away the wall of blubber without nicking into the meat. His dainty movements belied his scarred knuckles.

"So?" Wally said.

"I'm here to talk to your mum, not you."

Wally leaned toward her with his elbows on the plastic partition that separated them. "My mum's already been and gone, but I can see to answering your questions. I'm privy to her business."

Are you then, Teresa thought as Wally wiped the knife against his apron. At her prompt, he confirmed Mary's parting shot about a previous body, which was to say that poor Paddy was the *second* man dug up in the past week. The first man, like Paddy, had also fed worms for seven days before he was uncovered. However, he'd rested up around Galway, which explained why the Clare newspaper had missed the story.

Wally returned to his task and soon enough finished the trimming. He set aside the carving knife in favor of a cleaver, which he then slashed through the meat with a thwack of metal against wood chopping block. A perfect steak tipped over and Wally slipped it into the display case.

"The question being," Teresa said, "how Mary knew about the first body up in Galway."

"Ah-well, she's likely to be keeping her ear out, isn't she, what with her book missing? Besides, there's the rest of our clan out on Connemara. My mum put the word out for them to keep track of the gossip. So there you have it."

Teresa didn't have anything but confusion about the book's connection to grave tampering. Wally freshened his grip on the cleaver and raised his arm. "I can tell you this: His body wasn't meddled with," he said. "Was only the one leg pulled clear of the coffin and the top closed over the rest of the corpse."

Her uncle's photos had revealed the same image. What a perverse respect for the dead, Teresa thought, to protect everything from the elements but a leg.

"The man up in Galway, he wasn't cut?" she said.

"So I said." Wally smeared red goo across his forehead with an arm swipe. "Why, something different about your man yesterday?"

But his voice said he suspected as much. Or perhaps he knew? Could be he was putting her on with banter, but there was no telling, what with his Traveler accent. She pictured Paddy's skinny drumstick of a leg angled up and out of his coffin. It was obscene—and with the fresh-cut slice added atop that? Doubly obscene. They hid a fact or two, Wally and his mum. Mary's book must explain all and no wonder she worried over its loss. *If* it was lost.

"What would Mary say to a long rectangular strip of human skin from a corpse?" Teresa said.

"A strip, you say? She'd find a use for it, at that." Wally grinned in response to the revulsion Teresa couldn't hide. The cleaver bit through again and another steak toppled over.

Teresa sounded out a mounting suspicion. "I expect your mom visited the cemetery to discover for herself whether Paddy O'Grady had been cut. She have a vision it might relate to her so-called lost book?"

"That's obvious, I'd say, but a useless wankstain, your uncle. I'll pass on the good word about O'Grady's cut thigh, though, and me old ma will be appreciative. Might even gift you a love potion." He nodded back to the workroom where Gavin hid. "Not that you need it."

His snide tone implied that he knew a little something about her relationship with Gavin. But then, once again, she couldn't interpret him because of his accent. Bloody punter.

The cleaver thwacked again and Teresa twitched. Wally cradled a steak on his palm. With a wink, he asked if she wanted a free dinner as he'd sliced it too thin to sell. "I'll wrap it for you," he said.

"Grand." And later she'd gift the meat to her editor, he who had earlier that morning threatened to reassign *her* story. "What says Mary about the uncut Galway man? Why disfigure our man and not theirs?"

With a flourish, Wally tore a sheet of butcher paper off a roll.

"Maybe he forgot to sharpen his knife and fancied making a clean job of it," he said. "I could ask her, I suppose, it being a good question. And would you be coming around again for the answer?"

Gavin caught up with Teresa outside the shop. He eyed the packaged steak with a sour expression. "What did I tell you about Wally? Seduces with his meat, all right."

Teresa turned toward the *Challenger* office with a backward wave. Gavin insisted that Wally, or any ogling male, angled for a ride on her hips. Could be Wally favored a thought or two in that direction, but, Christ, if only Gavin would leave it alone already.

"I'll come by your place at the usual time tonight, then?" Gavin called after her. "I'll make you dinner!"

Ten aluminum caravans arrayed themselves in haphazard fashion around a fire pit. A gaggle of women in shapeless shifts cooked what smelled liked rashers while the men slouched around an old door lifted to table height by cement blocks. Dozens of children ran amuck between the corroded and dented caravans, and several horses that appeared better fed and cleaner than the inhabitants dozed under trees. Despite the burnt-out car husks and the rubbish piles, Teresa thought the site had its own kind of peace.

She surveyed the scene with Gavin lagging ten steps behind her. He'd navigated them to the campsite with little trouble, all the while grousing that of *course* he knew where Wally squatted because he'd provided an almost-address on his employment form, not that Gavin's father should have hired a sodding tinker in the first place. Gavin and his da had driven out to view the camp for themselves; the caravans confirmed that this batch of tinkers were in something akin to permanent residence, so Wally'd been hired.

Stepping past a slashed tire, Teresa reminded herself to be grateful that Gavin had insisted on accompanying her despite his discomfort and weariness. She'd awakened that morning surprised to discover Gavin curled on the floor beside her bed with skin pale to the point of translucence. He obviously hadn't slept well in her skinny bed, and he smelled gamey, too. She'd ordered him to the shower without asking what his mum would say about it when he landed back on her doorstep.

After another deathlike sleep and groggy aftermath, Teresa prayed she could manage Wally and what she'd discovered since yesterday to be his bullshit. Only he didn't work Saturdays, did he? So here she was, approaching three skinny girls who scrutinized her with ill-concealed disdain. Before she could speak, they pointed toward two caravans that perched outside the main circle. "Mary's there," one of them said, and on that dismissive note, they returned to plucking black and white feathers from a dead magpie.

Teresa had to wonder why they assumed she chased after one of Mary's alleged cures. Could be she exuded desperation that they took for man troubles—not entirely off the point, that—but they'd be spot-on if they instead guessed at her desire for a life bigger and brighter than that in County Clare.

One of the men at the table quit card flipping and approached them. Wally himself, the master of mistruths. Gavin cursed to holy Christ and rushed forward to place a proprietary arm around Teresa.

"Here to worry my mum, are you?" Wally said to Teresa.

"Listen, you blighter," she said, "I called my uncle this morning, and he confirmed the Galway body. Only, unlike you, he told me the man *was* cut. Nicks on the leg, he said. What do you think about that?"

"Said that, did he?"

"He did, and I want the truth from Mary."

Wally shrugged and led them toward a trailer with lace curtains. A lace-curtain Traveler? Teresa scoffed, and Wally admonished her to leave off, then; his mum had to set a welcoming picture for outsiders, now didn't she?

Potted herbs formed a path that led to a patchwork rug laid out before an open door. Mary appeared in layers of shapeless black cotton and wellies. She took one look at Teresa and shooed the men away.

"But—," Gavin said, alarmed.

"Off with you then, you fecking carp," Mary said. "Women's business."

Before Teresa could object, a push from Wally and a pull from Mary landed her in a tiny area that posed as a parlor. Two plush chairs sat across from each other with an unlit brazier tucked into the corner. Mary pulled a curtain to hide the rest of her home from view, but not before Teresa caught a glimpse of row upon row of jars filled with mysterious substances, some dried, some soaked in a briny stew.

Mary nudged her into a chair and took the second one for herself. She dipped her hand into a jar filled with lavender buds. Despite the network of wrinkles on her face, closer observation revealed skin that shone with a healthy gloss and not one errant vein or blemish. Her lips were full and her lashes long. Teresa saw the beauty of her lost youth and felt more uncomfortable rather than less.

"I called my uncle this morning," Teresa started, but Mary told her to shut her piehole.

"Tricky business, with the dead," Mary continued. She crushed lavender buds into her palm and held them under Teresa's nose. "Breathe; relax, girly."

Teresa waved a flustered hand, and the lavender scattered around her in a fragrant fall. "I'll not relax."

"I suppose not. Sleeping strange, are you?" Mary lifted a wooden box from the floor to her lap. "I'd say you've got a lovesick young twot on your hands. I've seen you along the street with him; I know what I see."

"You propose to play matchmaker, me with your son—is that it?"

Mary burrowed through charms, tokens, and glass vials as she spoke. "Don't be fecking daft. *That's* not my strength, not at all."

"Wally's the corpse cutter, isn't he?" Teresa said. "He's handy with a knife, I saw that for myself well enough, but like you said, it's different slicing on the dead. He failed with the first attempt."

Mary whistled under her breath as she untangled a black ribbon with a copper ball attached to one end.

Frustrated, Teresa's voice rose. "You've got a recipe in that book of yours that needs a grisly ingredient."

"There's a good guess, smarty girl." Mary smiled wide enough to reveal two missing molars. She held up a hand. The copper ball dangled from the ribbon. "Now we're on."

Teresa dashed for the door at the sight of the ball's pendulous swing—bloody hell if she'd fall into a trance and under Mary's control—but Wally jumped the steps to block her exit. She heard a bleat out of Gavin that was quashed by the slamming door. Teresa yelled and Gavin banged on the aluminum walls.

"Be a love, hold her still," Mary said. "I wish she had relaxed."

Wally was strong from manhandling meat, and he steadied Teresa's shoulders against his chest with no more effort than cuddling a bunny. Mary raised the ball, dangled it near Teresa's stomach, let it hang for a moment, then tucked it into her pocket. "We're confirmed, we are: You're not carrying."

Teresa sprang away from Wally. "What the devil are you on about? All I want—"

"I know what you want, girly, and I'm for helping. Had to be sure no wee one though. A baby can alter the sleep."

Gavin continued whaling on the aluminum siding. Mary broke into the secretive Traveler tongue, which Teresa knew to be a hybrid language that stemmed from Irish. As Mary spoke, Wally's amused expression turned serious. He left. A moment later Gavin's voice faded into the distance. After assuring Teresa that Gavin would be fine at his car, Mary set about arranging herself in her chair. "Now that we've got that sorted," she sighed.

She produced a chocolate-biscuit tin from under her chair and offered it to Teresa. Exhausted, Teresa sagged into the vacant seat with a head shake and the feeling that her first brilliant news story didn't have legs. It sometimes happened, she knew, that what looked to be a lead fizzled into nothing but a distraction. And, worst of all, her editor planned to reassign *her* story if she didn't come up with a workable angle by Monday.

"How many days did you say you were at this sleeping business?" Mary said.

"You mentioned my sleep habits, not me."

Teresa watched Mary munch biscuits while contemplating the ceiling. There had to be a way to salvage a story from this muddle. "You'll tell me about the book?" she asked. "If I tell you about my sleep?" A nod from Mary, and more munching. "Right then. For the past two nights I've slept like the dead until morning. Usually, I wake a few times in the night, you see. And, despite sleeping so well, I'm more groggy than rested when I wake up. That's it. And I don't see your point."

"I'm not supposing you do. Now." Mary groaned her way to her feet and slipped behind the curtain. Metal squeaked against glass as she opened various mason jars. She hummed, and soon enough a pestle chimed in against its mortar. A minute more, and Mary returned with a grayish powder in a plastic pouch. "This will lighten your sleep and strengthen your dreams."

"Right, thanks," Teresa said. "Now, about your book."

Mary grabbed the copious folds in her clothes and pulled out a worn leather-bound volume wrapped with twine. "Left on my step last night and only one page missing, not that I was surprised. Guess the dirty grubber was more like a borrower. And that's answer enough for you."

"How convenient." Teresa grabbed for the accursed thing, but Mary was more agile than she let on. "Show me where it's torn."

Mary patted Teresa's arm. "We remedy problems our way, as

you'll soon be seeing. Remember to mix the powder in with water right before bed. It counteracts the toxins. Off with you now."

Teresa left the encampment in a grumpy state that lasted well into the evening. She wavered between conviction that she almost had a story and futility about her chances for discovering its hook by Monday. The problem, she assumed, was the Traveler community: impenetrable.

"Or maybe I'm not cut out for journalism, after all," she said to Gavin, who stood at the other end of her tiny flat waiting for water to boil. "But, no, that's pure bollocks."

Gavin wore electrician's slacks with pockets at every seam, and Teresa felt a warming remembrance of weeks past when the sight of him turned her soft rather than itchy. Upon returning from Mary's trailer, Gavin had issued spit as he demanded to know what Mary said, what she wanted, and what the bloody hell happened anyhow? Teresa recalled the way he sagged when she described the pregnancy test performed with a scrying ball. His frantic interrogation proved his loyalty and protectiveness. As did his subsequent relief upon leaving the encampment. Any other woman, she thought, would relish a boyfriend like Gavin.

"We ought to tell my uncle about those two," she said, "and bring him along with us when we return tomorrow. I'd give the skin off *my* thigh for a look inside Mary's book."

Gavin stepped beyond her view from the bed, where she'd retreated to brood after picking at canned chowder and brown bread. From inside an alcove that served as a pantry, a cabinet banged closed. A second later Gavin reappeared with tea and biscuits on a tray. "Why bother?" he said. "Those tinkers, they're always shitting on us. They're dodgy that way."

She sipped tea while Gavin lounged on a rocking chair. He blinked out the window at passing feet, and every few minutes checked on her with a glance. Teresa sank into disturbing thoughts about the blasted skin strip. She couldn't help visualizing the skin as a hairy pork rind that was yellowed around the edges.

"What breed of potion requires human skin anyhow?" Teresa muttered.

Gavin blanched at the mere mention of skin, and Teresa held off further discussions. The gruesome possibilities were endless, and Teresa's imagination needed no help from Gavin. Perhaps Wally required a hex and nailed the skin to his enemy's door. Or, perhaps the skin was meant to protect a loved one from death; that would be a perverse little story about defiling a body on a good intention. Christ but she wanted this story.

Teresa sank deeper into the covers and let Gavin walk away with her teacup. "I'm that done in," she said. "Go grab a pint. Let yourself in later if your mum won't dump you in an early grave for it."

Gavin considered her for a moment before planting a kiss on her cheek. "Rough day for us both. You sleep. I'll grab that pint and be back to see you're okay."

Alone and relishing it, Teresa shuffled into the bathroom and stripped down for a shower. She bundled her jeans into a wad for the dirty clothes bin before remembering to clear out the pockets. She sniffed at Mary's herbs and who-knew-what-else. Licorice, she thought. Also something clean, purifying. She could do with a night's rest that didn't leave her groveling about in a daze the next day. Come to think on this, distressed sleep might explain why she couldn't get her head on straight about Mary and Wally. With a resolute nod, she decided to sample Mary's dubious goods. Real journalists opened themselves to new experiences, and, more important, she must be intrepid if she hoped to land in Dublin.

The concoction tasted benign if a tad gritty, but it didn't lessen her sleepiness. No worries though, for Gavin would return soon enough to check on her like the diligent boyfriend he was. As her eyelids sank, she wondered if she was too critical of him, if he deserved more of a chance. Soon afterward, she lost track of herself.

She startled awake sometime later. Without moving, she tried to decipher signals from her body. Mary had mentioned strong dreams, and, indeed, Teresa could swear she felt a slithery touch on her arm, something left over from a nightmare she couldn't recall.

"Gavin?" she whispered.

Across the room, layers of darkness parted. "Little shite dropped in, then lit out for the pub again. But he'll be back. I've no doubts about that." A lamp snapped on. "About fecking time you're awake. It's best to let the gits waken on their own is what Mary always says. Bloody nuisance banging around here in the dark, though."

There lurked Wally, all in black and with a stocking cap on his head. Teresa was too disoriented to be shocked.

"How are you keeping?" Wally rifled through an open dresser drawer. "Feel the love yet?"

A creepy sensation oozed its way along Teresa's spine—the cool hand of death that prowled her dream. "Not exactly," she said.

He turned a grin in her direction and winked his walleye. "Brilliant; I'd have to be worried otherwise. Mary's herbs were meant to waken you to the truth." He pulled out another drawer. "I'm here to get back what's ours. Mary said to check up on you, too."

"How did you find me?"

"Followed you this afternoon; nothing magical about that." He closed the drawer. "Guess I'll wait out your sad sack of a boyfriend. Meanwhile." Wally stepped toward the sink. A moment later, he returned with a glass of water. "Drink. It will clear your head."

She slipped a hand from under the covers, and as she did so, the slimy creepiness slithered down her arm. A meaty sourness filled her nostrils, and she tensed against the need to retch. Wally perched on her bed with the Traveler trickiness in his eyes. His gaze slipped to her outstretched arm. Her gaze followed his.

"Bloody hell! What is that?" Teresa screeched.

But she knew, all right. That was Paddy's thigh bit tied around her arm.

Teresa flung herself from the bed at the same time Gavin opened the door from the outside. Shrieking, she tossed her arm about in all directions until the skin flew off. "What are you, fecking crazy?" she yelled at Wally.

Gavin grabbed Teresa. "You're awake, are you?"

Teresa lurched away from Gavin with shaking finger aimed at Wally. By then, Wally stood in the kitchen nook sniffing at her teacup. "I'd leave off washing this," he said. "And you might want to ring that useless uncle of yours now."

"So you say, you bloody piece of—"

Gavin wrapped his arms around her in a hug. "Please, you weren't meant to wake up. It needed longer, one more night. Can't you go back to sleep until morning?"

Teresa struggled to regain her senses and release herself from Gavin's grip while Wally set his burly form to the task of rifling through Gavin's pockets. Gavin held Teresa tight rather than resist Wally's prying hands.

"Mary's a spooky old cow, she is," Wally said and raised a parchmentlike page with a torn edge.

Teresa gawked from over Gavin's shoulder, reading from the page, until Wally whipped it away. Gavin shook his head against Teresa's neck and hugged her tighter. She let him, as she'd have fallen over otherwise. "Holy Christ," she said. "Gavin, you?"

"He's known about my mum's bag of tricks since her first visit to the shop," Wally said.

Instead of further panic or queasiness, a rush of excitement startled Teresa. She inhaled long and hard to steady herself and then stepped away from whimpering Gavin. A quick scan of the room revealed the strip of thigh dangling from the lampshade. Backlit, it glowed from within like a macabre holy relic with faint shadows that could be veins or fat clumps.

Wally slipped Mary's page into his pocket. Then, he pulled out what looked to be a silver horn of plenty. "A gift from Mary," he said. "Sleep with this charm under your pillow for good fortune. Cheers then. Have fun, you two."

Teresa observed poor Paddy's missing bit for a while after Wally departed. She felt a newfound respect for Mary, and her write-up would reflect well on Mary's Traveler ways. She owed the old witch, after all; Teresa now owned a story worth the front page. And never mind poor Paddy: poor Gavin. His endearing face would make for a superb image above the fold. Truth be told, she was proud of him, overcoming his weak stomach all for her.

"Dear Gavin, I do adore you," she said.

He melted into another hug. She leaned against him, weak with contentment, and fixed what she'd read into memory: *Love charm to guarantee her lifelong ardor: a strip of skin from a man seven days buried, no more, no less; wrapped around the lover's leg or arm while she sleeps, for three nights running.*

Teresa would be ready with the heartfelt anecdote about her former boyfriend when she interviewed with the *Irish Times*, and she'd remain ever grateful to Gavin for kick-starting her career. She set aside a stab of remorse—the eejit had desecrated a corpse, after all—and reached toward the nightstand where her mobile waited with her uncle's speed-dial number.

ABOUT THE AUTHORS

Lisa Alber received a 2007 Elizabeth George Foundation writing grant, as well as a 2001 Walden Fellowship. She has completed two mysteries set in Ireland, featuring detective Danny Ahern, who makes a cameo appearance in "Paddy O'Grady's Thigh." One of her previously published short stories was a 2007 Pushcart Prize nominee. A UC Berkeley graduate, Lisa has worked in libraries, restaurants, multinational corporations in South America, major publishing houses in New York City, sports bars, newspapers, and high-tech firms. Now she relishes working from home in Portland, Oregon. You can find her online at www.lisaalber.com.

Linda Barnes, past president of the Private Eye Writers of America, is the author of the critically acclaimed Carlotta Carlyle series. A winner of the Anthony and American Mystery awards, she has also been a finalist for the Edgar and Shamus awards. Her latest novel, *Lie Down with the Devil*, is published by St. Martin's Press.

Julie Barrett is the author of one book, numerous short stories, and several audio dramas. When not at the keyboard, she can usually be found behind a camera or a microphone. She lives in Plano, Texas, with her husband, son, and cats. Home on the Web is at www.barrettmanor.com where she maintains a journal and a catcam. The cats get most of the traffic.

Stephanie Bond was seven years deep into a systems-engineering career and completing an MBA at night when an instructor remarked that she had a flair for writing. Intrigued, she began writing a novel in her spare time. Within four years Stephanie had ten sales under her belt and left her corporate job to write full-time. As of this writing, she has over forty romantic-comedy novels and humorous romantic-suspense novels to her name. Stephanie lives in Atlanta, Georgia, the setting for her humorous mystery series for Mira Books titled *Body Movers*. For more information, visit www.stephaniebond.com.

For two years, *Allison Brennan* worked by day in the California state capitol, writing every night after her kids went to bed in pursuit of her life-long dream of becoming a writer. Now a *New York Times* and *USA Today* best-selling author of nine full-length novels and a handful of short stories, Allison's suspense novels leave the reader with a sense of hope and justice when her protagonists find love in a violent world. Though Allison writes dark and gritty romantic thrillers complete with serial killers, mass murderers, and the worst man can do to man, she leads a rather boring life in northern California where for fun she plays video games with the kids (and by herself), goes wine tasting with her husband and friends, watches classic movies, catches up on crime dramas, and listens to classical rock. She's a member of Romance Writers of America, Mystery Writers of America, and International Thriller Writers.

Elizabeth Engstrom is a sought-after teacher and keynote speaker at writing conferences, conventions, and seminars around the world. She has written ten books and edited four anthologies, and she has over two hundred and fifty short stories, articles, and essays in print. Her latest book-length work of fiction is *The Northwoods Chronicles*. She lives in the Pacific Northwest, with her fisherman husband and their dog, where she teaches the occasional writing class and is always working on her next book. www.elizabetheng strom.com.

Patricia Fogarty is a former high school English teacher who lives in Orange County, California with her husband. This is her first published work of fiction.

Born in Philadelphia, Pennsylvania, ***Barbara Fryer*** graduated from Temple University with a bachelor of science degree in journalism. She spent most of her career writing for newspapers and teaching before turning her sights on fiction. She lives in Huntington Beach, California, with her husband and is currently working on a novel. Like the protagonist in "The Runaway Camel," Fryer is a rabid basketball fan, but there the similarities end.

Elizabeth George is the *New York Times* and internationally best-selling author of a series of sixteen crime novels set in Great Britain and featuring Detective Inspector Thomas Lynley and his partner on the police force, Detective Sergeant Barbara Havers. A former educator and recipient of an honorary Doctorate of Humane Letters, she has won the Anthony Award, the Agatha Award, France's Grand Prix de Litterature Policière, Germany's MIMI, the Ohioana Book Award, and has been named a Distinguished Alumna of both the University of California and California State University. Her novels have been filmed for television by the BBC and have been featured on PBS's program *Mystery!*

Carolyn Hart writes the Death on Demand, Henrie O, and Bailey Ruth mystery series. *Ghost at Work*, first in the series featuring Bailey Ruth Raeburn, an impetuous redheaded ghost, was published in 2008. Also published in 2008 was *Death Walked In*, a Death on Demand title. *Dare to Die*, nineteenth in the Death on Demand series and her forty-second published mystery, will be a spring 2009 title. Hart has won the Agatha for Best Mystery Novel three times. She received the Malice Domestic Lifetime Achievement Award in 2007. She lives in Oklahoma City with her husband, Phil.

Peggy Hesketh is a writer living under the shadow of the Matterhorn. A former journalist, she teaches writing at the University of California, Irvine. When she is not writing or teaching, she digs up dinosaurs in Montana.

Published internationally, **Wendy Hornsby** is the author of eight acclaimed mystery novels, but, as a writer, short stories were her first and remain her greatest love. She was awarded, among many others, the prestigious Edgar Allan Poe Award (the "Edgar") for a short story, and its French equivalent, the Grand Prix de Litterature Policière. Her stories are regularly included in anthologies of the year's best. By day Wendy is, as described by a National Public Radio interviewer, "a soft-spoken, genteel history professor." By night, she writes noir fiction that the *New York Times* described as "refreshing, real and raunchy." "The Violinist" comes from both aspects of the writer. While sequestered with the personal papers of Jack and Charmian London, questions began to emerge about their supposedly grand love and Jack's early death: Why would a bereaved widow build a house for herself and name it the House of Happy Walls? About what was she so happy?

Z. Kelley has published three short stories in literary journals— "Coaxing Sculpture" in *Aethlon* (2003), and "Autoerotica" (2005) and "The Light Offshore" (2006) in the *Southlander*. Additionally, she was awarded an honorable mention in the spring 2003 edition of *Peridot Books Literary Journal*. Kelley's collection of short stories, *Blue Lawn of Heaven*, is currently available at Barnes and Noble and on Amazon.com. She is currently working on her second novel. Z. Kelley is a pseudonym for Elaine Medosch, of Long Beach, California. Medosch is president and owner of em enterprises, a Long Beach PR company. She was city editor for a Long Beach newspaper for fifteen years and has a bachelor's degree from Tulane University and a juris doctorate from Western State University, College of Law.

Gillian Linscott is the author of the Nell Bray crime series, featuring a militant suffragette detective in Britain in the early years of the twentieth century. One of the series, *Absent Friends*, won the 2000 CWA Ellis Peters Dagger for best historical crime novel and the Herodotus Award. She has worked as a news reporter for the *Guardian* and as a political reporter for BBC local radio stations. She lives in a 350-year-old cottage in Herefordshire, England, and, in addition to writing, now works as a professional gardener.

Laura Lippman has published twelve novels—nine in the award-winning Tess Monaghan series and three stand-alones, including the *New York Times* best seller *What the Dead Know*. An anthology of her short stories is planned for fall 2008. She lives in Baltimore.

A native of the Detroit area, *Marcia Muller* grew up in a house full of books and self-published three copies of her first novel at age twelve, a tale about her dog, complete with primitive illustrations. The "reviews" were generally positive. Her literary aspirations were put on hold, however, in her third year at the University of Michigan when her creative-writing instructor told her she would never be a writer because she had nothing to say. Instead she turned to journalism, earning a master's degree, but various editors for whom she freelanced noticed her unfortunate tendency to embellish the facts in order to make them more interesting. In the early 1970s, having moved to California, Muller found herself unemployable and began experimenting with mystery novels because they were what she liked to read. After three manuscripts and five years of rejection, *Edwin of the Iron Shoes*, the first novel featuring San Francisco private investigator Sharon McCone, was published by David McKay Company, who then canceled their mystery list. Four more years passed before St. Martin's Press accepted the second McCone novel, *Ask the Cards a Question*. In the ensuing twenty years, Muller has authored thirty-five novels, three of them in collaboration with her husband, Bill Pronzini; seven short story collections; and numerous nonfiction articles. Together she and Pronzini have edited a dozen anthologies and a nonfiction book on the mystery genre. The Mulzinis, as friends call them, live in Sonoma County, California, in yet another house full of books.

Nancy Pickard, creator of the Jenny Cain series and the Marie Lightfoot series, has won Agatha, Anthony, Barry, Shamus, and Macavity awards. She is a four-time Edgar Award nominee, most recently for her novel, *The Virgin of Small Plains*, which was named a Notable Kansas Book of 2006. Several of her stories have appeared in previous editions of the year's best mystery and suspense stories. She lives in the Kansas City area.

S. J. Rozan, the author of ten crime novels, is a lifelong New Yorker. Her novels and short stories have won every major American crime-writing award, including the Edgar, Shamus, Anthony, Nero, and Macavity. Her new novel is *The Shanghai Moon*.

Kristine Kathryn Rusch is an award-winning mystery, science fiction, romance, and mainstream author. Her latest mystery novel, written as Kris Nelscott, is *Days of Rage*. Her latest science fiction novel is a science fiction mystery called *The Recovery Man*. To find out more about her, look at her Web site, *www.kristinekathryn rusch.com.*

Patricia Smiley earned a BA in sociology from the University of Washington in Seattle. She also holds an MBA with honors from Pepperdine University in Malibu, California. Her mystery series, featuring amateur sleuth Tucker Sinclair, earned critical praise and a place on the *Los Angeles Times* best-seller list. For more information, visit www.patriciasmiley.com.

Dana Stabenow was born in Anchorage and raised on a seventy-five-foot fish tender in the Gulf of Alaska. She knew there was a warmer, drier job out there somewhere, and found it in writing. Her first science fiction novel, *Second Star*, sank without a trace; her first crime fiction novel, *A Cold Day for Murder*, won an Edgar Award; her first thriller, *Blindfold Game*, hit the *New York Times* best-seller list; and her twenty-fifth novel and sixteenth Kate Shugak novel, *Whisper to the Blood*, comes out in February 2009.

Marcia Talley is the Agatha and Anthony award–winning author of *Dead Man Dancing* and six previous Hannah Ives mysteries, all set in Maryland. She is author / editor of two star-studded collaborative serial novels, *Naked Came the Phoenix* and *I'd Kill For That*, set in a fashionable health spa and an exclusive gated community, respectively. Her short stories appear in more than a dozen collections, including "With Love, Marjorie Ann" and "Safety First," both Agatha award nominees, and the multi-award-winning "Too Many Cooks," a humorous retelling of Shakespeare's *Macbeth* from the viewpoint of the three witches, in *Much Ado About Murder*, edited by Anne Perry. A recent story, "Driven to Distraction" won the Agatha Award, was nominated for an Anthony, and was selected for inclusion in *The Deadly Bride and 21 of the Year's Best Crime and Mystery Stories.* Marcia is immediate past president of the Chesapeake Chapter of Sisters in Crime, and serves as secretary for Sisters in Crime National. She is on the board of the Mid-Atlantic chapter of the Mystery Writers of America. She divides her time between Annapolis, Maryland, and living aboard an antique sailboat in the Bahamas.

Susan Wiggs's life is all about family, friends . . . and fiction. She lives at the water's edge on an island in Puget Sound, and she commutes to her writers' group in a seventeen-foot motorboat. According to *Publishers Weekly*, Wiggs writes a "refreshingly honest romance," and the *Salem Statesman Journal* adds that she is "one of our best observers of stories of the heart [who] knows how to capture emotion on virtually every page of every book." *Booklist* characterizes her books as "real and true and unforgettable." She is the proud recipient of three RITA (sm) awards and four starred reviews from *Publishers Weekly* for her books. Her novels have been translated into more than a dozen languages and have made national best-seller lists, including the USA *Today* and *New York Times* lists. The author is a former teacher, a Harvard graduate, an avid hiker, an amateur photographer, a good skier, and a terrible golfer, yet her favorite form of exercise is curling up with a good book. Readers can learn more on the web at www.susanwiggs.com.

ABOUT THE EDITOR

Elizabeth George is the *New York Times* and internationally best-selling author of a series of sixteen crime novels set in Great Britain and featuring Detective Inspector Thomas Lynley and his partner on the police force, Detective Sergeant Barbara Havers. A former educator and recipient of an honorary Doctorate of Humane Letters, she has won the Anthony Award, the Agatha Award, France's Grand Prix de Litterature Policière, Germany's MIMI, the Ohioana Book Award, and has been named a Distinguished Alumna of both the University of California and California State University. Her novels have been filmed for television by the BBC and have been featured on PBS's program *Mystery!*